Warriors of Gaia: Liberty's Cry

D.S. Northrop

RIO FLOJO PRESS

560 W. Rio Flojo
Green Valley, AZ 85614
rioflojopress.com

Cover art by Bradford Northrop

ISBN: 978-0-9883424-0-8

For Barbara, my steady light

Thanks Kristin, for all your help and support.

Within each of us lie seeds of glory.
Nurture them, and they will grow.

Prologue

Silvia was gathering berries for dinner when she realized with a sharp feeling of panic that the afternoon sun had long since disappeared below the treetops. She was about to break the most fundamental rule of her people: never be caught outside after dark. She had been distracted by dreamy thoughts of her upcoming wedding to Valentine. In a panic, she dropped the berries and began running for the safety of her village.

She broke into the clearing and saw the tall wood walls that marked her village and safety. Hope grew within her, only to disappear like the glimmering afterglow of fireworks when she heard the sound. She knew the sound well, and it sent icy fear rocketing up and down her spine and into those corners of the body reserved for the most primitive of emotions. The howling of wolves carried to her on the evening air. There were dozens of wolves, and their excited howls meant they had caught the scent of their prey. She continued to run, but a glance over her shoulder revealed gray streaks, light against the darkening forest, gray streaks that devoured the distance between themselves and her with impossibly long, lunging strides. She saw the luminescent yellow of wolves' eyes as she stopped, turned around, and, with stoicism common to her people, spread her arms wide to embrace her fate.

1

My name is Erin Taylor, but most people call me ET. My parents never had much money, so when they went on their honeymoon, they stayed in Tucson. They planned to tour the telescopes and go hiking in Madera Canyon. One night, they went to a classic movie festival at the Loft. The movie ET was playing. They loved it. When I was born exactly nine months later, it seemed appropriate to name me Erin so they could call me ET for short. So, I'm named after a dumpy little alien who made bicycles fly. I'm a soon-to-be junior at Sierra Vista High School ("Home of the Battlin' Rattlers") in Tucson, Arizona. The story I'm about to tell is true. I'm telling the story in the first person, but this shouldn't lead you to conclude I'll be alive at the end. In fact, the odds against me as I write these pages are pretty steep. Of course, as my friend Kennedy, the optimist, points out, all people die at the end of their stories.

* * * * *

"ET, there's something I need to show you," says Tyler the minute I open my front door.

"Okay, what would you like to show me?" I respond.

"I have to *show* you," he insists, "because if I told you, you wouldn't believe me. Please come with me."

"I have the second shift at work tonight, so I have to be home by four." I check my watch. It's only 7:00 a.m.

"No problem. I'll have you back in plenty of time."

"Just a second." I slide on a pair of shoes and check the mirror to make sure my hair looks roughly respectable. I pull my shoulder-length brown hair back into a ponytail when I realize it doesn't, and yell out, "I'm going with Tyler, Mom." I get a muffled, positive-sounding reply.

Tyler and I pile into his ancient Jeep. He's wearing his trademark round-rim glasses, and his curly blond hair peeks out in back from under his Diamondbacks cap. It's a warm Arizona morning, which promises to become another blazing-hot desert summer day. Ty's Jeep is far older than I am, but it runs like brand new because our friend Brianne, who knows how to fix almost anything, takes care of it.

"Can you give me a hint?" I ask.

"All I can tell you is that it's big. Huge. Enormous. Fantastic."

I can see from Tyler's body language that he's excited. And there aren't many things that get Tyler excited. Ty is our resident genius. He mastered high school calculus as a freshman, so he's taking integral calculus from Stanford online classes. He's also taking advanced physics classes from MIT.

"Are we picking up anybody else?" I ask. Tyler and I are part of a group of kids who have been best friends since third grade at Bessie Mae Reynolds Elementary School. Brianne, another member of the group, calls us the "Tucson Ramblers." I assume Ty will want to pick up at least a couple others for something that has him this excited.

"No, just you and me, for now. You have a level head, and I really need your advice on what to do next."

"Okay," I reply. I wonder if this is an attempt on Ty's part to bond more closely with me. I know he'd like us to become more than friends. But I'm not interested. It's not because Ty is a geek (actually, I really like that about him), and he's kind of cute in a distracted, scholarly sort of way. I'm just way too busy to have a boyfriend.

My dad is an alcoholic. He's not a get-drunk-and-beat-your-wife-and-kids kind of alcoholic. In fact, he's what his friends call a "happy drunk." He's very charming, drunk or sober. But he's chronically unemployable.

As a result, I work two jobs to help with the bills. And I need to get excellent grades in school because I'm determined to go to the U of A premed, and there isn't any money to pay tuition. So a scholarship is essential. I also run the 3200 for our high school track-and-field team. There's no way I can fit a boyfriend into my schedule.

Tyler is driving out of town on Speedway.

"Where are we going?" I ask.

"Midnight Mesa," Ty answers.

Midnight Mesa is a popular spot. Because it overlooks all of Tucson, it's a popular place for kids to hang out. From the serious look on Ty's face, and because it's early in the morning, I assume hanging out is not on the agenda. There's an old Indian medicine wheel on top of the mesa, but Ty isn't even remotely interested in Native American legends. I'm getting more and more curious about our objective.

We continue without speaking until we reach the track that leads toward the mesa. Calling it a track may be an overstatement. There are lots of dusty arroyos along the trail, and it's very easy to get stuck in axle-deep sand. Ty makes the turn and engages four-wheel drive. Even though Brianne has the shocks well tuned, we're bouncing up and down vigorously.

Two miles down the track, the rocks become too big to drive over or around, so we abandon the Jeep and strike out on foot. We weave our way around the rocks, carefully avoiding the cactus: fuzzy cholla, stout little barrels, and prickly pear. A few straggly mesquite and green-barked paloverde trees cast pathetically small pools of shade.

Tyler has a short metal rod hooked onto his belt with a C-clip.

"What's that?" I ask.

"You'll see in a few minutes," replies Tyler mysteriously.

The climb up the side of the mesa is not particularly difficult, but it requires some hand-over-head maneuvers to locate strategic handholds. This, of course, violates rule number one of desert safety: never put your hand anywhere your eyes can't see. Although I know people who've been bitten by snakes, scorpions, and the occasional Gila monster, I've never heard of anyone having a problem climbing up Midnight Mesa. So we defy convention.

Twenty minutes later, breathing a little harder than normal, we reach the top. There's a very impressive medicine wheel laid out on top of the mesa. Medicine wheels are a Native American creation and are thought to be places of great spiritual energy. The wheel looks like a wagon wheel, fifty feet in diameter, laid flat on its side. There's a large cairn of rocks in the middle, a circle of smaller rocks around the perimeter, and four spokes emanating from the center in the four cardinal directions. Each quadrant of the wheel is said to represent different life forces and different aspects of nature.

But I'm not thinking of the medicine wheel right now. I'm focused on something far more impressive. In the center of the medicine wheel is a huge circle of light standing about twenty feet high. The light shimmers like the heat mirages you see over pavement on hot summer days. Bolts of beautifully colored lightning crisscross the circle in every direction. If I look very closely, there appears to be a forest of trees buried deep in the middle, although the rippling air and colored lightning make it hard to tell for sure.

I'm stunned. Finally, I manage to stutter, "What *is* that?"

"I think," says Tyler, "that's a membrane."

I wait for Ty to continue.

"Lots of physicists today believe our universe is one of many. Some even suggest that different universes are connected to one another by thin membranes, or branes, for short. Now I'm not talking about a few fringe, wacko physicists. Some of the very best physicists in the world think our universe has lots of company."

I struggle to process what I've just heard. "So," I say at last, "you think what we're seeing here may be the window into another universe?"

"More like a door to another universe," Tyler explains.

"As in a door you can walk through?" I stammer.

"I think so."

"But how did it get here? We've been on Midnight Mesa lots of times, and this thing has never been here before." I study the shimmering light. "It's not like you wouldn't notice it."

"I don't know for sure. But it's sitting right in the center of the medicine wheel, and you know those things are supposed to be related to special forms of physical and spiritual energy."

Tyler is a scientist and has always been an empiricist. If a thing can't be touched, seen, or measured, it simply doesn't exist. I'm absolutely amazed that he's talking about Native American spiritual energy.

"Okay," I agree slowly, "but the medicine wheel's been here for a long time. Why did this brane pop up today?"

"Stay with me on this next bit," says Tyler, "'cause it's a little complicated. First, we're having hundred-year solar storms. That means the sun is throwing an enormous amount of electromagnetic plasma into space, and a lot of it interferes with things like radio and television signals here on Earth. But even more peculiar, there's a source of gamma ray activity in the center of our Milky Way Galaxy that's begun to randomly emit massive amounts of radiation. Scientists think that this should happen only once every million years or so, but it seems to be happening now. Usually, the earth's atmosphere screens out gamma rays, but maybe there's so much radiation, it's overwhelming the earth's ability to screen it all. So some radiation is leaking through. Not enough to fry everything, but enough to create quantum field fluctuations…"

Tyler sees the expression on my face and knows he's lost me.

"The bottom line," he says, "is I don't know for sure. But that's two very unusual things happening at the same time."

"Anyhow," he continues, "the *real* question is not how it got here, but what should we do about it? I suppose we should tell the police, or the principal, or somebody." He looks at me expectantly.

I now know why Tyler came to get me and not one of our other friends. I'm the adventurous one, the one who always plans the white-water rafting trips, the rock climbs, the trail bike expeditions. It's not that I'm reckless, because I always choose my guides and equipment with care. But life is meant to be *lived*. If there's another universe on the other side of that brane, I want to *see* it.

"No way are we going to the authorities," I say. "If we get them involved, they'll take the whole thing over, and that'll be the end of it for us. If that's another universe over there, let's take a look at it! Can we go through the brane?"

"Wait just a second. Let me get something." Tyler walks about a quarter of a mile, scanning the ground as he goes. He bends over and picks something up. When he returns, I see he has caught a lizard in a live trap.

"I set a few traps last night," he says by way of explanation. "I came up yesterday to look for geodes, and I found that thing." Tyler points to the brane. "I was pretty sure it was a brane, and I knew I wanted to go through it to the other side. But I wanted to be certain it was safe first."

Ty removes the rod he clipped to his belt. It's a telescoping rod, and he extends it until it has reached a length of about ten feet. It has a hook on the end. He places the caged lizard right in front of the brane and uses the rod to slowly push it through the pulsating light to the other side of the brane.

We can see the lizard underneath a bush on the other side looking very unhappy. Using the hook, Tyler drags the cage back to our side of the brane.

"Okay," he says, "the atmosphere on the other side must be breathable, 'cause the lizard looks pretty healthy. And we can tell the brane works in both directions. We can cross over and then come back." He opens the trap, and the lizard scurries away.

"Let's try it," I say. "Do you want me to go first?"

"I'll go," says Ty.

I watch him as he walks slowly through the brane. When he reaches the other side, he stops and looks around. He sniffs the air, then turns around and gestures for me to join him. I walk through the light and feel an odd tingling sensation, but it goes away when I emerge on the other side.

The first thing I notice is the heat. Anybody who lives through an Arizona summer knows what hot is, but this is extremely, outrageously open-the-oven-door hot. The next thing I notice is birdsong. Obviously, life exists on this side of the brane. There are lofty snowcapped mountains to our right side. The sun has just begun to peek over the mountains. The sky is similar to Earth's, but more white than blue. I hear the sound of a stream or brook to our left. The air feels heavy. There's no hint of a breeze.

There's a medicine wheel in this clearing as well. It's not as well maintained as the one on the mesa we left. Some rocks are missing, many are grown over by weeds, and still others are covered with lichen. But there's a cairn in the center, and the similarity to the medicine wheel on the other side of the brane is unmistakable.

"Hmm," says Ty. "Interesting."

A stone statue sits off to the side of the medicine wheel. It looks like a crying angel with hands lifted toward the sky.

"That's interesting as well," I say. "Let's go exploring."

"For all we know, there may be huge human-eating predators around here," says Ty. "Let's not get too far from the brane."

We move cautiously forward. The trees here are short and scrubby, none more than eight to ten feet tall. The leaves of most trees are yellowish, but others are green. There's underbrush in places, but none thick enough to keep us from moving forward. I take out my phone. No bars, of course.

My senses are tuned to high. I see, feel, and hear everything with crystal clarity. Every few moments, I glance nervously back over my shoulder to make sure I can still see the brane.

"Let's go just a little farther," I suggest.

Tyler looks nervously over his shoulder, but says, "Okay. Just a little farther."

We're still moving forward when we hear a noise behind us. I turn around quickly and see two small men dressed in black uniforms. The men are tiny, less than three feet tall. They're carrying bows and arrows. Fortunately, they're mesmerized by the brane and haven't yet seen us. But they're between us and the brane.

I don't know who they are, and I want to see what they're doing before I introduce myself. Tyler and I exchange glances. There's a thick copse of trees to our right. If we can reach them, we can hide from the blacksuits. I point to the trees, and Ty and I walk on tiptoe toward them. Ty steps on a stick, which breaks with a crack. The blacksuits spin around and see us. They quickly string their bows and aim them at us.

* * * * *

"Raise your hands slowly," says the taller of the two.

The black uniforms they wear have yellow braid on the shoulders and shiny gold badges marking them as either military or police. Their eyes are cold and hard.

"Raise your hands, by order of the Court," says the taller one. He has a scar running from his left ear to his chin. In addition to his bow and arrow, he has a horn slung over his left shoulder. His uniform is nicely tailored, his boots polished and shiny.

Ty and I glance at one another and raise our hands, slowly. In spite of my heart hammering away in my chest, I'm acute enough to be surprised that people in this world speak English.

"We're friendly. We mean you no harm," I say. "You can put the bows down. We're peaceful."

"We'll decide what to do with our bows," says the smaller one. He is very young, with just a hint of scraggly facial hair. "We have never seen giants before. Where have you come from?"

This is going to be a hard question to answer. "We come from far away," I explain." We come from a different world." I don't know if it's our size that causes their hostility, or whether they just don't like strangers.

"Another world! That's a good one," sneers the taller stranger. Both of the blacksuits laugh. Their laughter is harsh, devoid of humor.

The shorter one speaks again, addressing the taller one. "Let's take them back to the fort and see what the magistrate wants to do with them."

This strikes me as being a distinctly bad idea. I have no intention of seeing what the "magistrate" wants to do with us. Tyler and I make eye contact. His lips silently form the word "run." I nod.

"Go!" I shout.

We both take off running back in a direction perpendicular to the brane.

"Zigzag!" I holler, thinking we'll be harder to hit. The strangers' arrows are small, more like very long darts, but I'm sure they would be painful, at best, and possibly lethal.

"Halt!" shouts one of the blacksuits. "You are in violation of a court order!"

11

An arrow whistles by my thigh, just after I change direction. Tree branches claw at my face as I run. I see Tyler just ahead of me and off to my right. He's running a zigzag pattern as well. I see an arrow imbed itself in a tree, just missing his right ankle. It occurs to me that they are aiming low, so their intent must be to disable us so we can't run. I shudder at the thought of being captured. An arrow grazes the inside of my left calf. The pain is sharp, but quick. I can feel blood beginning to trickle down my ankle. A quick look down assures me that the wound is not serious.

I look over my shoulder and see we are pulling away from them. My foot catches on something in the undergrowth, and I go down, hard. Tyler helps me up. We reach a thicket where a dense snarl of brambles blocks our way. It's clear we're not going through it. I run to the left, hoping to find a way around. Tyler follows.

Despite our detour, we continue to pull away from the strangers. I breathe more easily as I realize that with their short legs, they won't be able to keep up with us.

My relief is short-lived. I hear a horn from behind us and answering horns to the left and right. There are at least three groups of strangers around us. I catch a glimpse of another pair of black uniforms on a hill ahead of us and to our left. They block our path around the brambles.

Ty and I quickly reverse directions. This will take us back toward the two blacksuits behind us, but there's no other way.

We're both breathing heavily now. Suddenly Ty cries out in pain. An arrow protrudes from the side of his right knee. He struggles to run, but can barely manage a limping walk. Putting weight on his wounded knee is obviously excruciatingly painful.

"Here," I say. "Lean on me."

He does, but with Ty gasping in pain every time his right foot touches down, it's clear we're not going to be able to move quickly enough to avoid our pursuers.

"Go ahead without me," he pleads.

12

"I'm not leaving you," I answer grimly.

"Please. There's no sense in them catching us both."

I hesitate, but Ty shoves me away. "Okay," I say, reluctantly. "But I'm going to get help and come back for you." I'm sure at least some of the Tucson Ramblers will be willing to help rescue Ty.

"That's good. Now go!" Ty hisses. He shoves me again for emphasis. My emotions rebel at the notion of leaving him behind. But I can't do anything to help him if they catch me, too.

I begin to run again. I gain about fifty yards and look back over my shoulder as a small group of men in black uniforms surround Tyler, who is now down on the ground. They begin to kick him. I hear horns all around me, and put every ounce of energy I have into a fresh sprint. I'm grateful for every one of the tens of thousands of laps I've run in track practice. Without them, I wouldn't have the stamina to keep going.

I run flat out up and down hills, around thickets, avoiding clearings where I would feel exposed. I run until my lungs seem ready to burst. The terrible heat is beginning to take its toll. I stop, bend over, and rest my hands on my knees. I gasp for air. Listening carefully, the horns seem far behind me. I examine my wounded calf. The wound isn't deep, and it's not bleeding anymore. Dried blood has turned the top of my white sock reddish black. At least I haven't been leaving a blood trail.

I regain my breath and force my way through a dense thicket. Coming out the far side, I run right into two blacksuits.

* * * * *

There'll be no running away from them this time. I'm less than six feet from the nearest stranger, and he has drawn a bead on my chest. One blacksuit looks young and frightened. The other is much older. He has a dark black beard and eyes like a cobra. There's no fear in *his* eyes.

"Raise your hands," says the bearded man.

I do as I'm told.

"Follow him," he says, referring to the younger blacksuit. "Let's take her back to the fort."

The younger blacksuit takes the lead. I follow him, and the bearded blacksuit walks behind me. A quick glance over my shoulder tells me he has his arrow pointed right between my shoulder blades.

We walk in silence. There's a rough trail through the trees. Soon the trail reaches a point where it runs parallel to a deep ravine to my left. The ravine is about fifty feet deep, and the slope downward is almost a sheer drop. Still, this might be my only chance. I throw myself over the edge of the ravine. I turn myself sideways, cover my head with my arms, and roll down. I'm airborne more often than not, and when I hit the side of the ravine, I hit hard enough to knock my breath out. I hit an exposed rock and feel a rib crack. When I come to rest at the bottom, I find myself in a fetid swamp. Bubbles of methane form and burst, releasing a horrendous stench that makes me gag.

A blacksuit arrow strikes the mud beside me, followed by another. The arrows remind me of my situation and bring me to my feet. I wade through the swamp, toward the far side of the ravine. Arrows continue to fall, but within minutes, they're falling well behind me.

I'm near the far side when I walk into a slimy brown pool of muck and discover I'm stuck. I can't lift my feet. Worse yet, I start to sink. The squalid pool is sucking me down.

Quicksand! I try to remember everything I know about quicksand. Rule One: don't struggle. *Good luck with that,* my instincts yammer as I start to panic. I force myself to slow my breathing and think. I'm in to my knees when Rule Two comes to me: lie down flat. Intuition rebels at this thought, but I force myself to lie on my back. With my weight distributed over a larger area, I stop sinking.

This is good! But I can't stay here. How do I get out? I see a large fallen branch to my left. I reach for it, but find my arm is at least a foot too short to reach the branch. Moving as little as possible, I struggle to remove my belt. I'm able to accomplish this, but at the expense of sinking a couple inches deeper. I feel the quicksand reach the level of the backs of my ears.

I hold the tail of my belt in my right hand. The branch on my left has a large snag protruding mere inches from its end. If I can catch the snag with my belt buckle, perhaps I can pull myself out. I cautiously cast my buckle at the knot. I miss, and the movement causes me to sink another quarter inch. On my second attempt, I miss again. The quicksand is now filling my ears.

On my third attempt, I'm successful. The buckle is caught on the snag. But can I pull myself out? The quicksand gives me nothing solid to push from. If I'm going to get out, I'm going to have to pull myself out using nothing but arm strength. I collect myself and take a deep breath.

I put every ounce of strength I have into one mighty pull. My effort accomplishes nothing but sinking me farther. The back of my head is totally immersed. Only my eyes and nose are above the slime. I continue to sink. In a matter of seconds, I find I can't breathe. My mouth and nose are covered with slime. I give another great tug and feel myself begin to rise. I need to breathe, but while my nose is now above the surface, it's plugged with muck. I'm blind as well. Mud has coated my eyes. I pull with my arms again. My head and shoulders come out of the quicksand. I'm beginning to black out due to lack of oxygen. I try breathing through my mouth, but my face is coated with muck, and it fills my mouth the second I open it. If I don't clear my nose and mouth, I'm going to suffocate. I spit mud from my mouth, and blow muck from my nose, but they're still clogged. If I remove my hand from the belt to clear my mouth, I'll sink back again.

With what little strength remains, I give one more pull. My shoulders come free. I use my left hand to clear muck from my mouth. I gasp at the air the instant my mouth is cleared. Then I reach out blindly with my left hand, slapping around, trying to find something to give me leverage. I find the branch and grab it.

The branch shifts and moves toward me. I'm putting too much weight on it. If it gives way, I'll have nothing to anchor myself, and I'll be back in the quicksand, sinking. I release my left hand and clear my eyes. I spot a tree root barely protruding from the ground. With my right hand still gripping the belt, I reach out with my left. The branch shifts again, and I sink a few inches back into the mire.

I grasp the root with the fingers of my left hand. Holding on to the root is difficult because my fingers are slippery with mud, and, since the root is buried, I can't wrap my fingers all the way around it. Nonetheless, I pull. I rise slowly, until my stomach clears the quicksand.

Just then, my fingers lose purchase on the tree root. I flail out with my hand until I find it again. I continue to pull. My waste and hips come clear. The tree branch I've been holding with my belt finally gives way, and I find myself teetering on the brink of falling backward into the fetid morass. Just before I overbalance and fall back, I release my hold on the end of my belt and quickly grasp the root with my right hand. With both hands pulling, I'm able to pull myself out of the quicksand altogether.

I lie on the ground, exhausted. I compose myself and peer at the ridge where the blacksuits were standing. They're still there, waiting. They haven't followed me down because they know how treacherous the bottomland is. But I'm well out of range of their arrows. I allow myself five minutes for rest, and then I stand.

I'm covered from head to toe with slime. I scrape off as much as possible.

I can outrun the blacksuits. I've proven that. I walk gingerly over the swampy bottomland toward the bank opposite the one I rolled down. On this side, I'll be out of the range of blacksuit arrows. I pay close attention before placing my feet. I find another pool of quicksand and walk delicately around it.

I look with anguish at the steep bank I must climb to get out of the ravine. The slope is near vertical, but, as I examine it, I can see places where the bank has eroded. I can use the washes to climb out.

Once I reach the top, I run a half mile directly away from the blacksuits on the opposite side. When I'm certain they can't see me, I turn left. I run about two miles in that direction. Then I double back to the ravine. I hide behind foliage as I near the edge of the ravine, checking the far side for blacksuits. There are none.

Quickly, I descend the bank into the swamp once more and pick my way carefully through the mud to the other side. I look up again, checking for strangers. I don't see any, so I begin to climb back out of the ravine. My heart pounds as I think what will happen if the blacksuits should suddenly appear above me. I'll be a sitting duck. But I reach the top without incident. I pause a moment to catch my breath.

Suddenly, I realize I have no idea where the brane is. A blind panic threatens to immobilize me. I fight it down. I have to think clearly. I need a plan. I force myself to calm down.

I try to remember any detail that might help me find the brane again. *There was a stream on my left,"* I remind myself. *"The mountains were on my right.* I hold my breath, listening for the sound of running water. I hear a stream, faint and barely audible. It's ahead of me. Is it the right stream? I have no idea. I have a hazy memory of splashing through a brook as I was putting distance between myself and the blacksuits.

I walk as quickly as I can in the direction of the stream, making as little noise as possible. If there are blacksuits around, I don't want them to hear me. The stream noise is getting louder. The sound of voices in front of me brings me to an instant halt. I fight down the feeling of panic again.

Crouching down low, I can barely make out the blacksuits through the undergrowth. Obviously, they haven't seen me. I lie down flat, making myself as hard to see as possible. Their voices are barely audible, but I catch a few words.

"…lost her," one of them says.

"…back and get Tracker. He'll find…"

"…horn…"

17

One of the blacksuits blows two short bursts on his trumpet. To my relief, they turn and walk slowly away. I realize I've been holding my breath. I let it out. If I interpret what I've heard correctly, they're going back to get someone named Tracker to hunt me down. This fills me with a new sense of urgency. I have to find the brane and get away before Tracker can find me.

I reach the stream. It's only ankle-deep, so I splash into it. I bend over in midstream and scoop up water in my cupped palms. I'm incredibly thirsty. But something about the smell of the water causes me to hesitate. It smells faintly of rotten things, so I ignore my thirst.

I cross to the far side of the stream. *Okay*, I say to myself. *I'm between the stream and the mountains. But is the brane in front of me or behind?* With all the running I've done, I must be past the brane. Praying this is the right stream, I orient myself with the stream to the left and the mountains to the right and begin to walk.

I move quickly, but quietly.

Fifteen minutes later, I have to fight down a gibbering panic that threatens to turn my knees to water. There's no sign of the brane. The thought of being stranded in this blistering hot world, pursued by vicious little men, is unbearable. And without drinkable water, I won't last long. My mouth and throat are parched. I continue walking.

Moments later, I see shimmering light through a break in the trees. I nearly cry with joy. I advance very slowly, trying to stay behind the cover of trees, but I see no sign of blacksuits. Finally, I break into the clearing and sprint as fast as I can through the brane and back into my own world.

2

With the familiar Tucson desert around me and the brane behind, what I want to do most is sit down and cry, cry with relief but also in anguish for Tyler. But Tyler is the reason I can't give in to weakness. I have to get my friends together, and I have to convince some of them to go back with me to get Ty. I simply can't bear the thought of Tyler spending the rest of his life in a strange world with the blacksuits, especially since I was the one who talked him into walking through the brane.

I look at my watch and am amazed to find it's only a little after 10:00 a.m., only three hours since I opened my front door to find Tyler with his urgent message. How quickly life can turn upside down. I briefly wonder what will happen when Tracker hunts me down and finds the brane. Will he come through? I can't imagine small men armed with bows and arrows will want to stay in this world very long. Still, I feel uneasy.

The favorite meeting place for the Tucson Ramblers is the Shake 'n' Burger Restaurant. I do a little computation. It'll take me about half an hour to get down off the mesa and back to Tyler's Jeep. Fortunately, the Shake 'n' Burger is on this side of town, so it'll take me only ten minutes to get there once I'm back to the Jeep.

I take my phone out of my pocket and pray that it hasn't been ruined by quicksand. I rub the muck off it and see the screen glowing faithfully. I speed-dial each of the five missing members of the Tucson Ramblers. My message is the same to each one: "Tyler is in big trouble. And I mean *big*. Meet me at the Shake 'n' Burger in forty minutes. I'll explain everything there." The bond between the seven of us is a strong one. I know everybody will come. But I'm not sure everyone will be willing to go back through the brane. The slime on me has dried, and I'm able to brush most of it off. Even so, I must look frightful.

I descend the mesa as quickly as I can and run to the place where Tyler parked the Jeep. I say a silent prayer that Ty has left the keys in the ignition. If not, I'll have to ask somebody to come get me, and that'll take time. And I have a feeling we need to rescue Tyler quickly, or we may be too late.

I reach the Jeep and breathe a sigh of relief. The keys are in the ignition. There's also a plastic bottle of water. It's warm, but I chug it down. Warm as it is, it's delicious.

* * * * *

The Shake 'n' Burger is a teen hangout. George Becker and his wife, Maureen, own it, and they work the counter every night except Sunday, when they close at seven. Two of my friends, Jules and Bree, work a couple nights a week waiting tables. The decor is strictly old and dated. *Star Wars* posters and pictures of Elvis, James Dean, and Marilyn Monroe cover the walls. Albert Einstein also has a place on the wall in the corner, but he seems out of place among the pop culture icons. One of the world's few surviving jukeboxes sits along the back wall. It too is outdated, but kids pump quarters in anyway. As a result, conversations at the Shake 'n' Burger are always set against a background of "Hound Dog" or "Blueberry Hill."

Despite the dated nature of the decor, the booths are comfortable, and George and Maureen dote on their regular customers. They are childless, so we serve as an extended family. George is short, almost totally bald, and he carries a large belly around. He has a great memory. He knows that my favorite color is royal blue, that my mom works at Applebee's, and that I like my hamburgers pink on the inside with lots of ketchup and mustard but no pickles. Maureen, his wife, is an exact physical opposite: tall and slender with a mountain of hair. Both are in their late fifties, and they've owned the Shake 'n' Burger forever. I remember my mother bringing my twin brothers and me here as toddlers for a chocolate malted, served in a tall, ornate glass.

One of the nice things about George and Maureen is that they are patrons of young art. One wall is dedicated to teenage art. George and Maureen have standards—there can be nothing irreligious, and subjects must all be clad—but the teenage art wall is impressive. There are some very talented young artists in Tucson. They also let teenage bands play on the slow nights: Monday, Tuesday, and Wednesday. Tyler plays guitar for a band that often performs here.

Ten minutes later, I walk into the Shake 'n' Burger to find my friends already assembled and waiting for me in our usual booth in the back corner. They are alarmed to see the muddy apparition I've become.

"What happened to you?" says Grizz, concern in his voice.

* * * * *

I should take a moment and introduce you to the Tucson Ramblers. You'll come to know each of them well as I tell the story, but let me give you a brief sketch of each. Horrible things have happened to some of them, and, because of this, there are scars on my heart that will never heal.

To my immediate right in the booth is Kennedy Carlson. She is as good at chemistry as Tyler is with physics. Although only a sophomore last year, Kenny took classes from Arizona State on the computer, with a trip to the campus in Tempe for a face-to-face every Saturday morning. Her idea of having fun after school is finding interesting new ways to blow things up. At five feet eleven, Kenny is a tall girl, and she has shoulders like a linebacker. This does not discourage boys from flocking around her. Kenny goes through boyfriends the way most girls go through clean underwear. When I ask her about it, she shrugs and tells me she never does anything to lead anybody on. And she doesn't. "Boys have this thing about the big smart girl," she says with a shrug. It doesn't hurt that she's also blonde and gorgeous.

Seated next to Kennedy is Brianne Stone. She's African American with short hair and a beautiful smile. Bree works part time in her dad's garage and hangs around the metal shop at school in her spare time. She owns three ancient

MGBs, *two for parts and one that she actually has running. When she needs a part that isn't made any more, like an air filter, she improvises. There's nothing Bree can't make or fix. She keeps all our cars running, which is quite a job. My F-150 has more than 250,000 miles on it, and Bree has come to know it well. She's barely five feet tall, and thin. Her outsize personality makes her seem larger. She wears glasses with dark rims. They give her a very scholarly look.*

Across the booth from me is Julia Ramirez. She speaks Spanish at home and English everywhere else. She has no trace of an accent, probably because she started kindergarten here in Tucson. She plays number two singles in tennis for our school. Her major is in biology, and she is very active in the drama club. Jules plans to get a PhD and go on to do genome research. Her father works two jobs and her mother does daytime child care and takes in laundry to make ends meet. Like many Arizonans from Mexico, Jules's parents are in the country illegally, so Jules lives under constant threat of being deported. "In our village in Sonora, there is no work," she says. "If the weather is good, people eat well. If the weather is not so good, we live with the hunger. Our lives in Tucson are hard, but so much better." Jules will be the first person in her family to graduate from high school. We hope.

Next to Jules is Fitzhugh Kerrigan Kennedy. His parents call him Fitz, but everybody else calls him Chase. How he got that nickname is a secret lost in the mists of time. If, from his given name, you guess that his parents might be Irish, and very much into the proud-to-be-Irish thing, you would be correct. His close-cropped black hair and bushy black eyebrows make him, in the words of his father, "black Irish." He has two brothers with red hair, which makes them just "Irish." Nobody will ever accuse Chase of being handsome, but he has a thousand-watt smile, and he's one of those folks who can make friends with anyone at any time. We have pointed out that it would be impossible for Chase to marry our friend Kennedy Carlson, because then her name would be Kennedy Kennedy. Chase is also our überjock Although just a sophomore, he's an all-conference defensive end on our high school football team. He's 6 feet 4 inches tall and weighs around 240. He's all-conference because he's on very intimate terms with every quarterback in the league. He enjoys knocking them down. Repeatedly.

On Chase's right is his girlfriend, Charity Wylbur, an extremely pretty cheerleader. Blonde-haired and blue-eyed, she has the face of an angel. But an angel she's not. She's not a charter member of our group. In fact, she doesn't really like us at all. I once overheard her asking Chase why he wanted to be friends with such "little people" when there were so many more important people he could cultivate. She doesn't deign to speak with us except when she has to. We are kind to her because she is Chase's girl, but I don't think any of us really like her. Oh. And her father owns a big tech company out in Research Park. So she's rich as well as beautiful.

And finally, there is Grizz. His real name is Shane Walker, but everybody calls him Grizz. All these people are my close friends, and I'd do anything for them, but Grizz is special. He lives across the street from me, and two doors down. We have been friends forever. I still remember racing tricycles with him when we were four years old. He has the biggest heart of any person in the world. If your car won't start and you need a jump, you call Grizz. If your heart is broken and you need a shoulder to cry on, you call Grizz. If you're nervous about giving an oral presentation, Grizz knows just the right words to say to pump up your confidence.

Grizz got the nickname because of his unruly mop of blond-brown curls that defy the best efforts of every comb to tame them. He would have a beard to match if it weren't for school rules against facial hair. Grizz is a little more than six feet tall, and his pale blue eyes and chiseled features make him very popular with girls, although he doesn't seem particularly interested in finding a girlfriend.

So that's the Tucson Ramblers: three geeks, three jocks, and Grizz. We're an odd bunch no matter how you look at it.

Our group has never been a clique. We've always welcomed newcomers. In fact, Bree didn't join us until fifth grade, and Jules didn't come on board until we were well into middle school. We've never been exclusive. But our odd combination of jocks and geeks has put off a lot of people. And there is also the fierce loyalty we have always had for one another. Most people just aren't ready for that kind of intensity.

You should understand that although there are both boys and girls in our group, there's never been anything romantic between us. Our group has very strong chemistry, and nobody wants any boy-girl nonsense messing that up. We're as close as friends can be, but there's absolutely no romance.

* * * * *

"Tyler needs our help," I begin. I proceed to tell them the story, leaving nothing out. I tell them about the brane, the men in black uniforms, the chase, Tyler's wound, the swamp, and my last view of Ty, surrounded by blacksuits. I also tell them about Tracker.

The expressions on their faces are easy to read. As I began the story, my friends have a look of puzzled concern, trying to figure out why I am telling them this outrageous story, waiting for the punch line. But as I continue, they began to realize I'm deadly serious, and their faces register worry, even shock. Chase's girlfriend, Charity, is the lone exception. She looks at me as if I'm demented, and is planning an exit strategy if I start frothing at the mouth.

When I finish, nobody says a word. I've given them a lot of information to digest. They're trying to fit all the pieces together.

"I'm going to go back for Tyler," I say emphatically. "This could be very, very dangerous. The blacksuits are vicious, and they aren't squeamish about hurting people. There's no shame in staying behind. But I caused the problem, and I need to fix it. Come with me if you will, but there are no hard feelings if you decide not to come. It's a tough decision, so think it through carefully."

Grizz is the first to speak. "So, let me be sure I understand: Tyler is in danger. He's wounded and has been captured by a bunch of creepy little bad guys. And you want us to go with you to help him." He looks at me expectantly.

"That's right," I confirm.

"Well this is a total no-brainer," says Grizz. "Of course I'm going. I'm hurt that you even *thought* I wouldn't go."

"A new universe to explore? Ohhhh yeah. Count me in," Kenny says. This isn't a surprise, as Kenny is always game for an adventure.

Bree adds, "We can't leave Tyler there without trying to help. Count me in."

Jules is cautious by nature. But finally, she says, "I'm coming, too."

This leaves Chase. We all look at him. "There's absolutely no way you're gonna leave me behind. I'm in," he says.

Charity looks at Chase as though he's gone crazy. "No way, Chase. It's way too dangerous. You can't go. I forbid it."

She hasn't yet figured out that telling Chase he can't do something is very bad strategy.

"Look, babe," explains Chase. "Ty and I have history together. He's always been there for me when I needed him. I'd never have passed a single math or science class without his help. He's the guy who taught me how to ride a trail bike without killing myself. I have to go. There's no two ways about it."

Charity isn't ready to give up yet. "How do you know he's still alive? You could go through that brane thing and find out he's already dead."

I patiently explain to her what I'd already made clear: The black suits didn't want to kill us. They were purposely aiming for our legs. Giant people have just shown up on their turf. They want to find out who we are, where we came from, and whether we're a threat. And there's no way Tyler can answer those questions with a story they'll believe.

"Okay," Charity sighs. "I'm coming too."

Charity doesn't care a bit about Tyler. But she's very jealous that Chase has four friends who happen to be girls. She can't believe that we're not all hot for him. So she's not about to leave him alone with a band of Jezebels. I'm sure she's planning to keep her head low, and to run at the first sign of trouble.

"Okay," I say. "Here's the plan. I want everybody to go home and pack a backpack with anything you can think of that might help us get Ty away from the blacksuits. Let's meet at the base of the Mesa in one hour. Be sure to bring water."

* * * * *

The minute I hit the door of my house, I head directly for the shower. My parents aren't home, and that's good, because I won't have to explain how I came to be so dirty and foul smelling. I limit my shower to sixty seconds, although I'd like to spend a lot more time under the soothing jet of warm water. I dry off, dress, and begin to pack.

One of my jobs is as a nurse's aide at Verde Valley Medical Center. I own a very extensive first aid kit, so I throw that into my backpack first. I take a compass (hoping that the new world has a magnetic field) and a pedometer, which is a device that you hook to the front of your belt, just over your thigh. The pedometer keeps track of the distance you've walked. The fear I felt on my first trip through the brane when I thought I might not be able to find my way back to the brane is fresh in my memory. I want to know exactly where I am at all times.

I fill a canteen with tap water and thread my belt through its straps. I rummage through the twins' junk drawer in the basement and find a Boy Scout knife and a pack of matches. My next stop is the attic. We have a great-uncle Aloysius who was evidently quite an adventurer. He made several trips to Africa and was on a polar expedition, along with various other adventures and misadventures. One of the heirlooms he left us is a bowie knife. Calling it a knife is really a misnomer, because it's more like a sword. Three feet long and razor sharp with a wicked serrated blade, it's an impressive weapon. I slide it into its scabbard and strap it to my belt as well. It bumps the side of my leg when I walk, but its solid weight does wonders for my confidence.

I hesitate before throwing a flashlight in my backpack. I'm hoping to get Ty and be back home by nightfall. But in reality, I have no idea where Tyler is. For all I know, the blacksuits may have taken him miles away. I throw the flashlight into the pack.

As I head for my beat-up old red F-150, I'm filled with doubt. What happens if we can't find Tyler? What happens if they've taken him someplace miles and miles away? What happens if they have him surrounded by an army? I choke down the doubt and turn the key in the ignition.

D.S. Northrop

3

I'm the first one to arrive at the base of the mesa, but I see several dust clouds coming down the access road. The whole party joins me within a matter of minutes. We compare backpacks.

Kenny has brought a huge backpack housing a chemistry lab. "I thought we might want to blow something up," she says with a mischievous smile. Inside her backpack is a jumble of bottles, jars, tubes, and wadding. "Everything the modern girl needs to build a bomb," she says cheerfully.

Bree has brought the emergency kit she keeps in the trunk of her MG. She has a small tool kit, ropes, flares, a small collapsible shovel, mosquito repellent, sunscreen, matches, dental floss, and clean wipes. Strapped over her shoulder are a bow and a quiver of arrows. It takes a moment for me to remember that she had a crush on a boy in middle school who was a bow hunter. She took lessons for months, until she broke up with the boy (or maybe the boy broke up with her. I don't remember).

"Can you still shoot that thing?" asks Grizz.

"Yeah, I've kept in practice. Hay bales in the barn," she explains. "I'm Robin Hood in a teenage girl's body."

Jules has brought snacks: energy bars, trail mix, Ho Hos and, of course, Skittles. She has a .22-caliber rifle slung over her shoulder with spare ammunition in her backpack. She also has a blackjack, a weighted bean sack attached to a wooden handle. It's used for bopping people over the head and sending them off to dreamland.

"Jules," says Kenny, "what are you doing with a blackjack? Have you been mugging people at night and not telling us about it? Working out some hostilities, maybe?"

"Nah," says Jules. "Do you remember when I was stage manager for the presentation of *Our Town* we did last year? Well, I was so bossy the cast bought me this thing. They really wanted to get me a whip, but they couldn't find one. If those blacksuits have hurt Ty, I'll definitely enjoy using it."

Chase also has a .22 rifle. He and Jules enjoy blowing holes in aluminum cans and plastic jars together. "A twenty-two doesn't have much stopping power," Chase explains, "but it may be just what we need. If the little folks you ran into are using bows and arrows, just the sound of a rifle may be enough to slow them down."

Grizz has brought a wicked-looking machete. His great-grandfather fought in the Pacific during World War II, he explains, and a machete was standard gear for troops who had to hack their way through jungles. It seems Great-Grandpa didn't bother to return it to the Marines. Grizz has also brought binoculars, a slingshot, ball bearings (for the slingshot, I assume), a hatchet, a walking stick with a loop that fits over his wrist, and a huge Swiss Army knife.

Charity has brought her purse, but she doesn't seem anxious to share its contents with us.

It doesn't matter. Between us, we have assembled a pretty impressive arsenal. "Okay," I say. "Let's go."

Twenty minutes later, we're atop the mesa. My friends are staring at the brane. There's a look of slack-jawed awe on everyone's face, just as there was on mine a few hours ago.

"Let's do this thing," I say. I take a deep breath and walk through the brane.

* * * * *

"Good grief, will somebody *please* turn on the air-conditioning!" complains Kenny.

My grandparents live in Phoenix, which is at a lower altitude than Tucson, and thus somewhat hotter. When I visit them in the summer, it's not uncommon for the temperature to hit 120 degrees. This is worse. Much worse.

"This is hotter than most saunas I've been in," says Bree, exaggerating slightly.

"You gotta be kidding me," complains Charity. "This is unreal. Chase, let's go back."

"Can't do that, babe," he responds. "You can leave if you want to."

Charity stays put.

Jules looks frightened. Grizz notices this and moves to her side. He talks with her in a soft voice. Typical Grizz. Always aware of the feelings of others and always knowing just the right words to say.

"What's the matter with these trees?" asks Kenny. "They're scarcely taller than bushes."

"Everything here seems to be smaller," I explain.

Everybody is nervous. Perspiring. Swallowing hard. Jittery. And no wonder. They *know* there are bad things around. Ty and I didn't.

"Which way do we go, ET?" asks Grizz.

Everybody looks at me. I set my pedometer to zero, and I'm pleased to discover the compass seems to work here. I have no idea whether the magnetic pole is north, south, east, or west of us, but the compass says the direction ahead of us is north and the brane, behind us, is to the south.

"Arm yourselves," I advise.

Jules and Chase unsling their rifles. Bree reaches for her bow and notches an arrow. Chase and I unsheathe our knives. Grizz loans Kenny his walking stick. It's sturdy enough to use as a club. He offers his slingshot to Charity, but she declines.

"Don't make any more noise than you have to," I caution.

"That way," I say.

The forest is exactly as I remember it. Trees are far enough apart to make walking easy in most places, but dense undergrowth forces us to circle around in others. Birds sing in the trees. We stop and listen every few minutes. We hear nothing but birdsong. Occasionally, a small animal makes a rustling sound in the undergrowth. Every unfamiliar noise sets my heart pounding.

I check my pedometer. We've come two miles. I begin to worry because there's no sign of blacksuits. Perhaps they've taken Ty miles away.

I stop abruptly. I smell something that can only mean humans are near: wood smoke, drifting through the trees.

"Do you smell that?" I ask.

Everybody nods.

"You stay here. I'll go and scout ahead," I say.

"I'm not letting you go alone," declares Grizz.

Grizz has always had this instinct to protect me. I'm not a helpless girly girl. I can take care of myself. So Grizz's protectiveness is annoying, but also a little sweet. I know there's no way to stop him from coming, so I simply shrug. "Okay, let's go."

We crouch down and move slowly forward, careful to place our feet where they won't snap branches. I'm surprised at how little noise two desert kids make in the woods when they're scared. Through the trees I see a clearing. We go down on all fours and crawl very slowly toward the tree line.

When we reach the edge of the forest, we get down on our bellies and peer out from behind the foliage. Before us are hundreds of acres of cultivated land. There is a fenced area where the villagers keep a few scrawny-looking little sheep. It must be near high summer here, because the sheep have been recently shorn. They look naked without their wooly coats.

In the center of the clearing is a fortress made of logs. The logs are placed vertically, with one end sunken in the ground. It's not great architecture, but it looks solid nonetheless. I estimate the height of the walls at about six feet. Looming over the walls is a watchtower, easily thirty feet high. There are hundreds of people working in the fields. The people here are no taller than the blacksuits, but nobody is dressed in black, and, as far as I can tell, nobody is carrying a weapon. The men are all bearded, and the hair of the women is knotted in buns. There are hundreds of children in the fields.

Sprinkled throughout the fields are a number of round structures with inward-sloping roofs. Irrigation tanks, I think.

Grizz hands me his binoculars. I examine the watchtower. Two men are manning it, but neither wears a black uniform. So far, so good. Still, there's a good chance that the blacksuits are somewhere inside the fortress.

"How many people, do you figure?" I ask.

"I'd guess maybe four or five thousand. And that's just the ones we can see. No telling how many are on the other side of the fort."

"Or inside," I add.

There's a part of me that wants to turn around and run and keep running until I'm back on Midnight Mesa. Then I think of Tyler: wounded, on the ground, surrounded by blacksuits. And I know I'm responsible for getting him into this predicament. So I fight down my fear.

"Can you think of an idea better than standing up and walking into the field?" I ask.

Grizz thinks for a moment. "Nope. Why don't you wait while I go out there?"

That's Grizz-the-Protector-of-Erin speaking. "That's not gonna happen," I reply. "Remember, at the first sign of trouble, we run like crazy. These people can't run nearly as fast as we do."

* * * * *

I stand up. Grizz stands as well. We walk slowly into the field, arms spread wide with palms out, a gesture that shows we're not carrying weapons. My heart is pounding in my chest, and my mouth is beyond dry. Grizz looks nervous as well.

Two young girls a few yards away take one look at us, scream, drop their tools, and run toward the fortress. I can't blame them. If two fifteen-foot tall giants suddenly appeared on my front lawn, I'd be scared too.

The men in the watchtower spot us and blow their bugles. One long burst. People all over the fields drop their tools and run toward the fortress. An old man about twenty yards away stands his ground.

"Wait!" shouts the old man. "They are not armed, and they look friendly."

People within the sound of his voice stop, turn around, and watch us with guarded curiosity.

The old man walks toward us. We meet him halfway. His hair is long and unkempt. Like all the men in the fields, he is bearded. Beneath the beard is a friendly face. Despite his short stature, he is a perfectly formed human in every other way, right down to his receding hairline. He smiles. He is missing several teeth, but his smile is warm anyway.

"My name is Bertram," he says.

"I'm Erin, and this is Grizz," I reply. "We've come from far away."

"Please, come with me," Bertram says. He turns and walks toward the fort.

Well I'll be, I think to myself. Grizz and I follow the old man.

"Geffrey!" the man shouts. "Run to the village and tell the elders the council needs to assemble."

A young man ahead of us, Geffrey, I assume, turns and runs toward the village.

I estimate the size of the fields around the fort to be several hundred acres. Short green plants are growing in most fields. Others look as though they have just been cultivated.

A series of dirt paths radiate from the fort in all directions. They provide access to the fields so people don't have to trample the crops on the way to or from the village. Nobody is on our path, except for the old man. People watch us from a distance, curious, but obviously not trusting us entirely.

"This is turning out well," I whisper to Grizz.

Grizz snorts. "Unless they're leading us inside so they won't have to drag us in from the fields before they cook and eat us," he whispers back.

"Why Grizz, what a nice thought." I smile despite my nervousness.

Bertram ushers us through the gates. The fort is much bigger than it looked from the outside. It's immediately obvious that these are poor people. The houses are small and made from mud and thatch. Most of the people are very thin. Clothing is made from rough homespun wool, and shows signs of patches and patches over patches. Many of the people have open sores on their faces, hands, and arms.

Smoke coming from chimneys provides evidence of cooking fires. They certainly don't need fire to keep their houses warm. The buildings are all made from mud and wattle. They are tiny. Everything about these people speaks of their poverty.

We are surrounded by curious villagers. Most appear a little frightened, but one little boy, about five years old with running sores on his face, cautiously walks up to Grizz and touches his hand.

"Your skin feels just like mine," he says, surprised.

"We're the same as you in every way," replies Grizz. "We're just a little taller. Do you want to see what the world looks like to a giant?" he asks.

"Yeah!" says the boy excitedly.

Grizz picks him up and hoists him onto his shoulders. The little boy squeals with delight.

My heart is still hammering away, but I'm encouraged because nobody seems to be threatening us in any way. The expressions I see are ones of curiosity, with a little fear nibbling around the edges. Grizz's easy rapport with the little boy has put many villagers at ease.

Bertram ushers us into a large round mud-and-wattle building. There's a rough-hewn round table in the center of the big common room. The floor is simple packed dirt. Small openings in the walls admit a faint light. Even so, the room is dark. Dark though it is, the room is vast. I suspect this must be the room where they hold town meetings. The ceiling is low, and we must duck our heads once inside. Seated around the table are a group of twelve old men and women. This must be the council Bertram spoke of. We can hear a soft buzz of voices from outside. The people of the village are waiting to see what's going to happen.

An elderly woman invites us to sit at the table. The members of the council appear to be as poor as the people we saw on our way into the village. They are tiny as well.

Grizz and I sit cross-legged on the floor because the benches around the table are much too small to support us. Bertram introduces us to the council. He tells us the name of each person at the table.

"We need your help," I begin.

"First, we must share water," says the woman at the head of the table. Her name is Muriel. She has beautiful blue eyes. Her back is hunched, and she seems to be the oldest person on the council.

Attendants bring us tiny earthen cups and fill them with water.

"Thank you, Mother, for the gift of water," intones Muriel.

Everyone at the table downs his or her cup. Grizz and I do likewise. These people don't *seem* sinister, but I can't help hoping that the water isn't drugged or poisoned.

"We apologize for the small size of the water offering," says Muriel, "but the monsoons are late this year."

Lack of water, I reflect, would also help explain the earthy smell of the bodies around us. The sharing of water finished, all eyes turn toward Muriel.

"So tell us, giants, why we should not kill you," she says. Her blue eyes are as cold as a glacier.

Six men and women armed with spears enter the building and stand behind Grizz and me.

* * * * *

Grizz tenses, ready to move into action.

I place my hand on his forearm. *Not yet, Grizz.*

"We mean you absolutely no harm," I explain, hoping my voice doesn't sound as shaky as I feel.

Bertram speaks next. "Muriel, they have been peaceful and cooperative."

Another woman, named Cressida, speaks. "Muriel, we can't kill strangers just because they're strangers. That would make us no better than the courtsmen."

Could these "courtsmen" be the same as our blacksuits?

Discussion continues. The majority of the council seems to oppose putting us to death.

Greatly relieved and sensing a favorable turn of events, I decide to take a chance. "We were hoping you could help us," I say. "As I have said, we are from a place far away. One of our people was wounded and taken prisoner by men wearing black uniforms. We just want to get him back. As soon as we rescue him, we'll go back to our home, and you'll never see us again."

Everyone on the council begins to speak at once. Bertram asks for silence.

"You have met the courtsmen?" he asks.

"If the courtsmen wear black uniforms, we certainly have met them," I reply, "and the circumstances were regrettable. They captured my friend and took him away."

Addressing the entire council, Bertram says, "The enemy of my enemy is my friend."

Even Muriel nods in approval.

"Who are these courtsmen?" I ask.

"They are lackeys of the Court," snarls Muriel derisively.

"And what is the Court?" I ask.

"The Court." Muriel spits out the words as though they have a bitter taste. "They are nine men who think of themselves as our masters."

Bertram adds, "Their hearts are as black as the robes they wear. We are nothing but slaves to them." His words are harsh.

"Do you know where they've taken our friend?" I ask.

"They have probably taken him to Fort Warren. That is the Court's outpost for our village. It is not far from here," explains Bertram.

I feel an upwelling of hope. "Can you tell us how to get there?" I ask. This could be a tremendous break for us.

"I will show them the way," says one of the guards who entered the room with spears. He is middle-aged and stands ramrod straight. His blue eyes match Muriel's in intensity.

"You are not a member of the council, Falstaff. Hold your tongue," says Muriel.

"There is no harm in showing the giants the way to Fort Warren," counsels Bertram. He gets murmurs of support from the council.

"No harm!" says Muriel, raising her voice. "Do you not know what will happen if the courtsmen find out we have helped these people? Absolutely not! It's too dangerous."

"There will be no danger of the courtsmen finding out," says the guardsman named Falstaff. "We will show them where to go, and we will make sure there is no trail for Tracker to follow."

Muriel is obviously displeased with this second interruption from Falstaff. But one by one, the members of the council speak. There are nine members in favor of helping us. Only three are opposed.

"The council has spoken," concedes Muriel reluctantly. She turns and addresses Falstaff. "You had best cover the tracks well. You know what the penalty will be if you don't."

"Tracker will never know the giants were here," promises Falstaff.

4

Preparations for our departure are completed in a matter of minutes. Falstaff and three helpers will accompany us to the blacksuits' camp. The three helpers carry tree branches still heavy with leaves. As we walk across the village's fields, they rake the ground behind us with the branches, obscuring our trail. I can see they've already erased the trail we made earlier, when we entered the clearing.

"We will go back to the point where you entered our fields," says Falstaff. "To Tracker, it will appear as if you looked in at us and decided to turn around and leave."

Once we reenter the woods, the sweepers stop sweeping. Falstaff wants a trail of giant tracks leading away from the village.

We rejoin our friends where we had left them. They jump to their feet when they see us.

"You were gone forever," says Jules. "We were afraid we'd lost you."

We introduce our friends to Falstaff and his companions. They eye each other cautiously.

"So now we have good-guy little people and bad-guy little people?" asks Kenny.

Falstaff is clearly not happy about being called "little." "We are *not* little," he huffs defensively. "You are big."

Diplomacy is not one of Kenny's strongest suits. Jules kicks her sharply on the ankle.

"Ouch! Sorry, I didn't mean to insult you," she apologizes abashedly. "It's just that in our world, we're normal sized. Well, except for Chase. He's pretty big everywhere. And I'm really big for a girl."

"Your apology is acceptable," says Falstaff.

I study Falstaff. Although short, he has the body of a wrestler: no neck, muscular arms, and a thick torso. His striking blue eyes stand out in a face otherwise dominated by a bushy red beard and a prominent hawk nose. He is a man to be taken seriously, a let's-get-down-to-business, no-nonsense man.

Grizz and I recount the events in the village. At the end of our explanation, we add, "These friends are going to lead us to where Tyler is being held."

"Then you know where Tyler is!" says Chase.

"We think so," I reply.

They immediately begin to pepper us with questions.

"How many blacksuits are defending the fort?" asks Kenny.

"The gleaning for this year is done," says Falstaff. "So there will only be twenty courtsmen guarding the fort, although some of them may be out on patrol."

"What's a 'gleaning'?" I ask.

"Once a year," Falstaff begins, "during the season of the long days, the courtsmen come and choose a hundred of our biggest and strongest young boys, and a hundred of our prettiest young women, and take them away from us, back to the cities. The young men are used for heavy labor. They call the young women 'breeding stock.' The men who are chosen for labor do not live long. Most live only a few years. So, they need the female 'breeders' to help replace the losses. They also breed our young women to produce courtsmen." Falstaff's voice is barely controlled. I can see the range of emotions he is feeling: sorrow, rage, frustration, bitterness. They're all reflected in his voice.

"No wonder you hate them so," I say softly. A long period of silence follows.

Chase finally breaks the silence. "And how are these courtsmen armed?"

Falstaff shakes his head to break his torpor. "Each courtsman will have a bow for fighting at a distance, and a sword for fighting at close range. Some of them are also trained in the use of spears."

"How big is their fort?" asks Bree.

"Not big," he answers, "a small fraction of the size of our village. You could easily fit fifty forts inside the walls of our village."

"Twenty little men with bows and arrows," says Chase. "I say we can take 'em."

Heads nod around the circle.

"Let's get Tyler back," exclaims Kenny.

"Show us the way, Falstaff," I ask.

Falstaff guides us about fifty yards through the forest, until we intersect a rough trail hewn through the trees.

"This is the trail the courtsmen follow when they come to pay us a visit, which they do every day," explains Falstaff. "It will lead us directly to Fort Warren."

"If this trail leads directly to the blacksuits' fort, you don't need to come any farther," I say.

"I want to come," responds Falstaff. "I want to see someone fight back against the courtsmen for once."

"That's just what you're going to see," I promise.

I dutifully read the compass and check the pedometer. I've been taking readings every step of the way so far, and am certain I can find my way back to the brane.

Falstaff's band walks in front of us now. "I don't want our footprints on top of yours," he explains. "That would tell Tracker a story I don't want him to know. Your prints on top of ours mean very little. The courtsmen use this trail as well, so our prints and theirs look about the same. With you walking behind us, your prints will wipe out most of ours anyway. The only real danger now is that we will run into the courtsmen coming the other way."

I shudder as I consider that possibility.

"Let's have our weapons ready," I suggest, "and be as quiet as we can."

We are all sweating profusely. Walking on the trail is less physically demanding than walking through the forest, but there is little shade out in the open. The sun beats down on us mercilessly. Occasionally, we pass through meadows and see plants with tiny yellow flowers. They are the only beautiful thing we've seen in this otherwise unattractive world.

We continue on for twenty-five minutes. I know it is twenty-five minutes because I'm constantly monitoring time, the pedometer, and my compass. The trail leads just west of south.

Finally, Falstaff raises his hand in warning. We stop dead in our tracks. Falstaff motions me forward. I join him, moving as quickly and quietly as possible. He points his finger. Through the trees, I can make out the blacksuits' fort.

* * * * *

We crawl on our bellies to the edge of the clearing. Everybody except Charity and Chase, that is. She stands on the trail, quietly. Charity has checked out. Not physically, but emotionally. She has a vacant stare, and I don't think she's said a word since we left the medicine wheel. I'm worried about her. Chase is at her side, arm around her, trying to comfort her. He's obviously devoted to her.

44

Each of us is careful to remain screened from view behind the foliage. Obviously, we don't want the blacksuits to know we are here. Grizz lends me his binoculars again. Falstaff was right. The wall in front of us appears to be about fifty feet long. There is a hammering sound coming from inside the fort. Somebody is making or fixing something. A thin plume of smoke rises in the still air. The walls are about six feet high, just like Falstaff's village. Also like Falstaff's village, there is a tall watchtower in the center. There is one blacksuit in the watchtower. I can make out the shoulders and head of another man, walking back and forth along an elevated walkway inside the wall in front of us. The fort is easily a hundred yards from our position at the wood line. There is no way to approach the fort without being instantly visible to the guards.

I'm frustrated because I can see only one wall. Slipping the straps of the binoculars around my neck, I find a tree set back from the clearing and climb it. Like all trees here, it is short and gnarled. Still, by climbing to the apex, I can see the tops of all four walls. There are guards on each wall.

I shinny back down, and signal my companions to join me. We retreat back down the trail far enough that we can speak quietly without danger of being overheard by blacksuits in the fort.

"We can't just walk up and knock on the door and ask for our friend back," I say. "Does anybody have any ideas how we can get Tyler out of there?"

Everyone looks thoughtful.

"We need to cause some sort of a distraction to get the guards' attention," suggests Grizz.

"Any ideas?" I look around.

Falstaff clears his throat. "The rains are very late this year. The timbers of the fort are very dry. If you could shoot a fire arrow into the fort, the courtsmen would have to move fast to put it out or risk the whole fort going up in flame."

"Bree," I ask, "can you put an arrow in the fort from here?"

"Not from here," she replies. "The range is too great. If I can get a little closer, I can."

"The minute you walk into that clearing, you'll have blacksuits swarming around you," I point out.

"That's not a bad thing," says Grizz. "Once they see Bree, they'll come charging out of the fort. You said they can't run very fast. Bree can draw them a mile or so into the forest, lose them, loop around, and rejoin us here."

"That's a great idea," says Bree. "Me, chased by a bunch of murderous little men in black uniforms. What's not to like?"

"That could very well empty out the fort," I muse. "But I doubt the sentries will leave their posts."

"Two diversions would be better than one, no?" suggests Kenny.

Kenny is a chemistry genius, and blowing things up is one of her many hobbies. So I know what's coming next.

Sure enough, Kenny continues, "Right after Bree gets their attention with a fire arrow and all the blacksuits go running after her, I can blow a hole in the wall on the other side of the fort. I can sneak up to the wall while everybody is watching Bree, plant the bomb, get out of the blast zone, but stay close to the wall. The sentries will never see me if I hug the wall. I can also set off a little smoke bomb to limit their vision." Kenny is obviously thrilled with the idea of building bombs that have a real purpose.

"I think this just might work!" says Chase. "While the guards are wondering who blew a hole in their wall, Grizz and I can sneak over the front wall, snatch Tyler, and climb back out."

"There's still going to be a guard on every wall," I point out. "Even if the guard is distracted, he's still going to notice a bunch of giant people climbing over his wall."

"That's where this comes in," says Jules, digging the blackjack out of her backpack. She hands it to Chase.

"And besides," adds Grizz, "who said anything about a bunch of giant people going over the wall? It's just Chase and I."

"I'm coming too," I insist.

* * * * *

Falstaff and his friends are unhappy to be excluded from our plans. But they agree it would bring great danger on their village if they were to be seen helping us.

"We don't want to hurt any of the blacksuits if we can avoid it," I say. "But Jules, if one of the guards sees us while we're inside the fort, can you hit him with your twenty-two?"

"You want me to hit a guy a hundred yards away while I'm perched in a tree," says Jules. "That's a tough shot, but I can try. Even a near miss will get their attention."

We spend the next several moments refining our plan, working out our timing. Everybody has a job. Bree hits them with a fire arrow. While they're watching Bree, Kenny comes up behind them and plants her bomb. While they're distracted by the bomb, Grizz, Chase, and I climb the wall and find Tyler. Jules is our sniper. Charity, I guess, watches.

We decide we'll need two fire arrows, in case one misses. I wrap gauze from my first aid kit around the tip of Bree's arrows. She watches carefully, and reminds me if the weight is lopsided, the arrow won't fly true. Grizz digs a can of lighter fluid and a Zippo lighter from his backpack. Bree stuffs them in the hip pocket of her Old Navy jeans.

Some of us bite lips or fingernails. Others shift their weight from one foot to the other and back again. Chase shakes his arms as they hang limp by his side. We're all nervous, more nervous than we've ever been before in our lives. Our plan sounds good, but who knows what's going to happen? If anything goes wrong, some of us could die.

"Are we ready?" I ask tensely.

Everybody answers affirmatively.

"Kenny plants her bomb when she hears the commotion Bree causes," I remind everybody. "Grizz, Chase, and I take off as soon as we hear Kenny's bomb explode. Everybody rendezvous back here. We wait until Bree circles back after she loses the blacksuits."

We all agree.

"Let's roll," I say.

* * * * *

We wait as Kenny quickly assembles her bombs. She hums as she works. Occasionally she stops and mumbles something about "combining reactants" or "controlling the blast field." She is done in a matter of minutes. "Ready," she announces. "This will definitely do the job." She is grinning from ear to ear.

Five of us wait as Bree and Kenny get to their jumping-off points. Jules climbs her tree.

Bree slowly and deliberately walks from the tree line toward the fort.

The guard in the watchtower sees her and blows his horn. "Giant coming from the west!" he shouts. A throng of heads appears along the west wall. Just as quickly, they disappear. Bugles sound. We hear running and shouting inside the fort.

Bree walks about halfway to the fort, douses the tip of an arrow with lighter fluid, lights the tip, and notches it. She lets the arrow fly, and it embeds itself in the watchtower, ten feet below the sentry's perch. The sentry cries out, takes off his shirt, and tries to beat out the fire with it. He's unsuccessful, because the fire is beyond his reach.

The gates of the fort open, and eleven blacksuits come spilling out. We've really poked the hornet's nest. Seeing the men coming, Bree turns and runs for the tree line. No need for a second arrow.

The sentries hold their positions. Eleven men pursue Bree, and there are five sentries. That leaves four blacksuits unaccounted for. They're either in the fort or out on patrol. I hope for the latter.

Less than a minute after the blacksuits leave, there is a resounding blast from the east side of the fort.

"Half the wall is down," crows Jules from her perch in the tree.

This is followed by a much less impressive-sounding pop. The hole in the east wall is now obscured by a huge cloud of black smoke. Kenny has set off her smoke bomb as well.

The sentries are looking at the billowing smoke with a look of terror, wondering, probably, what horrible apparition will emerge from that thick cloud. They've seen enough. They vault over the wall, land outside the fort, and run for the trees. This is a pre-gunpowder society, I realize. The appearance of a giant with fire arrows, followed by a huge explosion blowing a hole in their wall, has unmanned them.

Grizz, Chase, and I sprint for the fort. Just before we reach the wall, the sentry from the tower throws open the gate in front of us. Seeing us bearing down on him, he screams and changes course. He's headed for the trees to the east, leaving the gate open. Good luck for us. We don't have to climb over the wall after all.

Tyler is not hard to find. His hands are tied behind him, and he is lashed to a post in the center of the fort. He is slumped down. As we reach him, I see his face is a misshapen mass of bruises. His right eye is swollen shut, his lips puffy, and split in three places. He smiles when he sees us and instantly winces in pain. The blacksuits have not removed the arrow from his leg. In fact, his pant leg is stiff with dried blood from the knee down.

Grizz wastes no time using his pocketknife to cut through the vines that bind Ty to the pole. Tyler is obviously in no shape to walk, let alone run. Chase picks him up and carries him in his arms. We leave the fort and return to the trees.

Kenny is already there, and Jules has climbed down from her post in the tree. We settle down to wait for Bree.

"Why did they do this to you?" I ask Ty.

"They didn't like my answers to their questions," he replies. "They think I *made* the brane. They call it the strange light." He shrugs and winces in pain again. "I told them I came *through* the strange light, but I didn't *make* it. They didn't believe me. They think I must have used some magic or voodoo, and they wanted me to show them how I did it."

A crashing sound in the undergrowth heralds Bree's return. She is breathing heavily.

"When they heard the sound of Kenny's explosion, they stopped chasing me. They turned around and made a beeline back to the fort," says Bree.

Sure enough, as if on cue, the blacksuits who were trailing Bree appear at the edge of the clearing. The fire in the tower is now raging, and Kenny's bomb has caused a second fire on the east wall. The returning blacksuits, finding their fort afire and half a wall missing, mill around, frightened and disorganized.

We won't have to worry about pursuit. The blacksuits have their hands full.

Falstaff approaches me, tears in his eyes. I do a double take. Falstaff has been nothing but gruff and formal with us. His helpers are in tears as well.

"Falstaff, why are you crying?" I ask. "I thought you hated the blacksuits."

"These are tears of joy," he responds.

He seizes me in a tight embrace. The top of his head is level with my belly button.

"All my life I've wanted to see someone fight back against the courtsmen. Thank you. Thank you." He releases me and faces each of my friends in turn. "Mother bless you all," he says.

"You're welcome, Falstaff. But we have to leave now," I say.

"Mother go with you," Falstaff says. His helpers echo his words. They turn and head for home down the trail. There's a spring in their steps that wasn't there an hour ago.

Falstaff stops and turns around. "I hope you are not traveling far," he says.

"No," I reply. "Our journey will be short. Why do you ask?"

"In this land, you must never be out in the forest at night," Falstaff warns. "You won't live to see the sun rise."

That sounds creepy. "We'll be gone well before nightfall," I assure him.

"Okay," I say, "we head northeast until we cross the stream, and then we head due north until we find the brane. Mission accomplished!"

We all exultantly pump our fists in the air and turn to the northeast.

* * * * *

Tyler isn't very heavy, but dead weight takes its toll. Chase and Grizz take turns carrying him. We're talking and laughing, recounting our brilliant plan and the panicked way the blacksuits were milling around at the end.

Suddenly, I hear Jules cry out in fear. I look up to find four blacksuits ready to loose arrows. I dive and hit the ground so hard my jaw rattles. I hear two *thunk* sounds behind me. I glance over my shoulder quickly and find two arrows imbedded in a tree just behind me. Had I not gone down when I did, they surely would have hit me. A split second later, Jules cries in pain. There's an arrow buried in her left shoulder. Another arrow barely misses Chase, who is carrying Tyler.

At the top of a hill to our right, the four blacksuits are reaching for another arrow. One of them crumples as Bree's arrow takes him in the chest. Chase's .22 barks, and another goes down, crying out and clutching his leg. Grizz is brandishing his walking stick, swinging it in circles over his head. He yells and charges up the hill toward the remaining two blacksuits. The blacksuits think better of stringing another arrow. They turn and run in the opposite direction.

"Let 'em go," I holler after Grizz. "Let's just get to the brane and get out of here."

The wounded blacksuit is desperately crawling away from us. I recognize him as the man with the scarred face who stopped Tyler and I in the clearing this morning. I feel an instant impulse to take vengeance for all the problems he's caused us. I can't kill him in cold blood, so we leave him.

Grizz turns back. "I guess we found the four blacksuits missing from the fort's garrison," he says.

I turn to Jules. She's staring at the arrow in her shoulder. Her face is ashen. I examine her wound. The arrow did not penetrate deeply. No arteries have been hit.

"I think the wound is superficial. This'll hurt," I warn. I gently work the arrow loose as Jules yelps in pain.

I rummage through my first aid kit and find disinfectant, gauze, and tape. I splash on disinfectant, cover the wound with a wad of gauze, and tape it in place. Jules winces every time I touch her.

"I'll clean it and take another look at it after we get back through the brane," I promise. Jules nods.

I turn back and find Bree on her knees with tears streaming down her face.

"I just killed a man," she whispers. She begins to sob.

Grizz is at her side in an instant. He kneels, wraps his arms around her, and rocks her gently back and forth. "You had no choice," he says softly. "If you hadn't stopped him, he'd have killed one of us."

"But I k-k-killed him," Bree stutters.

Bree collects herself after a few moments. Grizz hands her his handkerchief. She wipes the tears from her face and blows her nose. "Let's just get out of this place," she murmurs.

I understand why she feels bad. If I find a spider indoors, I herd him onto a piece of paper and deposit him outdoors. The taking of a human life, even a bad one, is no small matter.

"You did the right thing, Bree," I offer. The others echo this sentiment.

Bree still looks miserable. We are a more somber group as we continue our march toward the brane.

We find the stream, and Grizz, who is in the lead, splashes across. Kenny follows. When she reaches the far side, she stops, scoops up water in her cupped palms, and takes a drink. She immediately vomits. She heaves again and again. When the spasms stop, she sits up, pale and sweating.

"I guess you shouldn't drink the water here." Kenny puts on a brave smile, but she looks weak. "I was so thirsty, and the water looked really good."

I remember my own experience with the water early this morning, and how I had thought it smelled of corruption. My suspicions have been confirmed.

When Kenny feels strong enough to walk, we continue onward. We've crossed the creek, so the brane will be to our north. We turn left.

I'm halfway across the clearing before I realize where I am. This is the clearing with the medicine wheel. The cairn of rocks sits in the middle. The crying angel is right where we last saw her.

But there is no brane.

5

It takes a moment for everyone to realize the significance of what we see, or, rather, what we don't see.

"This must be the wrong clearing," cries Charity. These are the first words she's spoken since morning.

"This is the right place, all right," says Grizz. "Look, there's the cairn of stones, and the crying angel is right there. The brane just isn't here anymore." He is clearly shaken.

My knees feel weak. My jaw chatters as my legs give out, and I suddenly find myself sitting down. The implications are enormous. We're stuck in this horrible world. I think of my family. How will they pay the bills without my paychecks? My room, my car, my clothes, my jobs. All gone. All my plans for premed, vanished.

Each of us reacts to this tragic turn in our own way. Charity is sobbing. Chase is trying to console her. Grizz is walking around, turning his head this way and that, as though he might be able to see the brane if he looks at it differently. Bree is biting her knuckle. Kenny is stomping around, kicking rocks and muttering. Most of us are crying softly. Tears well up in my eyes, but I am determined not to cry. I need to keep my head clear.

"Ty," I say, "why is the brane gone?"

Tyler blows his nose and responds, "I'm so sorry." Tears stream down his face. "The brane was open last night, and it was open again today. I had no way of knowing the parameters for keeping it open were so narrow. Earth is still getting hit by massive solar flares and substantial gamma ray radiation. That much isn't changing. I guess they have to be present in just the right combination and in the right range."

Seeing how guilty Ty feels, I put my arm around him.

"Not your fault, buddy," says Grizz. "You had no way of knowing."

"Ty, do you think the brane will reopen?" I ask gently.

"I guess it's possible that the conditions for opening the brane could reoccur."

"Is it probable or just possible?" I ask.

"There's no way to know," replies Tyler.

"What do we do now?" asks Kenny.

Everybody looks at me. I don't know how I became the leader of our little band. We've all been equals ever since grade school. I may have had a little tendency to be bossy at times, but I've never been our leader.

"We wait," I say.

* * * * *

Despite his enormous size now, Chase was a slow developer, and Grizz was the one who kept the bullies at bay in elementary school. Tyler, Kenny, and I have been tutors to everyone. Bree and Jules organize birthday parties and other celebrations. We are all givers.

I can tell one story about myself that illustrates how we look after one another.

Last year, I had a ferocious crush on Jared Cain, the quarterback of our football team. The amazing thing was that he was interested in me. I've never really had a boyfriend, so Jared's attention was as unexpected as it was wonderful. I knew that he had a reputation as a "love 'em and leave 'em" guy. But he seemed so in love with me, I knew I'd be different.

At the beginning, everything was amazing. He was attentive, interesting, funny, flattering, and handsome. I got flowers one day and chocolate the next. He wanted to be with me every opportunity he had. In short, he was everything a girl could want. I'd never felt so happy in all my life.

Storm clouds began to gather after about two weeks. He wanted to take our relationship to a level that I was uncomfortable with. At first, it was only a minor problem. But he became more insistent as time went by. Finally, we had a huge fight. He slapped me, hard, and stormed out of my house, slamming the door behind him. I had to put makeup on my face to cover the bruise before school the next morning.

Jared avoided me at school the next day. After school, as I left the building, I saw him sitting on a bench just outside the doors with his arm around Zoe Kerber. His eyes never met mine, but Zoe's eyes did, and her smile was a mean one. Jared never spoke to me again.

Grizz was the one who held me for hours as I cried my eyes out. He was gentle and kind. He didn't try to cheer me up with empty clichés. He didn't point out the fact that I'd been a silly fool to fall for Jared in the first place. He was just there. The girls brought me sympathy cards, Ho Hos, and Skittles, and they took me out to a couple shows to cheer me up. Ty came by after school every day and told me jokes until I was laughing so hard I'd had to hold my sides. Grizz called me every night to make sure I was okay.

Chase stuck up for me in a much different way. Chase plays defensive end on our high school's football team, and Jared is the quarterback. Chase is a specialist at crushing quarterbacks.

During football practice, quarterbacks wear red jerseys to tell everyone that they should not be tackled. Coach doesn't want his star quarterback to get hurt. Chase ignored the red shirt and leveled Jared. When he described it to me later, he called it a "slobber knocker hit." As he got up, Chase whispered to Jared, "That's for ET." Coach was hopping mad. Chase apologized. On the next play, Chase clobbered Jared again. Once again, Chase whispered to Jared, "That's for ET."

Coach told Chase to take a shower and wait for him in his office. When Coach came in after practice, he asked Chase what the problem was. After Chase explained, Coach simply said that even though Jared was a total jerk, he was still QB number one, and he didn't want him hurt. Chase explained that he had been careful to hit Jared high so injury wasn't likely. He said he'd made his point and promised it'd never happen again. They let it go at that.

This is what I mean when I say we're fiercely loyal to one another.

Of course, venturing into another world to save a friend from a bunch of homicidal pygmies is another pretty good example.

* * * * *

I examine Tyler's wounds. There's not much I can do for his puffy face. I clean out the cuts and put disinfectant on them. His knee is in terrible shape. Cartilage and muscle have been torn. I can see the bone exposed.

"The blacksuits kept twisting and turning the arrow to convince me to tell them the 'truth,'" Tyler explains. "It hurt so bad, and they wouldn't stop. I bled all over the place."

Bree and Kenny hold Tyler as I remove the arrow. Ty is doing his best to put on a brave face, but the pain is too great. He cries out in pain as the arrow comes out. There is not much bleeding afterward. I'm grateful for that.

If we don't get Tyler to a surgeon, he'll never again walk without a limp. And if infection sets in, he could lose the leg. I feel helpless. I'm the one who works in a hospital, so I'm the expert. But I don't have the skill or the tools to do what should be done. I clean and disinfect the wound and wrap his knee in gauze bandages. When I'm done, it looks as though Tyler is wearing a volleyball kneepad. I've done all I can.

"No skateboarding for a week," I tell him.

He smiles weakly. "Thanks, ET."

"We'll change that dressing every day," I say. Ty nods.

My heart breaks for Tyler. Knowing I'm the reason for his injuries fills me with guilt.

I take another look at Jules's shoulder. Her wound is a clean one. She'll be fine as long as we keep it clean and disinfected. "Is it painful?" I ask.

"Not really," she says. "It only hurts when I use my arm."

"Don't use your arm," I advise.

"Well thank you, Florence Nightingale." Jules grins.

None of us has much to say. Charity stops sobbing and stares vacantly at nothing. Chase holds her. I'm worried. I'd rather have her sobbing than catatonic.

Jules roots around in her backpack and emerges with energy bars and trail mix. She offers them around. Nobody has much appetite, but the food is welcome anyway. I choose trail mix and chew absently on nuts, fruits, and bits of chocolate.

Kenny walks over to Tyler and ruffles his hair. "You look terrible," she says.

Tyler smiles. "Why thank you for those kind words."

"Don't worry," says Kenny, smiling back. "As soon as the swelling goes down, you'll be as pretty as ever. In fact, you might have a couple little scars. Girls think scars are really hot. They make you look dangerous."

"Unfortunately, the girls on this side of the brane are all little munchkins," says Ty.

"I am *not* a munchkin." Bree pipes up. She is just short of five feet tall, and takes a lot of kidding about her size.

"I'm not talking about *you* girls," explains Tyler. "I'm talking about *real* girls."

Kenny snorts. Bree and Jules begin bombarding Tyler with Skittles. "So you don't think *we're* real girls?" says Kenny, feigning outrage.

"That sentence didn't come out right," Tyler says. "Don't make me laugh!" He struggles not to laugh. "It hurts."

We're silent for a moment. Then Kenny sighs, "I guess I won't be going on my date with Zach Martin tonight."

"You had a date with Zach Martin?" asks Jules. "I am sooo jealous."

"Zach Martin," Bree sighs dreamily.

Zach Martin looks just like Ryan Gosling, right down to the chiseled weight lifters' physique. He's evidently the latest of Kenny's many conquests. Or maybe she's the latest of his.

"Ahh, he's nothing but a pretty boy," says Chase.

"Yeah. He's in my English Lit class. Dumb as a box of rocks," adds Ty.

"All flash, no substance," observes Grizz.

Kenny sniffs. "Why, I believe you boys are jealous of Zachery."

After a moment, the boys agree, smiling sheepishly.

This retreat into teenage normality has done us all good. But we lapse into silence again as we watch the sun fall slowly toward the western horizon.

"Falstaff told us it would be dangerous to be out in the forest after dark." I throw the thought out for discussion.

"Okay," says Kenny, "if we don't want to be out in the open, we can either ask the villagers or the blacksuits if they mind putting us up for the night. I wonder who'd be happiest to see us."

"Good point," I admit. "We don't have much choice. Let's go to the village. We'll come back here in the morning."

Grizz takes his machete and cuts branches off trees. "Let's not leave a trail straight to the village," he suggests.

Charity refuses to join us. She speaks her first words since we discovered the brane was missing. "I'm not leaving. That brane thing is going to open up soon. I want to be here when it does."

Nothing we say changes her mind. Chase pleads with her to come, but she's determined to stay.

"I can't leave her," says Chase.

"There's no point in both of you getting killed," says Jules.

"I can't leave her," Chase repeats.

Reluctantly, we leave Chase and Charity behind. Bree, given her small knowledge of following tracks acquired during her bow hunting days, is our expert. "Don't worry about covering your tracks in the forest," she says. "You can't. We're going to leave broken twigs and loosened pebbles no matter what we do. Start sweeping when we get to the dirt path."

When we reach the path, Grizz points out the fact that a swept trail leading straight to the village isn't going to fool the Tracker guy. He volunteers to leave a more complicated trail. "I'll go a mile or two to the south, leave some false trails into the woods. Then I'll walk a mile or two north of the village and do the same thing."

Grizz's plan is a good one. We know Tracker will come after us sooner or later, and we don't want to leave evidence leading him to the village.

* * * * *

As we enter the fields surrounding the village, the watchman blows his horn and shouts, "Giants approaching!"

Taking us in for the night will doubtless put the villagers at risk. I'm afraid they'll turn us away. I am, therefore, happily surprised at their reception.

They throw open the gates and greet us with smiles, cheers, and booming applause. Bertram is in front.

"Falstaff told us what you did to the courtsmen. They've had their foot on our necks for so long, it's about time somebody had some sport with them. Thank you all!"

Even Muriel, who doesn't like us much, is smiling.

I explain that the door to our world has, at least temporarily, closed.

"That's terrible!" says Bertram sympathetically. "But, since you're going to spend the night with us, I would be a poor host if I didn't ask: have you eaten dinner?"

I admit we haven't.

"You heard the girl," shouts Bertram. "Let's get them something to eat!"

Falstaff asks me where my other friends are. I explain that they are still outside, but that at least one of them should be joining us.

He shakes his head. "They will not live through the night outside our walls."

A chill runs down my spine.

People push trestle tables into the village center and arrange them for a banquet. We sit on the ground, cross-legged, because the tables are so small. Bertram sits on my left, Muriel on my right. In a matter of minutes, we are treated to a bowl of mush, greens, and some berries. I taste the mush and recognize it as potatoes with a seasoning I can't quite place, possibly a garlic relative.

The plates and bowls are made of fired clay with no attempt at decoration or even color. The spoons we use are made of wood and are crudely carved.

I look around the table. My friends are involved in conversations with the villagers, and we're all feeling pretty good about our hero's welcome. Bree is surrounded by attractive young men who find her lack of height less intimidating than, say, Kenny's nearly six-foot frame. She's clearly enjoying the attention. Grizz is deep in conversation with Falstaff, and Kenny is happily explaining bombs to a fascinated audience.

Bertram introduces me to a middle-aged man to his left. "This is my son Henry," he says with obvious pride. Henry smiles and welcomes me.

"Do you have other children?" I ask.

"I had two others, a boy and a girl," Bertram answers. "But the courtsmen took them in a gleaning."

"I'm very sorry!" I exclaim. What a stupid question to ask, I berate myself. "Please forgive me for asking."

"It was a long time ago," says Bertram with a shrug. Still, I can tell, the memory continues to burn.

He asks me about my own family. I tell him about my father, the lovable drunk, and my mother, the waitress who works two shifts a day to make ends meet.

"I have twin brothers," I add. "They're a year younger than I. They're real pests, but they're also funny and nice at the same time."

"That's how it is with all siblings, I think," says Bertram. He is a careful listener. He smiles often, and I begin to really like his gap-toothed smile.

The conversation turns to water and its scarcity here. He's amazed when I tell him about my family's swimming pool, and how I use it nearly every day in the summer.

"You bathe every day?" he asks. He sounds astounded.

"No, I move through the water from one side to the other as fast as I can. The pool is ten yards long, the distance from here to the end of the table."

He looks at me with great skepticism. "Don't you make the water dirty when you move through it?"

"It doesn't matter," I explain. "We don't drink it. We have other water for drinking."

I hear the villagers behind us begin to buzz in whispered conversations. Bertram and his son Henry are speechless. The concept of a world rich in water is totally alien to them.

"Your world must be a wonderful place," Bertram says with awe. I agree.

Bertram asks if we'd like more food. I look at the scrawny, emaciated villagers around us and decline. I ask Bertram if the people in his village have enough to eat, because everybody looks so thin.

"We are hungry." His voice becomes angry. "The Court taxes us the same amount every year, regardless of the size of our crop. This last year has not been a good one. Still, the courtsmen come and take what they want, and we live in hunger."

"And there's no way you can stop them?" I ask.

"No. To defy the Court means death. We pay our taxes, or we die."

I feel guilty to have eaten so much. "I'm sorry, Bertram. If I'd known you were short of food, I would have eaten less."

"There is no need to apologize. Usually, we have only two feasts a year, one on the longest day of the year to honor the Father, and one on the shortest day of the year to honor the Mother. We haven't had a third feast in more moons than I can count."

"Isn't it cruel for us to eat in front of all these people? Especially if they're hungry?"

"No, it is not cruel," he says. "I eat with you because we wanted you to have someone at the table that you knew. The other spots were decided by lottery. Everyone has an equal chance to eat at the feast table."

"And Henry?" I ask.

"I was chosen by lot," he replies.

I'm at a loss for words. I decide to change the subject. I ask Henry if he has a family. He smiles and proudly points to a woman surrounded by three young girls who appear to be teenagers. They are a part of the crowd of villagers that surrounds our tables, hanging on every word.

Falstaff pounds the table. Everybody stops talking and looks at him. He stands on the bench and proceeds to tell the tale of our attack on the blacksuits' fortress. Again. He pantomimes Bree launching her fire arrow, and the flailing efforts of the blacksuit to put out the fire. He makes a huge noise to imitate Kenny's bomb. He describes the way the blacksuits milled about, dazed and confused, when they came back to find their fort in flames and missing part of a wall. The crowd of villagers laughs with glee.

The laughter is interrupted by a chilling sound.

I've never heard the sound before, but I recognize it instantly. Wolves are howling. The howls come from all directions. The villagers fall silent. There is no fear on their faces. They're evidently used to this bloodcurdling sound. But my friends look frightened. We've heard coyotes before, but nothing like this.

Henry sees the look of fear on our faces. "Those are dreadwolves," he explains. "But don't worry. The wolves cannot harm us as long as we stay inside the walls. But you must never be caught outside. Those who venture outside in the night never return."

Looking around in a panic, I realize that Grizz is still outside. And so are Chase and Charity.

6

Jules, Bree, and I huddle. We debate going out after Grizz. Bertram, who is eavesdropping, tells us this would be a bad idea. "The wolves are more likely to find you than you are to find your friend," he says quietly.

My feelings turn from despair to elation in the moment I hear the watchman holler, "Giant approaching!"

The villagers throw open the gate and then close it quickly after Grizz steps inside. I fly to Grizz and wrap my arms around him. "I was so worried," I exclaim. "When I looked around and saw you weren't inside yet, I…Well, I was worried." I know I sound lame. *Just what* was *it I was feeling*, I ask myself. "I'm just glad you're here," I say and embrace him again.

Grizz hugs me back. I feel what? Relief? Not exactly.

A moment later, the sentry cries again, "Two giants approaching the gate!" A moment later, Chase and Charity enter with expressions of sheer terror on their faces.

"Thank God you made it!" I say, relieved.

Chase looks sheepish. "Those howls were terrifying! We should've come back with you. I thought we were goners for sure."

Now that we're all here, we realize that the hour is late. Villagers are yawning and stretching.

Muriel organizes a party to find mattresses for us. It takes four mattresses apiece to accommodate us. The villagers spread them on the floor of the building where Grizz and I met with the council this morning. No blankets are necessary, as the evening is only marginally cooler than the day.

We turn in for the night, leaving a single candle burning. As exhausted as I am, sleep won't come. I lie awake for hours, listening to the sound of some of my friends quietly crying, and the howls of dreadwolves. I finally nod off.

* * * * *

We awaken to find sunlight streaming through the room's small windows. The windows don't admit much light, and, looking at my watch, I realize we've slept in late. It's already ten thirty.

Grizz is already awake.

"Why didn't you wake me?" I demand.

"Because I was having fun watching you snore," he replies.

"I do *not* snore."

"Yes you do," says Grizz. "But it's a cute girl kind of snore."

We're both smiling, something we haven't done much recently. For just a split second, we're teenagers again.

The others are stirring now as well. I examine Ty's and Jules's bandages. The wounds look clean. I'll change the dressings later in the day. I've led Ty across the room to examine his bandages, so the others won't have to look at blood first thing in the morning.

"ET," Ty says, looking at me earnestly, "if being trapped in this world means I'll be able to see more of you, then it's worth it to me. You know how I feel about you."

I think carefully about my next words. "I love you as a friend, Tyler, but I'm not in love with you." Still, thinking about Tyler's wounds, I can't help but feel extremely guilty because it's my fault he's

68

in this condition. I lift his chin with my finger and kiss him gently on the forehead. "You are dear to me, Tyler. I couldn't bear to lose your friendship."

Tyler smiles as best he can with swollen lips. "I love you, Erin. Even if you don't love me back. Maybe someday…" He trails off.

I smile in return and softly touch his cheek. "Come on," I say, "let's go back and join the others."

Life would be easier if I could love Tyler back. But I don't, and I wouldn't be doing anybody a favor by trying to fake it.

Seeing that we are awake, the villagers bring us breakfast: mushy potatoes, greens, and berries again. No wonder the villagers have running sores all over their bodies. If they eat the same thing for every meal, they must be suffering from major vitamin deficiencies.

"Great," Kenny grunts, looking at the tray in front of her. "Mush for breakfast."

"You expected eggs and bacon?" asks Bree.

"Personally, I'd rather have pancakes smothered in maple syrup," sighs Jules, wistfully.

"This food is just fine by me," says Tyler. Tyler will eat anything. He doesn't eat so much as he refuels. Pretty much any fuel will do.

Muriel enters the room. "What are your plans?" she asks politely.

"I guess we'll go back and see if the door to our world has opened yet," I reply.

"Of course," agrees Muriel, "you must be anxious to go home."

Just then, the watchman blows two blasts on his bugle. "Open the gates for the courtsmen," he shouts.

Muriel looks stricken. "Come with me right now. There's no time to waste. If the courtsmen find you here, they will surely kill you, and many of us as well." She gestures for us to follow. She leads us to the largest building in the village. It contains an enormous vat, perhaps ten feet high and thirty feet in diameter. Along the wall is shelving, covered with bowls, pitchers, and jugs of various sizes and shapes.

"Help me push this," says Muriel.

Chase and Kenny put their shoulders to the side of the shelving. It moves. Behind it, we see nothing but a wall. Muriel places a hand on the left side of the wall, near the floor, and presses. A hidden door creaks open. Muriel pushes harder on the door, and we follow her inside. The space was designed for smaller people, so it's a tight squeeze for us. We climb a rickety ladder and out onto the roof. The roof is shaped like a funnel, tapering from high walls at the outer edges downward to a hole in the center. I know where we are. This is the village cistern. This is where the villagers collect rainwater.

On the roof, Muriel turns to us once again. "You must not make any noise, and you must not leave this place no matter what you see or hear outside. Promise me." She looks me straight in the eye.

"We promise," I say.

"Swear a water oath," she insists. "You will not leave this room no matter what you see or hear."

I look at my friends. Everybody nods.

"We promise," I repeat.

Muriel turns and descends the ladder. We hear her close the door, and she grunts as she slides the shelf back in place.

We look around. There is a rickety barrier around the outside. There are small holes in it. By putting my eye next to a small hole, I have a view of the village square.

There are ten blacksuits in the square. One of them is hollering at the top of his voice, "We have found the tracks of two giants leading right to the gate of your village!"

How is this possible? We covered our tracks carefully. Then, with a sinking feeling, it comes to me. Chase and Charity. They were the last people in last night. Clearly, in their panic to escape the wolves, they didn't cover their footsteps. I want to be angry with them, but I remember how frightening the sound was. I'm not sure I'd have remembered to cover my trail either.

The blacksuits' leader is purple with rage. He strikes Bertram and Muriel again and again. They fall to their knees, bleeding.

"You will pay the Penalty of Nine," the blacksuit snarls.

The blacksuits drag nine villagers to the side of the square opposite our vantage point. There they bind them to nine poles, poles I had not noticed the night before. They tie their hands behind their backs. The blacksuits back up about ten yards, then face the bound villagers and string their bows. The villagers are all moaning and crying. The blacksuits let their arrows fly. Each arrow strikes a bound villager in the left shoulder. The crying of the villagers watching this awful show becomes wails. The blacksuits leisurely retrieve another arrow and aim. The second arrow takes each target in the right shoulder. Two more arrows follow. One for the left thigh and one for the right thigh.

I know what they are doing. They are putting these people to death in a very slow way. The villagers will bleed to death eventually, but they will die by inches. I look at the faces of my companions. Grief shows in their faces, shock and horror as well. But there is also something far deeper and much stronger: rage.

"These monsters have gotta pay," snarls Kenny. There's no risk of her being overheard with the crying and wailing below.

Every one of us nods a head in assent, even Charity.

"We can take these guys out," says Chase.

"No," I say. "Not now. Remember our oath. It will go badly for the villagers if we kill the blacksuits in their village. We'll deal with them later."

Muriel must have known we'd want to intervene and stop the blacksuits. That's why she was so insistent that we take the oath.

As I watch the nine victims suffer, I realize that they are all middle-aged or older. It makes sense that the blacksuits would not want to kill younger, more able-bodied workers. Suddenly I realize that I recognize one of the victims. He is Bertram's son Henry.

* * * * *

I'm amazed the villagers don't turn us in. How can they watch their loved ones suffer like this? And yet no one even glances in our direction. I scan the crowd and find Henry's wife. Her teenage daughters surround her. They're clutching one another tightly. All are in tears.

The blacksuits are now ransacking the village, looking for us, no doubt. They enter homes and throw furnishings in the street. They rip apart mattresses and clothing. We hear them ransacking the room below. We hear the sound of furniture being overturned and pottery shattering. Jules and Chase remove their rifles from their slings. Grizz pulls out his machete.

Bree strings her bow. We all hold our breath. The noise below fades as the blacksuits leave the building.

I breathe a sigh of relief. We could have made short work of the few blacksuits in the village, but the retribution the villagers would have suffered later would have been many times worse.

An hour later, the blacksuits give up. Most of the victims are dead now. A few, including Henry cling tenuously to life. They won't live much longer. We're startled as we hear someone open the hidden door and climb up the steps. Actually, it's two someones: Muriel and Bertram.

"Bertram, I am so sorry," I whisper. "We never meant to bring this on you."

"Hush, child. The blacksuits brought this upon us, not you." He continues. "The blacksuits are bringing an entire brigade from Fort Gentry to hunt for you," he warns. "That's a thousand soldiers. We cannot keep you safe here."

"It will not be safe for you at the shrine of the crying angel, either," says Muriel. "You must not go back to the place of your brane. Tracker will see that you have spent much time there, and blacksuit patrols will sweep the area several times a day. The only place you will be safe is in the Mother's Sanctuary.

"Then how will we get home? How will we know if the brane reopens?" I ask.

"We will keep a watcher near that clearing. If your brane opens, we will come and get you immediately," says Bertram.

"How do we know we can trust you?" asks Charity.

"We swear a water oath that we will come and get you if your brane reopens," answers Muriel. "I don't know about your world, but in ours, a person who breaks a water oath is a disgrace to his family and his village."

"These people just watched their friends die, and they didn't turn us in," I say. "I think we can trust them."

"What is the Mother's Sanctuary?" I ask.

"The Sanctuary is a place of peace and contemplation," answers Bertram. "The people you will meet there will welcome you warmly."

"Where is this Sanctuary?" asks Grizz.

"The Sanctuary is a quarter-day's walk away," says Bertram. "Not far. Follow me."

We descend the stairs and find Falstaff and two girls waiting for us. Falstaff introduces the girls as Beatrice and Persephone. They each have a bow and a quiver of arrows slung over their shoulders.

"We will lead you to the Mother's Sanctuary," says Falstaff. "Please follow us."

"Where are the blacksuits?" I ask.

"They are eating lunch," Falstaff replies. "They have left a guard at the gate, but he is being distracted."

Sure enough, as we near the gate, I see the guard surrounded by pretty girls. He's paying no attention whatever to the gate. Falstaff quickly lifts the bar while Beatrice and Persephone push the gate open and usher us through.

We follow Falstaff down the trail toward Fort Warren while Beatrice and Persephone erase our trail from behind. Once again, Grizz and Chase take turns carrying Ty. We reach Fort Warren, but pass it by. I hear the sound of axes ringing in the forest and realize the blacksuits are cutting timber to repair their fort.

"We could stop and blow that place to kingdom come," offers Kenny.

"That would be most enjoyable," admits Falstaff, "but not today, my friends."

The trail ends at the fort. Falstaff leads us into the forest and heads southwest. Beatrice and Persephone stop sweeping. We walk for a good two hours, until we emerge from the forest into a large clearing. The ground here turns to solid gray stone. In front of us is an eroded hill, rocky and craggy, but with a fair amount of stunted vegetation covering its flanks.

The stone surrounding the hill will keep Tracker from following us, I realize.

Falstaff begins to climb, and we follow.

We arrive at the entrance to the Mother's Sanctuary without seeing it. One minute Falstaff is in front of me, and the next minute he's gone. I look very carefully at the spot where I last saw him and discover an opening in the rocks, obscured by vines. I walk through the vines and into a fissure. In a few seconds, I'm through the narrow passageway and find it opens out into a vast cavern. Torches in sconces on the wall provide a flickering light. The ceiling is high above. In a moment, our whole party is assembled inside the cave. The cavern is cooler, providing a welcome break from the blazing temperature outside.

"This place is huge!" says Bree. "I could set up an archery range in here!"

"Or a bowling alley," says Chase. Carrying Tyler, he could barely fit through the opening.

An elderly woman enters the cavern from a side door. Like Muriel, she has striking blue eyes. She is dressed in a flowing white robe, and she welcomes us with a warm smile.

"Welcome, children," she says. Her voice is soft and melodious. "I am Helen, the first servant of the Mother."

* * * * *

"We are pleased to meet you, ma'am." I curtsy, feeling a little silly. I don't think I've ever curtsied before, but something about Helen's presence seems to make it an appropriate gesture. My friends bow and curtsy as well.

"There is no need for you to bow in my presence," says Helen. "I am only a humble servant. You must be tired and thirsty after your journey. Please follow me." She leads us into a smaller chamber, also illuminated by torches. Helen gestures for us to sit. I'm surprised to find chairs large enough to accommodate us comfortably.

"Who is this 'Mother' you serve?" I ask.

"In this temple, we serve Mother Earth," she responds.

Okay, I think, *fair enough*. I know that many primitive societies in our world worship the Earth Mother as well. I was paying attention during history class.

Two younger women bring us small glasses of water. I sniff the water suspiciously.

"The water is safe," says Helen. "Farther back in the caves, there is a tiny spring. The source of the spring is rainwater, and rainwater is the only source of safe water in our world. The spring is very small, but it is suitable for our simple needs. Please let us share the gift of water."

We all take a sip.

Once we have shared water, Helen says, "I have foreseen your coming."

"I beg pardon," I respond. I must have misheard.

"I have known for quite a while now that you would be coming to help us in our battle with the Court," Helen says.

My friends and I glance at one another uncomfortably.

I'm not sure I like the direction of this conversation. How could she possibly have known we were coming? And how can a small group of teenagers help fight the blacksuits? If the blacksuits can put a thousand soldiers in the field at a moment's notice, there's not much we can do to stop them. I fleetingly wonder if we've stumbled onto a strange cult. I dismiss the thought. Helen has a dignity and serenity that make it hard to picture her as a nutcase.

"In time, you will come to have faith in the visions," Helen vows. "For now, you may wish to consider why we have built these large chairs in which you are seated, when they are clearly too large for any of us."

That's a very good question, and it leaves me feeling uneasy.

"Please, children, let me tell you our story. You must not interrupt me as I talk. When I've finished, we can all talk about our plans."

Helen closes her eyes and begins her story, her face illuminated by the flickering torches. From the singsong voice she uses, I can tell she's repeating a story that has been handed down from generation to generation.

"Many, many seasons ago," the story begins, "mankind lived in a world where there was food and water enough for all. Humans had built many marvelous things. It is even said that men could fly.

"But humans ignored the needs of the Mother. Because we refused to confront the danger, we idly watched as our world became hotter and hotter. Great mountains of frozen water began to thaw. Most people in those days lived near large bodies of water called oceans. As the ice melted, the oceans rose, and they flooded the homes of billions of people. Whole cities disappeared beneath the rising waters.

"Every year, more and more people lost their homes. At first, people tried to find room for the homeless. The leader of our country, the president, declared martial law. He disbanded the People's Legislature because it was so riddled with dissension that it was unable to accomplish anything. The president declared that the troubles were so severe that the people would no longer elect the president until the after troubles were past. The judicial authority, the Supreme Court, appointed the president once every four years, and the president appointed a new member of the Court when a justice died.

"For a while, this government dealt with the problems. What it did was never popular, but it was often sufficient. But as the number of displaced people continued to rise, even this new government could no longer cope with the problems. Our economy fell into ruin. There were riots and lawlessness in every city that remained above water. Then, the world ran out of the energy sources known as fossil fuels.

"Faced with shortages and increasing lawlessness, nations turned on other nations. Wars were fought. Desperation caused nations to use increasingly lethal weapons. Some nations resorted to nuclear weapons. Others responded with plague. For a short while, it seemed that our own country was beginning to gain an upper hand. This caused others to fight with weapons that targeted our food supply. A plague that killed all plants in the grass family eliminated our grain crops and left us starving.

"Billions of people all over the world starved to death. Governments lost all control, and all vestiges of civilization disintegrated. The world fell into chaos. The only law left was the law of the strong.

"Our own government, with a small but effective militia, was able to sustain itself. But even with a small population, it was impossible to plant crops and feed the people, because lawless bands roamed the land and took what they wanted. We became a nation of hunters and gatherers. We stayed in one place to hunt until we exhausted the animal population and food from plants. Then we moved on.

"But this nomad life came with a price. We gradually lost the technologies of the old world. We lost the ability to fly. We had no reliable source of ores and minerals, so we could not make the things the old civilizations had made. With every available hour necessary to forage for food, we had no time for schools and libraries to keep learning alive.

"Finally, our people found this forest. Back in those days, the dreadwolves had not yet lost their fear of fire. We ventured deep into the heart of the forest. We began to build our forts. At night, we lit huge bonfires, and the dreadwolves left us alone. Half the trees we cut were used for building, and the other half for burning. It was slow going, but the fields we cleared were used to plant crops.

"Very few of the wild bands followed us into the forest. They did not have the resources or the patience to spend half their day cutting trees for bonfires. So, with only a few exceptions, the outside world left us alone.

"I think that is enough for now, children," she concludes.

Helen stops, and we're all silent for a moment. A sense of dread had been building in me as I listened to Helen's story.

"And what is the name of your country?" I ask, certain that I know the answer.

"We call ourselves the New United States of America," she replies.

"And the village where Falstaff lives, what is its name?" I ask.

"We call that village Phoenix," she responds.

"My God," I say, stricken. "We haven't come to another universe. This is our own world, hundreds of years in the future."

D.S. Northrop

7

For a moment, we are too stunned to speak. Finally, Chase breaks the silence. "So global warming actually happened. I don't think anybody really thought the consequences would be this severe."

"And nobody listened to the ones that did," Kenny adds. "Look, everybody knew about global warming, and everybody knew our political system was a gridlocked joke, but nobody had the guts to make the changes we needed to make. Jeez, a lot of people in our time wanted to do things that would make the situation *worse*."

Nobody argues with her.

"You can understand why people became smaller," says Jules. "As it became harder and harder to find food, a smaller body size would have been a very positive adaptive trait. Smaller body mass means less food necessary for sustenance. It's commonly known that people in *our* day were about a foot taller than our great-great-grandfathers at the time of the Civil War. All the protein in our diets made us bigger."

"The only thing I can't figure out is time's arrow," says Bree. "Time is supposed to move in only one direction, from the past to the future. But ET traveled into this world this morning with Tyler, and when she needed help, she came back to our own time. She moved forward *and* backward."

"That's been bothering me, too," agrees Ty. "Time travel backwards creates an opportunity for all sorts of paradoxes. Suppose ET went back to a time before she was born and killed her mother. That would clearly be impossible."

"But," says Kenny, riffing off Ty's thought, "ET left the past *today* and returned back to the *same* time. If she killed her mother, all it would mean is that her brothers would grow up without their mom."

"Can we use another example?" I ask. "I'm not going to kill my mom."

"Another kind of paradox," adds Ty, "is the one about traveling into the future, taking a look at stock prices, returning to your own time, and making loads of money."

"Not much chance of that," I scoff. "The stock market doesn't seem to be doing very well right now. About the only thing we *could* accomplish would be to go back and tell people to quit burning coal. *If the brane opens again.*"

"Like they'd listen to a bunch of high school kids who claim to have been time traveling," snorts Kenny.

Helen has been quietly listening to our conversation.

"You have quite a stake in our world," she says softly. "We are your grandchildren."

Helen looks straight at me. Why does everyone want to make *me* the leader? The only thing I ever led was Tyler into this world, and look how that turned out.

"I think," I say, looking to my friends for confirmation, "that we would be happy to help you. But our number one priority is to travel back to our own time."

"Of course you will return to your own time if the brane reopens. And we have sworn a water oath that we will keep a watch on that shrine every moment of every day. If the brane opens, our sentry will come here as fast as he can run," Helen vows.

"Can we trust these people?" asks Charity.

"Yes, child, you can," says Helen solemnly.

"I don't think we have much choice," I add bleakly.

82

* * * * *

"Perdita here will take your measurements," says Helen. "I hope you don't have to stay in our world for long, but if you do, you'll need more clothing. We will also bring you something to eat. You must be hungry after such a long day. We will finish our story after dinner."

Helen leaves, and Perdita takes our measurements and leaves as well.

"Okay, so we're stuck here," says Bree.

"Only until the brane reopens," I respond, sounding cheerier than I feel.

"Yeah," adds Kenny, "*if* the brane opens."

"What do you think of Helen's visions?" I ask.

"They're pretty creepy as far as I'm concerned," says Kenny.

"In our world," says Tyler, "there are people who seem to have accurate visions. We've all heard stories about how a psychic leads police to the place a body is buried, or tells them where to look for clues."

I'm stunned. Tyler is our empiricist. If you can't see it, it doesn't exist.

"The problem," Tyler continues, "is there are so many phonies and charlatans, we discount stories when people with the gift have legitimate visions."

"The Cassandra effect," adds Jules. "Oh," she says, seeing that she has lost us. "Cassandra is a figure in Greek mythology who was cursed. She has true visions, but because of the curse, nobody ever believes her."

"And they did build exactly eight big chairs," Grizz points out.

Three young acolytes bring us our dinner, mush with greens and berries again. Still, something is better than nothing.

Jules brings out the last package of Ho Hos. We carefully divide them up into equal pieces and consume them in a ceremony that feels almost religious. We know it'll probably be nothing but mush from now on.

"The one good thing about being stuck here," says Kenny, after dinner, "is that we'll be able to do some really nasty things to the blacksuits."

"We just have to be sure we don't do anything that'll get the villagers in more trouble," I caution.

Helen has reentered the room and overheard our last comments. She smiles. "Oh, we'll be able to come up with lots of ideas for doing nasty things to the blacksuits. But for now, I'd like to finish telling you our story."

We settle into our chairs, ready to listen.

"When I left off," begins Helen, "I told you that we had found this forest, and that we had been able to settle here and resume a farming life. In fact, the original purpose of the Disciples of the Mother was to maintain a seed stock of plants that we hoped to be able to grow someday.

"Once we had achieved this purpose, the Court officially disbanded the Disciples of the Mother. We defied the Court, because we knew we needed to keep alive the story of what happens when mankind neglects the Mother. Our order had to go underground, but hunters from Phoenix discovered these caves, and they made a perfect home for us. Tracker cannot find evidence of our existence here because of the stony ground surrounding the Sanctuary. And we are far enough from Phoenix that blacksuit patrols rarely pass this way.

"When our civilization was rebuilt, it had the city of New Washington at its center. On the outer edge, arranged in a great circle, were the villages. There is one village for every state in the old United

States, fifty villages in all. Your brane opened near the village that represents the old state of Arizona.

"Each city was built two dayswalks apart from the next city. A dayswalk is the distance a grown person can walk between sunrise and sunset on the shortest day of the year. At the time, the Court claimed distancing the cities would prevent the villages from exhausting the game in the forest surrounding it.

"Even when the villagers first heard this explanation, we knew it was lie. We compete with the dreadwolves for game, and after a short period of time, there was very little game left anyway. The true purpose was to keep villages from communicating with one another.

"You see, the courtsmen caught thousands of wolves in live traps, brought them into the city, and gradually conditioned them to lose their fear of fire. Once they had a large population that no longer feared fire, they released them into the forest. Within a generation, we could no longer move from one village to the next since fire no longer deterred the dreadwolves. Spending a night in the forest was suicide.

"The blacksuits have built a fort near each village. They call these the village forts. They use these forts to house small garrisons that patrol the area around each village, looking for any sign of disobedience. The blacksuits also constructed a ring of forts between New Washington and the villages. Each of these forts houses a brigade of blacksuits, and each fort is within a dayswalk of six or seven of our villages. The blacksuits respond quickly and brutally to the slightest disturbance in the villages.

"Before they released the dreadwolves, the blacksuits burned the entire forest between the ring of forts and New Washington. Without the cover of forests, the dreadwolves won't go there. So the Court, and its lackeys living inside the ring, enjoy a life without fear.

"With the villages isolated, the Court could impose draconian rules on the villages without worrying about them offering any coordinated opposition. Even so, there were two Great Risings in which we sought to overthrow the rule of the Court. Each rising was brutally suppressed. After the First Great Rising, the Court amended the New Constitution to outlaw the working of metal in the villages. After the Second Great Rising, the Court decreed that each village would be allowed to grow only one crop. That is why we eat potatoes at every meal. This limited diet weakens us and, in the Court's opinion, makes us docile.

"Believe me when I tell you that there is nothing docile about us. There is a fire burning inside each of us that will never be extinguished until we have ended the rule of the Court. We hunger for freedom.

"The Court needs us to grow its food and work its mines. But at each gleaning, they steal children from our families. They keep us sick, hungry, and impoverished. They murder our people for the smallest offenses. They say they need the labor of ninety-nine slaves to keep each citizen of New Washington living in comfort. We must end this tyranny, and you can help us."

Helen stops, and all is silent.

"But how can we help, Helen?" I ask. "There are only eight of us, and there are so many of them."

"I have foreseen your coming, children. I have also foreseen that you have knowledge of the old ways. You know how to build and create marvels that were once common but which our civilization has lost. Through you, we can hope to build the structures and weapons we need to overthrow the Court." Helen speaks softly, but there is steel in her voice.

"And yet, you would let us leave if the brane were to reopen?" I ask.

"If we were to keep you here against your will, or if we were to lie to you if the brane opens," Helen says, "we would be no better than the Court itself. I will pray every evening that your brane reopens. But I will also hope that it doesn't."

* * * * *

"To build the wonders you need, we need tools," says Bree.

"And raw materials like chemicals and ores," adds Kenny.

"I think we can provide the resources you need," says Helen. "Let me tell you another story. This will be a short one.

"When our people first moved into this area, we found a small group of people who had managed to stay in this area by herding sheep in the mountains. Their pastures were high up and hard to reach, so the marauding groups left them alone. The courtsmen, however, sent expeditions into the mountains looking for sources of copper and iron ore. They caught one of the shepherds.

"During their 'interrogation' of the shepherd, they 'convinced' him to reveal the legend of a workshop left by men who lived in the days of wonder. The shepherd told the blacksuits that the workshop contained many marvels from the old days. It was buried under a hill on the far side of the mountains.

"The courtsmen sent an expedition looking for this workshop, and they found it. To their consternation, they found that its door is protected by a strange lock. The locking device consists of an elaborate set of twenty-two dials, each of which can be tuned to a number or letter. The courtsmen tried thousands of combinations of letters and numbers, but were unable to find the correct combination.

"Every few years, the courtsmen send another expedition in an attempt to enter the workshop, but all have failed. One member of the last expedition later committed a petty crime in New Washington, and as a punishment, he was exiled to the villages. This is a very common punishment, and very effective, because no citizen of New Washington wants to lose the privileged life of the city for the harsh life of the villages.

"Be that as it may, the man who was exiled now lives in Detroit, which is the village immediately to our west. He will know how to lead you children to the workshop," Helen concludes.

"What makes you think we can find the right combination to open the lock?" I ask.

"I don't *think* you can open the lock, Erin. I *know* you can open the lock," says Helen mysteriously.

"How do you know about events in Detroit when you can't communicate with them?" I ask.

"The dreadwolves make it impossible to communicate directly, of course," Helen responds, "but they do not stop us from overhearing the conversations of the blacksuits. The last Rising was long ago. The courtsmen do not fear us. They speak openly, even when we can overhear them."

Helen asks an acolyte to summon Falstaff, Beatrice, and Persephone to join us.

A few moments later, they enter the room.

Helen addresses Falstaff. "If these young people will agree to help us, I want you to guide them to Detroit so they can speak with the man who knows the location of the workshop."

"I assume," Falstaff says, "that you must have a plan for getting us past the dreadwolves. We all know that it is a two dayswalk to Detroit and that we will have to spend a night in the forest."

"My plan is the same one we used at the time of the Great Risings. We will overwhelm the dreadwolves with numbers," explains Helen. "We will send more people than the dreadwolves can kill. Many will die, but some will make it through."

"As you wish, Mother" replies Falstaff. He appears unhappy with Helen's plan, but seems to trust her judgment.

"And this one," Helen continues, pointing at me, "will find a way to end the curse of the dreadwolves forever."

8

I am, to say the least, startled. "I'm not sure—" I begin, but Helen interrupts me.

"You must have faith in the visions, child," she implores.

Why does she expect this of me? I've never been outstanding at anything other than running. And that has more to do with a willingness to train hard and tolerate pain than it does to any natural gift. I feel overwhelmed by the pressure to do something when I have no clue how to go about doing it. How am I going to rid them of dreadwolves?

Helen continues, "The real question is, will you help us in our fight against the blacksuits?" Again she looks directly at me.

"I can only speak for myself," I say, "but I'll do whatever I can to help you."

Grizz steps up next to me. "Count me in."

"I'm up for any plan that'll let us settle some scores with those little black-suited monsters," says Kenny. "In fact, I'm looking forward to it."

"I'm in," adds Ty. "I have some issues with those guys, too."

One by one, Chase, Jules, and Bree agree as well. After a long pause, Charity says, "I guess I'll help, too." Perhaps there's hope for Charity after all.

"That's wonderful!" says Helen. "May the Mother bless you. But before you go anywhere, you must learn to fight blacksuits and dreadwolves. Falstaff, Beatrice, and Persephone will begin your training in the morning.

"The hour is late," she continues. "I suggest we all get some sleep, because tomorrow will be a busy day."

Two acolytes lead us to a room where eight mattresses have been laid out on the floor. Torches cast small puddles of light. There is food here and a small pitcher of water on a table. There are also chairs, and a colorful woven cloth on the wall.

"All the conveniences of home," says Kenny. "Oh, wait a minute. Where's my clothes closet? My TV's missing! Where'd my desk go? How do I plug my iPhone in? And where's my iPad? Tyler, did you take my iPad?"

"Just borrowed it for a minute," says Tyler. "Have to check the baseball scores."

"How'd the Diamondbacks do?" asks Chase.

"Beat the Cubbies in ten," says Ty.

I change the dressing on Ty's and Jules's wounds. I pick a mattress close to the door. I find it unexpectedly comfortable. It has an aroma that reminds me of freshly mowed grass. We talk softly back and forth until we begin to drift off to sleep. My last thought is, *How on earth did I get us into this mess?*

* * * * *

The Sisters rise with the sun, and so do we. The acolytes come in ringing bells.

"Don't they know we're on summer vacation?" grumbles Kenny. "How about we learn how to fight dreadwolves later? Like noon."

Chase hides his head under his pillow.

It does them no good. More acolytes come bustling in with breakfast. Mush again, of course.

"I could really get to dislike this stuff," mumbles Bree.

In the middle of breakfast, Perdita and another Sister come in with new clothes for each of us.

"These clothes are poor," she apologizes. "But they will provide you with a change of clothing while we make something more appropriate for you. The clothing the Sisters wear is made from softbark, and yours will be as well."

"Thank you," I say. I examine my new clothes. They have made us two sets for each of us. The material is homespun and feels rough to the skin, but, as I try mine on, I find it fits very nicely.

Helen comes in as we are finishing breakfast. She is followed by Falstaff, Beatrice, and Persephone, all looking bleary eyed.

"In the old days," says Helen, "when villages could still communicate, our people decided that each village would designate weapons masters. These people would keep alive our knowledge of how weapons are built and used.

"The Phoenix weapons masters, Falstaff, Beatrice, and Persephone, were up last night crafting weapons for you."

Acolytes bring in an impressive array of bows, knives, shields, and spears sized for "giants." We sort through the weapons, selecting ones that have a good feel in the hand.

"And here," Helen continues, "we have something very special." The last acolytes bring in three swords. "The big sword comes from the days before our people began to grow smaller. It looks like a good weapon for Chase."

Then they show us two shorter swords. "And these," says Helen, "come from the time of the First Great Rising."

The swords are indeed somewhat shorter, but Kenny and Ty heft them and decide to keep them. Grizz has his machete, I have my bowie knife, and Bree, Jules, and Charity don't seem anxious to become sword wielders.

I examine the quality of my weapons. The bow is firm, and it takes most of my strength to draw the string. The knives are made of flint, and I find them surprisingly sharp. The spears are nothing more than long, well-sharpened sticks, but they look lethal anyway. The shields have two straps on the inside. Falstaff shows us how to run our arms inside the middle strap and grasp the outer strap with our fist.

"You will use the shield with all weapons except the bow and arrow," Falstaff instructs.

The day is divided into structured periods. First up is bow practice.

Except for Jules, we are pathetic. Toward the end of the practice period, I actually manage to hit the target. Not in the bull's-eye, mind you, but I do hit the outer rim. Kenny almost shoots herself in the foot. The best pupils on this first day are Chase and Charity.

The main bow instructor is Beatrice, and she does her best to hide her exasperation. "Draw the string back to your cheek, just beside your right eye," she implores. "As you draw the bow, keep your right forearm parallel to the ground. Keep your left arm straight. Sight the target along the arrow!"

We take a half-hour break after bow practice, and then it is on to spears. This goes much better. The hardest thing is to thrust the spear with power.

"Human skin and wolf hide are both very tough," instructs Persephone. "If you want to penetrate them, you must thrust hard. Left hand under the spear. Right hand over the spear. No, don't hold it that close to the end!"

We have sacks full of bean-like material that represent the thickness of wolf hide. We destroy many, many sacks of beans.

After spear practice, we eat lunch. Mush with greens again. No berries this time.

We rest for a few minutes after lunch and then sword practice begins. After demonstrating basic technique for thrusting and parrying, Falstaff asks for a volunteer to practice what we've just learned. Kenny raises her hand without hesitation.

"You'll be fighting me," says Falstaff. She and Falstaff square off.

Kenny objects. "This isn't really fair, little guy. I'm a lot bigger than you are. I'm afraid I'll hurt you." And indeed, Kenny, who is almost six feet tall, armed with a long sword, paired against Falstaff, who is less than three feet tall and armed with a short sword, looks like a mismatch.

"Worry about yourself," warns Falstaff.

Kenny lunges at Falstaff and gets a sharp blow on the ankle as a reward.

"Ow!" she yelps.

Chastened, she goes on the defensive and awaits Falstaff's attack. She parries his first two thrusts and then takes another sharp blow, this time to the knee. By the end of practice, she is limping. There is much more to fighting with a sword than I ever could have imagined. We flail away at each other with varying degrees of success.

We use wooden swords for practice so we don't hurt one another. Another half-hour break comes after sword practice.

Knife practice is the easiest yet, and many more bags of beans die.

"Thrust, rip, and turn," repeats Persephone over and over again. "Penetrate the hide, rip through tissue, and then turn the blade."

Then Persephone tries to teach us how to throw a knife. Things go south in a hurry. "You're supposed to hit the target with the pointed end!" she says, exasperated. Throwing a knife and hitting the target with the pointed end is not nearly as easy as it sounds.

We are free to explore after knife practice. Helen warns us not to venture too deep into the caves. There is a vast system of caves and passages leading off from the caverns we have become familiar with, and it's easy to get lost. We're free to explore the forest around the caves. The Mother's Sanctuary is far enough south of Phoenix that blacksuits don't patrol the area frequently, but Helen puts out a screen of acolytes to provide early warning if blacksuits show up. We are instructed to keep our exploration within earshot and well to the south of the Sanctuary.

Bree borrows Grizz's machete. "There are some things I'd like to build," she explains, "and I need to find out what materials I have to work with."

When I look at the forest around us, I see trees, leaves, vines, shrubs, branches, and the occasional animal. When Bree looks at the forest, she sees Home Depot.

She spends her free time chopping down trees and whacking away at vines. She talks about properties like "tensile strength," "elasticity," and "load-bearing capacity." She is oblivious to everything else.

The forest has little animal life. With dreadwolves on the prowl, there are few large animals left near the Sanctuary. Birds are common, and we occasionally see squirrels, rabbits, and fat little skunks. We give a wide berth to the latter.

After an hour, one of the acolytes finds us and tells us it's time for dinner.

After dinner, we speak with Helen. This time, it's our turn to tell stories. Helen has an insatiable curiosity about our time. She stops us often with exclamations of surprise and questions. She finds our wristwatches fascinating.

* * * * *

Our days go by quickly, and we are soon pleasantly absorbed in our daily routine.

I think often of my family. How terrible it must be for them that I just disappeared. They won't know whether I'm alive or dead, which must leave them in a kind of emotional limbo. My father will drown whatever he's feeling in beer and bourbon.

I miss my mother. I miss them all. I realize I'm homesick. I even miss the twins, pests that they are. They could always make me laugh with their zany adventures and their razor-sharp sense of humor. With difficulty, I shake off the feelings of homesickness. They serve no purpose.

Each acolyte holds the title "Sister." The Sisters all dress in flowing white robes. We learn that there are twenty-five acolytes in the Mother's Sanctuary, ranging in age from two to forty. Nobody lives much past forty in this cruel future world. Every few years, the villagers send a baby girl to the Sanctuary. The Sisters raise them. Helen has already selected their next leader. A name is hidden inside a sealed envelope in her desk. Sister Juliet, who is never far from Helen's side, is the odds-on favorite.

* * * * *

I enjoy exploring the caves. I'm careful to heed Helen's warning that we not wander too deep into the caves for fear of getting lost. But I do visit each of the caves that are being used by the Sisters. I find a kitchen, meeting rooms, meditation rooms, a laundry of sorts, pantries, storage rooms, bedrooms, sitting rooms, and an armory where they both make and store weapons. One of my favorite rooms is the sewing room. One day I visit Sister Perdita, who is busy making tunics for us.

Feeling the fabric of a tunic that is almost complete, I marvel at how light and soft it is. "How do you make this so light?" I ask.

"We use fiber from the softbark tree," she replies.

"Doesn't the fiber decompose with time?"

"Oh, no, not at all," explains Perdita. "You have seen the baskets we weave?"

"Yes, of course."

"This is a similar material," she says, "but much softer."

"I've seen the villagers wearing homespun wool. Why don't they make their clothes from this fiber as well? It would be much more comfortable and far cooler," I observe.

"The making of clothes from fiber takes a very long time. Harvesting enough fiber to make a single tunic takes more than a week. And the sewing takes a lot of time because the threads are so slender. The villagers are too busy with their work in the fields. If they don't work, they don't eat. They simply don't have time," Perdita answers. "We would wear homespun ourselves, but the villagers insist we dress in robes. They say the priests and Sisters of old wore robes, and so should we."

We also learn that the villagers work hard to maintain their skill with weapons. Although they are forbidden to use them, the young ones continue to train daily.

"We are very good at hiding things from the blacksuits," Falstaff explains.

I ask him why the blacksuits don't live in the village instead of in a separate fort. Falstaff answers that the blacksuits know that, sooner or later, the villagers would find a way to cut their throats.

Every day, three or four more villagers arrive at the Sanctuary. They will be going with us to Detroit, a part of Helen's plan. We're hoping that a large force will prevent the dreadwolves from attacking, knowing that they will take very heavy losses. If they are not deterred, the idea is to throw more bodies at them than they can kill. A few of us will survive.

I ask Helen how so many villagers can leave Phoenix without arousing suspicions of the blacksuits.

"We all look alike to them," she explains. "From their perspective, we're interchangeable pawns on a chessboard. As long as the fields are full of workers, they won't notice a thing. Many of the villagers left behind work double shifts now, so the courtsmen are oblivious."

At the end of our first week, one of the villagers brings exciting news. The brane flickered twice during the day. The girl who brings the message says that the first flicker occurred so quickly she wasn't certain she'd seen it at all. Then she saw it a second time. She said we couldn't have passed through the brane even if we had been standing right next to it, because it came and went so suddenly. Still, this is good news.

* * * * *

Just before bedtime, we've established a custom of talking about what's on our minds.

Tonight Bree asks, "What do you miss most about home?"

"Boys," sighs Kenny. This is not a surprise.

"I miss my iPhone," says Jules.

"I miss my family the most," I add.

"Yeah," says Bree, "I miss Nana Joyce a lot. She's the only adult who ever treated me like a real person. Every other adult looked at me like I was slightly defective, somebody who didn't have the right stuff to sit at the grown-ups' table."

"You're right on that one," adds Jules. "My folks treat me as though being a teenager is some kind of disease that might get cured someday."

"I miss cheeseburgers," offers Chase.

"And pizza," adds Grizz.

"The mall," says Bree.

"Showers," says Charity, who has started to join in our conversations. "I hate that I'm never really clean. Splashing yourself with a little bit of water doesn't get the job done."

"Movies," says Kenny. "I miss going to the movies."

"Air-conditioning," says Chase wistfully.

"Playing tennis," says Jules.

"Skittles," I offer.

The thought that troubles me most as I drift off to sleep is that these things we miss are starting to feel like visions seen in a dream, as though they don't really exist.

9

Chase, Jules, and I played sports that put a heavy emphasis on physical training every day. We fall into the habit of running together every day during our afternoon break period. Our bodies need the endorphin high that comes with heavy exercise. Grizz, who has been my jogging buddy since I took up track, joins us as well.

One afternoon, as we are in the middle of our run, and about three miles south of the Sanctuary, we hear a strange high-pitched whine and a peculiar grinding noise coming from the south. We stop running and look in the direction of the noise. It grows louder, and after a few moments, we can see movement through the trees. We see something silver moving toward us and traveling fast. Chase, Grizz, Jules, and I look at one another. Curiosity and prudence go to war in my mind. Stay and see what's coming, or get out of here fast? Curiosity wins. We wait until we can see more clearly.

Prudence should have won. Coming toward us are two machines, each about four feet tall. The machines have a set of sharp, whirring, grinding blades set on top of treads.

"Run!" Grizz yells.

We sprint away from the blades, running toward the Sanctuary. The distance between us and the blades grows, but we are soon short of breath and have to slow down. As we slow to a walk, the blades close the gap between us. We begin running again, and find that if we jog, the distance between us stabilizes.

We break into a clearing and see two acolytes running as fast as they can. They have heard the blades coming, and obviously know they're bad news. "Bots!" they cry out to us. "Run!"

The Sisters are not going to reach Sanctuary Hill before the bots catch them. I reverse direction and head back toward the acolytes.

Grizz sees what's happening and turns as well. As soon as I reach the Sisters, I throw one over my shoulder like a sack of potatoes. Grizz picks up the other.

We turn back toward Sanctuary Hill and run. But the bots continue to gain on us. I'm tired and need to catch my breath. I place the Sister I've been carrying on the ground. "Go!" I yell, pointing toward the hill. The Sister takes off.

I bend over and put my hands on my knees, panting, and watch as the bots narrow the gap between us. They're still coming on too fast for the Sisters to reach the hill before being overtaken. There's only one thing left to do. I wait until the bots are ten yards away and sprint to my left, perpendicular to the path back to Sanctuary Hill. The bots wheel into a turn and follow me. I'm going to run them away from the hill and then double back. I have a sizable speed advantage when I'm sprinting. I reach the edge of the tree line, catch my foot on a vine, and fall. I catch myself with my hands and lose skin from the heels of my palms. I try to free my foot, but it's snagged on the vine that brought me down.

A bot is only yards away. I roll onto my side and grab a long fallen branch and hold it in front of me. The bot's blades tear up the branch, turning it into splinters. I finally jerk my foot from the snare and roll sideways, out of the bot's path. It makes a wide turn and comes after me again. That's okay. I'm no longer winded, so I'm able to dash away and increase the distance between us.

I turn for a sprint back to the hill, when I see Grizz climb a tree to avoid the bot that's been following him. He's winded and can run no farther. The bot begins to tear into the tree, making a whirring, thumping noise, a sound somewhere between that of an ax and a chain saw. The tree is only ten feet tall, and the bot's blades are almost long enough to reach Grizz's feet. The bot will have chewed its way through the tree in a matter of minutes.

I run toward Grizz. When I've covered most of the distance, I find a long, fallen branch. I pick it up, and when I'm within range, I hold it like a baseball bat and swing the branch into the side of the whirring blades. My blow knocks the bot on its side. It begins to right itself, but I've bought the time we need. Grizz is still breathing hard, but his moments of rest in the tree have given him time to regroup enough to run again. The bot behind me is only five yards behind, so we have no time to waste.

We reach the base of the Sanctuary and scramble up into the rocks. The bots have treads like a tank, but they aren't going to do any rock climbing. They stop at the base of the hill. They whir about for a while and then head off to the east.

"Those are bots," one of the acolytes explains. "Fortunately, they're not very smart. They don't wait for you to come back down. They lose interest and go somewhere else."

Bots are another weapon left over from the wars, no doubt. They must run on solar power, or they'd have stopped working centuries ago.

* * * * *

Our training continues, and we improve. Every time I begin to hit the archery target with some regularity, Falstaff moves it farther back. We develop blisters, but we tape them over and continue training.

I'm not happy with my progress with bow and arrow, so I sometimes use our time after dinner for extra practice. Tyler always joins me. He examines my form ("Keep your elbow up, ET"), fetches arrows, and cheers me on. With extra practice, I become much better. I begin to work on speed as well as accuracy. Falstaff tells us the ability to shoot rapidly is just as important as the ability to shoot straight.

I change Tyler's dressing daily. The Sisters have an herbal compress they use, and it seems to work just as well as disinfectant, if not better. After two weeks, it becomes clear that neither his eye nor his knee will ever recover from the trauma they've suffered. Tyler is very brave and puts up a good front, even though we know he must be despondent. My feeling of guilt grows exponentially. Grizz made an eye patch for Tyler. Ty loves it, and wears it everywhere. The Sisters tell him it makes him look like a roughneck.

I think the thing that bothers Ty most is that his injuries make it hard for him to progress in weapons training. With only one good eye, his depth perception is poor, and he can't plant any weight on his right leg because of his knee. This makes sword and spear work difficult, if not impossible. He refuses to be deterred.

"If I shoot the arrow straight, it doesn't matter how far away the target is," he says with determination. And he does very well. I watch one morning as he buries five straight arrows in the heart of the bull's-eye.

Tyler knows he'll never be able to fight with a sword, so during sword practice, he works with Beatrice fletching arrows. (Fletching an arrow involves affixing feathers to the arrow to balance it so it will fly straight.) Tyler is a quick learner and begins producing arrows at a prodigious rate. As Beatrice points out, you can never have too many arrows. When Ty is not fletching arrows, he's our number one cheerleader, always ready with words of praise and encouragement.

Kenny loves weapons training. One day after bow practice, she flops down next to me and says, "Don't mess with the warrior princess! I am Kenny the destroyer. Watch and fear."

"Aren't we full of ourselves?" I reply.

"Simply stating the obvious," sniffs Kenny.

Kenny has always steered well clear of any involvement in athletics. Our last conversation about the subject went something like this:

Me: "With your height, you'd be a natural for volleyball or basketball."

Kenny: "I don't like getting all sweaty and smelly. It scares away the boys."

Me: "Not if you shower afterwards."

Kenny: "Think what would happen to my nails."

The surprising thing is, not only does she enjoy training, she is good at it.

As days turn into weeks, a rivalry builds in intensity between Chase and Kenny with swords. Chase is bigger and stronger, and he has a greater reach. But Kenny is quicker and more agile. Chase wins a majority of their fights, but the competition makes them both better.

Charity and Jules excel with bow and arrow, but Bree is in a class by herself. She can hit the bull's-eye ten times in a minute, which leaves the rest of us feeling more than a little inadequate. Grizz's strength helps make him our best person with spear and knife, and he's almost as good as Chase and Jules with the sword.

Falstaff pays us the ultimate compliment when he tells us we just might actually survive for a minute or two in a fight with wolves or blacksuits. The blisters we had have been replaced by calluses.

We're in our fourth week when an amazing thing happens. "Two more giants have come through the brane," says an out-of-breath messenger. "We are bringing them to the Mother's Sanctuary."

* * * * *

Below us, I see Jared Cain and Zoe Kerber making the climb up to the mouth of the cavern. I am flabbergasted. Of all the people in the world, why did my ex-"boyfriend" have to be the one who suddenly appears out on nowhere? I can't think of anyone I'd like to see less. I give Jared a level stare when he reaches the top.

"Hiya, babe," Jared says when he sees me. These are the first words he's spoken to me since he hit me.

"Don't call me 'babe,'" I respond coolly.

"You know, you guys are famous now."

"How so?" I ask.

"The whole world is wondering what happened to you," he explains. "Your cars are parked at the Midnight Mesa trailhead, and there's no trace of you. We've had CNN and Fox News vans in town. Everybody has a theory about what happened to you."

"Great," I say. "So how did you wind up on this side of Midnight Mesa?"

"Zoe and I were on the mesa, planning for a little 'afternoon delight,' if you catch my meaning. Then there was this weird light. Zoe and I went to check it out, and we wound up here. We turned around, and the light was gone."

"I wish I could say I'm glad to see you, but I'm not," I say.

"Let's let bygones be bygones," Jared suggests.

"Not a chance," I reply.

"Your loss," he says with a shrug.

The acolytes rush Jared and Zoe into the cavern for an orientation with Helen. I can see that Grizz is very distressed by this turn of events. He pulls me aside, out of earshot of the others, and looks at me with deeply troubled eyes.

"ET," he pleads earnestly, "please don't fall for that weasel again."

"No need to worry, Grizz," I reply. "I'm totally over him."

"Erin…" he continues. I'm worried because Grizz *never* calls me Erin. "Erin, what Jared did to you was my fault."

I don't know what to think. Or say. I wait for him to continue.

"Jared has always hated me," Grizz continues. "I don't know why, maybe because he couldn't bully me like he did everybody else. Anyhow, one day last year, he and a bunch of his buddies caught me after school. With his buddies backing him up, he pushed me and told me I was piece of…well, never mind.

"Anyway, I pushed him back. And then I pushed him again and knocked him down. When he got up, I pushed him down again. I mean, I totally backed him down. He kept looking at his buddies, expecting them to step in. But they didn't. I don't know why. Maybe they were sick of the jerk. Or maybe they knew that I was Chase's friend and they didn't want to get into a fight putting them in the middle between two big-time football stars. Anyway, Jared got up again and backed away from me. When he was at a safe distance, he pointed at me with his finger and said, 'This isn't done.' He started hitting on you right after that."

"Grizz, I don't understand what all this has to do with me," I say, bewildered.

"What it has to do with you, Erin, is that Jared saw what everybody in the world sees. He saw that I was crazy about you, and if he could take you, he'd have his revenge."

I'm speechless. "You were crazy about me?"

"Wrong tense, Erin. I *am* crazy about you. Totally," he says. "The whole world knows it. Erin, I've been in love with you since we were five years old. And you're the only one who doesn't know."

"Why didn't you say something, Grizz? Why didn't you tell me?"

"I didn't say anything because you're always going on about how our group has such great chemistry and you're so glad that nobody gets romantic and messes it up." He stops and looks at me with such pain in his eyes that my heart melts. "I didn't say anything because I was afraid I'd scare you away."

I don't know what to say. Emotionally, I'm in a deep and troubled state of confusion.

"Erin," he implores, "I want to kiss you one time. And if you don't feel anything, I'll never mention my feelings again."

Before I can reply, he leans in and kisses me. He takes me in his arms. I feel a very pleasant warm sensation deep inside. I like this. But

105

then I think of Tyler. Tyler would be devastated if Grizz and I got together. Poor crippled Tyler, crippled because of me.

I push Grizz away. "Please, Grizz, I can't."

"Tell me you didn't feel anything, Erin."

I work hard to force the words out. "I didn't feel anything, Grizz."

I can see it in his eyes. He knows I'm lying.

"Please don't hate me," I plead, my voice choked with emotion.

"I'll never hate you, Erin. Never. I love you. I've always loved you. And I'll keep on loving you until the day I die." There are tears in his eyes. He refuses to let them fall. Instead, he turns and walks away.

I sit down, overwhelmed by emotion. I want to run after Grizz, to tell him that I care for him too. I never thought of Grizz that way before, but something happened when he kissed me. Something deep and profound and totally undeniable. But I can't run after him, because I can't do it to Tyler. I owe Tyler that much.

* * * * *

My friends and I make a point of watching as many of each other's performances as possible. Oftentimes, my friends make up over half the crowd at my track meets. Kenny and I were sitting at a table at the Shake 'n' Burger on a Tuesday night, listening as Tyler's band performed. Ty's band is better than average as teen bands go, and I always enjoy their shows.

Ty was singing the last song of their first set, which was unusual, because he wasn't usually the vocalist. The song had a lilting melody driven by a syncopated reggae beat. Eyes closed, Ty sang in his sweet, pure tenor:

106

Every night I dream of you,

Beautiful dreams that won't come true

Dreams in which you're holding me

Dreams I know can never be

Dreams imbued with the gossamer hue

Of deepest green and cerulean blue.

The song was by far the most beautiful one his band had ever done.

When the last note faded, the audience responded with applause. Ty and his band mates joined Kenny and me at our table. I learned long ago that whenever a girl goes out with Kenny, she's going to watch the boys flock around Kenny like bees to honey (or maybe like bugs to a zapper). The polite ones acknowledge my presence before they become lost in Kenny's glow. The phenomenon doesn't bother me, because it doesn't make any difference who the other girl is. Kenny is gonna be the center of attention.

Tyler is one of the rare exceptions to this rule.

"Did you like the last song?" Ty asked.

"Yes," I replied, "it was one of the most beautiful songs I've ever heard."

"I wrote it for you," Ty said, but he avoided my eyes and twisted a straw wrapper around his index finger.

Ty has a crush on me. I've been aware since third grade. But he never said much about it. Once in a while, he'd remind me, quietly.

"Ty, I'm honored, I'm…flattered. But, go on, you don't really dream about me. Do you?"

"Yeah," he said, "I do."

And then, being Tyler, he changed the subject.

Later, when the band was playing its second set, George, who owns the Shake 'n' Burger, sat down beside me.

"That boy would run through a brick wall for you," he said, nodding at Tyler.

"I guess I'm figuring that out," I responded.

"He's kind and he's gentle," said George. "He's about as nice as a kid can be."

"I know."

"Try not to hurt him too bad, ET."

"I won't hurt him."

"Good luck with that," said George, and he left with a smile.

I'd never thought Ty's feelings for me were strong enough that I should worry about hurting him. I knew I'd have to be very careful to avoid leading him on, and I'd have to be very honest with him when we talked about our feelings.

I couldn't help being flattered. What girl wouldn't want a song written about her?

* * * * *

The following day, Falstaff tells us that it's time to practice fighting dreadwolves.

"You fight dreadwolves with a sword and shield," he explains. "When a dreadwolf charges, its first inclination will be to tear out your throat. You will counter this by raising your shield to protect your throat. When the dreadwolf hits your shield, you will counter with an uppercut, driving your sword into the dreadwolf's belly. Thrust, rip, and turn, just like we taught you. We will need to work on balance, because a dreadwolf in full stride will knock you right over if you don't have your feet planted correctly."

We work for a long time on balance. When Falstaff is satisfied, he continues with another strategy.

"You fight dreadwolves in a circular formation. If you aren't in a circle, they will attack you from behind and in front simultaneously. You will quickly die. The thing you need to do is constantly be aware of what is happening around you. If you see your neighbor go down, shrink the circle and close ranks immediately. Stay shoulder to shoulder with the person next to you at all times."

I'm distracted during practice. I can't help thinking about Grizz. How can I have missed something so obvious? Why was I so stupid about telling people that I thought it was wonderful we had no romance in our group? Falstaff knows something is wrong. At one point he pulls me aside and asks me why I am so slow today. I respond that I didn't sleep well last night. That much is very true. I didn't sleep well, and when I did, I dreamed of Grizz.

I can't help noticing Grizz in ways I never did before: how his eyes are such a beautiful shade of blue, how his chest muscles ripple under the homespun clothes the acolytes made for him, how he's always so kind to the villagers. I force these thoughts from my mind and try to concentrate on closing the circle.

* * * * *

Several evenings later, Helen calls us all together for a war council. My friends and a few villagers sit around a large table.

"Falstaff tells me you are ready to fight." She looks at each of us in turn. "You will leave tomorrow."

I knew this moment would come, but I am still unnerved at the suddenness.

"We will not risk the lives of all our giants at once," Helen continues. "Falstaff tells me that Chase, Kennedy, and Grizz are our most formidable fighters."

I'm about to complain about not being included, when Helen says, "Erin will go, too. She must go if she is to rid us of the curse of the dreadwolves. But she must remain in the center of your fighting circle. We must not lose her."

How on earth am I going to end the curse of the dreadwolves? I can easily see it will do me no good to complain or express doubts. Morale among the villagers is high, and I can't say anything to change that. They've lived so long under the heel of the Court that the possibility of acting against it is intoxicating for them. I'm going to do everything I can to help them. If they think I can rid them of the dreadwolves, then I'll try.

Chase asks why he can't fight the dreadwolves with his rifle. Falstaff explains that fighting dreadwolves is a hand-to-hand affair. He'd never be able to take aim and fire before the dreadwolves were all over him.

I can see the rest of my friends are unhappy about being left behind. But Helen's logic is irrefutable. If anything goes wrong, she'll still have a core of "giants" to build around.

"You will leave at first light tomorrow," Helen says in conclusion.

Just before we retire for the evening, Perdita and another Sister bring us our new clothing. The tunics and pants are made of softbark. We try them on.

"This is the most comfortable thing I've ever worn!" enthuses Jules.

"I think we finally found something in this world that's better than anything we had in *our* world," says Kenny. "This stuff is softer than silk."

The boys grumble at how "girly" the clothes feel, but they seem pleased even so.

Between thoughts of Grizz and worries about the coming day, I sleep very little. I'm awake when the acolytes come to rouse us. We eat a quiet breakfast, and assemble for the day's march with the first hint of dawn in the eastern sky.

We've come to this world during the summer months, or the season of longdays, as the villagers call it. Detroit is two dayswalks from Phoenix. The length of a dayswalk is based upon the distance a person can walk from sunrise to sunset during winter, or the season of the shortdays. Thus, we can reach Detroit easily in two days, since summer days are so much longer than winter days.

Our strategy is to stop well before sunset, when we've found a clearing large enough to deploy our defensive circle. We'll leave time enough to cut wood to keep a number of bonfires burning all night. Even though dreadwolves no longer fear fire, fire enables us to see them. Since they are nocturnal, dreadwolves have much better night vision than we do. The bonfires should deprive them of that advantage and might even impair their vision. If we survive the first night, we press on to Detroit.

Falstaff introduces me to his second-in-command. "I'd like you to meet Valentine," he says. "He has a score to settle with the dreadwolves. His fiancée was killed by wolves just three days before they were to wed."

I shake Valentine's hand. "I hope you have an opportunity to avenge your loss," I say.

We assemble in our order of march. Falstaff leads, my friends and I follow behind him, and we are, in turn, followed by 120 villagers. We carry only swords and shields and a small amount of food and water.

The pace of the march is maddeningly slow. The villagers, with their short legs, cannot walk nearly as fast as we larger humans can. I have my compass, my watch, and my pedometer, and I keep careful track of where we are going. We travel in a line about five degrees north of west, but we must go around thickets and high, rocky hills. There are insects buzzing around us constantly, and we are soon drenched in sweat. The heat is merciless.

I am becoming familiar with the different species of trees and brush we encounter. We see birds flitting through the trees overhead, and I recognize many of them as well. We cross several streams, but know better than to drink from them.

Falstaff calls a halt at about 6:00 p.m.

Many of the villagers are extremely unhappy about fighting in this particular clearing. The carcass of a dead moose lies on the eastern side of it. Falstaff tells us the clearing is as big as we are likely to find, and advises everyone to stay well clear of the rotting corpse. We cut branches for the next three hours. As the sunset fades in the west, we have a number of impressive bonfires blazing. We form our defensive circle.

"You must not fall asleep," Falstaff warns. "You will not wake up if you do."

I muscle my way into the defensive line between Falstaff and Grizz.

"Helen was very clear. You are to remain in the center of the circle," Falstaff tells me.

"I'm not going to stand aside and watch you fight," I return.

Falstaff begins to speak again, but thinks better of it. Finally he shrugs. "Suit yourself," he says. After training me, he knows better than to argue with me.

Dreadwolves begin to howl. There are hundreds of them.

I settle in for a long, sleepless night.

When the dreadwolves come, they are on top of us faster than I ever would have imagined.

D.S. Northrop

10

One moment I am stifling a yawn, and the next there is a dreadwolf leaping for my throat. His open jaws reveal razor-sharp fangs. I barely get my shield up in time, and the wolf's momentum knocks me back two steps. Then training takes over. I put all my weight behind a thrust from underneath, into the wolf's exposed belly. Thrust. Rip. Turn.

I struggle to free my blade when I see another wolf, jaws open wide, lunging for my right thigh. I realize I can't get my blade free in time to stop this one. I breathe a huge sigh of relief when Grizz's machete nearly decapitates the wolf, inches short of my thigh. If the wolf had torn open my femoral artery, I would have died just as surely as if the other had torn my throat, and almost as fast.

Another wolf comes for my throat, but I'm ready for this one. Catch him on the shield, then thrust, rip, turn.

And then, as quickly as they appeared, the dreadwolves are gone.

While evolution may have driven humans to become smaller and smaller, it has done little to shrink the wolves. Their gray bodies are as big as German shepherds. I don't know how the tiny villagers can stand up to them. The dreadwolves are well adapted for hunting at night. Their luminous yellow irises surround huge black pupils.

In the instant the wolves disappear, cheers burst out along our lines.

"Stop!" shouts Falstaff. "They're not done. They were just probing our line, looking for weaknesses."

Many dreadwolf corpses litter the clearing, but half a dozen dead villagers are scattered on our southern flank, and even more on our northern flank. (Grizz and I, along with Chase and Kenny, face west.) Falstaff sees the weakness of our northern and southern lines and is shouting, trying to adjust our defenses to strengthen the line, but it's too late. The dreadwolves are on us again.

And just as we fear, they are concentrating their attacks on our northern and southern flanks. In less than five minutes, I watch helplessly as the dreadwolves slay brave young Valentine and break through the southern flank. Shortly thereafter, our northern flank disintegrates. Dreadwolves are inside our lines and behind us. In the next few moments, sections of our line disappear entirely, taken down by wolves attacking villagers from both front and rear simultaneously.

Moving quickly and frantically, we are able to reform four smaller circles, but dreadwolves separate the circles from one another, and try as we may, we cannot fight our way through to rejoin our comrades. The largest circle is our own, with my friends, Falstaff, and about a dozen villagers. Sister Juliet is still safe inside.

Over the next two hours, we watch the other three circles succumb one by one to the attacking dreadwolves. We try to cut our way through to join the other circles, but the wolves blunt every attack we make.

With only our own circle left, the wolves disappear again.

Just as quickly, they are back at our throats. This time, the dreadwolves employ teamwork. One wolf fakes an attack and then leaps backward, luring us into a thrust that catches only empty air, while a second wolf attacks while we're off-balance. I see Persephone go down, a victim of this strategy. A moment later, Beatrice succumbs as well. I grieve for these losses, remembering the hours those two spent teaching us to fight.

My friends and I face west and absorb the brunt of the dreadwolves' attack. They are choosing not to attack from the east, which is good, because the villagers are holding that part of our line and, as we've seen, their smaller size leaves them less able to stand up to the dreadwolves' attacks. Falstaff yells to the villagers behind us to keep up their guard.

On their next charge, two wolves leap for Grizz, one going high and the other going low. Holding my bowie knife tightly with my right hand, I swing as hard as I can at the bottom wolf. I catch him full in the chest, but the force of the collision sends painful shock waves up my arm and into my shoulder. I struggle to hang on to my weapon, but the blow leaves the dreadwolf fatally wounded and Grizz in one piece.

The dreadwolves attack relentlessly. My arms and shoulders tire, and it becomes harder and harder for me to parry their assaults. Every time they charge, the momentum of their charge forces us to give ground. I take a quick glance behind and realize we are only a matter of yards from the eastern edge of the clearing. We cannot let them drive us into the forest. We would be easily separated from one another, and the wolves would kill us one by one. But the onslaught continues. We leave dozens of dead dreadwolves on the ground in front of us, but the inexorable attacks force us back, step by step.

I impale another wolf on the end of my bowie knife, but the momentum of his charge forces me back again. I trip over something beneath my feet, and my nose tells me that I am sitting on the carcass of the dead moose we saw earlier. Some of the villagers unaccountably leave our circle and run right into the attacking wolves. The dreadwolves make short work of them. I see Falstaff start to charge the wolves, and I grab him by the collar and hold him back. He vomits uncontrollably.

There are more than a hundred wolves circling us, growling, snarling, and snapping their jaws. Our little party is down to eight people, four "giants," Falstaff, Sister Juliet, and two other villagers who are on the ground and heaving. With just four of us standing, we wait for the next attack, knowing that it will be the last one. Grizz is to my right, and I feel Kenny's back pressed up against mine. We are physically exhausted. It requires enormous effort to simply hold up my shield and sword. The wolves continue to pace around us as if looking for the chink in our armor, the best place to strike and finish us off.

For some reason, the dreadwolves do not charge again. I look back over my shoulder and see a faint light coming from the eastern horizon. Dawn! Slowly, the snarling dreadwolves back away from us and disappear into the forest. Falstaff and the villagers crawl away from us as quickly as they can, toward the center of the clearing.

The clearing is piled high with the intertwined corpses of dreadwolves and villagers.

And just as Helen has foretold, I now know how to stop the dreadwolves.

* * * * *

We have no time to rest, tired as we all are. We're sickened by the carnage around us. Good people died last night, and much as we might wish to, we have no time to bury them. We still have a day's journey to Detroit ahead of us. Nobody needs to state the obvious: we will never survive a second night in the forest. We begin to walk.

I mentally review the evidence I've seen over the last several hours. The villagers did not like the clearing because it had a corpse in it. When the dreadwolves forced us back onto the corpse, some of the villagers had inexplicably made a suicide charge at the dreadwolves. Falstaff had vomited when forced to stay near the corpse. And most important of all: The dreadwolves had not finished us off when they could have. They circled around us, but they kept their distance and never attacked.

These facts lead to an undeniable conclusion: animals in this world are deathly afraid of decomposing bodies.

As we walk, I explain my thinking. Falstaff confirms my theory. "If you get too close to a corpse you will die," he says.

"Of course!" says Kenny, picking up on the idea. "Helen told us that during the wars, after the oceans began to rise, nations used biological and nuclear weapons against one another. If a corpse was a carrier of plague, or if it was radioactive, you *should* avoid going anywhere near it. But by now, the plague has run its course. Animals today don't die from the plague."

118

Falstaff is skeptical.

"Well," I say, "I guess we'll find out. If we drop dead from the plague, we'll know Kenny is wrong."

"Now that's a pleasant thought," says Chase. "But how does this help us neutralize the dreadwolves? We can't walk around carrying corpses."

"The wolves don't fear the corpse," I say. "They fear the scent."

Turning to Kenny, I ask, "Could you make something that would mimic the smell of decomposition? Something that's portable? Something we can carry with us?"

"Hmmm," Kenny muses. "The smell of a decomposing corpse is caused by the release of a combination of gases: methane, ammonia, and hydrogen sulfide, mostly. That last one is the one that makes farts smell bad. If I could find a source for these, I could probably brew up something that would have a smell reasonably close to a rotting body." She lapses into silence as she concentrates. "What can I use to make that scent?"

"And who would want to walk around carrying something that smells like a corpse?" adds Chase.

"I think the Sisters could help us there," I say. "You've seen the pottery the Sisters make." We've been eating and drinking from it every day.

"Sister Juliet," I continue, "could the Sisters make a wide-mouth jar with a top to seal it? Could you make it with handles on the outside so we could slide a strap through and carry it slung over our shoulders? If we can close the container during the daytime, it wouldn't be so smelly. We'd only have to open the container at night!"

Sister Juliet answers immediately, "Yes, of course. We could easily do that."

"Poo!" says Kenny with excitement.

119

"Poo?" I ask.

"Yes! Poo! Excrement," continues Kenny. "It's an excellent source of methane and nitrogen! And we certainly make a lot of it. And skunk. I've seen some in the forest. Their spray contains sulfides! And ammonia and methane are by-products of decomposing plants as well as decomposing animals, so I can partially substitute dead plants for dead animals. Yep, I should be able to make the stinkum we need. It'll take some work, but I'm pretty sure it can be done."

Maybe we *can* help the villagers break the curse of the dreadwolves.

Tired to the point of exhaustion, saddened by the loss of so many villagers, and excited by the prospect of ultimately neutralizing the dreadwolves, I'm still aware of Grizz's presence next to me. I feel that strange, warm yearning in the pit of my stomach. I banish it at once.

* * * * *

We arrive at Detroit at about 6:00 p.m. It looks very much like Phoenix. A little smaller, perhaps. There's a fortress in the center surrounded by acres and acres of cultivated land.

Sister Juliet and Falstaff instruct us to remain hidden from sight at the tree line while they go into the village and talk to the village council to arrange for our arrival.

"The villagers would be very startled if you just suddenly appeared out of the forest, and there may be courtsmen in the village," explains Falstaff. "We'll send for you when everything is safe."

We watch as Sister Juliet and Falstaff walk toward the fort. The villagers eye them suspiciously. Cut off from other villages by dreadwolves, the only people who suddenly appear out of the forest wear black uniforms. An elderly man musters the courage to approach the strangers. They speak for a few moments, and he gestures for

Falstaff and Juliet to follow him. The gates of the village swing open, then close once our friends are inside. Detroit is much like Phoenix: thousands of workers in the fields, bearded men, women with hair pulled back into buns, and an enclosure housing dozens of scrawny, recently shorn sheep.

The people here are thin, and they look as unhealthy as the villagers in Phoenix. On the nearest workers, we can make out the same kind of running sores and abrasions we saw in Phoenix. The clothes here are patched and shabby, as well.

Sister Juliet and Falstaff are inside the village for a long time. I wonder if the villagers of Detroit are reluctant to have trouble-causing giants hanging around their neighborhood. I swat at insects and fight sleep. After perhaps an hour, the gates of the fort swing open again. Falstaff rejoins us and tells us the plan: we are to enter the village at dusk. That'll be before the dreadwolves are out and too late for blacksuit patrols.

At the appointed time, we rise and walk slowly toward the gates.

When we pass through the gates and enter the village, we are greeted with rousing cheers. Villagers surround us, smiling, whistling, and clapping. Clearly, Falstaff and Sister Juliet have been telling the villagers about our adventures. We are easily caught up in the moment. We smile and wave as we are ushered to the village center. A very happy-looking older man introduces himself as William. He is bald and has a large red nose. His smile reaches from ear to ear. He is the chairman of the village council.

He raises his hands and asks for quiet. The cheering slowly subsides.

"I introduce you to the giants who burned the courtsmen's fort in Phoenix!" he shouts.

Loud, rowdy cheering ensues. When it dies down several minutes later, he continues. He puts his arm around me and announces, "This is the Daughter of Gaia who defeated the dreadwolves and who will lead us in rebellion against the tyranny of the Court."

I'm speechless, but it doesn't matter, because I couldn't be heard above the noise of cheering even if I tried. Daughter of Gaia? Now where did *that* come from? I don't know how I could possibly lead a rebellion against the blacksuits, or why anyone would even think I could. These people don't seem to realize I'm just a girl from Sierra Vista High School. I'm not Joan of Arc.

When the noise quiets a bit, I start to explain that Kenny is actually the one who is going to build the weapon that will defeat the dreadwolves, but the minute I speak, the cheering begins again and drowns me out. I look at my friends, and they seem amused at my discomfiture. They're *enjoying* my embarrassment.

When the noise dies down, William tells the people to prepare for the feast. Trestle tables are pulled into the village center, and we are encouraged to be seated. Once again, my friends and I sit on the ground, cross-legged, because the table is too small for us. Food is brought out, and I almost cry with joy. It's not potatoes! The food is still mush-like, but it tastes like squash. Squash is not ordinarily one of my favorite foods, but after a steady diet of potatoes, squash tastes like manna, food sent straight from heaven.

Conversation is not possible over the noise and commotion, but when dinner ends, William invites Falstaff to tell the tale of the Battle of Fort Warren again. Falstaff stands on the table and tells the story. He is interrupted after every line by roars of approval. He then tells the story of our journey from Phoenix, fighting off the dreadwolves (and underemphasizing the deaths of over one hundred villagers).

When Falstaff is done, William invites Sister Juliet to address the crowd.

She stands and asks for quiet. When she can be heard, she points at me and says, "I'd like to introduce you all to the Daughter of Gaia, the one sent to lead us in rebellion against the despotism of the Court!"

The crowd goes wild.

Grizz whispers in my ear, "Stand up and take a bow, Daughter of Gaia."

"I'm *not* the Daughter of Gaia," I hiss back.

"Try and convince them of that," he says, gesturing at the villagers.

Uncomfortably and awkwardly, I stand and wave. After a few minutes, I wonder if the cheering will ever end.

Much later, after more speeches and toasts, William ushers us into the chambers of the village council. The air inside is hazy with smoke from the torches on the walls. Awaiting us inside is the man we came to see. He introduces himself as Orsino. He's an old man with a shock of white hair. Like most villagers, he's dressed in patched homespun and has running sores on his face and arms.

"They tell me you want to try to solve the riddle of the workshop," he says without preamble in a scratchy voice.

"Yes, we do," I reply.

"I can tell you where it is, but I doubt it'll do you any good. The courtsmen have been trying to open that door for years."

"We'd still like to give it a try," I insist.

"I can show you how to get there better if we go outside," he says.

We oblige him. It's dark, but there's a full moon this evening.

"Do you see those two peaks right next to each other?" He points at the mountains. The two peaks are not the tallest mountains in the range, but are nonetheless lofty and snow covered. They glisten in the moonlight.

"We call those peaks the Twins. Be very careful as you approach them, because the courtsmen mine the northern Twin for copper and iron ore. You must cross the saddle between the Twins," he continues. "Descend the far side, and travel toward the rising sun. You will come to an ancient road that is now mostly in ruins. Follow the road in the direction of the constant star, and you will pass through an old, ruined town. Just to the north of the town, you will see a steep, rock-covered hill. On the side facing the rising sun, you will find the door."

"How far away is this workshop?" Grizz asks.

"It will take you four or five dayswalks to travel from Detroit to the base of the Twins. You will need another day to cross the saddle between the mountains. Add another dayswalk to the ruined city." That translates into a three-and-a-half or four-day walk for us.

"Just what did you do to get yourself banished from New Washington?" I ask.

"I was accused of giving water to a thirsty slave," he says.

We wish Orsino luck, and he leaves.

William says, "It'll take us a day or two to get a force together to escort you back to Phoenix. We have many young men and women who will be proud to serve with you."

"You do realize," I warn, "that we don't yet have the weapon we need to keep the dreadwolves away from our throats? Many of your villagers will die."

"We understand. But we are willing to fight and die for you, Daughter of Gaia," replies William.

"Perhaps that won't be necessary," says Grizz. "We 'giants' can travel much faster than you smaller people. I think we can make it all the way back to Phoenix in one day."

"Are you certain you can do this?" asks Falstaff skeptically.

"I think Grizz is right," I say. "We had plenty of daylight left when we stopped yesterday and again today. And we will move much faster alone."

Chase and Kenny agree.

Falstaff and Sister Juliet are not happy at the prospect of being left behind in Detroit, but I promise them we'll send for them as soon as Kenny has perfected her "stinkum."

"Let's get some sleep," says Chase. "We'll have a long day tomorrow."

Sleeping quarters are arranged for us. I take some good-natured ribbing about being the "Daughter of Gaia," and then fall asleep the moment my head touches the pillow. My dreams are haunted by dreadwolves and villagers lying in a field with their throats torn open.

* * * * *

Falstaff awakens us when the sky is still totally dark. We eat a quick breakfast (not potatoes!) and watch the light begin to brighten the eastern sky. When the wolves have stopped howling, I embrace Falstaff, say good-bye to Sister Juliet, and lead our group into the forest.

I monitor my compass religiously. A small error in bearing at the beginning of a long trip can leave you miles from your destination hours later. We alternate between jogging and brisk walking. The miles go by quickly.

I find myself in the "zone" that comes with strenuous physical exercise. I am both here and not here, high on endorphins. The sky is clear. I don't think I've seen so much as a single cloud in all my time here. Although the day is another scorcher, I'm getting used to the heat. It no longer seems as oppressive as it was. Sweat runs down my back. The air smells, as always, of moldering vegetation.

We make excellent progress. At 4:00 p.m., by dead reckoning, I have us about twelve miles away from the Sanctuary. With more than four hours of daylight remaining, we should make it with time to spare.

Then trouble strikes. I hear a thud behind me and hear Kenny holler, "Son of a gun!"

I turn around to find Kenny on the ground. She sits up, cross-legged, and begins to massage her left ankle.

"I thought I had safe footing," she says, "but it was just leaves and sticks on top of an animal's burrow. Dang!"

I kneel beside her and begin to rotate her ankle. She yelps when I move it to the left.

"You want to give me some anesthetic before you do that again?" she says, looking at me crossly.

"Well, it's not broken," I say. "Try to put some weight on it." Many times you can just walk off a sprained ankle.

Not this one. The minute Kenny puts weight on it, she grimaces. She tries to limp, but her ankle gives way, and she's back on the ground again. "Nuts!" she says.

"Okay," I say. "Don't try to walk on it. You'll just make it worse."

Grizz and Chase are going to have to help her walk. We arrange Kenny so she has one arm wrapped around Chase, and the other wrapped around Grizz. They move awkwardly at first, but with practice, they manage to keep up a respectable pace. Grizz and Chase set off at a good clip, and Kenny plants her right foot every other step. They appear to be a peculiar-looking three-headed, five-legged beast.

"What say you lose a little weight before you do this the next time?" suggests Chase.

Kenny, who has her right hand wrapped around Chase's shoulder, uses it to box his ear. "What say you stop whining?" she says.

I look anxiously at my watch. If we can sustain this pace, we should still make it back safely, but we won't have much of a cushion.

The sun sets below the trees to the west. The western sky turns salmon pink, and the first stars appear in the east. I begin to worry. I know better than to say anything. Grizz and Chase are moving as fast as they can. Finally, just as the western sky begins to darken, I see the rocky hill that houses the Sanctuary. We're about a half mile farther south than I'd thought, but I'm still proud of my compass skills.

Then the wolves begin to howl.

I reach the hill and quickly climb twenty feet up. When I turn around, I see that the odd five-legged beast that my friends have become is only ten yards short of safety. And then I see a chilling sight: dozens of dark shapes emerge from the tree line and move toward us at unbelievable speed.

* * * * *

The threesome reaches the base of the hill. Chase and Grizz shove Kenny up. Grizz scrambles up behind her, but the dreadwolves are quickly closing the gap. Chase clambers up, and I heave a sigh of relief.

My relief is premature. The leading dreadwolf leaps and closes his jaws around Chase's calf. Chase cries out in pain, but manages to climb another four feet, pulling the wolf along with him. He's now high enough that no other wolves can reach him.

I draw the flint knife from my belt, holding it by the tip, as I've been trained, take aim, and throw. The knife catches the dreadwolf full in the chest, a fatal blow, a result that surprises all of us, myself most of all. Even dead, the wolf won't let go. We pull Chase up until we can reach the wolf, and it takes all three of us to loosen the wolf's death grip.

We maneuver Chase onto a level surface, and I inspect the wound. The wolf has torn the soleus muscle, which joins ankle to calf, and cut through skin right down to the shinbone, but to my unpracticed eye, everything looks as though it should heal. Still, Chase is not going anywhere fast in the near future.

I look up to see our friends and many of the acolytes looking anxiously down at us.

When we join the others inside the huge cavern, I overhear the Sisters happily whispering about the return of the "Daughter of Gaia." Charity looks relieved to have Chase back in one piece, more or less. We're all giddy after our close escape.

Kenny looks at Chase and, smiling, points to his injury and says, "That's what you get for touching my butt."

Chase blusters, "The only reason I touched your butt was to shove it up the hill so the dreadwolves wouldn't eat it!"

"Yeah, but you enjoyed it, didn't you?"

"Don't flatter yourself," Chase replies with a smile.

Kenny looks at Charity and says, "You know your boyfriend was touching my butt."

Charity, who is slowly learning to like us, replies, "Better your butt than somebody *really* pretty."

Kenny grins. "Nice one, Charity, you got me."

Ty welcomes Chase and Kenny to the "Gimps Club."

Kenny and Chase will be graduating from that club, I think. Unlike Tyler, who's a permanent member.

The Sisters bustle Chase off to attend to his wounds. I'm more than happy to turn my medical practice over to them.

Helen appears and asks if we'd join her in her sitting room. I'm sure she wants to hear about our journey, and what happened to all the villagers who went with us. We recount our exploits of the last three days. Helen is relieved to hear that Falstaff and Sister Juliet are still alive, and saddened by the loss of so many others. Chase limps in with the aid of a crutch. The Sisters have bound his wounds.

When we've finished our story, I tell Helen our plans to mimic the smell of decomposing corpses to frighten the dreadwolves away.

"I knew you would find a way, child." She beams at me.

I point out the fact that Kenny is the one who will actually provide the weapon.

"Of course," agrees Helen, "of course. Your friends are brilliant. And we love you all. You cannot know how much we owe you for everything you have done and for all that you will do."

Kenny tells Helen all the ingredients she'll need to make her potion.

"I'll need a laboratory, and you'll probably want to make sure it's a long way away from where you live and work, because it'll get *very* smelly," she says. "I'll need several skunks. Be sure to kill them before they spray, because once they've sprayed, they're no good to me. I'll need lots of dead plant material. And, I'll need lots of poo."

"Feces," I explain, seeing Helen's confused look. I then add, "We'll need wide-mouth jars with tight lids. We'll also need straps on the jars so we can carry them over our shoulders."

"You will have everything you need," says Helen. "We will start working on it at first light tomorrow."

Then, Helen drops a bombshell on us. "Your friends Jared and Zoe disappeared last night."

11

"What happened?" I ask.

"When we rose this morning," Helen explains, "Jared and Zoe were nowhere to be found. We searched the lower caverns, thinking they might have gotten lost. As we were searching, the Sister on watch sounded her horn. When we came running, she said she spotted the two of them running away from the Sanctuary and into the forest."

"Did you tell them your story?" I ask. "The one you told us when we arrived?"

"I told them much, but I didn't tell them everything." Helen pauses. "I had a bad feeling about them. They didn't seem to be…good people."

"You were right about that," I say. "But did you tell them about New Washington, and how the people there live so well compared to us?"

"Yes," admits Helen, "I did."

"Well, if they think they can live a more comfortable life with the blacksuits than with us, that's where they've gone," says Chase bitterly. "No surprise there."

Tyler is grinning. "That's great news! The blacksuits are just going to torture them the way they did me. They won't be able to explain where they came from any better than I did. They'll get exactly what they deserve."

"That's not exactly true," objects Grizz. "They can give the blacksuits information that you couldn't have given them."

"What would that be?" asks Tyler, confused.

"They can tell them where the Mother's Sanctuary is," says Grizz grimly.

* * * * *

The cave is abuzz with activity the following morning. Mother Helen has two acolytes busy helping Kenny set up her lab. She sends another half dozen out to hunt for skunks. Still others are instructed to return with decomposing plant material. Although it's doubtful the blacksuits will be moving against us today, she sends more Sisters to screen for blacksuits marching down from the north.

She realizes she needs more help, and sends another Sister to Phoenix to ask for additional people. "Tell the villagers they should all take different routes to get her. We don't want to leave any hints for Tracker to pick up."

The rest of us are busy preparing defensive positions near the entrance to the caverns. We pile rocks to give ourselves positions of cover so we can hide as we shoot arrows at blacksuits climbing up to the Sanctuary. Nobody has any doubt: The blacksuits will come. It's just a question of when.

When I'm satisfied with our defensive positions, I walk down into the lower caves to see how Kenny is doing. The smell emanating from her lab is terrible. I don't need anyone to show me the way. I can simply follow my nose.

Two young Sisters emerge from Kenny's lab as I arrive. They give me a very nasty look. These are the two responsible for bringing Kenny the poo she needs. They seem unhappy with their assignment.

The smell in the lab is overpowering.

"How can you stand to work in this smell?" I ask.

Kenny looks up from her work, sleeves rolled up, hair a mess. "What smell?" she asks cheerfully. "Actually, my sense of smell was never very good to begin with, and you can get used to just about anything."

"Okay," I say doubtfully. "How's the work coming?"

"Great!" she enthuses. "They just brought me my first skunk."

There, on her table, lies a skunk. Kenny is cautiously cutting into its rear end. "Have to be a little careful about this. Don't want to spray myself," she mutters, more to herself than me.

Her lab looks very impressive for a makeshift operation. She has shelves covered with all manner of pots, jugs, crucibles, tongs, and stirring and mixing utensils. She has even rigged a makeshift Bunsen burner. I notice things she must have brought with her through the brane: thermometers, scales, Pyrex test tubes, clear plastic tubing, droppers, and even a calorimeter. The backpack she brought to Midnight Mesa was a big one, I recall.

Kenny hobbles from shelves to tables with the aid of a crutch. "The trick is going to be finding the sources that will produce the exact combination of gases I need," she explains. She spoons a foul-looking green substance from one container to another, and then mixes it with an equally vile-looking runny brown material. I don't even want to know what they are. I don't even want to *think* about what they are.

She is humming merrily and mumbling to herself as she works.

I take my leave. I think she has forgotten I'm even there, but as I turn to leave, she says, "Good-bye, Daughter of Gaia," with a teasing smile on her face.

"You too," I mutter.

* * * * *

I stop by Helen's sitting room and find her sitting with Tyler. Ty has become Helen's near-permanent companion. She finds him essential as a science adviser and a sounding board for her ideas. This is terrific. Tyler is self-effacing and endlessly patient. He'll make a great adviser.

Helen looks a little frazzled today, and no wonder. The Sanctuary is usually a place for quiet contemplation. But today, it's as if someone stirred an ant's nest with a stick.

"You look troubled, child," Helen observes.

"Why do the villagers and the Sisters call me the Daughter of Gaia," I ask, and feel tears forming.

"They call you the Daughter of Gaia because you *are* the Daughter of Gaia," explains Helen.

This is not what I want to hear. "But—" I begin to protest, but Helen cuts me off.

"I have foreseen your coming," she says quietly. "And even if you don't believe in my visions, look what you have done for our people. For the first time in their lives, they have *hope*. They have been poor, starving slaves, living lives of misery and desperation. Now they *believe* in something. Surely you don't want to take that from them."

"What I don't understand is how they expect *me* to end their suffering. I'm only a young girl, and I don't have any special talents. How can I possibly avoid disappointing them?"

"You underestimate yourself," Helen responds. "And as for how you will end the suffering, that's simple. Follow your heart, Daughter of Gaia. That's all you need to do."

Tyler says, "I've known how special ET is ever since I met her. Believe me, ET, you've got something inside you that makes you different from the rest of us."

I'm confused and still in doubt. Follow my heart? Follow it where? How will that help anything?

At last, I ask, "How do you foresee things, Helen?"

"First of all," she explains, "one must have the gift. And then one must clear the mind, meditate, and listen for messages from the Mother and the Father. This is not an easy thing to do. It takes years of practice and hard work. Only one of our Sisters has this gift, and I work with her every day, and every day she practices."

"But how do you *see* the future?" I ask.

"I don't have someone whispering words in my ear." Helen smiles. "But I *see* things. Sometimes I see things very clearly, but sometimes what I see is clouded, like trying to see something through the morning mist."

"Do your visions always come true?"

"Almost all of them come true. But the future is determined by the things people do in the present. If someone does the wrong thing today, the future vision may not come to pass. And sometimes the visions are mostly true, but wrong in some detail."

"Are your visions of my friends and me clear or blurry?"

"My visions of your friends are *very* clear. But the ones of you are the clearest of all."

"Helen," I ask, "you just said you listened to the voices of the Mother *and* the Father. Do you worship the Father as well?"

"Yes, of course we do," she answers. "The problems we face today exist because people stopped listening to the voice of the Mother. Therefore, if we expect to restore the world to its proper harmony, we must listen to both voices."

"Is there a sanctuary for the Father somewhere?" I ask.

"Yes, child. Near New Haven, there is a system of caves similar to ours. There, the Brothers maintain a sanctuary for the Father. I wish we could visit them."

We fall silent for a moment.

"You have the gift of visions too, Erin," Helen says. "One day, when our people are free, I would like to teach you how to use it."

I'm still baffled, overwhelmed, and more worried than ever. I try to frame a question, but don't know what to ask.

We're interrupted by Bree, who is standing in the entrance to Helen's chambers.

"Come in, come in," says Helen, smiling.

Bree takes a seat. "Helen," she asks, "is there is any other way to get into these caves from the outside, other than the entrance we already know about?"

"There is one other entrance," says Helen. "It is on the south side of the hill. The entrance is totally useless, because it opens out from a cliff face. It's a sheer drop down and a sheer climb up. There's no way to get into the caves that way."

Bree explains her curiosity. "If the blacksuits send a couple thousand soldiers our way, there's no way to fight them off forever, is there?"

Helen nods in agreement. "Sooner or later, they will overwhelm us with superior numbers."

"And if you lose this Sanctuary, there will be no place for the Sisters to go?" asks Bree.

"You're right," agrees Helen. "I'm not sure where we would go if we lost the Sanctuary. Perhaps we could send a few Sisters to nearby villages. If Kenny can perfect her dreadwolf's brew before the blacksuits drive us from here."

"Let's say we could use the back entrance to this place. Is there a way we can get from here to the other entrance? Inside the caves, without going outside?" asks Bree.

"As I said, we cannot use the back entrance, but yes, there is one very narrow passage that leads from the caverns on this side of the hill to the caverns on the other side."

"I think I can make that back entrance usable," says Bree. "I've spent my rest periods combing the forest for building materials. And I think I've found something we can use to make a rope ladder." Seeing Helen's puzzled face, she adds, "A rope ladder is a flexible ladder we can let down when we want to get up into the caves, and pull back up if uninvited guests come along."

"You can build such a thing?" Helen asks.

"I'm certain I can," assures Bree.

"What would you need to build such a ladder?" asks Helen.

Bree produces a vine. "I would needs lots and lots of these," she says, handing the vine to Helen.

The vine is brilliant green, glossy, and rough-edged. The cut ends are weeping sap. I've seen many of these vines growing in the forest.

Helen examines the vine. "But child, this vine cannot support the weight of one of us, let alone you giants."

"It can if we put several of them together like this." Bree cuts the vine in four separate pieces and begins twining them together.

"You are braiding them!" says Helen. "And you could build a ladder doing that?"

"Yes," Bree assures her. "I'm certain it could be done. I would need enough vines to run around the grand entrance cavern six times."

"That's a lot of vine," says Helen thoughtfully. "But there is an abundance of it in the forest. Our problem is we have no one left to harvest vines. All of the Sisters are working on other projects."

We sit in silence for a moment. The light from the sconces flickers, sending shadows dancing across the cave floor.

"I've sent a Sister to Phoenix to ask for villagers to help us," says Helen. "When they arrive, we can send them to harvest vines." Helen reflects for a moment and then asks, "If the courtsmen take these caverns from us, what will keep them from coming through the passageway that links this side to the other? They could attack us from behind."

"That's where Kenny comes in," says Bree.

Helen, Bree, Tyler, and I go together to visit Kenny in her lab. Our noses tell us when we are near. Kenny is sitting on a chair looking perplexed. Her clothes are stained with unpleasant substances. She hears us and glances up.

"How's it coming?" I ask.

"Pretty good, actually. I need to figure out how I can produce a phase change in the rotted vegetation so it'll release ammonia," she says absently.

"Would you be willing to take a break and walk with us?"

"Sure," she replies. "Sometimes when you're stuck, it helps to take a break. What do you have in mind?"

"Follow us," says Helen.

We each take a torch, because the connecting passage is far from the caves we use. Two acolytes smell us coming and quickly reverse direction. Walking next to Kenny requires discipline.

We travel through a series of winding passages. Sometimes we're going downhill, but much more frequently we're climbing. In about fifteen minutes, we arrive at the passage that leads to the far side. It's very narrow, less than three feet wide at its narrowest point and about four feet high. It's about twenty feet long, and we can just make out the place where it opens out into a broad cavern on the other side.

"Kenny," asks Bree "can you create an explosion that will permanently close off this passage?"

Kenny examines the passage. She crawls around on the floor examining rocks that have fallen from the walls. She looks carefully at the ceiling. "I can bring the whole thing down. Piece of cake," she replies.

"Oh dear," remarks Helen as a thought comes to her. "Before we close this off, we will have to move everything we own from our side of the hill to the other. That will not be a small chore!"

* * * * *

I spend the rest of the afternoon with Tyler, fletching arrows. If the blacksuits send a brigade our way, and we all know they will, we'll need thousands of arrows.

We hear the villagers from Phoenix arrive. Bertram is among them.

He greets me warmly. "Erin, my good friend, it's good to see you again."

I tell Bertram how sorry I am that so many of his villagers were killed in the battle with the dreadwolves.

"Do not trouble yourself with those concerns," he reassures. "We give our lives willingly in the struggle against the evils of the Court. Every one of those people volunteered for that journey, and they all knew it was likely they would die."

There are only about a dozen villagers with him.

"The courtsmen still have a full brigade stationed in Phoenix. They've evicted us from our beds, and they eat what little food we have. So it's very hard for large numbers of us to slip away. More villagers will be joining us soon. We'll slip away in small groups."

Helen and Bree explain what we need the villagers to do. "Get me the longest vines you can find," instructs Bree.

The villagers take flint knives and climb back down the hill.

* * * * *

As we are preparing for bed, Kenny walks into our chambers. We had smelled her long before we saw her.

"Ewwww," says Bree.

"What?" asks Kenny, looking around the room. "What?"

"Ewwww," we say in unison.

Kenny sighs and drags her mattress out of the room and down the hall toward her lab.

I'm troubled, and sleep eludes me. I feel as though I'm being crushed beneath the burden of expectations. When I finally drift away, my dreams are troubled by visions of villagers lying dead in the clearing where we fought the dreadwolves.

* * * * *

After breakfast, Helen assembles us in the main cavern.

"Today, the blacksuits will come," she says. "We must use our time well. Those of you who are gathering vines, keep well to the south of the Sanctuary. If we hold the blacksuits off, they will be leaving early, because they have a quarterday's journey back to the safety of the walls of Phoenix. Wait until they are gone and then rejoin us."

She gives out detailed instructions to each group. When she is done, my friends and I gather with three acolytes who are skilled with the bow. Because our arrows travel farther and with greater velocity than the natives', we "giants" will form the bulk of our defensive force. Kenny, of course, is not with us. She is working feverishly in her lab.

We exit the cave, blink in the bright sunlight as our eyes adjust, and examine the defensive positions we built yesterday. We have built ten of them spread in a rough line, with five to the left of the cave opening and five to the right.

We agree that Chase and Ty will man the two positions closest to the cave's entrance. If the blacksuits threaten to overwhelm us, we'll need to retreat quickly into the caves. Tyler and Chase will be slowed by their injuries, so they'll be closest to the entrance. I'll hold down our right flank, and Bree will hold down the left. Chase and Jules will be armed with their rifles. The rest of us will use bows.

I scramble over to my position and examine the terrain around me. The tree line is about a hundred yards from the foot of the hill, and there is little cover for attackers after they leave the trees. The south side of the hill, behind us, is too steep for the blacksuits to climb, but there are places on the east side where they may try to climb and outflank us. I satisfy myself that I'll have a clear field of fire if they attempt this strategy. While I'm not as skilled with the bow as Bree, I've become good. I can hit targets with accuracy up to a distance of about fifty yards. And I can get off six arrows with accuracy in a minute. The air is totally still, as usual. I won't need to make adjustments for wind.

We reenter the caves and go to work twisting vines into rope. There's no conversation. I'm feeling butterflies in my stomach, and it's hard to keep my hands from shaking. A thought turns my blood cold: I could well be dead by nightfall.

We hear the sound of the acolytes' horns coming from the forest to the north. The blacksuits have arrived

D.S. Northrop

12

We race to the cave entrance. From there we can see the leading elements of the blacksuit brigade arrive at the edge of the forest. Within an hour, there are a thousand blacksuits gathered before us. I look through Grizz's binoculars and can clearly make out Jared Cain and Zoe Kerber standing out like two giraffes surrounded by a thousand chimps. They've sold us out. We move to our defensive positions and wait for the blacksuits' next move.

Jared and a group of blacksuits, officers I assume, move a few yards into the clearing and examine the hillside. Jared is pointing to the place where our cave opens. The blacksuits would never have been able to spot it from the ground without his help.

Our positions are forty feet up the side of the hill at roughly the same height as the cave opening. Chase aims his .22 at Jared. He squeezes off one round. At this range, he'd need luck to hit him, but his shot has the effect of making Jared and the blacksuits scamper back to the safety of the tree line. And, in this pre-gunpowder society, the crack of the .22 undoubtedly instills a certain amount of fear in our opponents.

I wait nervously. Ten of us against a thousand of them seem like bad odds, but we have the advantage of strong defensive positions and modern firearms. In addition, the rocky hillside below us provides only a dozen paths up to the caves, and each of the paths has choke points where only one or two blacksuits can pass through simultaneously.

The blacksuits finally begin their attack. Fifty of them emerge from the tree line and walk slowly toward the hill. Their black uniforms stand out against the gray rock of the forest floor. They don't know the effective range of our weapons, so at seventy-five yards, they break into a trot. At fifty yards, Chase and Jules cut down two blacksuits with their .22s, and the rest begin to run forward.

At a range of fifty yards, I loose my first arrow. I hit my target in the leg, and he falls. I bring down another one just as the blacksuit line reaches the base of the hill. At this point, the advantage of our positions really begins to tell. The blacksuits face a forty-foot climb, the equivalent of a four-story building, up a very steep slope. I select my targets carefully. I miss my first shot, but hit the next two. A few blacksuits string arrows and take shots at our positions, but a forty-foot shot uphill against opponents behind cover is pointless. There are rock outcroppings, which provide shelter for the blacksuits. But after another few minutes, they break off and retreat back toward the trees. Of the fifty who began the charge, fewer than half return to the tree line.

The blacksuits have probed our defenses, and now they know where our firing positions are and the range of our weapons. For a half hour, nothing seems to happen. Then, out of the corner of my eye, I see movement to my right along the tree line. The blacksuits have decided to try to outflank us rather than mount a mass charge. Our success in turning back their first probe has caused them to consider their options.

Approximately two dozen blacksuits leave the cover of the forest and charge the hill from the east. They are trying to go around us, with the objective of climbing above us and firing down into our positions from above. If we allow them to accomplish this, our position will be untenable. We'll be like ducks in a shooting gallery. My arrows strike three blacksuits in rapid succession before they can reach the foot of the hill.

Jules, who has the position next to mine, sees what the enemy is doing. She clambers into my blind and starts picking off blacksuits with her rifle. I begin to think we have a handle on the problem, when a blacksuit emerges from behind a rocky ledge less than five feet below me. I have no idea how he got there. I have an arrow ready, and I can't miss at that range. But as soon as he falls, there is another blacksuit in his place. We eye each other for the merest split second. The first person to retrieve an arrow and shoot will live. The other will die. I beat him, and say a prayer for the many days of practice I have had.

Jules and I have inflicted severe punishment on the flanking party. We see them break and retreat back down the hill and into the trees. Once again, less than half of the group that started out returns.

For a long time, nothing seems to happen. We can hear the moans of wounded blacksuits coming from below. After what seems like an eternity, we hear enemy officers hidden behind the trees begin to bark out orders. The blacksuits assemble themselves into a series of skirmish lines. An officer gives out a final command, and well over nine hundred blacksuits begin to cross the clearing, heading directly toward us.

* * * * *

Chase and Jules open fire when the range is seventy yards. I shoot arrows when they reach fifty yards. I bring down two before they reach the hill. They are not tentative this time. They are coming after us at full speed. The next few minutes dissolve into a blur. I shoot, grab an arrow, and shoot again. I don't have any idea how many blacksuits I have hit. Their first line has reached a height of about twenty feet. I can accurately shoot six arrows in a minute, and that's what I do. There's no lack of targets.

Then, with the sound of a horn, the blacksuits break off their attack and retreat. There is carnage below our positions. Dozens and dozens of dead and wounded blacksuits lie on the hill beneath us. Some appear to be peacefully sleeping. Others are splayed out in awkward, unnatural positions. The cries of the wounded are the only sounds in the still afternoon air. There is also the coppery smell of freshly spilled blood.

I feel emotionally numb. I take no joy in our success at holding our ground, and I feel no remorse for the lives I have taken. I'm overwhelmingly tired. I'd like to rest my head, but know I mustn't. I look along our line and see my friends. They look as exhausted as I feel. Although we are on the north side of the hill, the late-afternoon sun peeks over the crest of the hill. It's brutal. I take a sip of water from my canteen and wait for the blacksuits' next move.

They begin another charge, and there seem to be fewer of them this time. They have been clever, however. After the last charge, many blacksuits took cover beneath rock outcroppings below us. They never retreated back to the forest. We discover the point of this maneuver as the black line charges across the plain. The blacksuits lean out from their cover below and pepper our positions with arrows. They want us to keep our heads down.

But we can't. There are too many of them. If we don't keep up a steady rate of fire, they will swarm over our positions. I hear a sickening wet sound to my left. I look and see Jules lying on her back with an arrow protruding from her left eye.

I fight down the urge to wretch. I have no time to feel anything now. I'll feel later. Nevertheless, I miss my next two shots. I'm vaguely aware of Charity, who has now moved to Jules's blind. There's no sense in letting that .22 go to waste.

I gather myself and pour a steady stream of arrows into the advancing blacksuits. I hear an arrow whir as it passes my ear. Another one bounces off the rock in front of me, rebounding to take a divot out of my left cheek. I feel the warmth of blood trickling down my face. I ignore it. I have become emotionally detached, nothing more than an unthinking, unfeeling arrow-shooting machine. I have no concept of time passing.

And then the blacksuits are in among us. I drop my bow, slip on my shield, and draw my sword. I cut down two blacksuits who appear directly in front of me. Another charges in from my right, and I use my longer reach to run him through before he can strike.

To my left, Charity falls. A blacksuit arrow has punctured her neck. She makes a mewling noise, and her fingers scrabble at the rocks as her life's blood pumps in spurts from her ruined neck. There are no more blacksuits in my immediate vicinity, so I scramble to my left, carefully stepping over both Jules's and Charity's bodies. My foot slips on loose pebbles, and I do the splits, barely able to recover my balance before I pitch over and roll backward down the hill. An arrow grazes my right wrist. I regain my footing and continue moving to my left toward Grizz's position. He is under severe pressure with blacksuits in front of him and also to his right. I catch the two on his right from behind and dispatch them before they know I am there. A little voice inside me tells me it's not sporting to stab a man in the back. I tell the little voice to go away, that rule doesn't apply to this situation.

We have a moment to look down our line. Two of the Sisters have been overrun and are down. Chase is wielding his sword, evidently not feeling the pain of his leg in the urgency of the moment. The blacksuits have not overrun Bree's position yet. She is still firing arrows down the hill. Tyler has a sword in one hand and a spear in the other. Bad knee notwithstanding, he buries the spear in one blacksuit's chest and hacks at another with his sword.

Four more blacksuits appear in front of Grizz and me, and there are half a dozen more behind them. I see more approaching from my right. We cut down the first to reach us, but I realize, with crystal clarity, this is the end. Dozens of blacksuits close in on us, and there are more behind them. There are too many of them.

* * * * *

I'm distantly aware of a horn blowing far down below us, and suddenly, a miracle occurs. The black suits turn around and retreat down the hill.

"It's too late in the day," Grizz exults. "They have to pull out and head back to Phoenix or risk being caught in the forest after dark!"

"But they had us beaten," I say thickly.

"Maybe," says Grizz, "but you know we could have retreated into the cave, and with the help of the villagers, we could've kept them from coming through that narrow cave entrance for a long time. A few of us could hold an army there, at least for a while. The blacksuits couldn't risk being held up long enough to be caught in the open after dark."

The villagers and acolytes emerge from the cave and stare in wonder at the scene below. The hillside is littered with black uniformed bodies. The villagers and Sisters break into a cheer, jumping up and down and slapping each other on the back. A few are bawling tears of joy. It takes them a moment to realize that our side has suffered casualties as well.

Chase finally realizes what has happened to Charity. He cries out in agony, rushes to her, and cradles her body in his arms. Grizz and I leave him with his grief and carry Jules's body into the cave. There is no joy or celebration for us. Ty limps down the passage toward Kenny's lab to break the news to her.

One of the Sisters catches me and says, "You are wounded, Daughter of Gaia." She attends to my cheek and my wrist. I don't feel a thing.

I walk dejectedly toward our quarters. I sit on my mattress, and for a while I feel nothing but numbness. When the tears come, they flow and flow. These are not "I lost my boyfriend, boo hoo" tears. These are hot tears, angry tears. Grizz, my usual source of solace, is sitting on his own mattress crying bitter tears as well. Kenny enters the room, and despite her pungent smell, we can't deny her the comfort of grieving with friends.

Helen visits our chambers, realizes there is nothing she can do or say, and leaves.

I see many pictures of Jules in my mind: Jules laughing at some silly joke Tyler has told. Jules with her plans to go to college and do DNA research. Jules thrilled and excited after being named stage manager for the school play. Jules working my shift at Safeway when I was down with the flu. And Jules lying on the ground with an arrow through her eye. Jules, who will not be the first member of her family to graduate from high school. I find some small comfort in knowing she died instantly with no time for fear or pain. I grieve for Charity and Chase as well. Charity, who was just becoming a friend.

Chase stumbles into our room. His tunic is soaked with Charity's blood. He collapses in agony.

I fall into a deep and dreamless sleep. The Sisters try to wake me for dinner, but I wave them away. I wake hours later. It must be late, because there's no sound. The rest of the world is asleep. I know I'll not find sleep again, so I rouse myself and go outside for a breath of fresh air.

I find Grizz sitting on a large rock just over the entrance to the caves. I climb up and join him. Neither of us speaks. What could we say? After a few minutes, he puts his arm around me. My tears begin to fall again. I hear Grizz sobbing as well. Insects in the forest below fill the world with shrill songs.

Dawn finds us still sitting together on the rock.

"This whole thing just got personal," I whisper.

Grizz agrees. "Very personal."

* * * * *

The blacksuits return in the late morning. My friends and I move slowly to our defensive positions. Two villagers occupy the positions that Jules and Charity held yesterday. Tyler has inherited Jules's rifle. Our blinds are on the north side of the hill, so we are spared the worst of the blistering sun for most of the day.

The blacksuits send a hundred men onto the field waving white flags. Why? I wonder. The answer soon comes: they are removing the bodies of their fallen comrades. And no wonder, I think. This is a society that equates the smell of decomposing flesh with plague. They will want to bury their fallen comrades right away.

We help them out by rolling the bodies near our positions downhill. Actually, I'm not really helping them. I just don't trust them enough to let them anywhere near our lines. We watch them work for the next two hours.

I expect them to attack again. As badly as we mauled them yesterday, they still outnumber us forty or fifty to one. And we are down to our last twenty rounds of .22 ammunition. But the blacksuits simply mill around, looking dispirited and disorganized. At five o'clock, they turn around and head back to Phoenix. Their objective today was simply to keep an eye on us and ensure we didn't go anywhere.

* * * * *

Dinner tonight is a quiet affair. Beneath our grief, I sense something quite different growing: anger and a determination to avenge the deaths of our friends. Helen sits at the head of the table and respects our silence.

Two things happen in close succession, shattering our meditation. First, Kenny comes in (an event that destroys whatever small appetite I had) and announces she has the scent she's been looking for. We rise in unison and follow her to her lab to analyze her invention. I question whether her sense of smell is discriminating enough to distinguish one scent from another after her prolonged exposure to powerful odors.

We have no sooner risen than a messenger from Phoenix arrives, looking for Helen. He is out of breath, but in between gasps for air, he manages to deliver his message. "Three brigades of blacksuits arrived in Phoenix today."

* * * * *

This is dreadful news. We were lucky yesterday to hold off an attack by one brigade. Three brigades will brush us aside like flies at a picnic.

There is no time for any more wallowing in sorrow. We have to finish Bree's rope ladder, we have to move the Sisters' belongings to the other side of the cave, and we have to close the passage connecting the caves on the southern side of the hill from those on the northern side.

Tyler and I check out Kenny's new scent, and agree that it does, indeed, smell like the moldering flesh of the animals in the clearing the night we fought the dreadwolves. Helen joins us, sniffs carefully, makes a face, and agrees. She orders two acolytes to prepare a nice warm bath for Kenny. This is an extravagant use of water, but one that's been well earned.

The Sisters and villagers have spent the past two days working on the rope ladder, and others have already moved many of the Sisters' belongings to the other side of the hill. Still, I'm disheartened when I realize how much is left to do. Food stocks, furniture, cooking utensils, clothing, torches, sconces, mattresses, Kenny's lab, and hundreds of pots full of various and assorted things are still on this side of the hill. And the rope ladder is only half as long as it needs to be. Nobody will sleep tonight.

In a way, I'm grateful for the work because it keeps my mind occupied. There's no time to dwell on my grief.

* * * *

We are done moving the Sisters' possessions by sunrise. Kenny places her charges in the tunnel, but hands me the matches. "I can't move fast enough on this ankle," she explains.

I light the fuses and run like crazy. The explosives go off with a satisfying *crump*, and the ceiling falls in. The blacksuits will need years to clear out that passage, should they try, but they won't because they don't know what lies behind it. From their perspective, we will have vanished into thin air.

After breakfast, I join in the work on the rope ladder. We'll finish it today. Bree tests every knot after it has been tied. Helen sent scouts into the forest, and two more lie under cover on top of the hill. While we're working on the ladder, they bring us news that the three blacksuit brigades have arrived. They storm our old positions and, finding them abandoned, swarm into the caves. I can only think, with merriment, how frustrated they must be to find us gone.

Sentries bring news of their trackers scouring the forest around the hill to find the trail we must have left when we abandoned the Sanctuary. *Good luck with that*, I think smugly.

The blacksuits don't return to Phoenix today. All three brigades are spending the night in our old caves. This is bad news. When they were based in Phoenix, we had three hours of daylight in the morning and three hours of daylight in the evening when we could move freely outside. With three thousand blacksuits for next-door neighbors, we'll be sealed up in the caves all day, every day.

"We can't let them stay here," says Helen. "But I don't know how to get rid of them."

"I do," I say.

13

"Do you have enough material to make another bomb?" I ask Kenny. "I want to close the entrance to the caves on the south side of the hill so the blacksuits can't use them."

"I probably have enough," she replies. "I'll need to take a look at the rocks around the cave entrance to be absolutely sure."

"The rope ladder is done," says Bree, "but there's no way we can go outside with blacksuits crawling all over the place."

"We'll go after dark," I say. "We'll see if Kenny's stinkum works."

With a few hours before nightfall, I try to take a nap. But despite my lack of sleep last night, I'm too keyed up. I give up trying and pay a visit to Helen.

"Won't this be dangerous?" she asks. "You know the courtsmen will have posted guards at the entrance."

"It could be difficult, but you're the one who told me to follow my heart. And right now, my heart says this is the right thing to do."

"Be careful when you listen to your heart, Erin. Be certain that it is your heart that speaks and not something else."

I consider this advice. Part of me wants to do something—anything, really—to avenge the deaths of Jules and Charity. I'm pretty sure this plan to keep the blacksuits from using the caves is a good idea even without a revenge motive. The retribution we extract is just a positive by-product.

Our plan is to slip Bree, Kenny, Grizz, and I down the ladder after dark. No rifles on this mission, we'll need to kill silently.

We wait until four hours after dark to descend the ladder. We want to give the blacksuits plenty of time to get to sleep. We each have a lidded jar of Kenny's wolf bane. We pull off the tops and are immediately assaulted by the smell of death and corruption. I fight down an automatic gag response. I see my friends doing the same.

We deploy the ladder. With my flashlight, I see it has not been caught on any snags and it reaches all the way to the ground.

Bree asks who wants to be the first one to test her ladder. "The vines are plenty strong, but there may be some problems where the steps are joined to the sides," she warns.

Grizz immediately volunteers, but I'm standing nearest the ladder, so I go first.

As I descend the ladder, a step gives way, and I find myself hanging on with only my hands. The ground below the cave entrance is a good sixty feet down, so a fall will be fatal. I calm my breathing and probe with my foot until I locate a sturdy step.

"Be careful," I whisper to the three waiting above. "There's a step missing." I reach the bottom without further incident. I worry about Grizz and Kenny because they weigh more than I do. Two of us are already dead, and that's more than enough. Fortunately, there are no further problems.

Within ten minutes, we are all on the ground. The moon is waning, but it casts enough light for us to see what we need to see. The plan is to head for the tree line on the south side of the hill. Since Kenny is still limping, we plan to deposit her on the southeast side of the hill while we move around through the trees to the north side. From there we can see where the blacksuits have posted their sentries.

By the time we're halfway to the tree line, we hear the first chorus of howls from the dreadwolves. As we reach the trees, we see dozens of glowing yellow eyes, but the wolves don't attack. Kenny's stinkum is working.

Grizz, Bree, and I work our way through the trees until we're standing due north of the hill. Using the binoculars, I count six sentries. Ironically, they're sheltered in the defensive positions we built. I hand the binoculars to Grizz so he can take a look as well. Then it's Bree's turn.

"I make out six defenders," I say. Bree and Grizz agree. The blacksuits have not posted anyone above the cave's entrance, and this is a stroke of good luck. They have three sentries on each side of the cave's mouth. "We'll climb until we're above them and can shoot down into their positions," I continue in a whisper.

"I'll take out the two on the east side, nearest the cave mouth. Bree, you can have the three on the west side. Grizz, when you hear things start, you'll be in a position to take out the sentry farthest east. I only saw two sentries with horns. We target them first. We need to make sure each shot is a kill shot, because we don't want to give them a chance to sound an alarm."

We work our way back around to the southeast side of the hill, where we left Kenny.

"Boy, am I glad you're back," whispers Kenny. "These wolves just keep howling, and they're creeping me out."

Standing alone surrounded by howling dreadwolves would give anybody the jitters, I reflect.

I recall the way the two blacksuits came out practically on top of me during the fight two days ago when they were trying to outflank us. This tells me there's a way to get near the defensive positions without being seen. I examine the east side of the hill with the binoculars. It's hard to tell with parts of the hill hidden by moon shadows, but I think I see the way.

"Kenny, stay here," I whisper. "It makes no sense for you to be up there if things go south on us. I'll signal you with the flashlight when it's safe to come."

"Alone with the wolves again. Great," says Kenny.

We cover the distance from the tree line to the foot of the hill in seconds. There's no danger of us being spotted because the defensive positions all face north, and we're coming from the southeast.

We climb slowly. We watch our foot placement very carefully. The sound of a loose rock falling downhill could be fatal. We reach the place where the blacksuits surprised me. I peer cautiously above the rocks at the sentries' positions. In another stroke of luck, they haven't posted anyone in the defensive position farthest to the east. Unless one of the other sentries looks directly to the east, we can get up above them without being seen.

I motion for Bree to follow and for Grizz to stay put. Once the arrows start to fly, Grizz can stand up in his position and deal with the last sentry.

Bree and I continue to climb. I dislodge a stone and listen, holding my breath, as it falls downhill. The blacksuit nearest me turns around and looks up. I will myself to become part of the hillside, invisible. The sentry walks a few steps and peers around. I'm afraid to breathe. He takes one last look and decides an animal must have dislodged the stone.

I continue on more carefully. I reach a position from which I can see all three sentries on my side. As I wait for Bree to reach her post, I overhear the guards talking.

"Something has the dreadwolves riled up tonight," says one.

"I hope they're feasting on giants," adds another.

"Strange how the giants disappeared without leaving any trail," says the first.

"Scary. Say, do you smell something funny?"

They sniff the air inquisitively. They've caught the scent of our stinkum.

Bree has reached her position. I point to my eyes with my middle and forefingers. I can see my targets. In a moment, Bree returns the sign. Watching her, I silently draw an arrow and notch it. I aim at the guard with the horn. Having done the same, Bree looks back at me. I nod one time.

I let my first arrow fly. In disbelief, I see I've missed.

* * * * *

The arrow strikes the rocks right next to the sentry. But instead of blowing his horn, the guard turns around to see where the arrow came from. That's the only break I need. Within a matter of seconds, all three sentries are dead. Bree scrambles down from her perch. For her it was three arrows, three down, of course. I turn around and aim the flashlight toward Kenny's position at the tree line. I turn it on and off three times in quick succession. There's nothing to do now but keep a notched arrow aimed at the cave mouth and pray none of the blacksuits decide to come out for a breath of fresh air.

God made Kenny big, and he made her beautiful. But he did not make her quiet. We hear her coming from the minute she starts to climb the hill. She joins us a moment later.

"Let's take a look at how these rocks are sitting," she whispers.

She examines the rocks immediately below the cave mouth, and then she climbs up over the cave entrance and scrambles around, releasing small landslides of pebbles and small rocks. A rock the size of a volleyball rockets past me. I can only hope the contours of the winding, narrow cave entrance dampen sound.

Accompanied by a shower of pebbles, Kenny scrambles down and rejoins us.

"I just wish I had a rock drill so I could place those charges exactly where I want them," whispers Kenny.

Grizz pats the pockets of his tunic with his palms. "Gee, I didn't bring my rock drill with me," he whispers.

"And I left my long extension cord back in the other universe," hisses Bree.

"Aren't we sarcastic tonight?" says Kenny.

"Can you seal this?" I ask.

"I can bring the whole side of the mountain down on these guys," she says. "They'll never dig their way out." She looks at me expectantly.

I hesitate at the thought of burying three thousand people alive. But then I think of the way the blacksuits tortured Tyler, and how they cruelly killed those nine villagers. I think about how they turn the villagers into slaves, and how they wrench children from their families. I see Jules lying dead with an arrow in her eye, and Charity with her neck pumping blood all over her face.

"Do it," I say.

Kenny quickly assembles four bombs, and then stops. She looks for a moment at her fusing and does some quick mental calculations. She inserts the fuses into the bomb material and climbs back up. I follow her, because I know she's still a little slow with her sprained ankle, and she'll need me to light the fuses. She plants one bomb on either side of the entrance, stuffing them into crevices. She plants the other two bombs beneath rock formations above the cave entrance. She braids the four fuses together and hands me her matchbox.

"The fuses are plenty long, but the minute you light the fuse, run like the devil."

I listen as Kenny scrambles back down and joins the others. They disappear down the side of the hill.

I light all four fuses and follow my friends as fast as I possibly can, being especially careful not to slip. Thirty seconds later, I hear a series of four *crump* sounds in rapid sequence, then a very loud sound made by falling rocks. The rockslide sends up a huge cloud of dust, and for a minute, I can't see anything. Kenny, Grizz, and Bree appear at my side.

"Let's take a look at my handiwork," says Kenny cheerfully, not bothering to whisper.

When the dust settles, we see no sign that a cave entrance was ever there.

"Let's get out of here," I say.

14

We climb the ladder just as the eastern sky begins to brighten. Helen, Ty, Chase, and a crowd of anxious Sisters and villagers greet us.

"Everything went according to plan," I explain. "Those blacksuits won't cause any more trouble."

Everybody cheers. Everyone slaps us on the back. Many Sisters embrace me and say, "Thank you, Daughter of Gaia." I'm tired of the Daughter of Gaia stuff, but I hold my tongue.

I'm exhausted. I haven't slept much the last two nights. Still, I'm troubled by the fact that I've just killed three thousand human beings in cold blood. What makes me any different from them? Am I becoming as bad as the blacksuits? I finally fall into a fatigued sleep, but have a nightmare. I'm buried alive, and I can't claw my way out. I awaken with a scream.

I'm startled to find Helen sitting in the chair beside my bed.

She strokes my forehead gently. "The thing that makes us different from the courtsmen is we feel bad when we do terrible things, and they don't," she says.

I wonder if she has read my thoughts.

She smiles down at me. "Now rest, child. And don't trouble yourself with guilt. You did what you had to do. Nothing more, nothing less. That's exactly what we expect of our Daughter of Gaia."

I fall asleep, and for once, I'm untroubled by dreams.

* * * * *

I awaken in the afternoon, yawn, stretch, and go looking for my friends.

The whole cave is busy preparing for our expedition to the workshop.

"After everything I went through to make this stuff, I think it should have a more dignified name than 'stinkum,'" says Kenny.

"Wolf-B-Gone?" suggests Tyler.

"How about wolf bane?" proposes Chase. "That's what they call the stuff that's supposed to keep werewolves away."

"Sounds fitting to me," says Kenny.

Kenny has made several jars of wolf bane. "I've refined the way I make wolf bane," she says. "Wolves have a very keen sense of smell, so *you* won't be overwhelmed by the smell when you use it."

I examine the wolf bane. It looks a lot like the fish flakes I used to feed my guppy. I sniff. It's almost odorless.

"To use it, add about a tablespoon of water to a quarter cup of the stuff in the jar. If you're camping, spread it on a plate so it'll have maximum exposure to the air," she instructs. "But if you want to move around, you'll have to smear it on your arms."

"That sounds gross," says Bree, wrinkling her nose.

"So does being eaten by dreadwolves," says Kenny. "Being alive is a good thing, no? Besides, like I told you, I've gotten this stuff to the point where it doesn't have much smell."

"How long does it take before it loses its effectiveness?" I ask.

"It'll be good for at least eight hours," replies Kenny, "but you shouldn't trust it any longer than that."

I look at the size of the jar. "One jar has enough wolf bane to last a month, even if you use it every day," I observe.

* * * * *

In the afternoon, we bury Jules and Charity. We carry them far to the south of the Sanctuary, because we don't want their graves found by blacksuits. We cry for our lost friends, but Chase is hit the hardest. I'm depressed because I was the one who brought everyone into this world. We sit for more than an hour after the burial without speaking.

Finally, Chase rises. "We'll make them pay," he says harshly.

We make our way back to the Sanctuary, eyes full of tears and hearts heavy with grief.

* * * * *

A small party of Sisters carrying wolf bane heads off toward Detroit to retrieve Falstaff and Sister Juliet. I ask them to pick up Orsino as well. In our battle with the Court, it'll certainly help to have someone who knows New Washington inside out.

Bree is feverishly working on a set of drawings for an elevator to lift heavy things from the forest floor to the cave. The ladder is fine for getting people up and down, but it's impossible to carry anything in your hands while you're climbing. I look over Bree's shoulder and see a diagram with an assortment of pulleys and a cage made of poles and vines.

Bree is explaining her diagram to Chase and Tyler. Chase's calf won't heal quickly enough for him to join our expedition to the workshop. The elevator project will keep him occupied, and that will be a good thing. Chase's face is white and haggard. There are huge black smudges beneath his eyes, and his eyes are swollen and red. He's taking Charity's death very hard. I imagine his guilt over Charity's demise must be similar to my own toward Tyler. Probably even worse, since Tyler is still alive and Charity isn't.

Discussing the lift, Bree advises, "The Sisters' tools are surprisingly good. The hardest part will be rounding out and grooving the pulleys."

"We'll manage," says Chase.

I hear an unusual sound coming from the cave entrance. As I approach the mouth of the cave, I recognize the noise. I haven't heard it in a while, but it's utterly familiar. Thunder coupled with heavy rain. The monsoon has arrived. Rain comes down in sheets. Lightning forks cross the sky. Within a matter of moments, the storm is over, and the sun reappears.

"That's how the monsoon is," says Helen, who has silently materialized by my side. "The rain never lasts long, but even so, it blesses us generously with the gift of water."

When I return to our chambers, I find Kenny with her belongings spread out on her mattress. "I'm trying to decide what to take with me to the workshop," she explains.

I insist on checking her ankle. I want to be sure she's up for the journey.

"All right, Nurse Ratched," she says. She sits obediently on the mattress and bares her ankle. I'm happy to see that her bruises, which were purple and red, have progressed to yellow and green. She's healing fast.

I join Kenny in packing. In a few minutes, Bree and Grizz join us and begin packing as well.

"So how long do you think it'll take to get there?" asks Bree.

"Orsino said it took them about a week. But we'll move a lot faster than he could. I'd guess about three or four days," I answer.

"I hope it's not too cold when we reach the saddle between the two peaks," says Kenny. "You may not have noticed, but I didn't bring my winter wardrobe with me." She pauses for a moment. "On the other hand, it'll be really great to get out of the heat for a while."

"What do you think we'll find when we get there?" asks Grizz.

"I don't know," I reply. "Orsino said there's a door built into the side of a hill. The lock is a set of dials, and you have to enter some kind of code to get it open."

"And you think we can break the code?" asks Kenny.

"I don't know," I admit. "Helen seems to think we can."

I run through my mental list of things to pack.

First aid kit. Check.

Clean change of clothes. (Clothes never get truly clean in this place of limited water and no laundry detergent.) Check, anyway.

Three-week supply of dried potatoes. (Yum!) Check.

One-week supply of water. (We'll be able to make water by melting snow once we reach the saddle between the mountains.) Check.

Toothbrush. (The natives use a plant with a bristly stem. No toothpaste, though.) Check.

Pot full of wolf bane. Check.

Bow, quiver, and arrows. Check.

Sword. (Bowie knife, technically.) Check.

Flint knife. Check.

Compass and pedometer. Check.

Flashlight. (I hope the batteries were fairly new when I packed it back in Tucson.) Check.

Matches. Check.

Boy Scout knife. Check.

Pen and paper. (Don't know why, exactly, but it seems like a good idea.) Check.

I have everything I need for our voyage.

* * * * *

On our last night with the Sisters, we go over our plans at dinner. Grizz, Bree, Kenny, and I will leave at first light. We'll find the workshop, figure out how to get it open, and see what's inside. Once we know what the workshop contributes to our fight with the Court, we'll return to Phoenix and plan our next move.

Everybody left behind will stay holed up in the cave for a few days. If the blacksuits see four sets of giant footprints heading away from the cave area, and no other prints at all, they may figure we've gone, and maybe they'll leave us alone. One way or another, we know that over the next few days, they'll go over this hill and the surrounding forest with a fine-tooth comb. They'll definitely be in an ugly mood when they discover we've eliminated three full brigades of their brothers. But, since the new cave opening is sixty feet up a sheer cliff, the blacksuits are not likely to pay it much attention.

Messengers from the brane have been reporting in every day despite all the drama we've had. The brane hasn't so much as flickered, and the blacksuits are still watching it closely. I've given up hope at this point. I'm adjusting to the idea that this world is now my home.

Once the blacksuits give up and go, Tyler and Chase will build the lift with help from the Sisters.

Helen kisses all of us good night and wishes us luck on our journey. We turn in early.

* * * * *

We rise before the sun and eat a quick breakfast. Helen stops in and brings us a huge tarpaulin made from animal hide.

"You'll need this now that the monsoon season is here. Storms blow up fast, and if you're not under cover, you'll be drenched all the way down into your bones," she explains.

Knowing how scarce game is around here, the tarp must be ancient and highly valued. Grizz carefully rolls it up and lashes it to the top of his backpack.

"Heavy," he observes.

Grizz will take Jules's .22 and the last few rounds of ammunition. Kenny is taking the raw materials and lab equipment to make more wolf bane. Even though we think a jar of the stuff should last a month, we'll play it safe.

We finish breakfast, descend the rope ladder, and head toward the twin mountains. We're going to swing around to the south to avoid blacksuit patrols.

We find a walking pace that suits us all. Grizz has been my running buddy ever since I took up track, but Bree and Kenny don't exercise much. I tried to talk Kenny into running with us at one point. Her answer was that she couldn't see any benefit in learning to run fast because she *wanted* the boys to catch her.

I'm happy that my relationship with Grizz hasn't been harmed by his confession. I feel a little more uncomfortable than I used to, mostly because I see him in a new way. I'm more aware of his beautiful blue eyes, and his dimples when he smiles. I like to watch the way his muscles shift beneath his tunic, and the easy, athletic way he walks. When the warm feeling starts to grow deep inside me, I ruthlessly choke it off. My friends and I have enough problems, without adding romantic intrigue to the mix.

Still, Grizz and I walk side by side and banter back and forth the way we always have.

"I like you with that scar on your check," he says, referring to the wound I got fighting the blacksuits. "It makes you look sort of edgy, dangerous."

"Maybe I can get the little people to stop calling me Daughter of Gaia," I suggest. "How does Scarface sound to you?"

"You may be on to something there," he answers. "If I were a blacksuit, I'd be more worried about somebody called Scarface than somebody called Daughter of Gaia."

"When are we going to stop for lunch?" asks Bree.

"Right now suits me," I reply.

We don't bother to set a fire. We eat our dried potatoes cold. Cooking doesn't improve the flavor much anyway.

Late in the afternoon, storm clouds build behind us. Big purple clouds the color of new bruises roll in and tower high above us. When the wind begins to pick up, we unroll the tarpaulin Helen gave us and stretch it out over our heads. Very quickly, we discover this isn't the way to protect ourselves from a storm. The wind blows the rain parallel to the ground, right underneath the tarp. We're totally soaked within seconds. The sound of thunder is deafening, as is the drumming of water on our tarp.

The storm lasts only fifteen minutes, and, after it goes, we continue our walk. We find that, while the storm lowers the temperature for a little while, the hot air comes back with a vengeance. Only now it's worse because the humidity is higher. Our drenched clothes seem to take forever to dry. After an hour or so, we tell Grizz to turn his back while we shuck our clothes and wring them out. We repeat the favor for him.

"Won't need a bath tonight," observes Kenny.

We make forty miles the first day. At this pace, we should reach the foothills tomorrow. When we stop for the evening, it takes a long time to get a fire started because the wood is wet. We finally manage to get a small fire going, but it gives off more steam than heat. However, it's warm enough to heat our potatoes.

As I wait for sleep to come, with my backpack scrunched up for a pillow, Bree whispers, "If the brane opens up again, would you go back home?"

It takes me a second to answer. "Yes. No. I don't know. How about you?"

"I feel the same way," she says. "I miss my home, but we're doing something *good* here. We could never do anything this important back home."

Kenny and Grizz are sleeping already, but I'm willing to bet they feel the same way.

As I wait for sleep to come, I realize Kenny was right. The smell of wolf bane is barely perceptible. But it works. I fall asleep surrounded by glowing yellow eyes.

15

After lunch on the next day, we hear a troubling sound behind us. It takes me a second, but I place it: bots. "There are bots behind us," I say urgently.

I strain my eyes as the sound grows louder. Then, through the trees, I see a glint of silver: flashing blades.

"Run!" shouts Grizz.

We break into a trot.

The problem is, bots never get tired. After an hour of jogging, Kenny looks exhausted, and Bree is clearly ready to collapse. I no sooner think the thought than she doubles over and goes down on her knees, gasping.

"Stitch!" She wheezes.

Anybody who has ever had a stitch knows they are excruciatingly painful, and they last a long time.

"Leave"—*gasp*—"me," she says.

"We can't do that," I demur.

The sound of the bots grows louder.

I see them clearly, about two hundred yards behind us. They'll reach us in minutes.

Grizz aims the .22 and fires four shots at the leading bot. We see sparks where the bullets strike the churning blades, but it doesn't even slow the bot down.

Grizz talks quickly. "We can't lose Bree, 'cause she's our engineer. We can't lose Kenny, 'cause she's our chemist. And we definitely can't lose the Daughter of Gaia, or Helen will kill us."

Grizz drops the .22, turns toward the bots, and charges straight at them.

"Grizz," I cry, "What are you doing!"

Grizz doesn't answer. What he's doing is obvious.

"I'm coming with you!" I turn to follow him.

"You stay there," he yells over his shoulder.

I start to follow him, but Kenny grabs me by the collar and stops me cold. Grizz jogs to within ten yards of the bots, turns sharply to his left, and sprints away from them. The bots pause for a moment, then wheel into a turn and follow him.

I struggle to break free.

"I can't stop Grizz," Kenny says grimly, "but I can stop you."

"Let go of me!" I cry.

"There is absolutely no point in two of us dying," she whispers in my ear.

When I continue to struggle, she throws me to the ground and sits on my chest.

"Get off me, you gorilla!"

"Nope," she says simply.

I quit struggling and begin to cry.

After I'm cried out, I ask her when she's going to let me up.

"As soon as we both know that there's no way you can catch up to them," she answers evenly.

In a few minutes, she lets me go. She's right. At this point, there's no way I could ever catch Grizz and the bots. Even worse, I don't think I could stand finding what would be left of Grizz when the bots were finished with him. Because sooner or later, Grizz is going to tire. And the bots never will.

The thought that we've just lost Grizz hits me like a sledgehammer. I have to sit down again. The tears start all over. Only this time, it seems as though they'll never stop.

Bree and Kenny wait patiently until I'm too weak to cry any more. When I look up at them, I can see that they've been crying as well.

"Grizz," I whimper.

* * * * *

The rest of the afternoon passes in a blur. Grizz has been my best friend since we were preschoolers. And he could have been much more. I realize I'm not going to feel right for a long, long time.

As we continue our journey, changes in our surroundings penetrate the fog I'm in. Trees are becoming few and far between. The ground is becoming much more broken. And we're beginning to climb. Just a little incline at first, but soon it starts to get steeper.

I hear a clanking sound coming from our left.

"Wait here," says Bree. "I'll go see what's making the noise."

Even in the haze I'm in, I think, *Good idea. Don't send Kenny. The blacksuits would hear her coming a mile away.*

Bree's gone for about ten minutes.

When she returns, she tells us that the clanking noise is from the blacksuit's mining operation. There are a bunch of people with picks over their shoulders riding a cart down into a mine.

This brings me out of my mood. I remember Orsino warned us to be careful around the mine. We move out quickly and quietly.

We follow an old game trail up toward the saddle. The ground is much steeper now, and we begin to see evergreen trees. Within an hour, we're in a forest of evergreens. Unlike the shrunken trees on the plain below, these trees are big, thirty or forty feet tall.

Bree is in the lead, and she holds up a hand for us to stop. She strings her bow, aims carefully, and shoots. We follow the flight of the arrow, and it ends up lodged in a rabbit. Kenny and I are thrilled. Fresh meat tonight! The forests around the villages are teeming with dreadwolves, who do a very thorough job of depleting the wildlife. Up here, we may find more of it.

There is no storm today, so it's easy to build a fire when we stop for the night. We've put enough distance between ourselves and the blacksuits' mine that we don't worry about the smoke. The smell of cooking meat and the sound of fat dripping into the fire make me forget about Grizz for about ten seconds.

Rabbit is delicious!

I don't sleep well. Nightmares of Grizz and bots bother me all night long.

* * * * *

I wake up in the morning feeling groggy.

I check my pedometer. By dead reckoning, I figure we should cross the saddle today and be down the far side by the end of the day. We can't see the saddle from here because we're surrounded by trees, but we follow old game trails, hoping they won't lead us into a blind canyon or a sheer cliff.

By midday, the evergreens begin to thin out, and the only sign of life is lichen growing on rocks. By the middle of the afternoon, we've reached the snow line. We stop and put on our second set of clothes over the ones we're wearing. We're still cold. That's okay, I think. It'll give us real inspiration to get over the saddle and down the other side before nightfall.

By dinnertime, we're still climbing up, and there's no sign we're getting near the top of the saddle.

"Oh jeez," Kenny says. She stops walking.

I'm not paying attention, and I run right into her.

She's looking back over her shoulder. I turn around and see what she's seen: huge black cumulonimbus clouds. Within twenty minutes, the wind picks up, and the air turns bitter cold. After another few minutes, we see the first snowflakes. They grow thicker and thicker, and within moments, the trail is buried under snow. Bree and Kenny gather around me.

"Hold on to my backpack!" Kenny hollers.

It's almost impossible to hear anything over the wind. I nod my head to let her know I heard. Bree grabs Kenny's backpack, and I hold on to Bree's. Within minutes, we lose sight of the game trail we've been following. All we can do is make sure we're climbing uphill.

"Whatever happened to monsoons being *short* storms?" I holler.

I don't think anybody can hear, and I'm surprised when I hear Bree's answer. "It's just like the mountains back home," she yells. "The mountains make their own weather."

It's true, I think. We get a dusting in Tucson, and the mountains around us get a blizzard.

My ears hurt, and my fingers are frozen. I hold on to Bree's backpack with my left hand until it gets so cold I can't stand it anymore. Then I put my left hand in my pocket and grab the backpack with my right hand. The wind swirls around us and blows snow into our eyes. Not that we can see where we're going in the first place.

I'm down to the point where all I can do is put one front in front of another. The wind and cold have blown every thought from my head other than, *Left, right, left, right…*

I'm surprised when I bump into Bree. Bree stopped because she bumped into Kenny. Kenny points in front of us. There, through the blizzard, we can vaguely make out a cliff, right smack-dab in front of us. There's no way for us to go on.

* * * * *

Bree is hollering. "Let's make camp! We can put up the tarp to block the wind and build a fire!"

We realize the problem with this plan immediately. The tarp is with Grizz.

Bree begins to cry. Her tears freeze as soon as they fall.

"We have to keep moving!" Kenny shouts.

All I can do is nod. Kenny turns to the left. Maybe there's a way around this cliff. I grab Kenny's backpack, and Bree grabs mine.

A half hour later, I can't feel either my fingers or my ears. My toes are beginning to go numb as well. But things are looking better. Kenny has found a trail that leads up.

Walking becomes more difficult as the snow piles up. Soon, we're wading through two-foot drifts, which rapidly become three-foot drifts. I lose all sense of time. I've been plowing my way through the snow forever.

I begin to feel warm all over. This is a bad sign. I've read that when you start feeling warm when you're really cold, it means your body has about reached the end. It's ready to shut down. And still the wind cuts through me like a knife. I want to sit down. I'm so tired all I can think of is sleep. It would be very easy to give in to the desire to stop and lie down.

Kenny feels my hand drop away from her backpack. In a second, she's in my face hollering. "Keep moving, ET! If you stop, you die!"

Dying doesn't sound like such a bad idea. But Kenny is behind me now, pushing me forward. She stops, and I realize she has gone back to drag Bree to her feet and push her along as well. That's all that's keeping both of us going: Kenny pushing. She pulls us up when we fall and pushes us some more.

The world goes silent. I can't hear a thing. Then I realize my ears are buried under wet snow. In fact, the whole back of my head is covered with snow. *Frosty the Snowman*, I think. This strikes me as being hilarious. I begin to giggle.

Kenny's face is suddenly three inches from my own. "Snap out of it, ET! *Right now!*"

I stop giggling. The melody of "Frosty the Snowman" plays nonstop in my head. I don't mind. There's nothing else to think about. I start to hum.

I see Jules ahead. My foggy mind knows this can't be Jules. After a moment, I remember why: Jules is dead. And, oh yeah, this Jules is floating ten feet above the ground. I'm puzzled. This Jules-who-can't-be-Jules is looking at me the way Mr. Burton used to look at students when he found them goofing around in chemistry lab. It's a look that made 285-pound wrestlers quiver. Jules-who-can't-be-Jules glowers at me, raises her left arm, and points. Uphill. Jules wants me to keep climbing.

I find this energizing. I struggle forward. I can do this, I tell myself.

A short while later, I find something very nice is happening. I'm walking downhill! Within minutes, the wind dies down, blocked by the shoulder of the mountain, which is now behind us. The snowflakes are drifting straight down. Big snowflakes. Big, lazy snowflakes. I like these snowflakes. The piles of snow become more and more shallow.

Finally, as we descend, we leave the snow behind entirely. Wonderful! And then I collapse.

* * * * *

I wake up and am groggily aware that a huge bonfire is blazing. I face the fire, and the front of my body is nicely warm. My back is really cold, but that's no big deal. I drift off to sleep again.

I awake in the morning, and the fire has died down some. Bree is beginning to stir as well. Kenny, looking totally exhausted, sits next to Bree.

"Are you two sleepyheads about ready to join the world of the living?" asks Kenny. She has deep purple shadows beneath her eyes.

I sit up and look around. I see the snow line about a half mile above us. I become aware of the fact that the side of my body that is not facing the fire is very, very cold. We may be out of the snow, but we're not out of the cold.

I piece together my memories of last night.

"Kenny," I say, "you saved our lives."

"Yep," she replies. "ET, ever since we came through that brane, the responsibility for our group has been resting on *your* shoulders. I saw that losing Grizz really knocked the slats out from under you. So I figured it was my turn to step up." She shrugs her shoulders. "I got your back."

"Thanks," I say with gratitude. "Did you sleep at all?"

"Not much. I didn't want the fire to go out."

Bree, who has awakened as well, also says, "Thanks, Kenny. I'd be frozen like a Popsicle if it wasn't for you."

"Don't mention it," says Kenny. "I thought about letting the two of you freeze, but then who would I have to admire my great intelligence, wit, and beauty?"

We're still in the mountains, but below the snow line. As I look to the east, I see a vast dun-colored plain stretching as far as the eye can see. Serious desert, I think.

"This side of the mountains doesn't look a thing like the other side," I observe.

"This side of the mountains is in what they call a 'rain shadow,'" explains Kenny. "The clouds hit the west side of the mountain, and the cooler air near the tops of the mountains forces the clouds to drop their moisture. No clouds make it over to this side. That whole area down there"—she waves her hand vaguely toward the east—"probably gets less rain than Tucson."

"Especially when you consider that the side we came from doesn't have all that much water to begin with," Bree says.

We eat a breakfast of cold potatoes and consider our plans for the day. We scatter the remaining coals of the fire. Then, we climb back up to the snow line and stuff our canteens full of snow. We're not going to find any water below. Once we leave the warmth of the fire, we are cold again, but not nearly as cold as we were yesterday. Canteens replenished, we begin working our way down the mountain. We have to be very careful of our footing here, as the descent is very steep.

Thoughts of Grizz hammer away at me incessantly.

There is little vegetation. The plants here remind me of the ones near Tucson, cactus and scrub, mostly. There is none of the scraggly grass we know, but that figures because Helen's stories told of a plague that killed all the grass. The air is thin and still here. There's no more wind than there was on the other side of the mountains.

As we continue to descend, the air gets hotter. By the time we reach the talus slope at the foot of the mountains, we are every bit as hot as we were on the other side of the mountains. Sweat runs down my back, and I frequently stop to mop my forehead to keep sweat out of my eyes.

The land levels off, and we leave the mountains behind. There's still not much in the way of plant life. Bree manages to kill a large lizard with an arrow. When we stop for the night, she skins and guts him.

"I'm not touching that thing," says Kenny. "Aren't lizards poisonous?"

"I don't think so," Bree responds. "If we keel over dead, we'll know I was wrong."

The smell of cooking meat is irresistible, and in the end, Kenny gives in and digs into a lizard leg. "Mmm," she says. "Tastes just like chicken."

It doesn't taste like any chicken I've ever eaten, but I hold my tongue. Arguing with Kenny is a lot like playing tennis with Jules. No matter how good your shot is, the ball is going to come right back.

Later, as we lay with heads propped up on backpacks, we enjoy the night sky above us.

"Why are all the blacksuits men?" I ask.

"Oh," Kenny says, "I asked Helen about that. She says that the Court has rules against women serving in their military. They say fighting's not a fit thing for a woman to do."

"Maybe they'll learn something when they realize that girls were a big part of the army that just kicked their butt," Bree says.

I think of my vision of Jules during the blizzard. "Did you guys see anybody else on the saddle during the blizzard?" I ask.

"Nope," says Bree.

"What would somebody be doing on the mountain during a blizzard?" asks Kenny. "Funny things happen when you're tired. You must have been hallucinating."

I don't think so, but I don't pursue it. I don't want my friends to think I've gone soft in the head. And Kenny is right. I was not all there mentally. But Jules seemed so *real*.

Sleep comes easily tonight, but I wake after an hour or two. The rest of the night, I'm awake, aware that Grizz is not with us. I cry again. I never would have thought it possible for a person to hold so many tears. I'm dead tired, but sleep won't come. Finally, I doze.

I wake next morning with an ache in the pit of my stomach. The ache isn't physical. It's the ache you get when you want something with all your heart, but know you'll never have it.

* * * * *

Shortly after Grizz's family moved to Tucson from Texas, our parents realized that we were going to be best friends. Grizz's family moved into a house on the other side of the street and two doors down, so we had to cross the street to play. My parents changed the rule from "don't go out in the street" to "look both ways before you cross."

Behind my house, there's nothing but open desert. About fifty yards from the crushed rock that marks the end of my backyard stands an ancient mesquite tree, made for climbing. High up in the branches of that tree was an imaginary fort from which Grizz and I fought off hordes of al-Qaeda, Russians, Germans, and kids from Phoenix. The fort was our place, and magical.

On a hot desert summer day when we were seven years old, Grizz and I climbed up into our fort. There was a cool breeze blowing, and a cactus wren was calling his mate. Grizz had brought a lukewarm can of Mountain Dew, and I brought two Bit-O-Honey bars. We had to peel the wrappers off the Bit-O-Honey because they were sticky from riding in my back pocket all morning. I liked Bit-O-Honey because you had to work hard at getting a chunk to chew on. They lasted longer than Hershey bars.

Earlier that day, I overheard our neighbor, Mrs. Warton, tell her husband, "That Erin Taylor is a terrible tomboy." I had no idea what a "tomboy" was, but from the tone of her voice, I could tell it was not meant as a compliment.

So, relaxing in the fort, gnawing on my Bit-O-Honey, I asked Grizz, "What's a tomboy?"

"I think it's a girl who likes to do a lot of boy stuff, like climbing trees and playing baseball."

"Well what the heck's the matter with that?" I asked, indignant and genuinely curious.

"Beats me," said Grizz.

"Hey! If I'm a tomboy, that means we can be blood brothers, doesn't it?" I said, brightening.

"Guess it does," confirmed Grizz.

I dug a penknife from the front pocket of my Old Navy jeans.

I solemnly opened the knife and drew it across the ball of my thumb, wincing. I was rewarded with a bright plume of blood.

Grizz drew blood from his thumb. We pressed our thumbs together, allowing our blood to mingle.

"Blood brothers forever," Grizz intoned.

"Blood brothers forever," I repeated solemnly.

16

Orsino told us we'd find an old, broken-up highway if we headed east. By late morning, we reach it. The concrete is cracked and jumbled, so when we turn north, we walk beside the road, not on it. Everything is deathly quiet here. With groundwater polluted and almost no rain, there aren't many living things on this side of the mountains. Heat and sand, however, exist in abundance.

Toward late afternoon, we find the old town that Orsino had mentioned. The town is remarkably well preserved. We can make out a gas station and a restaurant. There are some ancient mobile homes with broken windows and doors ajar. Down a street that stretches from west to east, we see a few more abandoned and broken-down buildings, old homes and businesses mostly. Even in its heyday, this town was just a speck on a map.

"Considering the buildings are hundreds of years old, they're well preserved," I comment.

"The climate is so dry on this side of the mountains that everything is way better preserved than on the other side," explains Bree. "They find stuff in the Egyptian desert that's thousands of years old, and it looks like it was made yesterday. They dug up this one thing called Pharaoh's Needle in the desert. They moved it to America and set it up in Central Park in New York City. When they brought it to New York, it had all sorts of carvings on it. Those carvings had been there for thousands of years. But after a few years in Central Park, the carvings were eroded away."

"I hope we don't find any mummies," says Kenny.

"Not much chance of that," says Bree. "Those Egyptian mummies were very carefully preserved. Anything organic, plant or animal, rots away. It takes longer in a dry climate, but it happens."

We see a large, rocky hill north of town, just as Orsino had predicted.

We leave the road and move slowly around the base of the hill. The door into the workshop is easy to find. It's very large, easily ten feet tall and six feet wide. It's made out of gray metal. Three rows of dials are set on the front door. In my excitement, I almost miss the footprints.

I hold my arms out like a safety patrol at elementary school to stop Kenny and Bree. "Look," I say, pointing at the prints.

"Somebody's been here," says Bree.

"There's not a lot of wind around here to wipe out prints, but even so, those prints look fresh," agrees Kenny.

We stop and look around suspiciously. No sign of anybody. Even so, we begin to whisper.

"Could you blow this door off?" I ask Kenny.

"I'm out of bomb-making material," she reminds me. "And even if I could build a bomb, this door looks like it's made out of the same stuff they use for ATMs. You'd need a diamond-tipped drill to get through it. There are no hinges or handles anywhere. This would be a tough one to crack."

I examine the dials. There are four dials in the top row, six dials in the second row, and six more dials in the bottom row. Beside each row is a green plastic bubble. A little experimentation shows that the dials work like the rotating dials on a suitcase lock. The top row dials are all letters, the second row are numbers, and the bottom row has letters again.

The only clue is a set of four numbers painted above the dials. The numbers are 02, 91, 21, and 51.

"Okay," I say, "what do those numbers mean?"

"Some kind of code," proposes Kenny.

"There are four numbers, and the top row has four letters," I observe. "Maybe the numbers correspond with the letters."

"True," says Kenny. "But there are only twenty-six letters in the alphabet. The numbers can't correspond to numbers. What do you do with fifty-one and ninety-one?"

We rack our brains. Fibonacci sequence? Common divisors? Common multiples? Common factors? Some number system other than base ten? Nothing.

We sit down in the shade. The door opens out of the north side of the hill, so we don't get direct sunlight. How do you *make* ideas come?

Suddenly I sit up straight. "Wait a second! What if you turn the numbers around? Then you have twenty, nineteen, twelve, and fifteen!"

"Okay," says Kenny, interested, "that gives us *T*, *S*, *L*, and *O*. TSLO. Is that some kind of acronym?"

"Turn South Last One," I mumble. We all come up with possible acronyms. Nothing makes any sense at all.

"Okay," Bree says, "how about a word scramble?"

"That gives us 'slot,' 'lost,' or 'lots.' Do you see any slots on the door?" I ask.

There are no slots. Except for the dials, the door is perfectly smooth.

We dial the four letters on the top to "SLOT." Nothing happens. We move the dials to "LOST," and are rewarded by a sound coming from inside the door that brings to mind hamsters on exercise wheels. The green bubble next to the four letters lights up.

"Bingo!" shouts Kenny. She looks around with eyes wide. "Bingo," she says again, in a whisper this time, remembering the fresh footprints.

But brainstorm as we may, we can't come up with any more ideas.

"Lost," says Kenny. "We're lost, all right."

We decide to eat dinner. Because of the prints we found, we decide against a cooking fire.

Bree is gnawing on dried potato mush when she suddenly sits up straight. "Wait a second!" she exclaims. "Lost. And then six numbers."

Bree is visibly excited. Kenny and I are still clueless.

"Did you guys ever watch that TV series *Lost?*" she says excitedly.

"Yes," I say slowly. "What does the TV series have to do with the door?"

"I loved that show," says Bree. "I got the DVDs and watched the whole thing three times. I had this huge crush on the guy who played Sawyer! Think about 'six numbers.'"

Suddenly, I understand Bree's thinking. "The hatch! The computer! They had to type in six numbers every so many minutes. Six numbers just like our door!"

Energized, Bree hops up and spins the dials to 4, 8, 15, 16, 23, 42. More noise like hamsters on wheels and another green light. We fist-bump.

That leaves us with the last six letters to solve. We rack our brains trying to come up with a six-letter word. Island? No. Dharma? No.

Bree tries "Sawyer." That doesn't work either.

"I think I've got it," I say. "Hurley was the character who was jinxed by those six numbers. I dial up "HURLEY." There is a hissing sound followed by a cool breeze blowing out of whatever lies inside. The door is open.

* * * * *

"That hissing air is a good sign," says Kenny. "I think the breeze came because they sealed the room. That'll mean things inside are well preserved."

We peer inside. We see steps heading down. The workshop is buried deep beneath the hill.

"Should we close the door?" Bree asks.

"Probably not," replies Kenny. "If this place was sealed, and I think it was, there won't be any source of fresh air other than the open door. They've probably got an air vent you can open from inside somewhere. We should leave the door open until we figure out how to open the vent."

As we start to descend the steps, we realize we're going to need a light. I fumble around in my backpack until I find my flashlight. I turn it on and aim the beam downward. I say a silent prayer that the batteries are fresh.

As we follow the steps downward, the temperature declines. "That's another good sign," says Kenny. "They've buried the workshop deep enough so it'll stay at a constant temperature. That's good for preserving things as well."

Just when I begin to believe the steps will never end, they end. I play the flashlight around. It illuminates a vast room filled with all sorts of equipment. On the wall next to the stairwell is a throw switch about a foot long. I pull it down. Nothing happens. As I move around the switch, I stub my toe on something. We find a box that looks something like the old ice-cream maker with a hand crank on the side my dad used to make peach ice cream.

"That'll be a hand-crank generator," says Kenny, excited.

She immediately begins to turn the crank.

Within moments, we see overhead lights begin to flicker, emitting a wan light. As Kenny continues to crank, the lights get brighter. When she stops, they burn brightly for a moment and then begin to fade.

"We're gonna have to crank this baby up," says Kenny.

We take turns turning the crank. The lights grow very bright. After an hour of cranking, we stop, and the lights continue to burn brightly.

"We've built up enough charge for the lights to burn for a while," I say.

We begin to explore.

Along one wall are dozens of shelves loaded with canned goods: Del Monte peaches, Libby's pineapple, Chunky soup. There are containers of food that I recognize as MREs, "Meals Ready to Eat," made for the military. I begin to salivate.

"If that food's been sitting there for hundreds of years, it's probably not good anymore," cautions Kenny.

There's a can opener dangling on a string attached to the nearest shelf. I grab it and open a can of peaches. The peaches are bluish brown. I open a can of soup, and its contents are black. I open a can of green beans. I hate green beans. But when I open the can, the beans look perfectly good.

"Figures," I mutter. "Everything is spoiled but the green beans." But as I sniff the beans, I realize they aren't any good either. The MREs are no better. We are in a room with thousands of tantalizing meals, and they're all absolutely worthless.

I can't remain disappointed too long, because there is much to explore. This room is huge, at least three times larger than the gym at Sierra Vista High.

"Found it," says Bree triumphantly. "I'll bet this handle is the control for the air shaft." She's found a pull switch at the bottom of a large vent that disappears into the ceiling. Kenny and I join Bree. We agree that it does indeed look like the switch that will open the fresh air shaft. Bree pulls down hard on the handle, and we hear a grating sound from far above. A warm breeze blows down through the vent.

We continue to explore.

I find a huge tank along the wall to the right. Kenny joins me. I knock experimentally on the tank. Kenny finds a spigot and turns it. Clear liquid comes out. I catch some in my hand and smell it.

I sniff. "Smells like water."

Kenny touches it with the tip of her tongue.

"It is water," she says.

"Is it drinkable?" I ask.

"Water's water," answers Kenny. "It doesn't degrade over time. The only thing that might ruin it would be the container it's in. But this," she says, knocking on the tank, "looks like plastic to me. The water should be safe."

"There's enough drinking water here to last a hundred years," I exclaim as I size up the huge tank.

Kenny is staring happily at two stacks of fertilizer bags piled all the way to the ceiling, which is at least twenty feet high. Next to the fertilizer are brown bags without labels. Kenny opens one and examines the contents.

"Black powder!" Kenny cries. "These people were really into making bombs. The powder has probably broken down, chemically, but it's full of sulfur and potassium nitrate. I may be able to synthesize wolf bane without using skunk and poo. I'll still need the decayed plant matter, though."

She opens the doors of a large locker and yelps with delight. "Plastique! C4, Semtex!" she exclaims with glee.

"What's Semtex?" I ask.

"Plastic explosive!" she chortles. "And look here, detonators!"

"Uh-oh," she continues in a more sober voice, "they were gonna set these things off with mobile phones, and there isn't a working phone battery left on the planet. Well, I'll just have to figure something out. Maybe I can create some sort of voltaic pile..." She trails off with a look of deep concentration on her face.

Bree is equally rapturous. "Tool and die makers! Lathes! Milling machines! Drill presses! And look at the woodworking machines: table saws, routers, punches, jigs, spindle turners, faceplate turners— everything I could ever want!"

She is equally thrilled by the piles of lumber and metal she finds. "I can make anything," she crows.

Kenny locates several hundred jerry cans. "Gasoline?" she asks curiously. She unscrews the cap of one and takes a sniff. "Smells like gas. It's amber and crystal clear." She takes a stick and stirs the contents. "Too bad. Now it's cloudy. There must be lots of sediment at the bottom." She pours some liquid from a jerry can into a clear beaker. I watch with her as sediment slowly settles out of the liquid and falls to the bottom of the container.

"That's not gonna work in those generators over there," she says, disappointed, indicating a row of machines that must be generators without cranks. "Those generators were built to run on gasoline."

Bree has found radios. "Eight of them!" she exclaims.

"Could we use those radios to communicate with Mother Helen on the other side of the mountains?" I ask.

"This is strictly line-of-sight stuff," explains Bree. "But if we built a relay tower up on the saddle, and another tower by the caves, yeah, I think that just might work."

I store that bit of knowledge and continue my exploration of the room. "Wow!" I say in wonder. "Look at all these guns!"

I'm familiar with the banana clip profile of an AK-47 from watching action-adventure movies. I also recognize grenade launchers. There are dozens of lockers with AK magazines and grenades. There are a variety of handguns and some large tubes I don't recognize.

Kenny picks up an AK-47. "I wonder if this is the safety," she muses. She fiddles with it, and the rifle discharges a round that ricochets around the room several times before coming to rest in a can of creamed corn.

I dove for cover the minute the round was discharged. "Nice one," I say, picking myself up and dusting myself off.

Kenny looks sheepish. "I guess we should go outside when we play with these."

Undeterred, Kenny pries opens a wood crate on the floor. "Tear gas. These dudes were ready for war." She moves the crate and opens the one beneath it. "Launchers for the tear gas," she says happily.

Not being particularly handy at anything, I have nothing to focus my attention. Examining the machines, I realize I don't even know the names for most of them.

There is a large gray door about halfway down the left wall of the main room, and I open it to find a dark room. There is another hand-crank generator near the door. Twenty minutes of cranking leaves me with a tired arm, but gives me enough light to explore the room. It's very large, perhaps half the size of the main room, and it's filled with worktables. Cabinets along the wall are full of hand tools and electronics gear: computers, televisions, wires, circuit boards, and the like.

Leaving the workroom, I discover yet another gray door at the far end of the big room. I open the door and am once more greeted by a dark room. Another twenty minutes of cranking and I'm absolutely thrilled to find a smaller room filled with a dozen bunks with real mattresses and real pillows.

"Hey!" I holler excitedly. "Look at this! There are real beds in here!" I dive onto one and revel at the bounciness of a real mattress with box springs. After a few minutes of bliss, I notice a row of sinks against the wall and something that looks suspiciously like a shower. I turn a valve experimentally. The pipes groan, and a burst of air comes out of the faucet, followed by a stream of water. I sample it carefully. It's good! There are lockers on the wall opposite the sinks. I open one to find a walk-in closet with drawers on one side and a bar to hang clothes on the other. All in all, in this last room, I've discovered a little piece of heaven.

I return to the other room. I want to find candles, because I don't want to waste the power we've generated, and I don't fancy sleeping down here when it's pitch-dark. I work my way back toward the entrance and freeze when I see a man standing in the doorway.

17

Terror turns to exhilaration when I realize the man standing in the doorway is Grizz.

"Grizz!" I shout and run to him. I throw my arms around his neck. I kiss him on the forehead, on the cheeks, even on his nose. I don't kiss him on the mouth because, despite my sense of delight, I know that kisses on the mouth will take us to places we don't want to go.

"Whoa." Grizz grins. "You missed me."

"Of course I missed you, you big goof! We thought you were dead."

Bree and Kenny hug Grizz in turn. They are almost as delighted as I am.

"What happened?" I ask, looking at Grizz. "How did you get away from the bots?"

"I found a steep hill and ran up it. When I got to the top, I discovered a lake. It looked like the kind of lake the copper mining companies used to dig to store wastewater after they were done with it. The lake wasn't deep. In fact, it might not have been there at all without the monsoon rains. I dove in and began swimming to the opposite side.

"Fortunately, it turns out bots are not very smart. They could easily have rolled around the lake and met me when I came out the other side. But instead, they watched me for a few minutes, turned around, and rolled away. I guess they're programmed to lose interest if they can't follow you."

I'm beaming from ear to ear, probably looking like an idiot.

Grizz gestures toward the food. "So we're gonna eat real food tonight?"

"Not exactly," I say. I let Kenny explain the problem.

Grizz groans.

"How'd you like the snow up on the saddle?" I ask.

"Actually, I sort of enjoyed being cold after all the heat," he responds.

I take my flashlight and climb the stairs. Best to keep the front door locked, I decide. After making sure that we can open the door from the inside, I close it. The hatch closes with a hiss followed by a solid *thunk*.

Over a late snack, we tell Grizz about our dramatic crossing of the saddle. I don't say anything about seeing Jules, of course.

Grizz expresses surprise. "It only took me a few hours to get over the saddle," he says. "The snow was deep, but the sky was beautiful blue."

After our snack we find candles and matches, turn off the overhead lights, which are looking perceptibly dimmer, and go to the dorm room to enjoy the comfort of real mattresses with real box springs. The walls of the dorm are painted a cheerful shade of yellow, but there are no decorations on the walls. Everything in the workshop is utilitarian. The people who built this place built it with a serious purpose in mind.

"Who do you suppose built this place?" I ask.

"I figure it was probably some wacko survivalists," says Bree.

"Well hurrah for wackos" says Kenny.

"I'm guessing," I say, "that they may have foreseen how bad things were going to get, and they wanted to give themselves a chance after surviving Armageddon. They probably died before they had a chance to get back here."

"Why use *Lost* clues to open the door?" asks Kenny.

We have to pause a second and bring Grizz up to date with the story of the workshop's security system. We wait for Bree, our expert in all things *Lost*.

"I suppose *Lost* went into syndication and got a kind of cult following," she says. "Sort of like *Battlestar Galactica* and *Star Trek*. If the folks who built this place were fans of *Lost*, the clues wouldn't have been that hard to figure out. After all, we cracked the code without working up much of a sweat. And there's no way anybody is going to guess the combination if they don't know about *Lost*."

This sounds more plausible than anything else I can think of.

For the first time since we left the Sanctuary, I sleep comfortably and have no nightmares.

* * * * *

We are very busy the next day. Bree has an idea for making a weapon we can use to fight the blacksuits.

"If we had some sort of cannon, we could attack the blacksuit forts," she suggests.

I nod in agreement, as do Kenny and Grizz.

"But cannons are heavy, and they'd be hard to haul around in the forest. So I'll come up with something smaller and lighter, maybe even modular, so the villagers can disassemble it and cart it through the forest. Besides, casting a cannon barrel and getting the rifling of the barrel right is difficult. So I'm thinking of something along the lines of a trebuchet."

"I beg your pardon?" I have no idea what a trebuchet is.

"A trebuchet is like a catapult," explains Bree. "Only I'd like to make one that's more powerful than the ones they used in the Middle Ages. Something with hydraulics. Something we could use to fling Kenny's bombs at the blacksuits."

"That's a great idea," I say enthusiastically.

Bree removes a notebook and pen from her backpack and starts making sketches. Within seconds she's entirely absorbed and wouldn't hear one of Kenny's bombs if we set one off right next to her.

"What are you going to do?" I ask Kenny.

"I thought I'd work with the gasoline. Maybe I can make it useful again."

"Do you think you can turn it back into gasoline?" I ask.

"Not really," says Kenny. "Refining oil is a very complex process. Turning this back into gasoline is sort of like trying to put Humpty Dumpty together again. Once an egg is broken, it's broken. But I thought I ought to give it a try. I should be able to make it explode at the very least. After that, I'll see if the tear gas is any good."

"Just don't make any noise," I caution. "Remember the footprints."

Grizz and I go to work on the hand-crank generators. By lunchtime, my arm is ready to fall off.

We eat a lunch of cold potatoes, and Bree asks Grizz to help her move some sheet metal.

Later that afternoon, I decide to explore the immediate surroundings outside the workshop. I look for Grizz and find him taking a nap in the dormitory. I consider waking him, but decide to let him sleep. The last twenty-four hours have been hard on him.

"I think I'll go into the old town and poke around," I announce to Kenny and Bree.

"Be careful," they caution.

Remembering the footprints we found yesterday, I make sure the .22 is loaded, sling it over my shoulder, and put our last few bullets in my pocket. I'd take an AK, but I don't know how to use them, and I don't want to make a lot of noise practicing. I don't know who might be within earshot.

I climb the steps and throw the door open. Before I close it, I run through the combination in my head to be sure I'll be able to let myself back in. Then, I walk into town.

I find the old diner and decide to see what's left of it on the inside. The answer, I find, is not much. Everything is covered under inches of dust. There are some booths, but the cushions are in tatters. A stack of ancient menus sits on a table by the door. The kitchen is a bit better preserved. The grill is covered with dust, but looks as though it could be fired up and used to turn a pink meat patty into a hamburger. There's also a huge oven, but the door is sprung. There are broken dishes all over the floor.

I leave the diner and examine the old mobile home in the backyard, the home of the restaurant's owners, I assume. The inside of the trailers is in shambles. Furniture is broken and overturned. There's no trace of a kitchen left, except for a hole in the floor where the sink once drained. Incongruously, there's a calendar on the wall, curled and brown with age. The year is 2189. So civilization dragged on for almost two centuries, I think. I wonder what the year is now.

There's a magazine on the floor. I sit down next to it and carefully pick it up. Most of it crumbles in my hands, but a couple of the inner pages remain relatively intact. This must have been one of those magazines that idolize celebrities, because, even though the pages are brown, I can make out pictures of smug-looking people preening in outrageous clothing.

I hear a noise behind me. I spin around to see a small man standing in the doorway. He's much too short to be Grizz, and he has a crossbow pointed directly at my chest.

18

"Don't move, girly, or I'll put a bolt straight through your heart."

When he talks, he reveals a mouthful of rotten teeth. He is small, just like the villagers. His head is shaved, and he has tattoos on his beefy arms. There's a tattoo on one bicep that looks like an old American flag, one with only thirteen stars. The other bicep has a coiled snake with the motto Don't Tread on Me. He is dressed in clothes that look fairly new. There are no patches in evidence.

I raise my hands. "No need for that crossbow. I'm not going anywhere." Despite my words, I'm looking for a way out. I might be able to dive through what's left of the living room window, but I don't know what I'd be landing on outside. Unfortunately, if the man with the crossbow is paying attention, and he seems to be, I'd be dead before I hit the ground.

The man with the crossbow moves two steps in my direction. He keeps the crossbow trained on the middle of my chest. Another man steps into the doorway. This one is a little taller and is also dressed well. Like the first man, he has a shaved head and tattoos. The tats are identical to the first man's. The two of them are not gaunt like our villagers, but look well fed, fat even.

The taller one eyes me coldly. "Would you look at the size of this one!" he says. "The Leader will want her, no doubt about it."

"Oh yeah," says the other man. "He'll have fun with her for sure." He leers at me.

I don't like the way the second man is looking at me. He walks all around me, eyes traveling from head to toe and back again.

I search my mind desperately for a way out of this situation. I draw a blank. They've got me. I'll just have to wait for them to get careless.

"Put your hands behind your back," orders the first man.

I do as I'm told, and he quickly ties my hands together with insulated wire. I move my wrists, testing the bonds.

"Go ahead and try to get 'em off," he whispers, lips less than an inch from my ear. "All you'll do is cut your pretty wrists." His breath smells foul.

"I'll go with you, and I won't cause any problems," I say. "You don't need to tie me up."

"Oh," the man behind me whispers in my ear, "I like tying girls up."

Fear starts to knock on the door. I can't give in to it. I have to keep a clear head. Sooner or later, they'll make a mistake, and when they do, I need to be ready.

"Now walk," instructs the man with the crossbow. He gestures toward the door. He keeps the crossbow leveled as I move around him. The man behind me gives me a shove, and I struggle to stay on my feet. I descend the steps with care. The man behind me pushes me again. This time I can't keep my balance, and I fall. With my hands tied behind me, I can't use them to break my fall. I twist to the side so I won't fall on my face, and try to take as much impact as possible on my shoulder, but the side of my head cracks the ground, and I see shooting stars.

The bigger man drags me to my feet by my collar. "You're clumsy," he whispers.

I don't respond. Holding me by the collar, he drags me through the backyard of the trailer and across open desert to an abandoned building that must have been a warehouse. It has an elevated dock that would have been the perfect height for unloading trucks.

He pushes me upstairs and through an opening where a door once stood. The inside of the warehouse is dark, and it takes a second for my eyes to adjust.

"Hey, Walt, look here what *we* found," says the man with the crossbow.

Once my eyes adjust, I become aware of a third man and a young girl.

I size up the third man. He's attractive, but short, like most people in this world. His eyes are gray and cheerful.

It takes a moment for me to tear my eyes away from the third man, Walt, I assume, and examine the young girl.

Her face is directed at the floor. She is not looking at me. Around her neck is a dog collar. A heavy chain runs from the collar to a pipe on the wall. The end of the chain is wrapped around the pipe and secured with a padlock. Her hands are bound behind her back.

"You got here just in time, honey," says Walt amiably. "We were just getting ready to leave for HQ. Put her in her proper place,".

The taller man kicks the backs of my knees, hard, forcing me to kneel.

Walt walks up to me, examining me appraisingly. His smile is pleasant. "The Leader's going to like you," he says in a light, conversational tone.

The taller man speaks. "We ought to leave now, Walt. We want to make it to HQ on time."

Once again, panic starts to rise. If they drag me off into the desert, my friends will never find me. *Gotta stay calm*, I tell myself. *Gotta stay calm. Wait for your chance.*

"There's plenty of time," says Walt. He looks me in the eye, still smiling kindly. Maybe he's a sane one, I think hopefully.

"What's your name, sweetheart?" he asks, his voice gentle.

"I'm Erin," I reply.

"Well, Erin, I'm pleased to meet you. My name is Walt."

When I say nothing, he continues. "Just what are you doing in this pimple of a town in the middle of nowhere, Erin?" he asks kindly.

"I just crossed over from the other side of the mountains," I reply.

"Now that's a lie, darlin'. The Old Ones crossed the mountains, and there's nothing there, except wolves who'll tear a man to pieces in seconds. The Old Ones lost a lot of men on the other side of the mountains. And the Old Ones are never wrong." Once again, his voice is soft, gentle, even.

"I'm traveling cross-country." I improvise. I've never been a convincing liar, and I can see in Walt's eyes he knows I'm lying.

"Is that so? Where's your traveling kit?" he asks.

"I dropped it at the edge of town. It's pretty heavy, so I left it there so I could go exploring."

"Now you wouldn't happen to be in town because of the workshop, would you?" he asks pleasantly.

"I don't know anything about a workshop."

He slaps my face so hard I see bright flashes of light. I taste blood in my mouth.

"Does that help your thinking any?" he asks amiably. "Tell me how you know about the workshop." He is still smiling affably.

"I don't know what you're talking about," I say.

This time he punches me with his fist. I feel the cartilage in my nose bend. Tears come to my eyes. My face is throbbing with pain.

"I didn't like that answer," he says.

"It's the truth! Please, if I knew anything about this workshop of yours, I'd tell you."

This time his fist strikes me right between the eyes.

"You can do better than that," he says, sounding as though he were a parent, slightly disappointed with a wayward daughter. When I don't respond, he hits me in the mouth. I feel my lip split. Now I really taste blood. I can't think because the pain is overwhelming. All I know is that I can't let him know about my knowledge of the workshop, or they'll wait outside the hatch and ambush my friends when they open the door.

I remain silent. I'm determined not to cry.

"The workshop belongs to us," says Walt in a reasonable voice. "The Leader's great-great-great-great-great-granddaddy built it, along with his friends."

"Don't mess her up too bad," says one the other tattooed men, sounding worried. "The Leader won't like it if you hurt her too bad."

Walt ignores this advice. He pushes me down. He kicks me in the ribs. Twice. I can't believe how painful this is.

"Now," says Walt, sounding cheerful, "do you want to tell me what you know about the workshop?"

"No clue," I say.

He drags me to my feet. He walks around behind me and lifts my bound hands. I can feel him grasp the pinkie finger of my left hand. He forces it backward until it snaps. The pain is indescribable. Despite my best efforts, tears roll down my face. *I will not tell him anything*, I say to myself, over and over.

"Not too late to start talking, sweetheart," he says.

He takes my right hand, and I stand helplessly as he prepares to give my right pinkie finger the same treatment.

* * * * *

Before he can do this, I hear three explosions. Ears buzzing from the noise, I look over my shoulder and see Grizz standing in the doorway with an AK-47 in his hands. The three tattooed men are down on the floor, bleeding.

"Don't shoot the girl," I say weakly. I collapse and roll over on my side. The movement sends waves of pain rocketing through every cell of my body.

In a moment, Grizz has my hands untied. My body is alive with pain. The pain is so intense it drives every thought out of my mind except for gratitude that no more pain is coming. I'm aware of Grizz rocking me in his arms.

"Who are you?" he asks the bound girl.

She doesn't say a word. Her eyes are still fixed on the floor. I don't think she has looked up once since I entered the room.

"Will you be okay if I leave you alone for a second?" Grizz asks me.

I nod. This, the smallest of all possible motions, sends pain searing through my head.

Grizz props me up against the wall and turns Walt's pockets inside out. A lighter, a pocketknife, a rag, and a key fall out. Taking the key, Grizz unlocks the padlock fastening the silent girl's chain to the pipes. He takes out his pocketknife and saws through the dog collar. He throws it away into the corner. He unties her hands, which are bound behind her back.

"We have to get you back to the workshop," says Grizz. "Can you walk?"

I'm actually not too sure I can. "Yes," I answer.

Grizz helps me up. Once I'm on my feet, the pain is not as bad. My ribs are crying out, and my finger throbs, but most of the pain is located in my face.

"I'll be back to help you in a few minutes," says Grizz to the silent girl. She is still looking at the ground, but her head nods slightly. "Stay put. I'm your friend."

The walk back to the workshop seems to take hours.

When we reach the bottom of the stairs, Kenny and Bree cry out in surprise.

"ET!" exclaims Kenny, looking concerned and confused. "What happened?"

"I ran into some mean people."

Grizz picks me up in his arms, carries me into the dormitory, and places me gently on my bed. Right behind Grizz are Kenny and Bree.

"Can you take care of ET for a few minutes?" asks Grizz. "I have another job to do."

"Sure," says Kenny. "Of course. Bree, can you warm up some water?"

Bree nods and leaves right behind Grizz.

I wait until Bree returns and then explain what happened.

Kenny soaks a cloth in the water and dabs at my cuts. I manage to tell the story between cries of pain as she cleans each wound.

"This is gonna hurt," warns Kenny, "so be ready."

"Okay," I say. I grit my teeth.

Kenny quickly grabs my nose and straightens it. The pain sets off Fourth of July fireworks behind my closed eyelids.

Kenny looks at my pinkie. "What should we do about that, ET?"

"You're gonna have to splint it. Splint it from the tip of the finger all the way up to my wrist," I say.

"Just a sec," says Bree.

Bree leaves the room and comes back a moment later with a piece of wood that's about half an inch thick and four inches long.

"Get the tape out of my backpack," I instruct.

Kenny is ready to splint my finger.

"Just do it fast," I say.

I scream when they straighten my finger. When the splint is on, the pain subsides. A little.

I sit up on my bed and rummage through my backpack with my good hand. I find a bottle of Extra Strength Excedrin and dry swallow two of them. Then I dry swallow two more.

By this time, Grizz has returned with the silent girl. He brings her into the dormitory with his arm around her shoulders. He removes his arm, and she runs into a corner, turns around, and crouches down. She is terrified. Her eyes travel from one face to another, never resting more than a split second.

Grizz sits next to her. He talks to her softly. "These are friends. They want to help you."

She is clearly unconvinced, and Grizz continues to talk to her gently. After a while, she seems to relax a little. Her eyes stare at the floor. Her body is still coiled, ready to spring at the slightest hint of danger.

Bree leaves us and comes back moments later with warm potatoes, five plates, and five spoons.

The silent girl looks at the potatoes apprehensively, but begins to eat when she sees Grizz eating.

After supper, Grizz explains that he left the workshop shortly after I did.

"I took an AK and a couple spare clips," he begins. "I was going into town to look around when I saw the two guys push you out of the trailer. I hid behind the corner of the building. When they were all looking the other way, I followed you to the warehouse. I would have come sooner, ET, but one of the guys was standing in the doorway of the warehouse, and he kept glancing back over his shoulder. I knew I had to take them all down at once, or I'd be in a firefight, and I didn't know how many were inside. As soon as the guy in the door went inside, I crossed the open ground between myself and the warehouse. One quick peek in the door showed there were only three of them, and you know the rest.

"I'm sorry, ET. I got to you as soon as I could." There are tears in Grizz's eyes.

"You did good, Grizz," I say. I smile at him through puffy lips. Pain makes me wince.

On my bed that night, body throbbing with pain, waiting for sleep to come, I decide I've had enough. I can't do this anymore. Maybe Helen will take me in as an acolyte. I'm not cut out for this. They'll have to find another Daughter of Gaia.

19

I never make it into the deep sleep that brings true rest. I nap and wake the whole night through.

I finally give up on sleep. I lie on my bed, staring at the bottom of the bunk above me. I rethink my decision to give up. I've had a terrible experience. That much is plain. But I can respond to it in one of two ways. I can either let it break me or I can use it to make myself stronger. I have a choice between giving up and anger. I find a sense of cool determination. I'm not going to give in. I'm going to come out of this experience a tougher person.

I get out of bed and look at myself in the mirror that hangs over the sinks in the dormitory. I look awful. Both of my eyes are black, my nose is swollen an angry shade of red, and my lips are split and puffy. My finger and ribs throb. I use the pain to fuel my anger.

I dig the notebook and a pen out of my backpack, move into the workroom, and begin to write. I'm convinced we have, or can make, the tools we need to fight the Court. But I want to get my plan down on paper because it has a lot of moving parts, and they need to be coordinated.

I come up for air at lunch and eat sparingly.

Grizz has been working with the silent girl all morning. She sits down with us for lunch, looking almost at ease.

"Eva," he says gently, "I'd like to introduce you to my friends."

He introduces each of us in turn. We smile and tell Eva we're pleased to meet her. Eva smiles shyly at each of us. She doesn't meet our eyes, keeping hers averted, looking down. She is young, no older than we are. Her face bears scars, but is still pretty. Eva is the tallest person we've met on this side of the brane, almost five feet tall.

"Eva," Grizz says," can you tell my friends the story you just told me?"

Eva nods and begins her story.

"I can start with stories my people tell about our past," she says. "My home is a three-quarter-moon's walk from this place. When the waters rose in the old days, the land all around my people was flooded, but our lands had been on a hill, and the waters never rose to cover it. We found ourselves on an island, far away from others. We knew we were lucky. The world around us was in chaos. Neighbors fought neighbors, and there was much killing and starvation. My people were left to raise crops and tend our animals in peace.

"Our good fortune ended when the Leader's people found us. They call themselves the Sons of 1776. Before they found us, the Sons moved like the winds, never staying in any one place over a season or two. They never intended to leave this area because the workshop and the chem lab were here. However, a group of people called the Salvadorans came to these lands and drove the Sons away. During the next hundred seasons, plague weakened the Salvadorans, and the Sons were able to push them out and reclaim their lands.

"On one of their journeys, the Sons murdered a band of people who had a far-seeing tube. For us, this was a disaster. When the Sons looked at our island through the far-seeing tube, they could tell people lived on the island. The Sons had never lost the ability to travel across water, and within one season, they invaded our island and conquered our people.

"The rest of my story I can tell from my own memory," she says. "The Sons killed many of my people and made slaves of the rest. They allowed us to continue growing food, but now we grew it for the Sons. Once the Sons had a steady source of food, they didn't need to wander as much as they had before.

"Every season, the Sons visit the workshop and the chem lab, hoping to find strangers who have solved the mystery of the doors."

They almost did, I think, but I don't say anything.

"Every member of the Sons is taught the secret of the door. They can recite the code: L-O-S-T-4-8-15-16-23-42-H-U-R-L-E-Y, but they've lost the ability to identify written letters and numbers. To them, *L* is just a sound. They don't know how to match up the sounds and the dials on the door, because they don't know the sound *el* corresponds to the symbol *L*. My people kept alive some of the old learning. But we played dumb when the Sons brought us to the doors. We never knew what lay behind the doors, but we knew that if the Sons wanted it, we didn't want them to have it. Once in a while, one of our people would run away, hoping to open the door and find miracles inside that we could use to free ourselves from slavery. But the Sons always caught and killed them in the desert. And now that I've seen what lies behind the door, I realize we wouldn't have known how to use the workshop even if we had gained access to it."

We thought the workshop had been built by crazy survivalists, and we were right. And the survivalists had a great plan. As years went by, the workshop and the chem lab would have given the Sons of 1776 great technical superiority over their neighbors. They could easily have built an empire. Eva's story also explains why she is as tall as she is. Isolated on their island, tending their farms and animals, her people never wanted for food.

After absorbing all that I'd heard, I ask, "And so you were with a party that had come to check out the workshop?"

"Yes," Eva responds. "They brought me to cook meals and clean their clothes for them. They always travel with at least one slave."

"This chem lab you spoke of," asks Kenny, "do you know where it is?"

"Yes, I do," replies Eva. "I've been there three or four times."

"How far is it from here?" asks Kenny.

"It is not very far," answers Eva. "It's a two-sun walk from here."

Kenny is wearing a smile that stretches from ear to ear. She can't wait to get to the chem lab. We embrace Eva. She flinches at the first embrace, but realizes we mean the contact as a sign of friendship and affection. She responds with a small smile.

"You're one of us now, Eva," Grizz says kindly. "We'll do everything we can to keep you safe."

Eva looks at my swollen face, and I can tell she wonders just how safe she will be.

Grizz grabs a shovel and an AK-47 and leaves us. He's going to drag the bodies of the three Sons of 1776 out into the desert and bury them.

I go back to work on my plan for making war on the blacksuits. By dinnertime, I'm done. Over dinner, I outline my plans for my friends.

"Am I missing anything?" I ask. "Is there anything we should add to the plan?"

"I like it," says Bree. "I like it a lot."

"I can't wait to take the fight to the blacksuits," says Kenny fiercely. "They will be sooo surprised when *we* come after *them*."

"Think what this'll mean to the villagers," says Grizz. "After hundreds of years of suffering, they'll finally be able to fight back."

We speak for a while about details of the plan, and I finish up by summarizing, "I'll leave tomorrow and discuss the plan with Helen. If she agrees to it, we'll set everything in motion. Kenny, we'll need wolf bane. Tons of it. Bree, we'll also need those radio towers. I'll leave all my extra food here so you can continue to work uninterrupted. We'll send a party back with more food, and a bunch of people to help you make more wolf bane."

Grizz says, "I'll go back with you, ET. Traveling alone is dangerous."

"I'd like the company," I reply. I've always enjoyed Grizz's company. I just hope we can keep things from getting awkward.

"Eva, would you mind staying here and helping Kenny?" I ask. "She's going to need lots of help making the wolf bane. I promise you that once we've dealt with the Court, we'll help you free your people from the Sons."

Eva seems uneasy about staying. She anxiously looks at Grizz.

"Kenny will take very good care of you," Grizz assures. "I'll be back in eight or nine suns. I also promise you that we'll do everything we can to free your people once we've beaten the Court."

"We'll have fun, Eva," says Kenny enthusiastically. "We're gonna get smelly, but we'll have fun."

Eva nods, eyes still averted.

"ET, don't forget that I'm gonna need lots of rotting plants for the wolf bane," Kenny reminds me. "There aren't many plants on this side of the mountains, so people are gonna have to bring them from the other side."

"I'll make arrangements with Helen. I'm sure we'll find lots of villagers happy to keep you supplied."

Before we turn in for the night, Grizz enters the dormitory carrying a long rod with a brush on the end, a soft-looking white cloth, and a bottle of black liquid, which he identifies as gun oil.

"If we want to keep our AKs working, we'll have to learn to clean them," he says as he stuffs the cleaning supplies into his backpack. "I cleaned the barrel of mine before I left the workshop this afternoon. It was full of gunk, but once I cleaned it out, it worked."

Thank heaven for that, I think.

* * * * *

Grizz and I leave in the morning as soon as there's enough light to travel. We carry AKs, and we've each strapped an extra one across our shoulders. Our packs are crammed with extra clips. It'll be nice to beef up our firepower at the Sanctuary. If we'd had these the day the blacksuits overran our positions, the battle might have turned out very differently. Due to my cracked ribs, Grizz is carrying most of our supplies on his back.

Traveling with Grizz is pleasant, and I'm very careful to keep my feelings under tight control.

"You did a brave thing, Grizz, when you led those bots away."

"Like I said at the time, we couldn't afford to lose either Bree or Kenny. And I couldn't have stood losing you," he says.

"How did you think I'd feel about losing you? Grizz, you've been in my life since we were barely out of diapers. You're a part of me. When I thought you were gone forever, it was like a big piece of me died."

Grizz thinks this over. I know he wants to talk more about his feelings for me, but he promised he'd never mention them again. I want to talk about my feelings for him, but then I bring to mind a picture of Tyler. Tyler, who had trusted me. Tyler, who will live the rest of his life as a cripple. I swallow the words I want to say.

So neither of us says anything. How did we let it come to this?

We climb up to the saddle and peer cautiously at the sky on the other side. If there is so much as one dark cloud in the sky, I'm going to turn around and head back down. I'm not about to get caught in another blizzard. We can try again tomorrow. The sky turns out to be bright blue from horizon to horizon. We cross the saddle and begin to descend the other side.

My finger is throbbing, and my ribs ache, but the pain is manageable. We make it almost all the way down the western side of the saddle, and it's almost time to stop for the day.

"Grizz, let's see if we can climb the face of the mountain over that way," I say, pointing north. "The blacksuits have a mining operation going on over there, and I'd like to take a look at it."

We pick our way across the face of the mountain until we're several hundred feet above the blacksuits' mining camp. We do our best to keep behind rocks and trees, to avoid being seen from below. We find a spot with a good view of the terrain off to the west, and I train the binoculars on the scene below.

The mining camp is huge. There is a village for the slaves that must easily be large enough to accommodate forty or fifty thousand people. No walls surround the village, because the forest is not dense enough here to support dreadwolves. The buildings are the same mud-and-wattle structures we have seen in Phoenix and Detroit. At least ten thousand acres are under cultivation. There is a road leading off to the west, back toward the Court's cities. I can easily see from here the way the scattering of trees around the settlement below gradually thickens into the forest we know so well.

At the western edge of the encampment is a blacksuit fort that looks about twice the size of their fort near Phoenix. Even without the fear of dreadwolves, the blacksuits have built a fort here, probably to keep villagers from cutting their throats in the middle of the night. There's another large building adjoining the fort.

"Do you think that fort looks about twice the size of the blacksuits' village fort near Phoenix?" I ask.

Grizz studies the fort for a moment. "I'd say so."

"If the fort near Phoenix is built for a garrison of twenty, then this fort should have a garrison of about forty?" I ask.

"Sounds reasonable."

"Any idea what the building next to the fort might be for?"

"I was wondering about that, too," says Grizz. "An arsenal? Storage? A jail? I don't know."

I've seen all I need to see. Grizz and I scramble back the way we came and set up camp near the bottom of the mountain. We decide against a fire, because of our proximity to the mining camp. We don't need to use wolf bane this far from the forest.

I fall asleep with my head full of plans and schemes. I wake during the night because I've managed to roll over onto my broken finger. I doze again and dream of Walt and the other two Sons of 1776. I wake with a start, drenched in sweat.

* * * * *

"I'm sorry I couldn't get to you until after they'd hurt you," says Grizz the next morning.

"You got there as soon as you could," I reply. "Don't let it worry you."

I know this has been bothering Grizz. He has failed in his life's "Mission to Protect ET."

"If you hadn't come when you did, they'd have hurt me a lot worse," I say.

* * * * *

I think back to a day when Grizz and I were both fifth graders in Mr. Lawrence's class. Mr. Lawrence had this really cool ball that he used to demonstrate static electricity. There was red lightning that forked around inside the ball in a more or less random fashion until you touched the surface. Then, the lightning would be attracted to your fingers. Kids loved it.

One day at recess, Grizz and I volunteered to put mail in everybody's mailbox, the sort of elementary school mail that kids took home every day: graded papers, an announcement about the bake sale the PTA is running to buy playground equipment, a notice that somebody in third grade had head lice, and so on.

We finished the mail before the kids came back from recess, so I decided to play with the lightning ball. Only I dropped it. When I picked it up, there was a crack in it, and the lightning didn't work anymore. I carefully put the broken ball back on its stand and hurried to my seat because I could hear kids coming back from recess.

Later that afternoon, Mr. Lawrence noticed the ball was broken. He asked the class how the ball had been broken. I was sitting in my seat with a little devil whispering in one ear, "Don't say a word," and a little angel whispering in my other ear, "Confess."

I'm not sure which one would have won, because Grizz raised his hand and said, "I broke it."

At this point, I had to confess. I couldn't let Grizz take the blame for something I had done. So I came out and said, "No, he didn't, Mr. Lawrence. I did it."

To which Grizz, of course, said, "No, she didn't. I did it."

Mr. Lawrence found this highly amusing. "I'm sure it was an accident, whoever did it." He smiled.

This little experience taught me a lesson: Don't wait for somebody to ask. If you do something, confess right away. Otherwise, Grizz will take the blame, and I'll feel awful.

* * * * *

We arrive back at the Sanctuary near sunset on the fourth day of our journey. Acolytes quickly lower the rope ladder. "The Daughter of Gaia has returned," I can hear them say as they alert others in the

Sanctuary. Climbing the ladder is difficult because of my finger and ribs, so by the time I make it to the top, the whole population of the Sanctuary is waiting for us.

Helen is beaming until she sees my face. "What happened to your face, dear?" she asks.

"I ran into some bad people," I say. "Not blacksuits, different evil men."

We proceed to tell the story of my encounter with the Sons of 1776.

When I've finished, Helen notes, "It's near dinnertime. Why don't you have your wounds attended to and then come down for dinner?"

"I'm glad you're back." Tyler beams and throws his arms around me. The hug hurts my ribs, but I don't say anything.

"Good to see you again, ET," says Chase. "You look lovely."

I see my new friends Bertram and Falstaff as well, and they hug me too. Despite my split lip, I can't stifle a smile. It's good to be back.

Sisters fuss over my wounds for a few minutes, and then I head to the main cavern for dinner.

"I have two pieces of bad news for you," says Helen once we have been seated. "The brane has not opened again. And the blacksuits took their revenge for the three brigades we buried. They have killed every man, woman, and child in Phoenix."

I feel as though someone has punched me in the stomach. I look at once to Bertram and Falstaff.

"Fortunately, Bertram and Falstaff were with us at the time. We have pieced together the story from six villagers who escaped by tunneling under the outer wall," Helen continues. "The blacksuits killed them all slowly. It took them three days to kill everyone. They made parents watch as they killed their children. Then they made wives watch as they slaughtered their husbands. And then they killed the women."

I'm speechless. "I'm so sorry," I blurt at last. "If I had known, we never would've blown up the cave entrance."

"There is nothing to be sorry for," says Helen. "Those villagers died for our cause. The last words from their lips were: 'We die for the Daughter of Gaia and the revolution.' They died for the good of us all, and they knew it. How much better it is to die for something than for nothing."

I'm unhappy to hear that the villagers died for the "Daughter of Gaia." What makes me worth dying for? Why me? I ask myself again.

"Please tell them about the workshop," I ask Grizz. I don't want to talk right now.

Grizz describes the workshop. His voice rises in excitement as he runs down the list of things we found. His excitement is infectious. Each new revelation is greeted with a murmur of surprise and enthusiasm.

"Are we now ready to make war on the Court?" Helen asks when Grizz is finished.

"Yes," says Grizz. "And the Daughter of Gaia has a plan."

Helen looks at me. "Please, child. Tell us of your plan."

"If we carry out my plan, the reaction of the blacksuits will be brutal," I warn. "Thousands of us will die."

"We are ready to die," says Helen. "Our lives are short, hard, and filled with pain. We don't value life the way the city people do. If you had been among us through the ages of gleaning and hunger and brutality we've survived, you would understand us better."

"Helen speaks the truth," says Bertram.

"We are ready to pay any price," adds Falstaff. "To us, the deaths of those in Phoenix were noble."

"Please, Daughter of Gaia, tell us of your plan."

219

D.S. Northrop

20

"There are many parts to my plan, and each will be difficult," I begin. "First, we must realize that we now *own* the night. We can do things and go places the blacksuits cannot.

"Even as we speak, my friends at the workshop are making wolf bane. But they will need help, because we will need thousands of pots of wolf bane to support all of our plans. So we must send at least a dozen villagers to the workshop to help Kenny.

"If we move quickly, twenty suns from now, we'll have enough wolf bane to support two very important missions. One mission will be to head west to spread the word of our plans to every village. And the other mission will be to send a group to the east, also spreading the news. Tell every villager to sharpen their weapons and their skills.

"As your messengers reach each new village, tell them we need whatever food they can spare. We will also need at least ten young people from each village. And, tell every village we need more empty jars for wolf bane. Have them make as many jars as they can. We'll also need extra food to keep our workers at the workshop fed, and we'll need people to move full jars of wolf bane back to the villages.

"Within three moons, we should have enough wolf bane in the villages to allow us to start the second phase of our war. I understand that the blacksuits change the guards at each of their forts every new moon. They send a party from the outer ring of forts to relieve the blacksuits who have just spent a month in the village fort."

Helen nods in agreement.

"Then, on the night before the third new moon, counting from today, every village must send out warriors with wolf bane to find good positions to ambush the blacksuits. When the blacksuits come out of their forts in the morning for their daily patrols, we'll be waiting for them. On the next day, we'll ambush the blacksuits' relief force coming from the inner ring of forts. This done, we'll storm the forts and kill any blacksuits remaining inside. When this is done, we'll burn the forts to the ground."

I pause and look around the table. "Does everyone understand what I have said so far?"

"Yes, Erin, we understand," says Helen. "By the end of that day, the blacksuits will no longer have forts to launch their daily patrols." Others nod enthusiastically.

I continue. "The blacksuits will try to rebuild their forts. But they'll need to leave their construction sites well before sunset each night to avoid the dreadwolves. When they leave, your warriors will destroy whatever they have built during the day. At this point, you will have broken the blacksuits' ability to watch over your every move."

"On a daily basis, you must hide a part of what you have harvested outside the village. Hide it well, because the blacksuits will look everywhere for it. Hide only enough food to keep you from hunger. Leave the rest for the blacksuits.

"Even though the blacksuits will no longer be able to watch over you as they do now, there's no way we can prevent them from collecting taxes. No single village can fight off four or five brigades of blacksuits.

"So, the third phase of our war will be to set up a string of runners reaching from the blacksuits' outer ring of forts to our villages. Because we have the wolf bane, we'll be able to position our runners right next to the fort, so they'll see the moment the blacksuits open their gates in the morning to begin their march. At the first sign the blacksuits are coming, your runners must relay the information that the blacksuits are coming. When the warning comes, evacuate the village. Hide your people in the forest. If you stay a half dayswalk from the advance of the blacksuits, they'll never be able to catch you without being caught by dreadwolves on their return march. When the blacksuits arrive, they can collect their taxes, but they'll never again be able to glean our young ones."

I pause for a moment. People around the table begin to buzz with excitement.

"But why not hide all our food from the blacksuits?" asks Falstaff.

"Because we must keep the blacksuits dependent on us. If we don't, they'll burn our villages to the ground and destroy everything we've planted. They won't let us win if they have the means to defeat us."

"What if the blacksuits stay in the village? What if they stay and wait for us to return?" asks Bertram.

"Let them," I say. "Spread your people among the neighboring villages. Help them clear more land to plant more food. The blacksuits will tire of waiting once they realize you won't return until they leave.

"In the fourth phase of our war, we'll take the blacksuits' outer ring of forts. In order to succeed we'll need two things: new weapons, which we're now building at the workshop, and an army of trained soldiers."

Helen looks dubious. "We cannot possibly feed such an army. If we don't work our fields every day, we starve."

"I think I have a partial solution for that problem as well. We'll soon know."

"For the final phase of our war," I say, "we'll take New Washington itself. To do that, I'll need the help of my friend Orsino."

Orsino looks up, startled.

"I need Orsino to teach me the layout of the Court's forts and cities inside the outer ring. We need to know the strengths and the weaknesses of the blacksuits' inner defenses.

"And since there'll be at least two more gleanings before we can put a stop to them, I want every child who might be gleaned taught to deliver a message to the slaves of the inner villages. Tell them we'll need their help when the final moment comes. We'll tell them what we need when the time is right. And be sure to let them know: the Daughter of Gaia is coming."

* * * * *

When I sit down, the room explodes in cheers. The cheering continues for a long time. People chant, "Bless the Daughter of Gaia," over and over again. I'm embarrassed. It's not that I don't enjoy the adulation, but I haven't done much to earn it.

Helen takes the seat next to me.

"You have done well, Daughter of Gaia. Our rebellion begins tonight." Tears stream down Helen's face. "Will you please come with me? I have a matter of extreme importance I want to discuss with you."

I follow her to her sitting room.

"I would like you to join our order," Helen says. "You are the Daughter of Gaia in name, and I would like to invite you to become the Daughter of Gaia in practice, as well. If you agree, you will become a member of the sisterhood."

I'm surprised. I struggle for a moment to understand what Helen has just said.

"Let me be clear. If you join the sisterhood, you will pledge to remain on this side of the brane. You would also make a pledge of chastity. Sisters never marry."

I think about my situation with Tyler and my feelings for Grizz. I can never marry Grizz without wounding Tyler deeply. The vow of chastity is not a serious concern, given the Ty and Grizz situation.

More troubling by far is the vow to remain on this side of the brane. I think of my family and all my dreams back in Tucson. The brane might never open again, but if it did…

"May I think about your offer for a few days before I answer?" I ask.

"Of course, child," answers Helen. "I would have worried if you had made a decision on the spot. You are far too practical to make a decision of such consequence without due consideration."

"Thank you, Helen. I'll give you my answer soon."

* * * * *

Later that evening, my friends and I are sitting on our mattresses, catching up on what has happened since our group left for the workshop.

Grizz tells Chase and Tyler about our journey to the workshop, and I fill in the details about the Sons of 1776. We describe the blacksuits' mining operation, and I tell them that with their help, we'll be taking the blacksuits' mines away from them.

Tyler and Chase have nearly finished the elevator. It needs a few finishing touches, but the Sisters can do all the remaining work. It should be operational within a day or two.

Then, I ask them if they object to all the special attention I've been getting.

"We're a team," I conclude. "The villagers can call me the Daughter of Gaia all they want. Without you, I won't accomplish a thing."

"From the looks of your face and your finger, I'd say being the Daughter of Gaia is a pretty tough job," replies Tyler. "*I* don't want it."

"That's good, Ty," laughs Grizz. "I don't think you're cut out to be the Daughter of Gaia."

"I don't have any problem with the Daughter of Gaia thing as long as you don't start telling us to fetch your breakfast or wash your clothes," says Chase, smiling.

"Okay," I agree. "No breakfast fetching or clothes washing. I'll make a note of that."

"You aren't going to start having scary visions like Helen, are you?" asks Tyler.

"The only vision I have is of me getting a good night's sleep," I answer.

I lie on my mattress, staring at the ceiling, long after my friends have gone to sleep. I listen to the sounds of their breathing.

Do I want to commit myself to live in this world? I think of how the people of this world have cheered for their "Daughter of Gaia," and how they have put so much faith in me. Can I deliver what they need? And can I abandon my family, if the brane were to reopen? In my mind's eye, I picture my mother, my father, and the twins. My mind is in deep turmoil. Neither option seems acceptable. Finally, I close my eyes, force my mind to clear, and breathe deeply. The answer still eludes me.

* * * * *

First thing in the morning, I spend a couple hours with Orsino. He explains to me that more farms and a ring of factories are located inside the outer ring of forts. Then, there is an inner ring of three forts surrounding the "suburbs" of Bethesda, Chevy Chase, and Arlington. And the Court's quarters are surrounded by the largest fortress of them all. The "wealthy" live in the suburbs. The *very* wealthy live in New Washington itself. As he describes the layout, I draw a map.

"There is a map of all the fortifications and troop locations in the blacksuit headquarters located in New Washington," says Orsino.

"We may have to figure out a way to visit them and see if they'll make a copy of their defenses for us. All in all, it sounds like there'll be some hard work involved in the endgame," I say.

"That's putting it lightly," Orsino agrees.

After meeting with Orsino, I find Falstaff and take him with me to see Helen.

"I'd like to borrow Falstaff and about forty others who know how to fight," I say. "I want to take the blacksuits' mining operation away from them."

Helen looks startled.

"I assume you have a plan," says Falstaff.

"I do. It's at least two dayswalks from the blacksuits' outer ring of forts to the mines. I know this, because I just spent the better part of three days getting from the bottom of the saddle to the Sanctuary."

"It would be at least two dayswalks," agrees Falstaff.

"That means the blacksuits must have a fort between the outer ring and the mines. They need a place to spend an overnight safe from the dreadwolves," I say.

"True," Falstaff confirms.

"If we blow a wall off that fort at night, the dreadwolves will take care of the garrison for us."

Falstaff and Helen both nod. "That's correct," Helen agrees. "But how are you going to take the fortress that guards the mines themselves?"

"I have a little trick up my sleeve," I say. "I want Falstaff to lead the blacksuit relief column. Can the Sisters sew forty blacksuit uniforms?" I ask.

227

"Yes," says Helen. "We could make ordinary garments and stain them black with bitternut dye."

"How long will it take to make the uniforms?" I ask.

"We should have the clothes ready in six or seven suns."

"How soon can you find forty soldiers for Falstaff, and a dozen men and women to help Kenny at the workshop?" I ask.

"The courtsmen are repopulating Phoenix by imposing a special gleaning on the other villages," Falstaff responds. "They will, however, require many moons to bring Phoenix back to its former size. Since Phoenix currently has only a few inhabitants, we will need to ask for volunteers from Detroit, and from Seattle, which is the closest village to the east. We'll need at least three days to assemble the forces we need, if we travel both night and day."

"There's no need to hurry," I say, "as long as they're here by the time the uniforms are ready. Helen, can you put together enough food to keep our operation at the workshop going for a couple weeks? We'll need to have enough food to keep our workshop staff supplied until another expedition can reach them. Plus, Falstaff and his force will be in the field about two weeks. Remember, food supplies from the other villages should begin rolling in soon," I remind her.

"I'll take care of all the details right now," says Helen.

* * * * *

My next job is to corral Grizz, Tyler, and Chase.

"What do you guys say to a little AK-47 practice?" I ask.

"We're one ahead of you there, ET. We were out earlier," says Chase.

"I'll keep you company," offers Tyler.

228

One by one, I master the fundamentals of the AK-47. Single shot. Continuous fire. When you're on continuous fire, you have to work like mad to keep the AK level, because the barrel wants to climb. Release the clip and insert a new one. Tyler is the perfect teacher, patient and supportive. As I try to align the sights, I realize that the AK-47 was never meant to be a sniper's rifle. At least the one I'm using wasn't. Great for hosing down lots of bad guys at fairly close range, but if they're more than a hundred yards away, forget about it.

"I couldn't hit anything at long range either, ET," Tyler reassures me.

* * * * *

At dinner that evening, we review our plans. I also tell Helen about the radios.

"We'll have enough radios to place four of them in villages. That'll reduce the amount of time it takes to communicate with all the villages. We won't have to send runners from here to all forty-nine of the other villages. If we place the radios well, we'll be able to communicate with every village within a matter of five or six suns. That will be especially important once we launch our attacks on the outer ring."

Helen is, as always, awed by the technology. The concept of standing in the workshop and talking to someone in the Sanctuary seems like magic to her.

* * * * *

The following morning I awake to find Tyler seated in the chair nearest my bed, reading a book he brought with him from Tucson. He sees I'm awake.

229

"After breakfast, we're planning to learn to disassemble the AKs, and also how to clean them. Interested?" he asks.

After breakfast, we learn, by trial and error, how to dismantle and reassemble an AK-47. Once we've done it a few times, it seems easy. We take turns with the brush and rag, cleaning our barrels. And although we're not entirely sure what parts need to be oiled, we intuit by looking for places that look oily to begin with. We must not have done anything too ruinous, because after we've finished cleaning and oiling, the AKs still work.

Days go by quickly as we wait for the Sisters to finish sewing the uniforms. Every day my ribs feel better, and my face begins to mend. I spend a lot of time on top of Sanctuary Hill, mulling over Helen's offer. Life here is hard, but it's also rewarding. I have the ability to do important things. But I don't know if I want to become a Sister. Surely I could continue to help the villagers without joining the Sisters' order?

On our third day at the Sanctuary, Grizz comes up to join me as the sun is sinking in the western sky. The sky is already taking on a red-and-salmon hue, hinting at a beautiful sunset to come. Grizz plops down next to me.

"I found you," he announces.

We sit in companionable silence for a few minutes, watching the sky turn colors.

"How do you feel about being stuck on this side of the brane?" I ask.

"It's really not so bad here," Grizz responds. "I really like the villagers. They're so friendly and so…stoic. Falstaff is quite a guy. I'm getting to know him well. I guess, to answer your question, I feel really good about what we're doing here. Life here isn't so bad. Except for the food. But once we shut down the blacksuits' village forts, villagers will be free to grow anything they like."

"If the brane opened tomorrow, would you go back?" I ask.

"That would depend on what *you* did," Grizz replies.

I was afraid he'd say that. I don't know how to respond. To steer the conversation into a safer channel, I change the subject. "Look at that," I say, and point to a beetle struggling to carry a load three times his own size.

"He's an ambitious little guy, isn't he?" says Grizz.

I play the scene that happened next over in my mind a hundred times, and I still can't figure out exactly how it happened. One minute Grizz and I are leaning toward each other, looking at the little beetle, and the next minute we're kissing. Grizz throws his arms around me, and I throw mine around him. I pull him as close to me as my strength allows and want him closer still. I'm flooded with warmth and pleasure. I ache inside, the kind of ache that comes from wanting something deeply.

Finally, I get a grip on myself and pull away. "I can't, Grizz. I just can't," I whisper. There's Tyler to think about. And then there's the fact that I don't want Grizz to stay in this world just because of me. I want him to do whatever is best for him.

I climb quickly down the hill and go looking for Helen.

"I have the answer to your proposal," I announce when I've found her.

"I know that you will make the right decision, although I have to confess that I do not know what your answer will be. My visions have given me no indication of your decision. I have lucid visions of you leading us to victory, but I honestly don't know whether you will join the sisterhood. I will rejoice with you whatever you decide."

"The faith your people place in me binds me to them," I say simply. "They seem to need me. I'm terribly afraid I'll disappoint them in the end, but I pledge myself to do everything I possibly can."

Helen smiles. "Bless you, child. Would tomorrow be too soon for us to hold your initiation ceremony?"

"Tomorrow will be fine," I reply.

231

* * * * *

After lunch the next day, I follow Helen to a large room that I know is used by the Sisters for meditation. The sconces on the wall are dark. The only light comes from candles. The Sisters carry one candle each. They stand in two lines, one line facing the other, their faces made gentle by the soft glow of candlelight. At the end of the aisle formed by the Sisters' lines is a low table covered by a cloth made of softbark, light blue in color. A bowl on the table is flanked by two candles, glowing softly. Helen moves to stand behind the table.

"Please come," Helen urges gently.

I walk slowly down the aisle formed by the Sisters. I stop when I reach the table.

Helen holds her hands, palm down, over the bowl, which contains water.

"Mother, please bless this water, your gift to us, and the source of all life."

The Sisters repeat, "Mother, please bless this water, your gift to us, and the source of all life."

"Please kneel, child," requests Helen.

I go down on my knees.

"Do you, Erin Taylor, renounce all worldly goods and desires?" asks Helen.

"Yes, I do."

"Do you promise to serve our people to the best of your ability?"

"Yes, I do."

Helen dampens her fingers in the water. She reaches over the table and touches my forehead with her damp fingers. "I anoint you in the name of Father, the creator," she says.

She dampens her fingers a second time and touches my chin. "I anoint you in the name of Mother, the sustainer."

She dampens her fingers and this time touches my right cheek. "I anoint you in the name of Mother Earth."

Once more she touches me with water, this time my left cheek. "And I anoint you in the name of heaven above. You may rise, and face your sisters." She smiles.

"Please welcome Sister Erin into the Disciples of the Mother," concludes Helen.

One by one, the Sisters embrace me and whisper, "Welcome, Sister Erin. Welcome, Daughter of Gaia."

Afterward, Helen embraces me and whispers, "The Sanctuary will always be a home for you. Welcome to our order, Daughter of Gaia."

"Thank you," I reply. "I'll do my best."

I decide not to tell my friends about my decision to join the Sisters' order. I fear Grizz and Tyler would both feel bound to remain with me on this side of the brane, and, if the brane reopens, I want them to make the choice that's best for them. My friends are accustomed to the villagers calling me the Daughter of Gaia. They'll have no way of knowing that I've now become the de jure Daughter of Gaia.

I thought my feelings would be a mad jumble at this point. What I feel, instead, is a sense of peace. My life has a purpose. I'm still not certain I can meet everyone's expectations, but I'll do everything I can. There'll be no more self-doubt, just commitment.

D.S. Northrop

21

We're a large party as we leave the Sanctuary. We have a dozen villagers who will be harvesting plant matter and remaining at the workshop to help boost production of wolf bane. Falstaff has forty warriors who will help us capture the blacksuits' forts. Grizz, Tyler, and Chase are with us as well. Ty, though still hobbling on his bad knee, is no slower than the villagers. Chase is still limping almost imperceptibly, but I examined his ankle before we left, and despite an angry red scar, his wound is healing well.

We move slowly, our pace determined by Falstaff and the villagers. I fall in beside Falstaff as we walk.

"Will your men and women be ready to fight?" I ask.

"They'll be ready," Falstaff replies. "Remember, our people have kept their weapons skills. The courtsmen have forbidden us to practice, but we hide our weapons well. Every day, our young men and women spend time practicing. And Mother knows we have motivation. Don't worry about us, Daughter of Gaia. When the time comes, we'll fight like demons."

I avoid Grizz on the march. I can see the hurt in his eyes, but my own feelings are too strong, too raw. Close contact with Grizz would be agonizing for both of us. I desperately want to run to him, to hold him, to kiss him, but I know I can't. So I suffer alone.

During the march, I make a point of speaking with each villager in our group. I've never been great with names, but I want to know the names of the men and women who'll be fighting and dying with us. I've decided the Daughter of Gaia will be a hands-on leader.

At the end of our second day, Falstaff dispatches two of his soldiers to infiltrate the villagers' quarters near the mines. Their job will be to pass word among the villagers that, when the time comes, they should be ready to rise up and overwhelm their overseers.

Midway through our third day, I decide we've traveled far enough to the east. We make a turn and head north. This should bring us through the woods to the point where the blacksuits will have built their overnight fort, halfway between the outermost village fort and the mines. I send Grizz and Chase to scout ahead, ranging to the east and west until they find the blacksuits' fort. They return in the late afternoon. They've found it.

When we reach the blacksuits' fortress, I'm very happy to find they haven't cleared the trees to give themselves a good field of fire. Because this position is more than a dayswalk from the nearest village, the blacksuits are not expecting to be attacked. They haven't even bothered to build an observation tower. They do, however, post sentries on each wall. But with trees close to the fort, our bowmen will be able to target the sentries without breaking cover.

We've arrived a day before the relief garrison is due at the fort. We back off several miles and pitch camp for the night. The following day goes slowly as we wait for nightfall. We send spies to keep an eye on the fort, and they return late in the afternoon with news that the relief column has arrived.

* * * * *

Grizz, Chase, Tyler, Falstaff, and I go over our plans. From my backpack, I produce two bricks of C4 explosive, a spindle of wire, and a sealed jar with Kenny's "voltaic pile" detonator solution. My friends and Falstaff will each take a side of the fort. On my whistle, they'll take out the four sentries. I'll lay the C4 charges along the wall nearest our camp, string wire, and detonate the plastique. The dreadwolves should do the rest.

236

We wait nervously for darkness. We'll be using bows and arrows to eliminate the sentries. At the first sound of an AK, the walls will be covered with blacksuits, and I need a little time to place the C4 and run the wire to the detonating solution. Every shot must be a kill shot, because all four sentries wear horns. Fortunately, the sentries will almost certainly be relaxed because they'll never expect an attack so far from the villages.

We hear the first dreadwolf cry. In moments, we're surrounded by howling dreadwolves, but they never come closer than twenty feet. Nonetheless, there are a lot of them, they are noisy, and they make me nervous. We wait another three hours, giving the blacksuits plenty of time to settle in for the night. Falstaff brings his men close to the wall on the side on which I'll be planting explosives. If anything goes wrong, they'll provide me with cover by picking off anybody who pokes his head above the wall. I wait several minutes, allowing Grizz, Tyler, and Chase to get into position. I whistle. Time to go.

I sprint for the wall. Someone missed a sentry, because I hear the blast of a horn from inside the fort. I plant the first block of C4, insert the wire, and move down the wall to plant the second. I hear the noise made by blacksuits rolling out of bed and rushing to man the walls. I plant the second brick of C4 and insert the second wire. I scuttle backward toward the trees, spooling out wire as I go.

I'm aware of the sounds of battle going on around me. The blacksuits are on the wall above me, and are engaged with Falstaff and his men behind me. An arrow hits the ground right between my feet. I hear another as it whizzes past my ear. I'm almost to the trees when I feel a burning pain in my side. A brief glance tells me the arrow must have grazed me because there's nothing sticking out of my side. *Crud!* I think. *My ribs were just healing, and now I'm hurt again.*

I snip the wire from the spool, yell, "Everybody down!" and dip the end of the wire into the detonator solution. The two blocks of C4 go off in tandem. I feel the concussion from the blast and, afterward, raise my head to admire my handiwork. There's a gaping hole in the wall.

Dreadwolves are pouring through the breach. I listen to the cries of the blacksuits as the dreadwolves find them. It's an awful sound, and I'm grateful when it ends, moments after it began. Falstaff and his men take the golden badges from the dead blacksuits and pin them on their own shirts. The gold badges are the one thing we couldn't manufacture at the Sanctuary. Unless the sentry on duty at the fort at the mines is hyper vigilant, he'll never know we're not the real relief party, until it's too late.

By destroying this fort, we've made it impossible for the blacksuits to travel to the mines. We'll need to sweep the forest every night and burn down any new construction the blacksuits are attempting. But the mines will soon be ours.

My wound is painful, and I see why as I examine it with my flashlight. The arrow took a huge chunk of flesh along with it as it passed me by. Blood is flowing freely, and I dig around in my backpack until I find a wad of gauze I can stuff into the wound. Grizz is quickly by my side, and he keeps pressure on the wound until the blood begins to clot.

Falstaff's men and women are hacking branches from trees and piling them up along all four walls of the fort. When the piles grow large, they set them on fire. We watch the fort as it burns, crackling and sending sparks into the night sky. We bury what's left of the dead blacksuits, and two of our own soldiers, and make camp for the night.

* * * * *

We spend the next several hours on the march, stopping when we reach a point near the mines. As the sun rises, Falstaff, my friends, and I move cautiously forward to get a better look at the blacksuits' fort.

"This one looks like the other forts we've seen," says Chase. "It might be a little bigger."

Falstaff, who has never before seen the fort, agrees that, based on its size, the garrison inside will probably be about forty strong. "It'll be tricky trying to overwhelm the defenders before they know what's happening, but I think we can pull it off," he says. "If it's like other forts, there'll be a barracks, a dining area, officer's quarters, and an armory. I've split my force into teams, so we'll be hitting each building at exactly the same time. Another team will pick off the sentries."

My friends and I will wait outside the fort. In the heat of battle, we may not be able to distinguish Falstaff's soldiers from the blacksuits. Falstaff doesn't think he'll need us, anyway. And his people will be anxious to extract a little revenge on their own.

There are thousands of villagers working in the fields. Every few minutes, a party of villagers descends into or emerges from the mines that dot the foothills of the northern Twin. There are armed overseers at posts observing the laborers. We'll be able to take the fort, but overwhelming the overseers will be a task for the villagers themselves.

We wait patiently in the forest. Based on our experience with blacksuit practices, we guess the relief column usually arrives at the fort around 6:00 p.m. At 5:30, Falstaff forms up his column and advances on the fort. When they reach the gates, the sentry in the tower calls out, and Falstaff responds. The gates swing open, and Falstaff's party enters the fort.

I am exultant! Our ruse worked! Next, the gates swing closed, and we hear the beginning of the battle inside. All we can do is wait and watch. Villagers near the fort hear the commotion inside and begin to attack their overseers. Fifteen minutes after they closed, the gates of the fort open again. Falstaff appears and waves us in.

"The plan worked perfectly," says Falstaff. "We took three casualties, and five of the blacksuits surrendered. The ones who surrendered will make excellent farmers."

"Let's give the blacksuit prisoners a choice," I say. "They can stay with us or head out on their own. If they leave, they can either head back into the forest or climb over the saddle. Either way, they won't live long. I don't want to force them to work. If we did, we'd be just like them. We can't offer them *good* choices, but we can let them decide for themselves."

"As you wish," says Falstaff.

I can tell he doesn't approve of giving the blacksuits options, but I know he'll follow my instructions.

"The villagers did a good job of overwhelming their overseers," I say. "Let's take a tour and see where things stand."

As we walk among the villagers, they cheer enthusiastically. "The Daughter of Gaia has come!" I hear some of them say. Chants of "Bless the Daughter of Gaia!" begin, and become louder as more and more of our people join us.

I ask Falstaff to pass the word for the villagers to assemble near the fort. I want to speak to them. In the meantime, my friends and I take a tour of the area. There are at least a dozen mines, and the fields for farming are vast. There is a building behind the fort that had aroused our curiosity, because its purpose isn't immediately clear. When we enter the building, I whoop with joy. This is a storehouse for food. And the farmers here have been growing many different crops! No more potatoes.

"Well, well," says Grizz. "We won't have to depend on the villages for food. I've always felt guilty taking their food to feed ourselves, because it's obvious they don't have enough to feed themselves."

* * * * *

An hour later, the villagers are assembled at the fort. I find a perch on the wall where they can see me. I ask Falstaff to join me. I've always been nervous when speaking to large groups of people, so I'm jittery as I wait for the cheering to end. There are thousands and thousands of villagers. It takes at least half an hour for them to stop cheering. As they celebrate, I reflect that we've earned at least some of this applause. We've accomplished something very important. The blacksuits have lost their mines, and they'll now know they have a serious threat to deal with. I smile and wave.

"With your help, we have dealt the blacksuits a severe blow," I begin, voice a little shaky. Cheering interrupts me for another several minutes. When it's quiet again, I say, "But to defeat the Court for good, we will need your continued support."

"Tell us what to do!" villagers cry out.

"Anyone who doesn't want to stay here is free to go," I say.

I'm interrupted by a thunder of voices. "No! I'll stay!"

"If you choose to stay," I continue, "I would like our farmers to continue farming. We must have food to fuel our rebellion. But now, I want you to keep more of what you produce. I want to be certain that you never again go to bed hungry!"

I wait for silence again.

My nervousness has evaporated. I gather enthusiasm as I go. "If you work the mines," I continue, "I would like you to *stop* mining. We will need an army to end the rule of the Court, and I would like you miners to become the foundation of that army."

Once again, I'm interrupted by cheers and applause. "We'll fight for the Daughter of Gaia!" they chant.

"Tomorrow," I say, putting my arm around Falstaff, "Falstaff will begin to organize you and teach you to fight. When you've learned what Falstaff has to teach, we'll take our fight right into New Washington itself."

"And tonight, you will sleep as free men and women!"

Many cheer, many cry tears of joy, and it's clear to everyone this is the happiest these villagers have been in their entire lives.

241

* * * * *

We got no sleep last night, and my friends and I, along with Falstaff, are exhausted. But before we go to bed, we hold a war council. We now have just two months before we take the village forts, so we have no time to waste.

"Falstaff," I ask, "will you name a commander to accompany us to the workshop?"

Falstaff nods. "Gretchen is ready to lead. I trust her as I trust you, Daughter of Gaia."

I ask one of our guards to find Gretchen and ask her to join us.

"I wish we could take you with us, Falstaff, but I believe your talents are needed here. We need to turn miners into soldiers."

"I'm anxious to get started," responds Falstaff. "These men and women will work harder than they ever have before. And when I'm done with them, they'll be better fighters than the blacksuits themselves."

Gretchen sits with us.

I look at her. "Falstaff tells me you're the best officer to command our escort," I say.

Gretchen blushes. "I would be honored to serve, Daughter of Gaia."

"Please work with Falstaff to find a hundred men and women to take food enough to keep our people at the workshop supplied for two months. If the Sons of 1776 show up again, I don't want our people to starve while they wait for us to come and chase the Sons away."

Gretchen and Falstaff nod in agreement.

"Arm as many of them as you can," I instruct. "We'll also see if we can find the place the Sons call the chem lab."

We discuss details of our plans for the next hour. Then, we find places to sleep in the blacksuits' fort. *Actually*, I think with a smile, *it's now our fort.*

As we sit on our hastily improvised mattresses, my friends and I talk.

"You've done very well, ET," says Tyler. "I've always known you were something special."

I feel myself blushing. "There's nothing I'm doing that any of you wouldn't do equally well if you suddenly discovered you were the 'Son of Gaia.'"

"Maybe," says Chase, sounding doubtful. "But there's something special about the way you connect with these people. You mesmerize them. It's as though what you're doing was *fated* to be."

Grizz agrees with Chase's assessment. As he does, I catch his eyes and see sadness there. I'm sure he sees that same sadness in my eyes. Duty comes with a steep cost.

As I wait for sleep, I realize how tired I am. But it's not simply lack of sleep. A part of my exhaustion has to do with all the killing. I'm tired of people dying. I know we've done only what we had to do, but I'm still tired of it. I can't find joy in the deaths of people, even the ones who wear black uniforms.

* * * * *

We sleep in later than usual the next morning, but we set out for the workshop well before 10:00 a.m. Villagers collect decayed plant matter along the way, filling up burlap sacks with it.

The monsoon rains strike in the early afternoon. I don't use the tarp this time. Since we don't have enough waterproofing for everyone, I get drenched along with everybody else.

The villagers urge me to use the tarp. "The Daughter of Gaia must not catch a fever," they say.

I ignore them. This "Daughter of Gaia" wants no special treatment. I already feel guilty for wearing comfortable softbark clothing while they wear their poor homespun.

We've placed the villagers in the front of our marching order. When I lead, I often start thinking about other things, and when I look over my shoulder, I find I've left the villagers behind. When we're behind them, we avoid the problem.

As we approach the final climb to the saddle, we keep a close eye on the weather. The monsoons blow up fast, so there's no guarantee we won't be caught in a blizzard, but we're as prudent as possible. We've already had one rain today, but that doesn't guarantee there won't be another.

The villagers are awestruck when they feel the cold temperature as we climb toward the top of the saddle. They've never known anything but the blistering heat of their forest. At first they're pleased by the novelty of cold air, but as we climb, the temperature continues to fall, and they soon realize cold air can be very unpleasant indeed. I feel sorry for them, accustomed as they are to heat.

Crossing the saddle turns out to be uneventful, and we spend the night far down the eastern side. We build bonfires to keep ourselves warm.

* * * * *

On our march the next morning, we see a glowering red sky rising to our north. None of the villagers know what it is, but Ty, Chase, and I know what's coming. From time to time, the desert is struck by sandstorms known as "haboobs." High winds and stinging sand make it best to be inside during a storm.

Unfortunately, we don't have shelter close at hand. The desert around us is flat and featureless. The foothills of the mountains would offer at least some shelter, but they are at least a two-hour walk to our west. The abandoned city near the workshop would offer better shelter, but it's still a good three hours away.

"What do you think?" I ask.

"I say, let's try to make it to the foothills," Tyler offers.

Grizz and Chase nod in agreement.

"Okay," I say, "Let's give it a try."

We move as quickly as we can toward the mountains. But less than half an hour later, as we watch, the haboob rises until it covers the entire northern horizon. The wind picks up around us, and the first of the blown sand begins to sting our faces. I look up and see the storm has risen to a height of at least a mile. It literally towers above us. I find it hard to keep my eyes open as the sand begins to pelt us harder by the minute. Sand blown by a strong wind is every bit as abrasive as sandpaper.

The villagers, who have never seen anything like this, tremble in fear.

I shout to be heard over the wind. "Cover yourselves as I do!"

I sit with my back to the storm and bury my head between my knees. I raise my arms to cover the back of my head. And then, I wait. Despite my best effort to seal my eyes, nose, and mouth, the sand penetrates. My tongue is gritty, and my eyes begin to water. I can't hear anything over the howling of the wind.

And then, the storm begins to abate. Within moments, it's gone. I open my eyes and see the storm moving away from us to the south. The sand has left me with arms that look (and feel) like they've been sunburned. I spit sand out of my mouth, rub my eyes with my fingers, and blow sand from my nose.

I look up to see Grizz talking to me, but I can scarcely hear what he says. I begin batting the sides of my head to knock the sand out of my ears.

"Are you all right?" Grizz asks.

"Yes, I think so."

I turn my back so the men can take their clothes off and shake the sand out of them, and they return the favor. I shake my clothes vigorously, but they still feel gritty when I put them back on.

Sand-burned, red-eyed, hair in tangles, spitting and snorting, we're a pathetic-looking group. Grizz, Ty, Chase, and I spend the next half hour breaking down and cleaning our AKs. I'm glad we learned to do this at the Sanctuary, because we finish quickly. We return to our order of march, villagers in the lead, larger folks following.

We are within sight of the hill that towers above the workshop when a rain of crossbow bolts begins to fall around us.

22

In the first volley, six villagers fall. We hit the ground, but the barrage of bolts continues. I assess our situation.

Whoever is launching the attack, and I must assume it has something to do with the Sons of 1776, has laid out his ambush well. They fire from cover, and we're in the open. If we remain in this exposed position, they'll pick us all off. It's just a matter of time.

"Fall back!" I holler.

We retreat from the ambush, zigzagging as we go. When we're out of range, I take stock of our situation. We've lost eight villagers, although a couple of them are still moving. From the number of bolts fired, the enemy has a large force, perhaps as many as a dozen. Our situation is not dire. We outnumber them, and with our AKs, we outgun them as well.

"Let's move into town and find some cover," I say.

We circle around the ambush site. As we approach the diner, we discover the Sons have beaten us to the punch. We take fire from both the diner and the trailer. We give a wide berth to those buildings, only to take fire from the warehouse as well. Avoiding the warehouse, we find unoccupied buildings on the east side of town. The buildings look as though they were once part of a strip mall. We claim three of them. The buildings are set apart from the rest of the town, so we have a clear field of fire. Better yet, they provide a good view of the warehouse, the trailer, and the restaurant, so we'll know if the Sons move.

I run from building to building to ensure we have all doors and windows covered. Satisfied that the Sons will not catch us napping, I turn my thoughts to the workshop. With a rising sense of fear, I wonder if the Sons have gotten to Kenny and Bree. Do they now control the workshop? I have to find out.

I instruct Gretchen to sit tight and keep a sharp eye on all the approaches to our position. With my three large friends, I leave the safety of our buildings and find a spot with a clear view of the hill. Looking through binoculars, I can see the Sons have posted two sentries on top of it. We won't be able to make a single move without them seeing us. We have to eliminate them.

We run toward the hill and safely reach its base. I hear a few crossbow bolts clattering around us, but we're out of effective range. From the bottom of the hill, I see a number of ways we can approach the top without the sentries seeing us.

"Let's climb up as close to those guys as we can," I suggest. "We'll think of some way to flush them out when we get up there."

The hill is not a big one. We're halfway up in a matter of minutes. I poke my head out from behind a rock, trying to find the Sons' position, and two crossbow bolts hiss by.

"Okay," I say. "I'll break cover and draw their fire. You guys try to nail them while they have their heads up."

Grizz takes off running, heading uphill. Cursing him under my breath, I look to find what the sentries are doing. They have their heads up, shooting crossbow bolts at Grizz. I set the AK to single fire and adjust the sight. I go deaf as Chase squeezes off a round with the barrel of his AK right next to my ear. I squeeze the trigger, slowly, as I've been taught. My target falls.

We quickly reach the top of the hill and find both Sons down.

Grizz joins us. His huge backpack is bristling with crossbow bolts. "I used my backpack as a shield," he says with a smile. "Those guys were pretty good shots."

A part of me wants to chew him out. I said that *I* was going to draw fire. A wiser part of me knows that chewing out Grizz would accomplish nothing. He'd stand there smiling while I fumed.

Instead I say, "Grizz, would you please go back and ask Gretchen to send a couple of our guys up here? Let's put our own sentries on top of the hill."

Grizz grumbles and goes.

Looking down the east side of the hill, I see the Sons have left another two sentries posted on the hillside, right above the door to the workshop. They've heard the sounds of the AKs at work, so taking them by surprise is out of the question.

"I'll keep their attention up here," I say. "Try to stay under cover until you're close enough to get a kill shot."

Tyler and Chase move out. I poke my head up and spray fire in the direction of the Sons. I can't do much damage at this range, but they don't know that. They duck during the barrage. I spray them again for good measure. When they stick their heads up once again, Tyler and Chase cut them down.

We scramble down the hill, dial the lock, and swing the door open. I run down the stairs to find Bree, Kenny, and Eva, the girl we freed from the Sons, sitting languidly in chairs, smiling at me.

"About time you guys showed up," says Kenny.

* * * * *

I feel a great weight lift from my shoulders.

"I had this picture in my mind of those guys lying in wait outside the door and drilling you when you opened it," I say, heaving a sigh of relief.

"We were lucky," says Kenny. "I got stuck on a problem, so I stepped out for a breath of fresh air and climbed the hill. The top of the hill is my thinking spot, you see. I saw a whole bunch of those rascals crossing the desert, coming our way, and they didn't look friendly. Bald-headed guys with tattoos and nasty-looking crossbows generally don't make good neighbors. So, I came down the hill double time, slammed the door, and decided to wait for you to come and rescue us."

"How long have you been holed up?" I ask.

"They only got here a couple hours ago," answers Kenny.

"I never even saw them," grumbles Bree, sounding disappointed.

"Grab an AK and come with us," I suggest. "You'll get your chance right now."

Bree also grabs a grenade launcher and stuffs several grenades in her backpack.

"I've been practicing with this thing," she explains. "I'm getting pretty good."

We run, bent over, back to the buildings where we left Gretchen. I look over my shoulder and see we have two men posted on top of the hill. I wave to them, and they wave back.

I find Gretchen, her eyes glued on the buildings held by the Sons.

"Have they moved?" I ask.

"No," she replies. "They're going to make us come and get them."

I study the warehouse. This is the same building in which Walt tortured me. Time for a little payback. On the side I can't see from my current position are the loading dock and the door the Sons dragged me through. On the opposite side is a large window, glass long gone. The side in between has no openings whatsoever.

"They're blind on this side," I observe.

"How about I sneak up and blow a big hole in that wall?" asks Kenny. "There's no way they can see me coming."

"Give it a try," I agree.

"Give me a sec. I need to go back to the workshop and collect a few things. Chase, come with me and help me carry stuff."

We watch Chase and Kenny dash toward the workshop. I turn and carefully watch the buildings occupied by the Sons. I can see a few peering through the windows, waiting for us to move.

Ty takes aim at a window in the restaurant and fires a single bullet. It's impossible to know whether he hit someone. I tend to doubt it, as the range is too great, but it may encourage them to keep their heads down.

Kenny and Chase return. Kenny has two bricks of Semtex, a lot of wire on a spool, and some vicious-looking liquid in a clear bottle.

"Keep me covered," she says and darts through the door.

The men in the warehouse can't see her, but the ones in the restaurant and trailer do. They send a shower of bolts in her direction, but the range is too great for accuracy. We respond with AK fire so they can't focus all their attention on Kenny.

Kenny reaches the warehouse wall. She packs her explosives in gouges in the wall, near the bottom. Then she cuts off two pieces of wire and thrusts one end of each into a block of Semtex. She braids the other ends together and then braids the joined wire to the wire on her spool. She runs backward toward us, spooling out wire as she comes.

She cuts the wire from the spool and instructs, "Get down."

"Wait a second," I say. "Get ready to charge the wall as soon as Kenny blows it."

I wait for our people to get in position.

"Go!" I shout.

Kenny sticks the end of the wire into the foul-looking liquid, and the wall of the warehouse disappears in smoke. The concussion from the blast is so great it hurts my ears.

We run toward the warehouse firing AKs on rapid fire. By the time the smoke clears, we're in the warehouse and find seven Sons dead. One of the Sons is still alive, but badly wounded.

I kick his crossbow away from him and ask Gretchen to have him carried to the workshop.

The restaurant will be much harder to crack. There's no way to approach it without coming under fire from both the restaurant and the trailer. There is one large window, however.

"Let me try this," says Bree, brandishing the grenade launcher.

"Give it a try," I concur.

She eyes the restaurant carefully, fiddles with the settings on the launcher, loads a grenade, and fires. The grenade clears the roof of the restaurant by twenty feet, sails across the old highway, and explodes a good hundred feet on the other side.

"I'm glad you've been practicing," says Chase.

"Put a sock in it, big fella," huffs Bree. "That was just for practice." Undeterred, she loads another grenade, changes her settings, takes careful aim, and fires. This grenade goes straight through the window, a perfect shot, and...nothing happens.

"Dang!" says Bree. "A dud. Third time's the charm."

No sooner does she say this than we hear a massive explosion inside the restaurant.

"Sounds like one of the fellas in there decided to play with the grenade," says Bree.

I want to get into the restaurant to be sure the grenade blast didn't leave anybody alive. But we can't get into the restaurant without coming under fire from the trailer unless we circle around and come at the restaurant from the other side. I'm contemplating this move, when six men come out of the trailer with their hands in the air. They've seen enough.

* * * * *

In the aftermath of the battle, we find ourselves with seven prisoners, one of them badly wounded. We carry the wounded prisoner into the dormitory and handcuff him to the bed frame. I inspect his wounds and realize he's too far gone for my limited medical skills to do him any good. He has a sucking chest wound, and his breathing is labored and erratic. He's unconscious and not likely to gain consciousness again. I leave one of Gretchen's soldiers with him with instructions to call me if he wakes.

We don't have a good place to keep the other prisoners, but, thanks to the folks who built the workshop, we have handcuffs. For now, we'll keep them in the trailer, arms and ankles handcuffed. If they escape, they won't go anywhere fast. I ask Gretchen to release one of them so I can talk to him. She frees him from his fellow prisoners, cuffing him again before she leaves. Kenny and I move the man outside.

"I want to talk to this one," I say.

"You want to interrogate him?" asks Kenny.

"Yeah. If we're gonna fight these guys, we need to find out more about them," I explain.

"Ohhh," says Kenny. "Let me interrogate him."

This is something I'd like to see. "Be my guest."

"I'm Kenny," she says, looking at the prisoner. "Who are you?"

253

"They call me Snake," he replies. Snake has the typical Sons' look: short, shaved head, tattoos of a minuteman. He's young, though. His skin is like leather, so he's lived his life outdoors in the sun. He has small, close-set eyes, which may help explain his nickname.

"I know you're with the Sons of 1776," Kenny says. "Where are you from, Snake?"

"Now just why would I want to tell you where I'm from?"

"Because I have a gun and you don't," Kenny says, glancing at her AK, which is pointed directly at Snake.

"What *is* that thing?" Snake asks.

"I'll answer your question if you'll answer mine," she offers.

"Okay," he says, "I'm with the Sons of 1776."

"I know you're with the Sons," she says. "The question was, where are you from?"

Snake sits silently, a look of studied disinterest on his face.

"Eva," Kenny calls out. "Would you come in here, please?"

I've asked Eva to wait outside until we call her. Eva joins us.

"Do you know this man?" Kenny asks.

"Yes," says Eva. "His name is Snake."

"Eva," Kenny says, "show Snake your knife."

Eva has armed herself with a stiletto from the armory. She draws it from its sheath and points the blade at Snake.

"Has Snake ever hurt you?" Kenny asks.

"Yes," says Eva.

"Would you like us to leave you alone with Snake for a little while?"

"I'd like that very much."

"Okay," Kenny says, rising. "Let me know when you feel more talkative, Snake."

Kenny and I turn our backs and walk away. I won't let Eva harm Snake, but Snake doesn't know that.

"Wait," sputters Snake.

"Do you want to answer my questions now?"

"Yes."

"Eva, would you stand there beside Snake? Every time he lies, I want you to cut him. Now," Kenny says, turning her attention to Snake, "where are you from?"

"I'm from HQ," he replies.

"And why did you come here?"

"The Leader wanted us to find out what happened to a guy named Walt. He was sent up here on patrol, and he didn't come back to HQ when he should've."

"How long does it take you to get here from HQ?"

"Ten suns."

"And how long have you been here?"

"We just got here today."

"Who was the leader of your party?"

"His name was Gus. You blowed him up. He was in the big building."

"What's the Leader going to do when *your* group doesn't come back?" Kenny asks.

"Nothin'."

Eva takes her knife and touches Snake's Adam's apple with it.

"Try again, Snake," Kenny says patiently.

"He'll send his Patchees to find you."

Eva winces slightly when Snake says this.

"What are Patchees?"

"You know," he says. "Injuns."

I'm guessing he means Apaches.

"Why doesn't the Leader send a big army up here to fight us?" Kenny asks.

"Takes too much water to keep a big army goin' so far from HQ," Snake explains. "He'd have to keep half of us just haulin' water. He ain't gonna send no army up here till he knows what he's dealing with."

"So what happens if we ambush the Apaches?" Kenny asks. "He still won't know what he's dealing with."

"It's hard to ambush Patchees, even if you know they're comin'." Snake pauses, then sneers. "And don't never let no Patchee catch you. If you know something 'bout how to get into that workshop yonder, you'll tell it to the Patchees. I seen 'em break down tough men. Real tough men. They got a million ways to make men talk."

"How long before the Leader knows you're not coming back?"

"He won't miss us for maybe twelve or fourteen suns. He told us to stay here for a few days, just to see if somebody showed up."

"Thank you, Snake. And by the way, this 'thing,'" she explains, lifting her AK, "is called an assault rifle. It's does an excellent job of killing Sons of 1776 and Apaches."

"It's loud," he says. "You people make more noise than anybody I ever knowed."

Kenny smiles at Snake as the guard leads him away. I've found our ace interrogator.

"What do you know about these Apaches?" I ask Eva after Snake is gone.

"I know you don't want to mess around with them. They're expert trackers, and they're quiet. They can walk right up behind you, and you'll never even know they were there. They can run forever. I've heard stories of them running deer to death. And Snake was right. If they want you to tell them something, they'll make you tell."

I ask Gretchen to post a guard on the prisoners. We'll send them back to Helen and see what she wants to do with them. We can't send them to Falstaff for safekeeping because the minute they weren't being watched, they'd climb the saddle and be gone.

* * * * *

The next day passes quickly.

Bree has finished building masts for our radio antennae. She's already installed a mast on top of the hill above the workshop. We all troop to the top of the hill to look at her handiwork. At first I can't find it, and then I realize she's disguised it by putting it up through the branches of a scraggly mesquite tree.

Bree has also done an ingenious thing with the hand-crank generators.

"I knew we'd be getting help from the villagers," Bree explains, "so I added a second crank and a seat to the generators. The villagers can ride them like a bicycle. There'll be much less wear and tear on their arms."

We establish a schedule for villagers to "ride" the generators. We arrange to have them work for an hour and rest for an hour.

257

Later in the day, Gretchen approaches me with the news that the villagers are unhappy with their generator schedules.

"Should we give them a longer rest period?" I ask.

"No," replies Gretchen, "it's the exact opposite. They're unhappy because they want to work *more*. You have to remember, our people are accustomed to hard physical labor from dawn to sunset. With an hour break every other hour, they feel they're being profligate."

"Okay," I say. "Let them set up their own schedules." Once again, I'm impressed by how simple, loyal, and hardworking our people are. Working with them is an honor.

We try to train the villagers to use the AKs. But the rifles are simply too long for their short arms.

"Can you cut the AKs down?" I ask Bree.

"Not without wrecking them," she replies.

The villagers have no better luck with handguns. The recoil leaves nasty bruises on their foreheads. And they're unable to keep the barrel level when they attempt to depress the trigger for automatic fire.

At a meeting later in the day, I sit with my large friends, along with Eva and Gretchen.

"I've been trying to figure out how we can take the forts in the outer ring," I say. "Since the monsoons have started, the wood won't be dry, so I don't think we can get the walls to burn with fire arrows. Anybody have any ideas?"

"The trebuchets I'm working on won't provide enough velocity to bring the walls down with a bombardment," Bree muses. "We'd need to bombard a wall for hours to put holes in it."

"Ooh," Kenny says, inspired. "The gasoline we found won't work as gasoline, but I can distill out a liquid that will burn like mad."

"We could put Kenny's flammable gas into a container that would shatter on impact, like glass or pottery," says Chase. "We could hit the wall with Kenny Gas, and then hit the wall again with a firebomb. When the firebomb hits the gas, it should make it ignite. That should set the wall on fire, shouldn't it?"

"That ought to work," says Bree, excited, "especially if we had several trebuchets going at once."

Another problem solved, I think.

"One more thing before we break up," I say. "It's only a matter of time before the Sons of 1776 or their Apache scouts show up here. Eva tells me the Apaches are masters at extracting information from people. If they catch somebody who knows the combination to the door—well, we can't let that happen."

We ponder for a moment. Finally, Grizz speaks. "Let's keep the combination limited to a few people on a need-to-know basis."

"Everybody in this room already knows," I say. "Other than Falstaff and Helen, does anybody else need to know?"

"I can't think of anybody else," says Gretchen.

"Then that's settled," I declare. "Everybody else has to knock on the door to get in."

"There are some video cameras in the lockers in the workroom," Bree says. "It wouldn't take a lot of work to set up some surveillance cameras above the hatch. I'll disguise them so they'll be almost invisible."

"We could post sentries on top of the hill," offers Gretchen. "That'll give us an early warning if the Sons show up."

"Great idea," I say. "If the Sons show up, get everybody inside and seal the hatch. Get on the radio and let us know what's happening. We'll send a relief column from the mines."

Our radio masts are modular so we can easily carry them in pieces and put them together wherever we need them. I ask Grizz and

Chase to take half a dozen villagers with them and set up a mast atop the saddle. Since the radios work on a line-of-sight basis, we'll need a mast up there to relay signals from one side of the mountains to the other. Then, I ask them to oversee the construction of another mast at the fort by the mines. I'd also like to build a mast at the Sanctuary, but this will be more difficult. The placement of the Sanctuary mast will be critical. It must be close enough to the Sanctuary so it can be conveniently used, but hidden well enough that blacksuit patrols won't stumble across it. Once we burn the village forts, this won't be an issue.

After Chase and Grizz have shown the villagers how to set up masts and operate the radios, I ask them to instruct the villagers to set up radio stations at the forts farthest in all directions, one radio at our village farthest north, one farthest west, and so on. Instead of taking more than a month to send runners from the Sanctuary to all fifty villages, we can dispatch runners from each village with a radio. We'll be able to communicate with every village within a week.

* * * * *

On the night before Grizz leaves, I enter the dormitory to find him sitting on his mattress, alone in the room.

"Hey," he says.

"Hey yourself," I reply. I sit down next to him on his mattress. I take his hand in mine. For a long time we sit there silently. I'm filled with a longing so deep and fierce it threatens to consume me. Finally, I stand up and face Grizz. I hold his face between my hands and kiss him on the forehead.

"I love you, Grizz," I whisper. When tears start to form in my eyes, and in his, I turn and walk quickly away. I don't dare look back.

* * * * *

My mother and I began fighting about dresses when I was four years old. She wanted me to wear them. I wanted nothing to do with them. The battle of wills came to a head on a cold Sunday morning when I refused to go to Sunday school wearing a dress.

"It's too cold. My legs are gonna freeze," I complained.

Mom and I compromised on a pair of respectable-looking slacks. Every Sunday after that, I dressed in slacks. I was worried when the weather began to warm that Mom would want me to go back to the dresses again, but she never mentioned dresses again.

Many years later, when I was in middle school, our teachers threw a Spring Fling Dance. I decided not to go, because I knew I'd have to wear a dress. But Jules, Kenny, and Bree wanted me to go, and they finally wore down my resistance. And so, on a beautiful, warm May evening, I found myself self-consciously wearing a dress into the school gym.

The teachers had hung crepe banners from the walls and ceiling, the basketball backboards at either end of the floor were folded up, and the lights were dimmed. A big banner proclaiming the Spring Fling Dance hung across the room, and a sparkling ball was suspended from the ceiling.

At first, the boys stood along one wall, and the girls stood along the other. Some of the girls danced with one another, but the boys didn't do that kind of thing. After a half hour of gender separation, Mrs. Tyler, the girls' gym teacher, put on a slow song, took the microphone, and announced the next dance would be a "ladies' choice." The girls crossed the dance floor like heat-seeking missiles, grabbed their flustered partners, and pulled even the most reluctant onto the floor.

I was determined to stand my ground. If a boy wanted to dance with me, he'd have to ask, I thought haughtily. But when I realized I was alone on the girls' side, I was forced to reconsider.

I watched Grizz, on the boys' side, refusing the offer of one girl after another. I decided that if I'd be comfortable dancing with anyone, it would be Grizz, and he was still available. So I slowly walked across the floor.

"You wanna dance?" I asked, afraid to look him in the eye.

"I don't know how to dance," he replied.

"Neither do I," I said, shrugging. I'd be happy standing with Grizz, watching everybody else dance.

"But neither do they," said Grizz, nodding his head at the dance floor.

There were dozens of awkward twelve-year-old kids going through all sorts of contortions, and mostly figuring things out. Grizz took my hand, and we walked onto the floor, finding a corner where we hoped no one would pay us any attention.

Starch stiff, we hooked on to one another. Grizz touched my left hip softly, as though he were afraid he'd break it. I put the fingertips of my left hand on his right shoulder, and we began to shuffle our feet, more or less in time to the music.

I was surprised to find myself disappointed when the music ended. I walked beside Grizz back to the boys' side, where both girls and boys were now mingling.

"Hey, ET, nice legs," said Chase, probably thinking I'd feel complimented.

"There's nothing here you haven't seen when you watched my track meets," I pointed out.

"True," Chase replied, "but you're wearing nylons."

"If you don't stop talking about my legs, I'm gonna have to hurt you," I said with a sardonic smile.

Chase laughed, but he stopped looking at my legs.

The rest of the night passed in a blur. I danced with Grizz, Chase, and Tyler several times, and also with some boys I didn't know as well. By the end of the evening, I'd decided the skirt thing wasn't all that bad.

* * * * *

The next few days are relaxing ones. I visit Kenny in her lab and find that Eva has mastered the art of manufacturing wolf bane. As I watch, I'm surprised at how complicated the process is. Eva has to put the raw materials through several levels of purification, titration, and phase changes. Kenny is a genius. Eva is training several villagers in the process. In a few days, we'll have an assembly line mass-producing wolf bane.

Tyler has been complaining about pain in his knee. Knowing Ty, if he's complaining of pain, anybody else with his symptoms would be flat on his back in bed.

"How'd you like to stay here and help Eva with the wolf bane?" I ask.

"That would be great," he responds.

I've been observing Ty and Eva over the past couple days. The two of them are spending a lot of time together. Has Ty found a girlfriend? Eva, whose people have been well fed since the Great Collapse, is certainly tall enough to be a possible love interest.

Kenny sets up a wolf bane distribution schedule with the villagers. We'll soon have a constant shuttle system in operation. Villagers will pick up wolf bane at the workshop and deliver it to the Sanctuary. At the Sanctuary, they'll pick up empty jars, harvest decaying plant matter, and haul them to the workshop. From the Sanctuary, another set of villagers will deliver wolf bane to all the other villages.

We'll be ready to attack the blacksuits' village forts in two months' time.

* * * * *

After three days at the workshop, I find Kenny in her lab overseeing the wolf bane assembly line. She looks very pleased. I ask her, "Would you like to go find the chem lab?"

"I've been looking forward to it ever since we found out it existed," she responds. "Eva and Ty have this operation humming. They won't miss me."

I ask Eva for directions to the chem lab.

"You can find it easily," she says. "Head directly toward the rising sun. The desert you will cross is totally flat. You'll find a large hill late on the afternoon of the second day. It's easily recognizable because it's the only hill for miles around. This is *not* the hill you're looking for. A short walk will bring you to a second, larger hill by sunset. You'll find the hatch for the chem lab at the base of that hill on the side of the constant star."

"I think we should be able to find it," I say.

We arrange to have ten villagers join Kenny and I on the walk. We'll be carrying the radio, the mast, and enough food to keep Kenny working for at least a month. Since we know the Sons of 1776 will show up at the chem lab sooner or later, we also carry two cameras to set up a security system around the door, similar to the one Bree put up at the workshop.

The wound in my side is still painful. I carry my AK, my pocketknife, binoculars, two canteens, and my compass. I don't carry anything else. I feel guilty carrying so little when everybody else is fully burdened, but the wound will never heal if I keep aggravating it.

The first day of our journey is uneventful. The desert is so uniform in all directions that monotony sets in. We light a fire at sunset and warm up a meal of beans, squash, and tomatoes. We also have three rabbits Kenny brought down during the day. The pantry at the mines was full of different kinds of food. The variety is heavenly. I'll never eat another potato as long as I live.

Just as Eva predicted, we see a hill on the horizon late in the afternoon of our second day. I scramble to the top and see the second hill. I estimate it'll take us less than two or three hours to reach the chem lab. I don't know why I chose to train the binoculars back in the direction from which we'd come—the desert in that direction was mind-numbingly boring—but just as I'm about to put the binoculars down, I see a hint of movement. Looking closer, I see a man in dun-colored clothing with midnight-black hair. As I scan from side to side, I see nineteen more men. They're coming toward us at a slow run.

One of the men has blond hair, a couple of them have red hair, and several are brunets. The term "Apache" seems to be generic for people who have lots of stamina and are good at hunting people down.

The Leader didn't wait for the party he sent on his second expedition to vanish. He's already sent his Apaches, and they've found our trail.

D.S. Northrop

23

"Apaches are on our trail," I say.

"But Snake said they wouldn't come until his group came up missing," objects Kenny.

"Well, they're here." I hand the binoculars to Kenny. "Take a look."

It takes her a moment, but she finds them. "Dang!" she exclaims.

"As slowly as our villagers walk, the Apaches will catch us long before we reach the chem lab," I say. "Kenny, you take them to the lab, and I'll hold them off from here."

"I can't leave you behind, ET. Between the two of us, we can handle them," says Kenny.

"There are too many of them," I object. "You heard Snake. Those men can crawl right up next to you without your hearing a thing. Listen, you get to the chem lab and get that antenna up. Radio back and let them know what's going on."

Kenny hesitates.

"Snake said these guys can run down a deer," I remind her. "But I'm a distance runner on the track team. I can run for a long time, too. I'll lead them away from you. Now go!"

Kenny gathers up the villagers and reluctantly leaves. "Run!" she hollers.

I find a spot with good cover, unstrap my AK, and set it to single fire. I train the binoculars on the Apaches again. At their current pace, they'll reach me in less than an hour. If I can hold them off for another half hour, they won't be able to catch my people before they reach the chem lab. I settle in and wait.

A half hour later, the Apaches close in on me. They're spread out in a line forty yards wide. As they close the gap to one hundred yards, I lift my AK, raise its sights, and focus on the chest of the man in the center of the line. I wait for him to come a little closer, take a deep breath, exhale, and gently squeeze the trigger. The man in my sights drops. The other Apaches instantly dive for cover.

Through the binoculars, I see them talking animatedly with each other. One man in particular seems to dominate the conversation. All I can see of him are his head and shoulders, but that may be enough. I draw a bead on his head and squeeze off another round. His head slumps to the ground. The rest of the Apaches leap up and retreat. I manage to hit another one as he runs away.

They form a huddle about a half mile away. After a few minutes of discussion, eight head off to the south, and another eight head north. They're going to surround me. By now, they know they have only one opponent, and they know I can't look in all directions at once.

Okay, I think, *let them come.* I say a prayer of thanks that the desert here is so featureless. Quiet as they are, there's no way they can hide from me.

I follow their progress through the binoculars. I wait until they have me surrounded and begin to close in. I can't let them get within range, or they'll shoot me down the minute I stand up. I'm going to make my escape to the north. I set the AK to rapid fire and get on my feet and run as fast as I can.

I run straight at the Apache coming at me from due north. When I see him raise his bow, I spray him with AK fire and watch him fall. I sprint as fast as I can for a hundred yards and then risk a look back over my shoulder. The nearest Apache is fifty yards behind me.

Legs burning, lungs laboring, I sprint another hundred yards and look back again.

The Apaches have formed their line again. I watch anxiously as they turn to follow me. Eight of them follow me, while the other seven peel off and head toward the chem lab. This doesn't worry me because I've given my friends enough time to reach safety. The Apaches are all moving more slowly now. They now know the people they're trailing are dangerous, and they'll have to be careful lest we ambush them again.

I turn away from them and begin to jog. Although the Apaches are considerably taller than the other humans on this side of the brane, they appear to be well less than five feet tall. At five feet seven, I'll have the advantage of longer legs. Over a number of hours, this should help me outdistance them.

Where do I want to go? I turn this over in my mind as I run. My first thought is to return to the workshop. But the thought of Apaches setting up ambushes all over that hill, of them sneaking up behind us if we leave the shelter, discourages me. A better plan will be to head for the saddle. I'll reach it in a little less than three days if I can maintain a good pace. Once I lose the Apaches, I can slow down, because, as fit as I am, I know I can't run for three days straight.

I make a wide turn and head toward the saddle. Two hours later, I stop and scan the horizon with my binoculars. The Apaches are still coming on, but they're farther behind.

I'm dying of thirst, so I unscrew the cap on my canteen.

Water! I think in a panic. When we started out for the lab, we took only enough water for four days—two days' worth to get us to the chem lab and two days' worth to get us back to the workshop, just in case we couldn't get into the lab. I've already used up almost two days' worth! I'll have to conserve.

Darkness falls, and I continue to run. When my stomach begins to rumble, I rummage in my backpack until I find a dried carrot. There's only a sliver of a moon tonight, not enough light to see anything in the distance, but enough to see an Apache in the unlikely event he gets within fifty yards of me. A bigger problem is that I can't see the Twins or the saddle. I'll have to use my compass and dead reckoning.

I alternate between jogging and walking through the night, and by sunrise, I'm exhausted. During the night, I've run a little farther to the north than I should have, but I'm getting close to the Twins. I search the area behind me with my binoculars and am relieved to see no trace of the Apaches. As much as I want to sit and rest, I deny myself. I force myself to continue walking. At noon, I stop and sit for a half hour. When I rise, I look again, but still see no sign of Apaches. Maybe they've given up. I continue walking through the afternoon. I stop at dinnertime and treat myself to a sit-down meal and a large gulp of water. The wound in my side has reopened, and blood is soaking through the bandage. I stretch my tired legs and permit myself an hour of rest.

When I rise and scan the horizon, I see the Apaches following my trail, although they're several miles behind. *Jeez!* I think. *You can't shake these guys.*

The Apaches are advancing in their usual easy, loping trot. I'm going to have to jog all night. I groan and start running. Night falls, and I must stop for rest. My lungs are heaving, and my thighs burn as if they're on fire. Around midnight, I collapse. I simply can't run any farther. I chew on another carrot and check my watch. I'll give myself an hour, and then I'll start walking again.

Exactly one hour later, I struggle to my feet and walk. I'm starting to feel the results of exhaustion and, worse, dehydration. I've had to conserve water, so I've not been able to slake my thirst. My head begins to ache, and I feel dizzy all the time now. At sunrise, I scan for Apaches again. There are none in sight. I collapse in a heap, and sleep claims me.

I awake with a start. My head is pounding, and my tongue sticks to the roof of my mouth. I glance at my watch. How long have I been asleep? More than two hours. This time when I look for the Apaches, I find them. There are still eight of them, doggedly following me. I force myself to rise and run again. I quickly discover I can no longer maintain a constant jogging pace. So I jog for a while, and then I walk for a while. The Apaches are not gaining any ground, but I can no longer leave them behind. I take heart as the Twins grow steadily larger, until, by late afternoon, they fill half the sky. I'm at the foot of the saddle!

I hear the hoot of the great horned owl on the trail above me. The sound brings me to an abrupt halt. I grew up with a great horned owl living in the open desert behind our house, and I often listened to his call as I lay in bed before falling asleep. The hoot of the owl above me wasn't quite right. I hear it again, from a different location. This time I'm certain. The call was clipped too soon. That's not an owl.

Hope evaporates when I see the merest hint of movement on the path above me. Something is there and gone in an instant. A part of me wants to believe it's an animal, but the reality sinks in. If the Apaches found our trail between the workshop and the lab as I had speculated, they could easily have traced it back to the workshop and from there to the Twins. There's another party of Apaches ahead of me.

I want to give up. I'm exhausted and dehydrated. I can't push myself any farther. My lips are cracked and bleeding. My tongue is the size of a sub sandwich. But then I think of Snake, sneering, *"The Apaches got a million ways to make a man talk."* I can't let them catch me. I have only one chance, and that's to work my way across the east face of the northern Twin and down the side opposite the saddle.

I start again. I realize my walk has turned into a stagger. Still, I have a good lead over the men behind me. I force my way up the east face of the mountain. After a half hour, I stop to catch my breath. I've climbed about a thousand feet above the desert floor. The Apaches have just reached the foot of the mountain. I turn and scramble upward, trying to work my way up and to the right. I climb for an hour and then must stop for rest. The Apaches are somewhere below me. I can't see them because they're hidden below the rocky slope I just climbed.

At this point, they're probably moving faster than I am. I want to go more quickly, but my body is worn out. I scuttle upward again until I'm blocked by a cliff rising sheer up in front of me.

* * * * *

I begin to cry, but am too dehydrated to manufacture tears, so I dry sob. How can this be? I've worked so hard. I take a second look at the cliff and realize my situation isn't totally hopeless. The rock forming the cliff is old rock. It's weathered, and there are trees and bushes growing out of several crags.

My first experience in rock climbing came in middle school, when our gym teacher, Mrs. Tyler, had a climbing wall mounted on one side of the gym. After lots of trial and error, I learned how to climb. My friends and I took a good many rock climbing trips around Tucson. Of course, back then, I was always tethered to a safety line. And I wasn't on the verge of physical collapse.

I close my eyes, slow my breathing, and rest for a moment. When I open them, I see Jules. She's floating a few feet above the ground, to my left. She's frowning. As I watch, she points her finger up, toward the top of the cliff. And then she's gone.

I study the cliff face in front of me. I look where Jules was pointing and see a possible path. My head is still throbbing, and I'm still dizzy and exhausted, but I also feel a sense of renewal. I start to climb. How long do I have before the Apaches show up? If they catch me on the cliff face, they can pin me to it like a butterfly.

I mindlessly climb, remembering the rock climber's mantra: three points of contact at all times. Of your hands and feet, three must have sturdy purchase while the fourth searches for something to grasp or wedge. The fact that my pinky finger is still in a cast doesn't help. From time to time, I'm overwhelmed by dizziness and must stop. My *personal* rock climbing mantra is: never look down. When I look down, a kind of vertigo takes hold of me, and I know I'll fall. As much as I want to look behind me to see if there is any sign of Apaches, I know I mustn't.

Left hand. Left foot. Right hand. Right foot. Over and over. Ignore the headache blazing behind my eyes. Ignore my swollen tongue. My left calf muscle begins to cramp. I ride the pain and force myself to relax. Breathe slowly, in through the nose, out through the mouth. My calf finally relaxes. I wish I could massage it, but that's not possible. I feel the telltale tightness and know the muscle is going to cramp again.

My left hand reaches for purchase, but it finds only loose rock. I hear pebbles rattle down below me. Try the left hand again. The handholds aren't evenly spaced, so sometimes I'm stretched out with arms and legs splayed, while at others I'm scrunched up like an inchworm. I plant my right foot and stretch to find a handhold. The rock below my right foot gives way, and I find myself desperately clinging to the rock with my left foot and left hand only. I jam my chest into the cliff. My muscles are far too tired to tolerate this kind of strain. My calf muscle threatens to cramp again. I feel myself weakening, but finally find a place to plant my right foot. I rest after the close call.

And then I come to the ceiling. A rock juts out about a foot, perpendicular to the face of the cliff above me, blocking further progress. I can't see any way to climb around the ceiling. I have only one chance now. I push up hard with both feet and wedge my left shoulder into the junction of the cliff face and the rock above. I reach out blindly with my right hand and work it around the rock blocking my way. My hand scrabbles against the rock, desperately seeking something, anything to hold. There's no way to back out of this maneuver. I either find something to grab or I'm a dead girl.

At the extreme limit of my reach, my fingers find the gnarled root of a tree. I can touch it with the tips of my fingers, but I can't get my hand around it. I begin to whimper. My legs begin to shake with exhaustion, and I know I can't hold my wedged position any longer. With the last of my strength, I push off with both feet and manage to grab the tree root with my right hand. Will it hold? I hear the clatter of pebbles as part of the rock holding the root gives way. I'm now dangling with nothing holding me up but my right hand.

I work to swing myself out away from the cliff face and lunge at the root with my left hand. I grasp it, but can feel the root beginning to give way. I ignore the pebbles falling all around me. I squeeze my eyes shut, grit my teeth, and use every ounce of strength left to pull myself up. I lift my head just above the rock and see another root. I grab it with my right hand and pull myself up. My arms are beginning to shake with the strain, but I manage to reach the root with my right hand. I pull myself slowly upward until I can hook a knee over the top of the ledge.

A matter of seconds later I am lying on top of the rock that had been blocking my way, gasping for breath. I lay still for a long time. I open my eyes and realize I've reached the top of the cliff. I look at the stunted little cedar I used to get over the last hurdle and consider kissing it.

I remember the Apaches and force myself to sit up. How long has it taken me to climb the cliff? I had only about a half hour's lead. I quickly scramble to the ledge and look down. The Apaches are there, below me at the foot of the cliff. My hands are shaking too much to aim my AK, but I unsling it, set it to rapid fire, and point it straight down. I pull the trigger and hold it. I don't dare empty the clip, because I have no spare. But when I peek out, I see three Apaches lying on the ground and the rest diving for cover. Each of the three downed Apaches are groaning and moving. *Let them go*, I think. *They're in no condition to climb the cliff.*

I can hold them off forever in this position, and they know this as well. I see a number of the Apaches climbing back down. They'll search until they find a way around the cliff, and there almost certainly will be another way to get up here. I haven't solved the problem, but I've earned some rest. *Let them search*, I think. *If they find an easy way around the cliff, they can have me. Because right now, I can't move.* I drift off to sleep.

I awake to find an Apache grasping at the stunted cedar, ready to pull himself up on my ledge. I lash out with my foot and push him out, away from the cliff as hard as I can. He loses his grip on the cedar and falls. A second later, I hear a thump from the bottom of the cliff. I try to stay awake, but I can't. I drift off to sleep again.

When I awake, the sun has passed behind the mountain. I shake my canteen. Only enough water left for one swallow. I drink the last of the water, and it feels blissful to my parched throat.

In the twilight, I see a ledge running off to the southwest. The ledge is roughly four feet wide and is populated by the sorts of plants that can find a foothold in weathered rock: stunted, gnarled trees and shrubs. The path will lead me back toward the saddle. But since I'm higher than I was earlier today, perhaps I'll wind up above the Apaches waiting at the foot of the it.

Sleep has done me good. I feel a tiny surge of energy, not enough to start dancing, but enough to walk. As the sky darkens, walking the ledge becomes trickier. At some points, the ledge narrows until it's only inches wide. I turn and hug the cliff, shuffling sideways on tiptoe. Tiny baby steps. I can only pray that the ledge doesn't disappear altogether. My calf cramps again. I struggle to keep my footing, and finally, the muscle loosens, and the pain subsides.

After about fifteen minutes of inching my way along, the ledge widens again. I walk for hours. My burst of energy is gone. I'm back to slogging forward, one foot in front of the other. I find myself staggering side to side as much as I'm moving forward. I try to correct and keep going in a straight line. Dehydration makes me incredibly dizzy. I stop and rest, and then force myself to move again. I'm dimly aware of sunrise. I've walked all night long. But I'm in pain and exhausted. Finally, I fall to my knees. I can't go any farther. I've pushed myself to the limit. Without water, I simply can't continue.

At this point of unconditional surrender, I see Jules again. Once again she floats ten feet off the ground, and once again she's giving me a look that turns my blood to ice water. She's pointing to a narrow game trail leading down and to the south.

Go away, Jules, I think. *Let me die in peace.* Nevertheless, I force myself to crawl. I'm dimly aware of the rough rock shredding my palms and my knees. *Doesn't matter,* I tell myself.

And then I hear the voices. The Apaches again, only now I'm too physically battered to escape.

I hear Snake. *"The Patchees got a million ways to make men talk."* I can't let the Apaches take me. If they do, the Sons will have the secret to the combination for the workshop and the chem lab. My arms are too short to shoot myself with my AK. But if I take my shoe off, I might be able to pull the trigger with my toe.

The voices are getting louder. They're almost here. I fumble with my shoelaces and kick off my right shoe. I swing the AK around just as I see them appear from around the rocks above me.

24

Grizz appears. First Jules, now Grizz. I'm really hallucinating. But this Grizz isn't floating above the ground. And when he touches me, he feels distinctly real. I'm floating in and out of consciousness, but I realize, dimly, that Grizz is cradling me in his arms, rocking me back and forth.

I try to speak, but all that comes out is a croak. Grizz is holding a canteen to my lips, slowly pouring water into my mouth. My throat is so raw and swollen that I can take in only a trickle of water at a time, but it tastes like manna. I lose consciousness again. I awake to realize that I'm strapped to a makeshift stretcher and I'm being jostled down a steep incline. Did the Apaches get me after all? I hear Grizz's voice (what a relief!) and pass out again.

When I awaken, I'm on a mattress in a dark room. Grizz is sitting on the floor next to me, head on his chest, sleeping. I sleep, too.

I'm distantly aware of the sound of voices around me. I slowly open my eyes and see Grizz and Falstaff in conversation. Grizz sees my open eyes, drops to his knees, and holds me. He says something to Falstaff, who disappears. A short time later, a villager hurries into the room with a bowl and a wooden spoon. She hands these to Grizz, casts a worried glance at me, and leaves. Grizz props me up on pillows and carefully spoons the liquid from the bowl into my mouth.

Soup, I realize.

Grizz is very careful, giving me only a few drops at a time.

"I can't feed you too fast, or you'll throw it right back up. But we need to get some nutrition in you."

"Thanks," I say. My voice doesn't sound right. I sound like a frog.

Grizz continues spooning soup into my mouth until I lose consciousness again.

The next time I awaken, I see the sun shining into the room through small windows. Grizz is still sitting next to me.

I feel much better. "How long have I been sleeping?" I ask.

"This is the second day since we found you on the mountain," Grizz says.

"Oh. You carried me here," I croak, remembering being jostled around on a stretcher.

"That's right," confirms Grizz.

"Where are we?" I ask. The room around me is unfamiliar.

"We're at the fort by the mines," Grizz replies. "You'll be embarrassed, but the villagers have named it after you, so you're in Fort Taylor."

"That's nice," I say. I smile, but my lips are still cracked and blistered, so it hurts.

I see dark patches beneath Grizz's eyes. "You need sleep."

"I've been taking catnaps," he demurs. "I want to be awake so I can take care of you."

"Thanks, but you need sleep, too."

A moment passes as we look at one another. I'm sure that the care I see in his eyes is echoed in my own.

"What happened?" I ask. "How did you find me?"

"Pure luck," says Grizz. "We'd just assembled the radio mast at the fort when a call came through from the workshop. There were evidently some unfriendly-looking people hanging around, and they asked us to come and chase them away. So Chase, Gretchen, and I were leading a relief expedition over the saddle. We stumbled onto you. You were delirious and trying to take your shoes off."

The memory comes back to me. God, am I lucky Grizz got there when he did.

"Have you heard anything from Kenny yet?" I ask.

"There's been no news from the chem lab," Grizz says. "Chase and Gretchen cleared out the area around the workshop, and now they're heading to the chem lab."

I feel a cold sensation deep down in my stomach. Did the Apaches catch Kenny after all? I tear up at the thought.

Grizz sees my tears. "Don't worry yet, ET. They're probably holed up safely inside the lab. They probably didn't have time to get the mast up before they had to lock down."

I can only hope Grizz is right.

With Grizz's help I'm able to stand. My head feels full of cotton, and I'm immediately dizzy. The dizziness slowly clears, but the cotton remains. With my arm around Grizz's shoulder, I hobble to the door. Villagers are working in the fields. The ones closest to us break out in a throaty cheer and wave. I wave back.

I feel dreadfully weary. "Please help me back to bed, Grizz."

He does, and I sleep again.

* * * * *

I feel much stronger when I awaken again. I swing my legs off the mattress and struggle to my feet. My muscles are still aching, my throat is sore, and I feel as weak as a newborn baby. Grizz is asleep on the mattress next to mine. Remembering the circles under his eyes, I decide not to awaken him. I walk unsteadily to the door. I realize I'm starving. There's a sentry posted at the door, and he breaks into a smile when he sees me.

"Daughter of Gaia," he says, "are you feeling better?"

"Yes, thank you," I answer. "But I'm very hungry. Where can I find food?"

"You rest," says the sentry. "I will ask the kitchen to bring you something."

I watch as he runs toward the dining hall. Once again, workers in the field are cheering and waving. I wave back. Realizing that I'm dressed in a nightgown, I decide not to go out for a walk.

A young woman hustles through the door with a tray of food. I see sweet potatoes, lima beans, and a salad with tomatoes and carrots. Despite my hunger, I resist the temptation to gobble everything down. If I've been eating nothing but soup, as seems likely, I'd best not overdue the solid food. I nibble at all three dishes and set the tray aside.

"Is the food all right?" asks the girl who brought the tray, concerned.

"Oh yes," I assure. "The food is very good. I just need to be careful what I eat right now."

She smiles, nods, and takes the tray away.

I find my clothes in a cabinet and quickly change out of my nightgown, into my pants and tunic, which are freshly laundered.

Grizz is stirring.

"Good morning," I say when he opens his eyes.

"You're sounding pretty chipper this morning," he comments as he sits up, rubbing sleep out of his eyes.

"Let's go for a walk," I suggest.

"Feeling better?"

"Much."

We walk from the fort to the northern edge of the cultivated land, a distance of about two miles. We return workers' waves as we pass them by. By the time we reach the northern border, I'm beginning to tire, so we turn around and head back.

"You pushed your body way too hard up on the saddle," says Grizz.

"You think?" I say. I hurt everywhere.

When we get back to the fort, we walk to the dining hall, where I eat a bowl of hot vegetable soup. I tell Grizz the story of my flight from the Apaches. I've been too out of it to give him more than a thumbnail sketch before.

"This means we're either going to have to defend the workshop and the chem lab or we're going to have to abandon them," says Grizz.

"We have to hold them," I say. "We'll never defeat the blacksuits unless we have better technology than they do. Right now, they have every advantage."

I'm finishing my soup when I get my biggest surprise of the day.

* * * * *

Zoe Kerber walks into the dining hall surrounded by an escort of armed villagers.

Gesturing toward Zoe, the leader of the escort says, "She showed up outside the Sanctuary a couple days ago and asked if she could join us. Helen didn't know what to do with her, so she told us to bring her to you."

I turn my attention to Zoe. "So why do you want to leave the life of luxury at the Court?" I ask.

"I hate living in New Washington," Zoe says. "They have this really strange philosophy about women. They don't let us hold jobs, and they expect us to cook and clean like slaves. And Jared is turning into a tyrant. He expects me to wait on him night and day. I just can't face that life anymore. If you take me in, I'll do anything you ask."

Grizz looks at Zoe with suspicion. "Why should we trust you?" he asks flatly.

"You don't have to trust me," Zoe returns. "Just don't treat me like a slave."

"Come with me," I say.

I lead Zoe from the mess hall to the room where Grizz and I are staying. I point to the bed next to Grizz's and say, "Why don't you park you gear there? You can stay here with Grizz and me."

Seeing Grizz's expression of doubt, I ask Zoe if she can give Grizz and me a moment alone.

When she's gone, I whisper, "I don't trust her either. But you know what they say. Keep your friends close—"

"And your enemies closer." Grizz completes the old adage.

"I don't know which one she is," I say. "So we'll keep an eye on her."

We join Zoe outside. I'm very tired. My morning walk has exhausted me. "Grizz," I say, "can you introduce Zoe to Falstaff? Zoe, if you're going to be one of us, you gotta learn to fight."

"I'm good with that," agrees Zoe with a look of determination.

Grizz leads her away, and I sit down to rest.

* * * * *

The next day brings a more pleasant surprise. Luther, one of Falstaff's assistants, rushes to catch up with us on our walk and says, "I've just come from the radio room. We've received a message from the chem lab. Gretchen's force just got through to the lab and chased the Sons away. They've put up their radio mast and sent us a message to let us know everything is okay. They're going to leave a garrison at the lab and another at the workshop. Chase and Gretchen should be back here within seven or eight suns."

I breathe an enormous sigh of relief.

When we return from our walk, I visit the radio room. The operator, a young woman named Helga, shows me how to operate the radio.

I pick up the microphone and squeeze the button. "This is Fort Taylor calling the chem lab," I say, following the newly established protocol. "Repeat, this is Fort Taylor calling the chem lab." I release the button.

I listen to static for a moment and then hear an excited "Hey, ET, is that you?"

I'd recognize Kenny's voice anywhere. "Yeah," I say, "it's me."

"I was worried," Kenny says. "Chase and Gretchen told me you looked about nine-tenths dead when they found you."

"That's about right," I agree. "Apaches are persistent little demons. It took everything I had to stay a jump ahead of them. But everything worked out well. I'm feeling a lot better. I hear they've left some soldiers up there to keep you company."

"I prefer to think of them as my personal entourage," sniffs Kenny. "It's nice to open the hatch without worrying someone's gonna whack me over the head with a tomahawk."

"I imagine so. How's the chem lab?"

"*Oh my God!*" exclaims Kenny. "This place is *fabulous!* I have *everything* here. I feel like I've just had a lifetime's worth of Christmas mornings all at once!"

"Can you brew up a few things we can use to make life difficult for the Court?"

"The question isn't whether I *can* brew up some nasty stuff, but which nasty stuff I should make *first.*"

"That's great, Kenny. I'll try to pay you a visit in a week or two. But this time I'm gonna bring an army with me."

"No more flying solo?" Kenny asks.

"No more flying solo," I agree.

25

I regain my strength as the days pass. My side is healing nicely. Grizz and I walk around our entire complex every morning. It's a ten-mile walk, but I'm strong enough to handle it now. I'm especially impressed with the job Falstaff is doing training our army. A huge area has been set up for weapons training, and it brings back memories to hear Falstaff barking instructions at his new trainees. In another area, soldiers are practicing the tactic of advancing under fire. One line moves forward while a second one fires at the enemy, and then the advancing line goes down to provide covering fire while the other line advances. Recruits in another area are experimenting with different forms of camouflage.

We stop at the obstacle course as men and women run and crawl over, through, and around a variety of obstacles. At the end, they use ropes to climb a twenty-foot wall. Other recruits are running around the outer edge of the practice fields in lockstep formation.

"Falstaff is very strict about physical conditioning. When he's done with these recruits, they're going to be as fit as we are," says Grizz.

"I'll race you," I say as I run toward the obstacle course. I look over my shoulder to find Grizz staring at me as though I've suddenly gone crazy. But he chases me.

"We nurse you back to health, and now you're gonna hurt yourself," he hollers.

I ignore him and continue running.

He wins, as I expected, but I give him a serious challenge. We both fall to the ground past the finish line, out of breath.

"I guess you *are* feeling better," he says, breathing hard.

"Yep." I smile. "ET is back."

The day comes when I know it's time to remove the splint from my pinkie finger. I ask Grizz to do the honors. He's extremely gentle, and with the splint gone, I find my finger now curls up instead of down, but I can move it around and clench my fist.

"Looks cute," says Grizz, evaluating the finger. "Like it has a mind of its own. Kind of like the rest of you." He gives the finger a tender kiss.

* * * * *

In the days that follow, I set up a daily routine. In the early morning, Grizz and I go for a run around the farms and the mine area. Afterward, I work on my sword-fighting technique. Despite all the things he has to do, Falstaff insists on carving out time to help me with my swordsmanship skills. Falstaff tells me I'm getting pretty good. Coming from him, that's high praise. I still can't beat Grizz, but I make him work hard.

In the afternoon, I walk through the fields and the military training areas, getting to know our farmers and soldiers. They finally get used to seeing me and don't stop work to wave and cheer. This is a relief.

I venture down into the iron mine, riding the rusty old cart the miners used. We're not actively mining now—the miners are learning to be soldiers—but I want to get some idea what conditions in the mine are like. The conditions are cruel. The air is fetid, and the mines are stifling. We'll have to work on these problems when we resume mining.

As usual, Falstaff joins Grizz and me at dinner. We've now added Zoe to our dinner party as well.

286

"I have to tell you," Falstaff announces around a mouthful of peas, "I'm very impressed with this one," he says, nodding at Zoe. "Every recruit I have works hard, but Zoe works hardest of all. She's the first one working in the morning and the last one to leave at night. Her timings on the obstacle course are off the charts."

"I just want to convince you to let me help you fight the Court," she intones modestly. "I have some things to prove."

"You'll get plenty of chance to do that," says Falstaff. "You'll make a good officer someday, Zoe. You're a born warrior."

Grizz and I exchange surprised glances. "That's great, Zoe," I say. "We're glad to have you on our side."

* * * * *

Spending time with Grizz makes this one of the sweetest, and most frustrating, times of my life. I finally work up courage to talk to him about my initiation into the Sisters' order.

"Do you remember, before you left to set up the radio masts, when I told you I loved you?" I ask.

"Are you kidding me?" Grizz replies. "I think about it every day. I dream about it every night."

"I meant it," I say earnestly. "But there's no way we can ever be a couple."

Grizz waits for me to continue.

I pour out my heart. I share my guilty feelings about Tyler. I explain that I don't want Grizz to stay on this side of the brane just because I'm staying. And then I tell him about my initiation into the Sisters' order.

I expect Grizz to be angry. If the situation were reversed, I'd be furious. But, as often happens, Grizz surprises me.

"I knew about you and Ty," he says. "You wear your guilt like a cloak. I know you, ET. I know how to read you. And I also knew you wouldn't want me to stay on this side of the brane just for you. But what you *don't* understand is that I wouldn't leave you even if you tried to beat me away with a stick. And as far as the Sisters are concerned, I knew you were committed to their cause, whether or not you took an oath.

"But you know what?" he continues. "I love you, ET, and the only thing I want is to be with you. If we can't be romantic, so be it."

I feel tears on my cheeks. "Oh, Grizz, I love you so much." I throw my arms around him. The precious ache I always feel this close to Grizz is going to be a problem forever. I want much more.

With difficulty, I release Grizz. I look into his blue eyes and see he feels the same thing I feel. This is clearly not going to be easy for either of us.

"I love you, too, Erin," he says softly. In his voice, I hear a mixture of tenderness and longing.

* * * * *

The next day, Chase and Gretchen return from their expedition to the workshop and the lab. At dinner that evening, we discuss strategy.

"Sooner or later," I say, "the Sons of 1776 are gonna send an army against us."

"We're going to need fortifications at the lab and the workshop," says Falstaff.

Nobody questions the importance of holding on to the lab and the workshop. We all know we'll need a technological edge to defeat the Court.

"And while we're at it, we need to defend the saddle," I add. "The Apaches tracked us to the foot of it. You know the Sons are gonna want to know what's on this side."

"We should build forts at all three locations," says Chase. "We need defensive positions to fight off any move the Sons make."

There is universal agreement.

"I'd like to volunteer to oversee the construction of the forts," Chase offers.

"I think you're the perfect person for the job," I agree.

Falstaff says, "I'll assign a thousand men and women to work with you, Chase. There are tens of thousands of big evergreen trees just below the summit of the saddle on this side. They'll provide you with lumber, but you'll have to haul everything over the saddle and down into the valley. That's going to be a huge job, so we should get started."

"I'm ready," says Chase.

Everybody looks at me for approval. On one hand, I wish they wouldn't do that. On the other hand, I'm getting used to it. It goes with the job.

"We start tomorrow," I say.

I announce my plans to visit the chem lab and the workshop.

"I want to time my visits so I can be back in time to join Helen at the Sanctuary midway between the next two new moons." Zoe is dining with us, as usual, so I don't discuss the fact that this will be exactly two weeks from the day we attack the blacksuits' village forts. I'm growing to trust her more each day as she continues to work hard with Falstaff, but I'm not going to trust her with our strategic plans.

"In fact," I continue, "I think it'd be a good idea if all of us met at the Sanctuary, just to make sure everything is ready."

"I can leave the training of our troops in Gretchen's hands," says Falstaff.

"And I should have the construction of the forts well under way by then," says Chase.

"I know Bree will be ready for a break," I say. "Knowing her, she's been working twelve hours a day, seven days a week at the workshop. She'll need to come up for air."

Nobody needs to be reminded that taking the village forts away from the blacksuits is the most important project we have going. Burning those forts to the ground is the only way we can end the gleanings and the butchery of our people. By my calculation, we should have supplies of wolf bane delivered to all the villages in plenty of time to launch our attacks. Because of the distances we have to travel, our radio masts on the far western, far southern, and far northern villages are not yet operational, but I expect the southern fort to come on line in under a week, and the others should be working no more than four weeks from now. That'll be two weeks before our attacks on the village forts.

* * * * *

A day before I'm scheduled to leave for my tour of the lab and the workshop, Falstaff asks me to meet him on the training fields. When I join him, he introduces me to the Daughter of Gaia's Guard.

"I've selected one hundred of our best fighters," says Falstaff. "Wherever you go, they go. We can't have Apaches chasing our Daughter of Gaia around the desert anymore."

He introduces me to Rosalind, the captain of the Guard. Rosalind's hair is beginning to gray, and she has the stern look of a person with a mission.

"We have all taken an oath," says Rosalind. "We'll gladly lay down our lives in your service, Daughter of Gaia."

I don't like the idea of people dying for me, but I don't want to be chased around by Apaches anymore, either. "Thank you, Rosalind," I say. "I pray you'll never have to make that sacrifice. And you must understand that I pledge my life to you as well."

I walk back to my quarters, and Rosalind and the guard follow me.

"Are you going to follow me wherever I go?" I ask.

"Yes, Daughter of Gaia," replies Rosalind. "We're under orders from Falstaff. Where you go, we go."

So much for privacy, I think.

When I head for the dining hall, all hundred guards follow me. When I enter, I'm relieved to find only Rosalind accompanies me inside. The rest of the guard watches the hall's doors and windows. I'd feel self-conscious if I had a hundred people watching me eat.

I ask Rosalind if she'd like to join us for dinner.

"Oh, no, Daughter of Gaia," she demurs. "I must always be visually scanning the room, looking for possible threats."

I shoot Falstaff a withering look.

"We just want to keep our Daughter of Gaia safe and sound," he says, suppressing a smile. He knows I detest special treatment.

When one of the cooks drops a pot, creating a terrible clatter, Rosalind wrestles me to the ground and lies on top of me.

I get up and dust myself off. I look at Rosalind with one eyebrow raised.

"I'm just doing my job," she explains.

* * * * *

Grizz and I leave for our tour of the technology labs on the east side of the mountains the following morning.

Rosalind falls in beside Grizz and me. She has outriders on all our flanks, so she can relax a bit. I ask her about her life before joining the guard.

"I was gleaned when I was twelve," she says. "The courtsmen wanted me to become a household slave. But I was too unruly. I was supposed to be the handmaid for one of the justice's daughters. But when she told me to fetch her a snack, I told her to get it herself. So they whipped me and sent me to work in the mines."

"I'm guessing," I say, "that when Falstaff tells you to do something, you don't tell him to do it himself?"

"Absolutely not!" snorts Rosalind indignantly. "A good soldier always follows orders."

"What was working in the mines like?" I ask.

"Well," she says, "you spend all day underground breathing air that smells rotten. And believe it or not, the mines go so deep that the air down there is even hotter than it is on the surface. You swing a pick or dig with a shovel all day long. If you stop working when you're not supposed to, an overseer gives you a taste of the lash. I worked fourteen-hour shifts, and by the time my shift was over, my muscles shook from exhaustion. I'd have to say I didn't care for it. I much prefer soldiering."

* * * * *

Late in the afternoon, a monsoon blows up. I'm immediately surrounded by a platoon of young soldiers who insist on holding a tarp around me. When I move, they move.

"This isn't necessary," I say. "The Daughter of Gaia isn't going to melt in the rain."

"We're just following our instructions," says a young man. "Please, Daughter of Gaia, if Rosalind sees you out in the rain, she'll be very unhappy with us. We'll wind up on guard duty all night long."

"Very well," I sigh.

Grizz is grinning. I fume in silence.

* * * * *

When we reach the tree line on the western side of the saddle, we hear hundreds of axes ringing out. Chase's workers are busy. As we march on, we pass large groups of our people hauling logs up the mountain and down the other side. Moving in the opposite direction are soldiers bearing wolf bane, bound for the villages. The foundation for the fort on the west side of the saddle is already laid, and at the workshop, we find the foundation being prepared. Chase and his people are working fast. I ask if Chase is around, and am told he has moved on to the chem lab, where another party is at work.

* * * * *

I visit with Bree for an afternoon. "We're going to have two trebuchets built for each village," she says. "And we're also working on large catapults that will be much more powerful than the trebuchets. We'll have much more difficulty moving them through the forest, but

293

from everything I've heard, we'll need the extra power when we tackle the forts of the inner ring," she says.

She also has the wolf bane assembly line humming. They're manufacturing hundreds of pots every day.

"We weren't getting enough new pots from the villages," Bree explains, "so I've trained some of our people to make wooden pots with the machinery here. The pots are much lighter and easier to carry. We'll soon be producing enough of our own pots that we won't need the villagers to make any more."

As hard as the villagers work just to harvest enough food to stay alive, I'm certain they'll be relieved to have the pot-making burden lifted.

I'm pleasantly surprised to discover Tyler and Eva have become inseparable. Tyler is as happy as I've ever seen him. Watching Eva dote on Tyler fills me with joy for both of them. I'm glad for Tyler, but I can't help noticing the irony of the situation. No sooner have I joined the Sisters and taken a vow of chastity than my problem with Tyler seems to have resolved itself. The romance between Grizz and I is just not meant to be, it seems. And the longing I feel for Grizz will become even more intense without my feelings of responsibility for Tyler helping me to extinguish it. When Grizz sees Ty and Eva nuzzling one another, he smiles sadly at me.

* * * * *

Before we leave the workshop, we receive an urgent radio message from Falstaff.

"Zoe has deserted," he announces angrily.

"What do you mean? " I ask.

"She didn't show up for training this morning. We searched everywhere for her, but she was gone."

I can't say I'm terribly surprised. "Do you think she went back to the Court?" I ask.

"I don't know where else she could go," says Falstaff. "And worse yet, she took several jars of wolf bane with her. I don't know what her plans are, but I've doubled patrols in the forest between us and the outer ring of forts."

"You should warn Helen as well. She'll need to post more guards, too."

We press on to the chem lab, which turns out to be a carbon copy of the workshop, but with chemical paraphernalia instead of machines. There are arms and ammunition here, as well as another huge water tank. More useless food and fuel line the walls. We find Kenny busy at work.

"What are you cooking up for us?" I ask.

"I have three projects going right now," she says. "First of all, Bree tells me that she needs a bomb that can be launched from her catapults that will explode on impact, so these people here are working on that." She gestures at a group of people hard at work.

"And these people over here are working on tear gas. The tear gas the Sons left was too old, but the launchers still work. So we're working on the gas and canisters. Right here, we're working on flashbangs."

"What's a flashbang?" I ask.

"Our military used to have them. Basically, they explode with a brilliant flare of light and an earsplitting noise. Anybody within a radius of about fifty yards is pretty much blind and deaf for five minutes after they go off."

"So," I summarize, "when we attack the blacksuits, we'll be able to knock down their walls, make them cry, and turn them blind and deaf?"

"That's about it," Kenny says. "Oh, I almost forgot. You know how our tunics are made from softbark and how light they are?"

"Yes."

"Well," continues Kenny, "softbark is almost perfect for making a hot air balloon. Unfortunately, a little bit of gas leaks out when the softbark is exposed to high pressure. I'm trying to rubberize the softbark without adding too much weight. I figure an air force might be a good thing, no?"

"You're the greatest, Kenny."

Kenny grins.

"I don't suppose you'd want to join us at the Sanctuary in about three weeks?" I ask.

"No way," says Kenny. "I'm having too much fun here."

＊ ＊ ＊ ＊

We spend one night at the chem lab and then begin the long march back to Fort Taylor. I've seen everything I need to see. We'll soon be ready to become the aggressors. The blacksuits have no idea what's about to hit them.

Our return journey is delayed by a blizzard over the saddle, so my journey to the Sanctuary is delayed by two days.

We are within a day's march of the Sanctuary when disaster strikes.

Standing idly in the path in front of us is Jared Cain. "I'm so glad you finally came," he says.

Zoe steps out from behind him.

26

"You're late," she says. "We've been waiting for you several days now. We're almost out of wolf bane."

Rosalind and my bodyguard quickly string arrows and point them at the pair blocking our path.

"I wouldn't do that if I were you," Jared warns. "You see, we have a thousand arrows pointed right at the Daughter of Gaia."

Hundreds of blacksuits step out from behind trees.

Seeing the confused look on Rosalind's face, Jared explains, "We ambushed your scouts. They're dead."

"What do you want with us?" I ask.

"We want you and Grizz to join us," Jared explains pleasantly. "I have some friends who'd like to meet you."

"I'll bet you do," jeers Grizz. "And you," he says, glaring at Zoe, "we took you in and made you one of us."

Zoe laughs. "How could you ever think I'd give up life in New Washington for your dirty, primitive fort?"

"We'll come with you peacefully," I say, "if you'll let Rosalind and the others go."

"Of course," agrees Jared. "This way." He gestures to the north with his arm.

"Daughter of Gaia," says Rosalind miserably, "I've failed you." She looks stricken

"This isn't your fault," I reassure. "Go on to the Sanctuary and tell Helen what's happened."

Blacksuits bind my hands behind my back, and they do the same with Grizz. They also bind our feet. The shackles on our feet are long enough for us to walk, but we can't possibly run.

"Surely you don't need Grizz," I say. "I'll come willingly if you leave him alone."

"Can't do that," says Jared. "Grizz is a big part of our plans."

Blacksuits roughly shove Grizz and me northward. We've walked less than five minutes when we hear the sounds of battle behind us. The fight is a short one. Rosalind is badly outnumbered, and the blacksuits have the advantage of cover. The thought of my friends being butchered fills me with grief.

"Still a liar," I hiss, looking at Jared angrily.

"No need to call names," says Jared. "You didn't really think we'd let them live, did you?"

I don't answer.

As we walk, Jared tries to strike up a conversation. When he sees that Grizz and I are not going to respond, he falls silent. I can't help but wonder what the Court has planned for me. They don't want us dead, at least not yet, because Jared could kill us right now, if that was the plan. I try to find some means of escape, but draw a blank. With our legs shackled, the blacksuits would quickly run us down if we tried to get away.

The blacksuits look at us with unveiled hostility. I'm sure their enmity has something to do with the three thousand blacksuits we buried at the Sanctuary. I'm sure they're itching for revenge.

* * * * *

We spend the night at Fort Gentry, one of the blacksuits' outer ring forts.

"We've been instructed to take good care of you," Jared says as he shows us to our rooms. My room is right next to Grizz's. Once the door is closed behind me and bolted, I examine the accommodations. They are fine indeed. The bed has a thick mattress, cotton sheets, and a quilted bedcover. There are paintings on the wall, a dresser, and on top of the dresser is a pitcher filled with water, along with a large bowl. A washrag, a towel, and a bar of scented soap sit next to the bowl.

The room has a barred window, but it's large and admits lots of light. I look out the window onto a courtyard. I imagine it must be a parade ground. The barracks I see surrounding the courtyard are solid, whitewashed, and well constructed. Blacksuits and a few civilians linger in the courtyard. Four sentries have been posted just outside my window. Even if I could somehow get through the bars, I couldn't escape.

I sit in a plush chair and reflect. Things could be much worse. I worry about what this gentle treatment might mean. Why didn't they throw us into a dirty cell with straw for a mattress?

My thoughts are interrupted as the door is unbolted and a slave woman brings me a tray of food. She sets the tray on the table, curtsies, and leaves without a word. The food smells delicious. There's meat that looks like beef, mashed potatoes with brown gravy, and mixed vegetables. For the first time since we passed through the brane, I'll be eating with silverware. I eat heartily, but can't help feeling guilty when I contrast my meal with the meals the villagers are eating this evening.

Later, the woman who brought the tray brings another one, this one bearing sugared strawberries and a small pitcher of cream. She exchanges this tray for the one with empty dishes.

I fall asleep still puzzled by the generous treatment. Why are they treating us so well?

* * * * *

Breakfast consists of an orange and a slice of something that looks like bread, but isn't. I recall Helen telling us that the world's grain crops were destroyed during the wars. Whatever I'm eating tastes something like bread, and it's generously buttered.

After breakfast, Jared and Zoe enter my room along with several blacksuits.

"I hope you slept well?" Jared asks.

I don't respond. I have nothing to say to Jared and Zoe.

"Silence becomes a girl," Jared says with a shrug.

The blacksuits bind my hands again and usher me through the door, where I find Grizz, also bound.

Jared and Zoe lead us out of the fort and northward, toward New Washington. We leave the familiar forest behind. The first mile inside the forest is barren. Nothing but a few weeds grows. People will never venture within a mile of the forest after sunset, lest they be attacked by dreadwolves.

The barren zone gives way to cultivated fields. Slaves are growing a variety of crops, including citrus groves, fields of strawberries, peaches, grapes, cotton, and sugarcane. Luxury crops. They make the villagers grow the staples and keep the luxuries for themselves. The slaves in the fields are thin, much like our villagers, but they don't have the running sores we know so well. Obviously, they aren't fed much, but what they do eat is more nutritious. We pass a huge lake that smells so bad it causes me to gag. Jared and Zoe hold handkerchiefs over their noses.

Scattered through the fields are dozens of small forts, with blacksuits keeping watch from towers. Clearly, they guard their slaves as closely as they guard the villages. From a tactical standpoint, if we are ever to get close to New Washington, we must first capture these forts. The garrisons aren't large, based on the small size of the forts, but there are lots of them.

We pass foul-smelling villages. The houses are made of mud and wattle, just like those of our villagers. These are the houses of slaves. By late afternoon, the cultivated fields give way, and we see a large castle. As we get closer, I can tell it's made of concrete, and it gleams white in the sun. Glistening turrets rise from the walls, which are more than twenty feet high. This is clearly one of the inner-ring forts. Taking this one will be difficult. I hope Kenny and Bree are working hard on new weapons. We'll need them. Flags hang limply from flagpoles atop the turrets.

"There's someone inside I'd like you to meet," says Jared.

The gate is lowered and we enter the castle. The castle is clearly a military facility. Everything is neatly organized. Barracks, a mess hall, offices, and an armory are all whitewashed and lined up in perfectly straight rows. We're headed for a building with a sign in front that reads: Officer's Club. Jared ushers us into a large room where a small party of men wait.

I'm struck by the fact that these men are tall. Every one of them is nearly six feet.

"I'd like to introduce you to the chief justice of the Supreme Court, Oskar Salieri."

Jared falls to his knees. The blacksuit behind me whacks me across the back of my knees, and I find myself involuntarily on my knees as well.

"Please rise," says the chief justice. "Untie her."

A blacksuit loosens my binding, and I rub my wrists to restore circulation.

Salieri is a plump man, balding, perhaps fifty years old. He's not bad looking, and his clothes are impeccable. But there's something about him that turns my stomach. His eyes are hard and cold, and he seems...oily, smooth, slippery, and utterly toxic.

"You must be the Daughter of Gaia," he says pleasantly.

"I'm sometimes called that," I confirm.

"I've been anxious to meet you," says Salieri. He steps up and kisses me once on each cheek.

I recoil as I would from a snakebite. I slap his face, hard.

"Don't ever touch me again," I say evenly.

I see rage in his eyes. He slowly regains emotional control. "Now, now," he says calmly. "That's no way to treat your future husband."

* * * * *

I'm speechless. I laugh at the outrageous thought of marrying him.

"I don't know what you think you're doing," snarls Grizz, "but—"

Grizz is silenced by a blow to his stomach, which leaves him breathless and doubled over.

Jared, who administered the blow, says, "You don't address the chief justice unless he speaks to you. You have a lot to learn, Grizz, and I'm gonna enjoy teaching you."

"How can you even *think* I'll marry you?" I ask Salieri incredulously.

"You will marry me," explains Salieri, "because you want to save your friend here from a very, very painful death." He gestures at Grizz.

My sense of defiance deflates as I digest this threat. I can't let them hurt Grizz.

"Don't do it, ET. Just—" Grizz starts, and receives another blow to the stomach.

"You're a slow learner, Grizz," says Jared.

"Come with me," orders Salieri.

He leads us out into the street, where we find a carriage being borne by twelve slaves.

"Please," Salieri says, opening a carriage door and gesturing for me to enter.

"I'd rather walk," I say.

"Jared," says Salieri, looking over his shoulder at him.

Jared punches Grizz again, this time in the face.

"Now," says Salieri, "as I said, please enter."

I give Grizz an anguished look.

"Don't—" Grizz begins, but is once again interrupted by a blow to the midsection.

I step up into the carriage. Salieri closes my door and walks around to the other side, where a slave opens his door. He steps into the carriage, which perceptibly sags under his weight.

Salieri looks at me. "We knew you and your friends were going to cause trouble for us when you murdered three thousand of our soldiers at your so-called Sanctuary. But we might have been able to overlook that bit of…unpleasantness."

Sure you would, I think sarcastically.

"But when you took our mines away from us," he continues, "we knew we had to stop you. We need our mines, you see. Without them, we can't live as comfortably as we would like.

"And we've also noticed that our slaves have become surly and unproductive recently. They keep mumbling about a 'Daughter of Gaia' as though she were coming to free them. And we certainly can't continue to live in luxury if our slaves don't do their part."

I remain silent, waiting for him to continue.

"Fortunately, Jared and Zoe helped us make our plans to stop this silly little revolution of yours. They told us who this Daughter of Gaia is, and that we can control her through her boyfriend. All that remained was to catch you. You made this easy by taking Zoe into your circle and discussing your plans in front of her."

This surprises me, because we'd been very careful to avoid discussing our plans to take over the village forts while Zoe was within earshot. But did I mention my travel plans while she was near? I must have.

"How do you plan to use me to stop our rebellion?" I ask. "The villagers don't need me to continue their fight against you."

"I think they do," says Salieri, "but let's not quibble. Here's the plan. You and I will wed, a symbolic joining of our two peoples. Then, we will launch a new era of cooperation between your people and mine. We will permit the villagers to grow a healthy variety of crops in their fields. We will turn the village forts into centers where we can educate your young and provide medical care for your old."

I'm not buying a word of this. "And what would you expect us to give you in return?"

"All we require is the return of our mines and the secret for making wolf bane," he replies. "And, at some point in the future, you will tell us how to get into the workshop on the other side of the mountains."

"Once you had the ability to make wolf bane, what would stop you from continuing to enslave my people?" I ask.

"Absolutely nothing," says Salieri.

"Then why do you expect my people to trust you when you make these promises?"

"Oh, they won't believe *me*. They will believe because *you* will be the one making the promises."

I'm dumbfounded. "I won't lie to them." I say emphatically.

"Fine," says Salieri. "Then we shall send you your boyfriend's right pinkie finger on your dinner tray this evening. Tomorrow, we'll send you his left. We can continue to provide you with dinner surprises for weeks. In fact, Jared will thoroughly enjoy doing this. I understand he doesn't care for Grizz."

I struggle to keep my expression neutral. "Is there any chance you'll keep any of these promises?"

"There is absolutely no chance."

Of course not, I think. But I give Salieri points for honesty. "And if I cooperate with you," I ask, "what will happen to Grizz?"

"You and he will live a long and happy life together in the heart of New Washington. You will be extended every comfort and convenience we can offer."

"And why should I believe you?"

"Because I'm telling you the truth," he says. "We would expect you to tour the villages from time to time. As a little reminder to the villagers that opposing us is futile."

"You say Grizz and I will 'live a long and happy life together.' How does that work if you and I are married?"

"I quickly tire of girls. If a slave girl is pretty, I may keep her for a month, or even two." He looks at me appraisingly. "I would guess you might last six weeks. Then you would be free to live with Grizz."

"Won't being married to me be an inconvenience when you find someone you'd really like to marry?" I ask.

"That's not likely to happen. I'm very fond of my slave girls. But I can always have the marriage annulled if it becomes inconvenient. After all, I have friends at the Court." He laughs at his own joke.

I can see I need to play for time. With Grizz as his captive, Salieri holds the high card. I need time to think and plan.

"I'll do whatever you want me to do," I agree. "My only condition is that you let me see Grizz every day, so I can see for myself you're keeping your word."

"A short visit every day can be arranged," he agrees.

* * * * *

Salieri enjoys describing his fiefdom as we travel.

"We are now traveling through the factory district," he says. "This is where cotton is milled, furniture is made, iron is smelted, and wine is bottled. Most of the things we need for a comfortable life are made in this ring."

The factories seem drab and dismal, and the few people I see are poorly dressed and miserable looking.

Within an hour, we leave the factory district.

"This," announces Salieri, "is the suburb of Chevy Chase."

The houses here are wood-frame structures, neatly painted and nicely landscaped. The streets are paved. The people in this suburb are well dressed. They bustle about busily.

"The people who live in the suburbs are very satisfied with their lives. They look at the fate of the slaves and feel very fortunate and prosperous by comparison. But they, too, serve us. These people are our doctors and nurses, our merchants, our midlevel military officers, our vintners and chefs, the ones who supervise the work of the slaves. We of the elite need these people, so we allow them to live well, and to believe they are both happy and fortunate."

You're despicable, I think, but I don't speak. I've already decided that my best chance for escape will lie in making them believe I've bought into Salieri's plan.

"You say Grizz and I will live in New Washington," I say. "You're going to allow us to live with the elite?"

"Yes, of course, my dear. We want the villagers to know that you are one of us," he says with a smile.

As we come closer to New Washington, the houses grow larger and the streets wider.

By late afternoon, we're within view of the Palace of the Court. The magnitude of the structure is enormous. The palace is surrounded by a defensive wall at least thirty feet high. Turrets overhang the walls and provide overlapping fields of fire. Near the top of the walls, I can make out embrasures and murder holes, narrow slits where archers can loose arrows from behind cover, firing down at the approaching enemy below.

"The walls are six feet thick, made of reinforced concrete," Salieri explains. "Ten thousand men defend New Washington from these walls."

I'm certain he's telling me these things to discourage any hopes I have for taking these walls. He's succeeding.

The drawbridge is lowered, and our carriage enters New Washington. There are dozens of buildings in the city, most of them simple barracks for defenders and a variety of small shops. The dominant structure, however, is the Palace of the Court. It rises sixty feet high and measures at least three hundred feet a side. Built of white stone, it stands gleaming in the sun.

"The slaves of our ancestors spent more than one hundred years building the palace," Salieri explains. I believe him.

The slaves bearing our carriage stop in front of a broad set of steps leading to a pair of massive wooden doors. A slave opens my door, and Salieri takes my hand as he leads me up the stairs. I have a visceral need to pull my hand away from him, but I remind myself I must appear to cooperate. I'll need them to let their guard down.

Inside the doors is a vast entry hall. Plush red carpet covers the floor, and portraits line the walls.

"The portraits are of men who have served as justices," Salieri explains. No women, of course.

The ceilings are vaulted and at least twenty feet high. Everyone we meet takes a knee in front of Salieri. The people inside the palace are very tall, some even exceeding six feet. These people have clearly eaten well, even during the years their people spent as hunters and gatherers. They've never known the kind of hunger that would have made growing smaller a necessary adaptive trait.

"We'll start our tour at the bottom," says Salieri as he removes a torch from its holder. He leads me down a narrow set of steps. At the bottom is a large, concrete-lined tunnel. There's no light but Salieri's torch. "This is an aqueduct," he says. "When our ancestors first arrived, they built the palace on the highest ground they could find. They did this so they could build sewers to flush waste away. We have our servants dump our refuse into the aqueduct, and every night we wash it away. The wastewater travels many miles before it is dumped into vast waste pools. Properly treated, the waste makes excellent fertilizer."

I think of the evil-smelling lake we passed on our journey. "Where do you get the water to flush the aqueduct every night?"

"There's a huge cistern which covers the entire roof of the palace," says Salieri. "If the rains aren't adequate to fill it, we have a system for pumping groundwater to the cistern. You can't drink the groundwater, of course, but it's entirely adequate for flushing the sewers. Many slaves are needed to drive the pump, but slaves are plentiful."

I can't help but be impressed by the magnitude of the sewer system.

"Tens of thousands of slaves died building this aqueduct," says Salieri. His tone of voice shows his pride in this dismal fact. I'm once again sickened by the low value these people place on human life.

Salieri leads me back up the steps. We continue our tour on the first floor. He shows me the grand room where the Supreme Court sits while in session. Furniture is large and well crafted, shining with polish. The walls are decorated with colorful banners. The seats occupied by the justices are elevated, allowing them to look down on everyone before them. The remainder of the first floor supports the operation of the Court: a bailiff's chamber, a small cell for prisoners awaiting hearings, rooms for storing records, and offices for the justices themselves. The size and richness of everything contrasts vividly with the pitiable homes and buildings of our villagers.

At the far end of the first floor is a museum dedicated to the history of the Court and its people. There are drawings of New Washington as it was being constructed; gavels first used hundreds of years ago;, robes worn by earlier justices; and the ceremonial swords of every chief justice since the founding of New Washington. The swords gleam in the sunlight that pours into the museum through large windows.

"This sword belonged to my grandfather," says Salieri proudly, pointing to a long sword with a jeweled handle and an edge that looks as sharp as a razor. "I'm the sixth member of my family to serve as chief justice."

We continue our tour on the second floor. This floor is where the work needed to support the justices and their cronies is done. There are kitchens here, tailors and cobblers at work, a large laundry, servants' quarters, and a warren of small shops and offices. Salieri leads me down a long corridor lit only by torches. I catch a foul smell in the air, which grows stronger as we proceed. Salieri ushers me into a room where men dressed in white are hard at work in what is clearly a chemistry lab.

"These are our alchemists," Salieri says. "They are hard at work learning the secret behind your wolf bane. We know it's the scent the alpha male uses to mark his territory, and it will take us only a short while to reproduce it."

Clearly, Salieri and his alchemists have no clue what the wolf bane truly is. "You're very clever," I say. "But if you're making wolf bane yourself, why do you need me to tell you how to make it?"

"Only to simplify the process," says Salieri. "We have other projects for our alchemists. The weapons we took from you when you were captured by Jared and Zoe are of great interest to us. We would like to make our own explosive weapons."

The third floor houses the military of the elite. There are rooms with huge maps on the walls, a hall for bow practice, a room for dueling, an armory, and residences for the senior military staff. I'd love to get my hands on those maps.

The remaining three floors of the palace are given over for residences of the elite. Salieri leads me to the top floor, where he shows me into my own suite. My rooms are luxurious and extravagant. The floors are made of polished stone. My four-poster bed is larger than my family's backyard swimming pool. The coverlet and pillowcases are tastefully embroidered. The walls are hung with painted landscapes and colorful cloth artwork. There's a large desk made of polished wood, and comfortable-looking chairs. Double doors with windows open onto a large balcony. On the wall opposite my bed is a painting of Salieri. That will have to go.

"We decided to put you on the top floor so you wouldn't be tempted to escape," explains Salieri. "Trying to climb down from here would be suicide."

I look down from the railing at the edge of the balcony. I'm at least sixty feet above the plaza below. There's no way to climb down.

"Your friend Grizz occupies the suite right below you," Salieri says. "Now you've seen the building where you will spend the rest of your life. If you are cooperative, the rest of your life could be a very long time. And if you are less cooperative…" He lets the sentence dangle in the air. "If you are *very* cooperative, after a number of years, we might give you liberty to leave the palace and wander the streets of New Washington as you please."

"I'll cooperate," I say, hoping I sound sincere.

"Oh yes," says Salieri as if he's had an afterthought. "We will be wed on the day of the first waxing crescent. I like the symbolism. Our relationship with the villagers will begin anew just as the moon begins to renew itself."

I have less than two weeks to escape.

D.S. Northrop

27

I'm contemplating what life with Grizz would be like in this gilded cage. I decide that he and I weren't built to live in any cage, no matter how pleasant. And we wouldn't care much for our neighbors.

A servant enters with dinner. "Veal stewed in tomatoes, caramelized sweet potatoes, and fresh young asparagus in a cheese sauce," the maid says. "For dessert we have chocolate mousse,".

The food is delicious. After eating, I stand on my balcony, which faces south, and think about the villagers, only fifty miles away. If I can't escape, can I allow the Court to keep them in slavery? I decide that I cannot bear to think of Grizz being tortured. I know this makes me selfish, putting my own happiness ahead of tens of thousands of villagers. I'll just have to find a way to escape so I don't have to make the choice.

I see a slave moving through the courtyard below my balcony in the moonlight. She stops in the middle of the square and lifts something that looks like a manhole cover. She dumps the contents of her bucket in the hole and replaces the cover. Access to Salieri's aqueduct, I speculate.

Just after dark, another maid enters. She's an older woman dressed in a full dress expensively embroidered. The Court dresses its house slaves well. Her silver hair is pulled back into a tidy bun.

"Daughter of Gaia," she says, "I am so honored to meet you." She goes down on her knees.

When she rises, I ask her for her name.

"My name is Mariana," she replies.

"In the future, Mariana, there's no need to kneel in my presence. I'm a simple servant of the Mother."

"Daughter of Gaia," Mariana says in a whisper, "we've heard it said you were coming, and we were to be ready to rise up against the Court. Is this the time for us to rise and fight?"

"No, Mariana, this is not the way I planned to come. I was captured by the courtsmen. The time for the rising will come, but not now."

Mariana looks crushed. "How can you lead us if you are a captive of the Court?"

"I'll have to figure out a way to escape," I say.

"Is there anything we can do to help you escape?"

"I don't have a plan yet. But I'll have one soon. And when I do, I'm certain I'll need your help."

"Please ask anything of us," she urges. "We'll do anything, even die, for you."

Mariana turns down my bed and produces a nightgown from the wardrobe closet. The nightgown is made of softbark.

"Daughter of Gaia, you must not trust the woman who brings your meals. Her name is Francisca, and she is a spy for the blacksuits. Anything you say to her will travel straight to Salieri's ear. However, Isabella, your morning maid, is one of us. You can trust her to be discreet. We even have ways to get messages to Mother Helen, if you should have that need."

"Thank you, Mariana. I'll certainly ask for help when I need it. How do you know that Francisca is a spy?"

"We've seen her talking in whispers to a blacksuit captain. In their arrogance, the courtsmen believe us to be simple and ignorant. Their arrogance will be their downfall," she says.

Other maids, with kettles of steaming water, enter the room and fill my bathtub. They empty a bottle filled with pink liquid into the hot water, and bubbles with a pleasant scent emerge.

"Do you require anything else before we leave?" asks Mariana. "I can scrub your back if you'd like."

"No, thank you. I'm fine." I don't like the idea of anybody staring at me while I'm taking a bath, even a nice person like Mariana.

Mariana bows as she backs out the door.

I sit in my bathtub and soak, letting the misery of my current situation slowly dissolve. After drying myself, I look around my room for something, anything, that will help me escape. I put on my nightdress and go to bed. Just before I fall asleep, I have an idea.

* * * * *

In the morning, I wait for the morning maid. She's a much younger woman than Mariana. She's dressed in a colorful cotton dress. Her blonde hair is cut severely short, and she wears no makeup.

When she enters, I ask, "Are you Isabella?"

"Yes, Daughter of Gaia, I am. How do you know my name?"

"Mariana told me," I explain. "Isabella, is there any way you can leave my soiled sheets here in the room rather than sending them to the laundry?"

"Yes, Daughter of Gaia, I think I can. You have two sheets. I can easily leave one in the room. Nobody will count the sheets I throw in the laundry tubs."

Isabella makes my bed. I start to help her, but she asks me to stop. "If my master were to enter the room and find you helping me, I would be punished severely. Maids are trained to behave in certain ways, and if we don't, we suffer harsh consequences."

I ask Isabella about her life in the Palace of the Court.

"I suppose I should be grateful I don't work in the fields," she says. "But how can anyone be happy when they live the life of a slave? I serve at the pleasure of the elite. You may have noticed my short hair and my lack of makeup. I try to make myself unattractive. Pretty girls attract the attention of the masters. Some women go so far as to scar their faces."

"The day of justice is coming," I promise. "You won't be a slave much longer."

When she's finished, Isabella asks, "Can I bring you some books, Daughter of Gaia? Your days must be long and lonely."

"I'd like that. Thank you, Isabella."

Thirty minutes later, she returns with three books.

When she leaves, I read the titles. *The Proper Role for Women in a Free Society* reads the first one. I'm definitely not interested in that one. The next is titled *Tax Policy: Why Heavy Taxation on the Slaves and the Middle Class Guarantees Economic Growth*. This is not one I'm looking forward to. The final one is *Why Slavery Benefits the Slave*. Not exactly my idea of compelling reading, either.

At two o'clock, guards knock on my door. They hurry me down a set of stairs and stop in front of a door on the floor beneath mine. The captain of the Guard has a key ring, which he uses to open the door. He enters the room and emerges with Grizz in tow. Grizz looks good except for the black eyes Jared gave him yesterday. I move to embrace him, but a guard lowers a spear between us.

"No touching," he says.

"Are they treating you well?" I ask.

"The food is great," Grizz says. "But I'm bored out of my mind."

We make small talk. With the guards watching, we can't say much.

"Time's up," announces the captain of the Guard after five minutes. They lock Grizz up and escort me back to my room.

In the evening, Mariana enters my room with a serious expression on her face. "Daughter of Gaia, I bring a message from Mother Helen."

"What's the message?" I ask.

"Mother Helen wants to know if she should postpone 'the attacks' we have planned. The woman who passed the message to me said Helen told her you would know what 'the attacks' are. Helen is fearful the Court might retaliate against you if they carry them out.'"

"Please send a message to Mother Helen saying the attacks must proceed exactly as planned. Also, ask her if she can have a party of soldiers waiting for me at the edge of the forest near Phoenix the night after the attacks. I won't have wolf bane, so I'll need someone to escort me through the forest."

Mariana looks ecstatic. "You have made plans to escape!" she cries out.

"I have a few ideas," I verify.

I take the two sheets Isabella has left thus far and lay them both on the floor. I roll each sheet up. I tie a knot joining the two sheets. I stand on one sheet and pull on the other with all my weight, tightening the knot. If I add a new sheet each day, in two weeks I should have a "rope" made of sheets that will reach the ground. I stash the rope in my wardrobe. Nobody goes in there except Isabella and Mariana, and they're trustworthy.

* * * * *

On my fourth day of captivity, Salieri bursts into my room. He hands me a sheet of paper.

"Memorize this," he orders. "You will be giving a speech to all the slaves in New Washington this afternoon."

I read the speech:

I have asked my fiancé, Oskar Salieri, to grant me the privilege of speaking with you. My marriage to Chief Justice Salieri will cement the ties of friendship between the men of the Court and my people, the villagers and slaves of the New United States. As a token of his generosity, Chief Justice Salieri will allow our villages to grow a healthy variety of crops. The Court will also use their village forts to provide education for our children and medical care for our sick. Slaves will be taught to read and write. In the spirit of this new age of cooperation, we will provide Chief Justice Salieri with the formula for wolf bane, and we will restore the Court's rightful claim to their mines. I know you will join me as we celebrate the dawn of a new age of cooperation between our peoples.

I work hard to keep my expression neutral as I read the speech. I remind myself that my only prayer for escape is to convince the Court that I've become their willing accomplice.

"I'll give this speech if you will repeat your promise that Grizz and I will be allowed to live together in New Washington."

"Of course I will repeat my promise," says Salieri. "Your people view you as their one great hope for freedom. Having the Daughter of Gaia living in luxury with us in New Washington serves our purposes nicely. We will have no more nonsense about revolution."

That afternoon, I stand on an elevated platform in a huge plaza that is jammed with servants and slaves. Salieri stands at my side, along with a military honor guard. I look out on a sea of hopeful faces, men and women who have been slaves all their lives, but now believe I will set them free. I deliver my speech in a strong voice. I make a simple addition. After I say we will provide the Court with wolf bane, I add the phrase "Which mimics the scent alpha dreadwolves use to mark their territory." When the content of my speech reaches Helen, and I know it will reach her soon, she'll realize I'm not cooperating with Salieri.

As I speak of the alpha wolf scent, I glance anxiously at Salieri out of the corner of my eye to see if he's upset with the addition to the speech. His face remains serene.

I watch as the expressions on the faces of the slaves turn from hope to despair. When I finish, the crowd stands in stony silence. They have no way to pick up my rebellious clue. They realize that once the blacksuits have the secret of wolf bane and their mines back, they'll continue to govern in the old way, and no military uprising will be possible.

Keep the faith, I think, but I can say nothing. I've sworn an oath to serve these people, and I will. When the day of the new moon arrives, I'll launch my escape plan.

D.S. Northrop

28

On the day of the new moon, I pace my room anxiously until nightfall. I force myself to wait until after midnight before tying one end of my sheet rope to the corner post of my balcony. I thread the remainder of the rope through a gap between the bars of the balcony. There's no moon tonight, but I can see far enough to confirm the white sheets reach all the way to the ground.

I carefully step over the balcony rail until I'm balanced on the outside. I follow ET's rule for dealing with frightening heights: don't look down. I know the ground is sixty feet below me, but it doesn't bother me as long as I don't actually see it. I carefully lower myself down the bars until I can grasp the rope. I release my hold on the balcony one hand at a time and wrap each hand around the rope. The rope begins to give way, and my heart pounds like a hammer in my chest until I realize that my weight has forced the knot above me to tighten. The rope remains firm. I climb down the rope, hand under hand, until I reach the balcony of the room below me.

The Court helped my plan enormously when they put Grizz in the room below mine.

"Grizz," I whisper. "Grizz!"

I hear nothing from inside. I take one hand from the rope and use it to bang lightly on the rail of Grizz's balcony. If I make too much noise, I'll awaken the guards, but I have to make enough to rouse Grizz.

At last, I hear sounds from Grizz's room. Grizz emerges onto his balcony, hair a mess, eyes squinting.

"ET!" he says. He takes one long look and realizes what I'm doing.

"Wait here until I'm on the ground," I say. I don't know if the rope will support two of us at the same time. I descend quickly. I watch as Grizz follows me.

I throw my arms around Grizz when he reaches the ground. We remain locked in an embrace for a matter of seconds, not nearly long enough.

"What's the plan?" Grizz whispers.

"I can't explain now," I whisper back. "Just follow me."

I peer around the corner of the palace and see a guard posted by the entrance about fifty yards from where I stand. He stands in a pool of light cast by torches on the wall behind him. That's good, I think. His eyes are not night-adjusted. There's no way he'll see us on a moonless night. I walk on tiptoes to a point about thirty yards from the guard, below a window.

"Give me a hand up," I whisper.

Grizz weaves his fingers together to form a stirrup. I place my foot in the stirrup and push off. I can easily reach the bottom ledge of the window. I say a quick prayer of thanks they haven't rediscovered glass yet as I boost myself through the window.

I'm standing in the History Museum. I move quickly to the sword exhibit. I carefully take the sword that belonged to Salieri's grandfather, and the sword next to it. I slide them into their sheaths and fasten one sheath to my belt. They also have an exhibit of shields, and I quickly take two of these as well. With my arms full, I glide back to the window. Grizz is looking up at me. I carefully lower the second sword until Grizz has a firm hold on it, and then I let go. Grizz quickly fastens the sheath to his belt.

"Catch," I whisper. I drop the first shield, and Grizz catches it neatly. I drop the second shield and feel a moment of terror when Grizz can't catch it and it clatters on the ground.

The guard on duty squints in our direction. He blows his horn, making a noise loud enough to wake the dead. The guard runs at us, but Grizz dispatches him quickly with his sword.

"Follow me," I say. I run quickly around the corner of the building and out into the plaza until I find the slab that covers the chute leading to the aqueduct below. There's a ladder, and after Grizz descends, I stand on its top rungs. I can hear the sound of feet rushing in response to the guard's trumpet blast. I can see shapes of blacksuits in the distance, but none are looking in our direction. I climb down and pull the cover back in place.

The sewers are squalid. Both Grizz and I gag. I pull out two cloths I've cut from my bed sheets and hand one to Grizz. I tie the other behind my neck and cover my nose and watch as Grizz does the same.

"The cloth helps a little," says Grizz.

Very little, I think. The stench is still overpowering. I orient myself. The ladder was on the side opposite my room, which faced south. So we need to move down the tunnel on the ladder side. The aqueduct is pitch-black. There's no hint of light, so there's no way to avoid stepping into putrid piles. I steel myself to ignore them as they squish beneath my feet. The sewer is round, with a diameter of about eight feet, so we can move quickly. Because of the darkness, we constantly carom off the sloping sides of the tunnel. Once again, I'm grateful for every single practice lap I ever ran, as Grizz and I are able to keep up an excellent pace as the hours roll by.

I can't see my watch in the darkness, but my internal clock tells me we've run for about six hours when I hear a roaring noise behind us. I know at once what the sound means. The sewers are being flushed.

"Brace yourself. We're about to be flushed!" I shout to Grizz.

I can't see his face, but I hear him mutter, "Wonderful," and then the torrent carries us away.

We bob around in the tunnel like corks. The rushing water bounces us off the walls as it carries us along. There's plenty of air between the surface of the water and the top of the tunnel. I gambled on being able to breathe, and the gamble has paid off. Had I lost, we'd have died a very unpleasant death. We're carried by the water for what seems like an eternity.

Finally, the tunnel ends, and we find ourselves deposited in a putrid lake. I squint until my eyes become adjusted to sunlight. I assume this is the sewage lake we passed on our trip to New Washington. We swim for the shore. I reach it and wade onto dry land. My sense of smell has long since been overwhelmed and stopped working, and I'm thankful. Grizz emerges from the lake and cries out in pain. He drags himself out of the water, and I see a snake wrapped around his leg with its fangs buried in his ankle.

* * * * *

Grizz draws his sword and beheads the snake. One look at his ankle tells me that his wounds are serious and need to be tended to immediately. A woman working in a nearby field saw us come out of the aqueduct and plunge into the lake. She joins us at once.

"Please," I say urgently, "I'm the Daughter of Gaia, and I need your help."

I can imagine the thoughts going through the woman's head. Is this foul-smelling apparition truly the Daughter of Gaia? And, if so, why did she just fly out of the sewer and into the waste pond? Our height seems to convince her. Far more likely for the Daughter of Gaia to come flying out of the sewer than a justice of the Supreme Court.

"Please," she urges. "Come quickly! The blacksuits must not see you!"

She leads us into a sugarcane field where we can bend over and disappear behind the plants. Grizz is moving slowly on his damaged

324

ankle. We emerge from the fields to find an ancient barn. She hurries us into the barn.

"Thank you," I say. "What is your name?"

"My name is Olivia. Please, wait here. I'll bring help."

Olivia disappears, and I remove Grizz's shoe and sock and roll up his pant leg. I want to clean his wound, but there are no rags to be found. We're both covered in filth, and I know Grizz's wound must be cleaned immediately, or infection will set in.

Olivia returns with five other women. They carry cloths, blankets, and large bowls of water. One of the women is evidently a healer. She cleans Grizz's wound and douses it with the contents of a small vial. The wound is already swollen and infected. The healer draws a knife and lances the swelling. Foul-smelling pus drains from the cut. Grizz grimaces in pain. The healer covers his wound with a poultice smelling of herbs and ties a bandage in place.

"Give us your clothes," says Olivia. "We'll wash them. Clean yourselves, and use the blankets to cover up."

Grizz turns around while I strip down to my skin and bathe myself using the fresh water and clean rags the women provided. It takes forever to clean the filth out of my ears, mouth, and nose. I wrap the blankets around me and avert my eyes so Grizz can clean up as well.

"Hide up there," instructs Olivia, pointing to a loft above our heads. We climb a rickety ladder that was clearly built for smaller people. We move to the back of the loft, where we can't be seen from the barn floor.

"We'll bring food," says Olivia as she climbs up the ladder to join us in the loft. "We've heard wonderful news. We've heard the villages have begun to fight back against the blacksuits. Blacksuit military units have been on the roads all night last night and all day today."

325

Grizz and I smile and high-five one another. "Then it's happening," I say exuberantly.

This is good news for another reason. I had hoped the rebellion in the villages would stop the blacksuits from concentrating on chasing Grizz and I. That seems to be happening as well.

The loft of the barn is used to store tobacco leaves. They hang thick from the ceiling to dry. The walls have numerous small openings where we can see dust motes dance in shafts of sunlight. We eat the food brought by the slaves and sleep fitfully through the day. When darkness falls, we leave the barn and head south again.

We are much slower now, with Grizz hobbled by his bad ankle.

"Go without me," he says. "I'm only slowing you down."

"Do you really think I'm gonna leave you?" I ask.

"No," he replies. "Did you really think I wouldn't offer to stay behind?" I can see his smile despite the darkness.

I thought we'd reach the forest by four or five in the morning, but we're clearly not going to meet that goal. Just before dawn, I hear noise behind us. The bleating of horns and the rhythmic sound of thousands of footsteps marching in unison can only mean a military unit is on the move. As dawn breaks, I see a force of several thousand blacksuits behind us. Grizz struggles mightily to pick up the pace, but the blacksuits behind us are closing the distance between us.

We're nearing the forest. If we can reach it before the blacksuits catch up with us, perhaps we can avoid them in the rough and broken ground of the forest floor.

I soon realize we aren't going to reach the forest before we're overwhelmed. The tree line is at least a mile away, and the blacksuits are closing in.

Like the professional soldiers they are, the blacksuits advance in lines razor straight. Spearmen form the first rank, followed by swordsmen. Archers bring up the rear. Each blacksuit has a specialized job. Spearmen carry spears, and they are trained in nothing else. The same is true of their swordsmen and archers. A lifetime of practicing with a single weapon makes each blacksuit formidable.

I stop walking and turn around. I draw my sword, as does Grizz.

"This is a good place to die," I say

Grizz nods grimly.

* * * * *

From behind us, I hear a boisterous roar. I look over my shoulder to see Falstaff leading three thousand of his newly trained militia as they emerge from the trees, shouting and cheering. They are running at top speed. The blacksuits in front of us see the threat and respond by picking up their pace as well. Falstaff's force reaches us, and Grizz and I are swept along with them.

"Halt!" shouts Falstaff. Our soldiers stop on a dime.

"Bows!" commands Falstaff.

Falstaff's militia takes up their bows and string arrows.

"Loose!" shouts Falstaff.

Our bowmen loose their arrows, and dozens of blacksuit spearmen go down. The blacksuits are advancing at double time. Their bowmen shoot while moving, and their arrows tear huge holes in the ranks of our militia.

"Loose at will!" orders Falstaff.

Our soldiers have been practicing. By the time the lines are within twenty yards of each other, the blacksuit spearmen have been almost totally eliminated. But the blacksuit bowmen have been at work as well, and our ranks have been substantially thinned.

327

"Swords!" shouts Falstaff.

Our soldiers drop their bows and draw swords.

"Charge!" Falstaff commands.

Our men and women descend on the blacksuit lines.

I see Kenny and Chase in the vanguard, AKs blasting away. There's a deafening roar when the two armies collide. The blacksuits maintain discipline, their lines still as straight as a ruler, with space between each man, perfect for the deployment of swords and shields. Their superior training begins to tell. Our soldiers, with six weeks of training, are no match for the blacksuits one-on-one.

"They outnumber us two to one," I cry. "We should fall back!"

"Not today, Daughter of Gaia," says Falstaff. "Not today."

No sooner has he finished speaking than a thousand of our soldiers emerge from the woods to our left, and another thousand appear on the right. These forces hit the flanks of the blacksuit lines and curl around behind them. All sense of lines and organization quickly disappear as the conflict turns into a hand-to-hand melee. Small groups of our men and women struggle with small groups of blacksuits, spread over the huge field. We can't match the blacksuits in skill if we fight their fight, but in the chaos of a melee, our superior motivation gives us the edge. We've been trained to cover the backs of our mates, but other than that, the battle is a free-for-all. Falstaff stands next to me, and Grizz has our backs.

A pair of blacksuits charges at me. I catch the sword of one on my shield and run the other through with my sword. The first blacksuit gives ground, but I step forward and cut him down, only to find another in his place. I parry his thrust and strike him in the face with my shield. Staggered by the blow, he is easy prey. Out of the corner of my eye, I see Chase and Kenny. They've abandoned their AKs, which are worthless in hand-to-hand fighting, and have taken up their swords.

The battle rages around us for an hour, with our forces steadily gaining the upper hand. We slowly push the blacksuits backward. But as soon as I sense we are on the verge of victory, I hear horns blaring. Another blacksuit brigade comes charging at us from the south, the garrison from Fort Gentry, no doubt. The tide starts to turn as the blacksuits' superior numbers begin to wear us down. But our force rallies. We adapt to the new threat and hold our own.

I see a blacksuit with dozens of ribbons on the left breast of his uniform, marking him as a high-ranking officer. The man is also tall, meaning he is a member of the New Washington elite. He sees me and yells, "Rally around me! Advance on the Daughter of Gaia!"

Dozens of blacksuits flock around him, and they drive toward us. Fortunately, Falstaff, who's standing at my side, sees what's happening and orders our people to rally around him. We are soon surrounded by several dozen soldiers wearing threadbare wool garments.

The blacksuit officer fights his way through the crowd until he reaches me.

"Your death will avenge the three thousand comrades you murdered at the Sanctuary," he sneers.

"And yours will avenge the hundreds of thousands of my people that your brutal rule has enslaved and murdered. Shut up and fight."

The man is an excellent swordsman. I go on the attack, probing for a weakness or an opening and find none. He retaliates, but I've worked hard on my technique, and I easily turn away his attacks. We fight hard, exchanging blows on an even basis for at least ten minutes, and then his weakness begins to reveal itself. This officer has lived the life of the elite, with rich food and all manner of luxurious indulgences. I've worked hard keeping myself fit every day, and my superior conditioning begins to show. His movements become slower as we fight on, until I'm able to launch a flurry of blows he's unable to evade.

He dies bravely, a worthy opponent.

The battle continues with both sides absorbing terrible losses. The blacksuits possess superior skills with weapons, but our advantage is one of motivation. Our people fight with a determination the blacksuits lack. We hunger for revenge. Hundreds of years of frustration and degradation provide us with a strength the blacksuits can't counter. Two blacksuits go down for every casualty we take.

Through the swirling groups of fighters, I see Jared Cain leading a group of blacksuits less than ten yards from us.

"Come with me!" I shout.

We cut through a crowd of blacksuits separating our group from Jared's. I see Grizz look at Jared with the expression of a starving lion who has just found a bleating lamb.

"He's mine," I growl, warning Grizz off.

Chase once told me that Coach called Jared a quarterback with a million-dollar arm and a ten-cent attitude. He was well known for dogging it at practice, and he got away with it because, with his superior athleticism, he could still dominate his opponents. I trust that he's done the same in his swordsmanship training.

When he sees me in front of him, Jared says, "Killing you will be a real pleasure, ET. The chief justice turned purple with rage when he found you'd escaped. I know he'll have a nice reward for me when I bring him your corpse."

"Shut up and fight," I return.

I can sense the fighting around us stop as both armies disengage and watch our confrontation, fascinated. The roar of battle is quickly replaced with silence. The Daughter of Gaia fighting the blacksuits' giant is a sight worth seeing.

Jared opens our fight with a series of powerful thrusts. He's a head taller and more than a hundred pounds heavier, so his strategy is to overpower me. His mighty blows force me to give ground. Despite his apparent advantage, his thrusts are powerful, but not skillful. I easily parry every one. Losing his temper at the failure of his first flurry, he intensifies his attack, putting every ounce of strength he has behind a new set of blows. Once again, I deflect his blows and sidestep, giving ground. But soon, his laziness in training begins to tell.

His attacks have left him breathless and tired. I begin my counterattack. My thrusts are short, economical, and quick. He struggles to deflect my blade, but his arm is tiring. Every blow is parried with more difficulty, and each of my thrusts comes closer to flesh. I see a look of fear rise in his eyes as I pursue him relentlessly. I give him no opportunity to regroup or gather his strength.

His right arm is so tired it's nearly useless. He drops his shield and grasps the handle of his sword with both hands. With another series of thrusts, I drive him to his knees. He knows he's going to die.

"Please, ET, I'll join your side," he pleads. "You can use a strong man like me. I'll do whatever you tell me to do."

I'm tempted to toy with him. I've enjoyed seeing his look of desperation grow. But if I give in to this temptation, I'll be no better than he is. Our eyes lock as my final thrust takes his life. His death is as quick and painless as a sword thrust allows.

Around us, the blacksuits begin to disengage and back away. The spectacle of their champion defeated has robbed them of their courage. Our own militia has suffered terribly, so we don't pursue the blacksuits as they retreat. The field is covered with dead, but despite our losses, our men and women raise a ragged cheer that goes on and on. They have fought the hated blacksuits, and they have won.

* * * * *

I warmly embrace my friends.

"I dropped what I was doing and raced to Phoenix the minute I heard Salieri kidnapped you," says Kenny. "Waiting for word from you was agonizing. When the message came through that you'd meet us at the edge of the forest, I literally jumped for joy."

"You had us worried sick," says Chase. "You should've seen how fast Falstaff quick-marched the militia to Phoenix. They ran so fast their feet barely touched the ground."

I feel tears in my eyes as I mull over the loyalty of these people. As the Daughter of Gaia, I've suffered my share of pain, but when I see the looks of love on the faces of my friends and my people, I realize everything I've endured has been worth the sacrifice. I relax and take pleasure in the joyful celebration of those I love deeply.

We arrive in Phoenix after nightfall, and the merriment continues. I sit with my friends, and we watch the villagers celebrate. They've waited hundreds and hundreds of years for this night.

Kenny sets off fireworks she's prepared, rockets that leave a red trail of fire behind as they climb and explode with an ear-shattering blast that releases a bright spray of colors. The fireworks amaze the villagers, who've never seen anything like them.

"How'd you know we were going to fight a battle and win? You left the chem lab before I'd even planned my escape," I ask Kenny.

"I had a vision," says Kenny.

"Really!" I say. Kenny must have the gift as well.

"Of course not," says Kenny with a grin. "I just like to build things that make lots of noise."

Much later, a breathless villager enters the village and rushes to me.

Gasping for breath, he says, "The brane has opened."

www.ingramcontent.com/pod-product-compliance
Lightning Source LLC
Chambersburg PA
CBHW020330180626
46812CB00001B/128